Abandon

Hope

The Ballad of
Tul'ran the Sword

Book the Third

Dale William Fedorchuk

Acknowledgments

Dedicated, as always, to El Shaddai, who inspired it.

Second, to my beautiful, patient, loving, and kind wife, Anika. We've spent many hours talking about Tul'ran, Erianne, Mick, Heather, Johan and Gwynver'insa, while our dogs rolled their eyes and googled synonyms for 'obsession.' Anika is my muse, editor, wife, and best friend. I couldn't have done this without her.

Third, to my personal "editorial board," who read the drafts and provided helpful insight, encouragement, and proposals: Anika Fedorchuk, Mike Bennett, Kendell Anquist, and Payton Goller.

Fourth, to my mom, Rose Fedorchuk. Mom encouraged me to read since I was five years old and now she's reading my novels. The circle is complete. Love you, Mom.

I am indebted to John MacArthur, who wrote *The MacArthur New Testament Commentary, Revelation 1-11* and *Revelation 12-22*. His books gave me a deep insight into the Tribulation period and what we can expect.

I authored this novel before August 2023. Since then, some distressing events in the world have paralleled scenes in my novels. If you find yourself distressed by current events, I encourage you to go to davidjeremiah.org.

The Tales

The Cast

Tul'ran az Nostrom
Tul'ran the Sword,

Born in 2037 BC, he became a famed warrior after Gutian renegades murdered his family and God assigned him as one of His Judges for the era before the time of Abraham.

Erianne de mi Corazon,
Lady az Nostrom

Born in 2067 AD, Erianne became a Time Historian for the Time Travel Initiative. She married Tul'ran and now rides at his right hand.

Quil'ton az Peregos,
Lamek Davis, "Mick"
Lam'ek az Peregos

Davis, a retired Navy SEAL, joined TTI as a Protector. He became lost in time in 2025 BC and assumed the identity of Quil'ton az Peregos.

Dr. Heather Wu, PhD

A brilliant Programmer, one of many who programmed the time and spatial coordinates for the Navigation Coins used by TTI's Time Historians.

Darian Ostrowski,
Darian O.

A former Controller for a terrorist group called the Order of Purity, who now searches for her own identity.

Dr. Johan Weinstein,
PhD

A brilliant physicist who became a Time Historian to restore his family's honor by trying to kill Adolph Hitler.

Major Coventry Quarterlaine	A retired U.S. Marine seconded to TTI as a troubleshooter.
Dr. Michael Sullivan, MD, "Sully"	Davis's former teammate on the SEAL Teams, now a physician specialist.
Jeannie Sullivan, BN	Sully's wife and a skilled trauma nurse.
Admiral Sylvia Oslo, USN	The President of the United States who became a Regional Supervisor for the global Government of Democracy.
Marjatta Korhonen	The Administrator of TTI, who reports only to the Supreme Global Leader.
Erasmus Hart	Head of Special Projects Division, a clandestine arm of TTI that reports directly to Korhonen.
Malchus Contradeum	The Antichrist.
Jezebel Brandt	Contradeum's Executive Assistant and his conduit to Satan.
G'shnet'el	Formerly an angel of Heaven who fell with Lucifer and became one of Satan's chief lieutenants in Hell. He rules in the Abyss over unjudged souls.

E'thriel	Formerly an angel of Heaven who fell with Lucifer but Tul'ran and Erianne redeemed him.
Gwynver'insa	A prophet of God trapped in the Garden on Spes Deserit until Tul'ran and Erianne rescued her.
Evo, She Who Was Not	Created as the first woman on the planet Everhome, she grew to resent God and seeks to destroy Him.

Of Ancient Nightmares

Before the creation of humans, he was. Before the creation of angels and archangels, he came. He was among the first of God's creation, designed to be a leader and formed to be a warrior. There was no other like him, not even Lucifer. He did not answer to Lucifer. Before Lucifer, he was.

He was mammoth, built much like a human, and dressed all in black. His face was a construct of rugged beauty, and framed by sweeping long, black hair. His eyes appeared a solid black, the pupils indistinguishable from the iris. He spread his great obsidian wings and shivered the feathers. In the angelic realm, it was their way of expressing pleasure.

Satan, the being once known as Lucifer the Light Bringer, sent him to this world to prepare it for Satan's rule. The thought edged a cold, hard smile on his lips. Satan was a fool and a lunatic. The black-armored angel who watched the new arrivals was not one of the puny tempters of people who slavered around Satan's feet like dogs. Before Satan, he was.

When he arrived on Spes Deserit, it was a beautiful world overflowing with humanity; humans who had shrunk the world's resources to a breaking point. He didn't have to tempt or deceive these people to sin against God. All he had to do was whisper a question into one farmer's mind: was it truly unlawful to wage a war of survival against others to reduce the surplus population and conserve resources?

The humans seized upon the new notion as if it were the very essence of life. Their initial attempts at killing were crude and indecisive. As the struggle for food, territory, and riches increased, so did their intellectual and immoral capacity for inventing new, more cruel means and methods of waging war. Their research led to the development of weapons not seen anywhere in the universe, drawing energy from Inter-Dimensional Space to power and create them.

Indeed, it had been necessary for him to restrain them in their burgeoning research and development; otherwise, there would be no planet on which to stand. This world would have suffered the same fate as the biosphere once orbiting Earth's sun between Mars and Jupiter, now reduced to a vast field of rubble known as the Asteroid Belt.

The brooding angel watching the new arrivals was an angel of judgment, but not Satan's angel of judgment. An angel, but not of the company of angels; a being who didn't serve evil, but who served death. He couldn't help it. The Father designed him to destroy. It was in his nature, the very essence of his being, and the very reason for his existence.

It was not his destiny to prepare Spes Deserit for a delusional megalomaniac; he was here to sharpen his skills. His target was Earth. Specifically, his target was every human being who lived on the Earth. They would die in his hands. That was his destiny. He cared not one whit who reigned after he laid the planet to waste.

There was just one last piece to resolve before he could leave Spes Deserit. The girl. She finally came out of her hole. He didn't know the humans who came out of the Garden with her, but it didn't matter. Once he killed all of them, he could return to Earth. The desire for the transition back to the first human world created by God bubbled in his body like boiling oil.

The need to sharpen his sword against the lives of humans had pulled him away from the Earth for a time, and times, and half a time. No longer.

The Earth would soon feel the wrath of Abaddon the Destroyer.

CHAPTER THE FIRST:

ABANDON HOPE

Spes Deserit, 3,700 light years from Earth
In the Year of Our Fight 2375
Mission Day One

It was a world well suited to its name. Everything, the sky, the buildings, the ground, was a uniform dingy gray. It wasn't dark outside, but it may as well be because of the murky sediment of pollution sitting on the air like a thick blanket. If dismal were a place, it would be called Spes Deserit. If depression had a name, it would be a planet called Abandon Hope.

No wind moved. There were thick clouds in the sky, to the extent one could see the sky. Big hulking outlines of buildings reached out from the gloom, as if offering solace and begging for tenants. Their silent pleas, unaided by lights or signs or any other form of warmth, fell upon no ears. All the buildings lacked activity. They lacked life.

A fine dust, like lunar dust, pervaded the air and covered everything in a haze of silent apprehension. There were no sounds. Birds didn't fly. Predators didn't search the alleys in pursuit of the next meal, for neither predator nor prey existed on Spes Deserit. The creatures in this world were like a moth flirting too closely to the flame. They flared into death like the paper used by magicians. A flash, then only ash.

Perhaps it's unfair to say no life existed. Some life commanded the mechanical monstrosities wandering the abandoned streets and killing all living things on the planet because the machines were not autonomous. Mortality lay patiently in wait for life in Spes Deserit. Just as it waited in hiding outside the Lord's Garden, just beyond the Crystalline Wall, eagerly hoping to unleash fury on anyone who dared to venture out of hiding.

Gwynver'insa, Tul'ran az Nostrom, Erianne de mi Corazon Lady az Nostrom, Dr. Johan Weinstein, and Darian Ostrowski slipped into a gloomy darkness through the shimmering veil separating the Lord's Garden from Spes Deserit. As the group walked away from the barrier, the sentient Crystalline trees ground and clashed their way into place, sealing the Garden from the planet. Chilling feet of apprehension ran down each of their spines as the Crystallines moaned their way back into place.

A flare burst over their heads, a dull, ruddy red splotch against a gray sky. In its dim light, they saw the muzzle of a gigantic cannon pointed at them.

Various machines with wheels, tracks, and too many sharp edges surrounded the cannon. A harsh voice crackled into the night.

"We have you now, witch. Prepare to die!"

The cannon hummed to life, as did devices on the machines surrounding it. Darian crawled in behind Johan, her eyes wide with fear. Gwynver'insa whirled as if to run back to the Garden and charged into Erianne, who caught her and folded her into her arms. Erianne looked at Tul'ran, her face a shade paler. Time to test their unfamiliar voices; a gift of telepathy from El Shaddai to be enjoyed only between husband and wife.

'Tul'ran, milord husband,' she thought into his mind, concentrating furiously. 'Time isn't stopping. Why is Time not stopping? If they fire those weapons, we'll all die.'

Her husband looked behind them at the Crystallines, standing tall and firm against the entrance to the Garden. His mouth set in a hard line before he looked up into his wife's green eyes.

'Whatever we are to do, my love,' he thought back, too worried to wonder at their new way of speaking privately. 'We must do it here. No one's getting off Abandon Hope now.'

Tul'ran drew Bloodwing from over his shoulder. He didn't know what he could do with a sword in the face of these things opposing him. All his life, he only waged war against men and beasts. He saw the fear these things generated in his wife. Tul'ran didn't need to know their purpose; it was enough they caused his wife to be afraid. It was enough to make him afraid.

A blade of light erupted from the cannon. Darian and Gwynver'insa screamed. The malevolent beam streaked to their position, then ponderously slowed to a halt. It hovered in front of them for a moment, pulsating an intense blue glow cackling mayhem. Without a hint of its intention, the entire bolt dove into Bloodwing.

The Blade, normally black steel edged with a bright blue glow, radiated an intense blue shine through the length of the sword. Wisps of azure danced on the surface of the weapon, as if steam twirled sensuously from its depths. The wisps rose into the air from the surface of the Blade and twisted towards the cannon, dancers in a winsome ballet of destruction. Like a phantom, the blue wisps from the Blade wrapped around the Advanced Energy Disruptor, covering its entire surface. They lingered over the surface of the most fearsome weapon ever created and then dissipated.

The cannon was gone. Nothing, not even blue wisps of energy, remained.

Abaddon turned away after he saw the Disruptor fire, but checked his turn when the energy beam stopped its flight. The sword in the small human's hands had absorbed the bolt from the advanced energy weapon. Not possible!

The angel focused his ethereal vision on the sword, and what he saw staggered him. A human carried Bloodwing the Blade! Abaddon knew the sword well. It was the most powerful ever created by God the Father. The Holy Trinity gave Bloodwing to Lucifer as a reward for the Light Bringer's love and devotion, but took it away when the Lord kicked him out of Heaven.

Abaddon wondered if the human knew he carried the Sword of Uncreation. He subconsciously took a step back from the scene. No weapon in Heaven or in the universe could end the eternal life of an angel... except that one. If used for its intended purpose, the edges didn't cut. They reversed the creation of the person or thing attacked by the Blade. Nothing existed after an act of uncreation. Perhaps the Father could recreate what Bloodwing left undone, but who wanted to tempt that fate?

Not even Lucifer had known the true potential of the weapon when he possessed it. They had not yet created Lucifer when the Father and the Son forged the sword the Son Himself would wield in the Last Days. Abaddon witnessed the forging of Bloodwing the Blade with a feeling of fear and exhilaration. They didn't build it for him, but he would give anything to possess it.

Abaddon could only imagine the damage he could do while swinging Bloodwing the Blade. He was one of the few angels who knew the true purpose of it and how to use it. His trip to Earth would have to wait.

He had to have that sword.

"How did you do that?" Erianne whispered as she stared down at Tul'ran's blank face. He turned to look up at her, the hands wrapped around Bloodwing's hilt trembling slightly.

"I know not, milady wife. I put no thought into what I would do. The blue light entered Bloodwing, and I could not move a muscle until the Blade did its work. Wait, what's this?"

The other machines rapidly executed a maneuver and ended it by pouring bolts of blue energy on their group. Dreadful, destructive beams rained down on them from every angle. But before their energies could extract death from life, they again stopped well short of their targets, paused, and siphoned into Bloodwing. The intensity of the Blade's glow increased substantially, lighting the surrounding area in sharp relief. The light made the scene seem more foreboding, bringing to stark relief the empty streets and the array of belligerent machinery.

Fists of smoke rose from the Blade, writhed, and turned in the air as if seeking a scent, before moving to the machines from which the attack came. The energy of this counterattack was far greater. Blue vapors rising from Bloodwing's surface became pillars of blinding sapphire light, with arcs of electricity crackling about its surface. Bloodwing's tendrils enveloped each machine attacking the group of humans. The night dimmed considerably as the specters did their work.

Their group was alone. Not one machine remained.

A large gong sounded in the air above their heads, and the harsh voice was back.

"Not fair! I lodge a complaint! The opposing force didn't dice fairly and now I have lost an entire company. I demand to have my complaint heard immediately!"

As the last of the loud voice faded, Gwynver'insa broke the ensuing silence with a sigh.

"Well done, Lord Tul'ran! If the truth were to be told, I half expected my death at this hour. We must go to my bolt hole with haste, for others seeking advantage will replace the forces you did so handily defeat. We must be away from here before the sun goes down."

Erianne glanced around at their dimly lit surroundings. Everything was back to a dull gray, and her sight barely penetrated beyond the nearest streetlamp.

"Are you saying the sun rides in the sky this very hour?"

Gwynver'insa nodded somberly.

"Even so. When young, this planet was beautiful. It resembled the Garden, with a vast array of flowers, plants, and living things. The sun shone upon us during the waking hours and the stars showered their glory upon us at night."

"Then the Fight came. It started with two farmers, each of whom needed an addition to their land to produce more of their vegetable wares for the market. In the heat of their argument, the one farmer beat the other to death. His neighbor came upon the bloodied men, killed the survivor, and claimed both their lands for his own. The ensuing violence was like a plague. To be infected, one merely had to take their eyes off Yahweh."

"The wars consumed resources like sheep consume grass. Our world was first stripped of its metals and minerals, then its forests and animals. You would not know it, but there is around our planet's atmosphere a thin layer of transparent ice. The ice layer acts as an ablative shield, directing heat and cosmic radiation away from the ground. The existence of the ice firmament protected our planet from harm, maintained an even temperature around the entire world, and created perfect conditions for growing and living."

"With the wars came fire, soot, and the release of toxic chemicals into the atmosphere. They created a dense, dark fog permeating every level of our atmosphere, closing out the sun and the sky forever. Our planet's ecosystem died, and life became a war for survival."

"When the Fight came to my village, my family and others fled instead of becoming wrapped up in the conflict. We joined other refugees and searched for places to conceal away from the conflagration claiming this world. Every time the Fight came near us, we ran away. Each time we bolted, the battles thinned our numbers as we became collateral damage. Years ago, a vicious conflict separated me from my family and friends. I found the Garden and have stayed in it ever since. I do not know if those I love yet live."

Erianne stepped back from Gwynver'insa to look at her up and down. She saw a short woman with long blonde hair and a slender, well-proportioned body. Her pretty face was small, as were her nose and lips. Her ears were slightly pointed, like a small elf. Gwynver'insa's large eyes were bright blue and filled with intelligence. Erianne wouldn't have placed her age past twenty years.

"Lady Gwynver'insa, if I may ask it, how old are you?"

Gwynver'insa pondered for a moment, then

raised her right hand into the air and sketched motions as if adding up numbers. Her face lit up with a smile, her teeth as white as goose down.

"I am one thousand, one hundred and twelve years old. In the language in which you speak, I am only now entering adulthood."

Darian tapped her ear twice.

"This translator must not be working right. Gwynver'insa, did you just say you are a one thousand, one hundred- and twelve-year-old young adult?"

Gwynver'insa beamed.

"Indeed, I did, Mistress Darian! One reason I am so happy to have you here is that I have been quite lonely. Yahweh is a wonderful companion, make no mistake, but I have longed for the company of women. My body is undergoing changes and I crave the advice of other females to help me transition into adulthood."

Tul'ran grinned at the look of discomfort on Erianne's face.

"Lady Gwynver'insa, Erianne only recently told me of her belief, now proven to be mistaken, she might be with child. She is keen on bearing progeny and delivering them into the world. I am sure she would be more than delighted to impart the wisdom of her age to a mere stripling."

Erianne lowered her eyelids at him in mock warning.

"Mischief is only funny when I do it to you, Lord of the Scalawags. Lady Gwynver'insa, it would please me to assist you where I can, but be aware you are many hundreds of years older than I. I am not sure how much help I can provide."

Gwynver'insa linked arms with Erianne, beaming her smile up into the much younger woman's face.

"Fear not, milady. I am sure we have enough commonalities between us, enabling you to render the perfect advice," she said, as she started leading the troupe away from the Garden. "For example, I have had odd feelings in my most recent past towards the thought of men. I hope to discuss my feelings with you, a married woman whom a mighty warrior follows slavishly, being so besotted with you as he is."

Erianne glared back at Tul'ran, from whom a sound had come, which may have been muffled laughter.

"I will do what I can, Lady Gwynver'insa, but you should know men often smell like goats and most frequently act like them, too."

The smaller woman giggled and then put her hand out to the rest of the group, her first two fingers raised.

"Friends, from this point forward, we are not safe. There are devices concealed everywhere on these streets monitoring warmth, carbon dioxide levels, movement, and sound. I found a path through these streets once when I journeyed to the Garden. Our technology is not self-sustaining, because it does not repair itself once broken. The means by which to repair the war machines are now limited since many of our scientists have died at the hands of the Combatants. Innovation and invention have perished, but they are the least of the Fight's casualties."

"It may be the case the Combatant who owns the devices on this street has taken the time to repair his surveillance equipment. Or not. Let us tread softly and not speak. Milord and Milady az Nostrom, draw your weapons, I beg of you. If the Combatants attack us, it will come of a sudden."

"A moment, Lady Gwynver'insa." Erianne shrugged off her cloak, which was as much a light-absorbing black as her husband's and shrugged a small pack from between her shoulder blades. From the pack, she withdrew the gun and ammo she seized from Darian. She offered the gun to her.

"I believe this is yours."

Darian took a step back, both hands at shoulder level and fingers spread wide.

"I'm not taking it. In fact, I'm not staying. I want to go back to Earth. We haven't been in this world for ten minutes and something tried to kill us. I didn't sign up for this. Send me home!"

Erianne put the bag back on her shoulders and wrapped the cloak around her frame.

"You can't go home," she said, striving for patience. "Look behind you. See those trees? They form the Crystalline Wall, sentient rocks unwilling to let us back into the Garden. The Garden has the only capacity to transport us off this world. Until we get back in, we're going nowhere."

Darian crossed her arms in front of her ample breasts, a pout forming on her lips.

"How do you know? Have you tried? I'm not going anywhere but back home."

Tul'ran let out an exasperated sigh.

"You're coming with us. The man in the Garden

on Earth, who introduced himself to you as Jay, told us you must come with us. Your destiny is here, whether you wish it to be so. Come with us or go alone. You can't return."

Darian glared at him.

"Who died and made you the boss?"

Tul'ran's eyes flared wide, and he took a half-step in her direction.

"I made me the boss," he answered, his voice a soft menacing growl. "No one had to die, but you still can if you continue to strain my nerves."

Darian swallowed and shrank back. She remembered the slaver in ancient Mesopotamia who found the end of his life on Bloodwing the Blade. Tul'ran didn't take a second to warn the guy before he walked up and ran a sword through his chest. She also remembered Erianne's warnings in the Garden of Eden to stay away from his temper. She nodded, reluctantly.

"Fine. Gimme the gun."

Darian cast a glance at Tul'ran's frozen features before she checked the gun for its load and configuration.

"The last time I had this gun, I tried to kill you with it."

"You won't have the opportunity again," Tul'ran said in a cold, grim voice. "I have your measure, Darian, for I've studied your movements since we met you. I know your facial expressions and the tensions in your body when you're angry, scared, or threatened. You wouldn't have sufficient time to draw your weapon against us before I'd leave your head on the ground."

Darian glared at the warrior, who seemed completely unaffected by the gaze.

"Thanks, 'friend'. Your faith in my character is heart-warming."

Tul'ran cocked an eyebrow at her.

"You're here because my wife is the Lady of the Second Chance. If your character proves less than stellar, you'll disappoint her, not me. I'd be more afraid of her rage than mine, were I you."

"Enough," Erianne said, interrupting the rising friction between the tall brunette and her ever-dangerous husband. "We've sufficient enemies without the two of you attempting to kill each other. Move out!" As she passed Tul'ran to take point, she said into his mind, 'I really must teach you the wisdom of diplomacy, love of my life and holder of my dreams.'

It made him smile.

They moved out, weapons drawn and tensions high. Gwynver'insa stayed one step back of Erianne, guiding her to their destination with silent touches to her shoulders. Darin followed, placing one hand on Gwynver'insa's back to let her know Darian followed and remained in contact.

Johan followed her with a hand on her back. Johan wasn't a fighter, so his anxiety resulted in heavier breathing, and his hand squeezed her shoulder in response to his rising fear. Darian turned to sneer at him.

"Back off. I can feel your breath on the back of my neck. We're not trying to make babies here."

"Shut up!" Johan said, his voice frantic. "There are things out there listening for us."

"Both of you shut up," Tul'ran said in a soft voice behind them. "Or I'll cut out your tongues."

The conversation ended. Tul'ran didn't have a hand on Johan's back because he held Bloodwing in his right hand and grasped El Shaddai's Knife in the left. His nerves sang with the need to find and dispatch hidden enemies in the thick, gray gloom twisting around them like a living thing. Behind every strange monument, in every weird building, lay the potential for ambush. It wasn't exhilarating. It was exhausting.

Tul'ran shook his head at the absence of sound. Even in the desert in his home world, something moved, made noise, or made you aware life existed. The silence in this place was unnerving. He gripped and re-gripped the hilt of his wondrous sword. At this rate, the hike would drain him more than combat itself.

Abaddon rested at one of the tallest spires in the city, from where he monitored the progress of the group of humans. The Sword Wielder was among them. His ethereal vision allowed him to pierce the darkening skies easily. The gloom didn't bother him; in fact, he preferred it. He developed a great fondness for darkness after God stationed him in the Abyss.

The Holy Trinity didn't create all angels to be equal, nor did He create them at the same time. The First Order of Angels, the Highest Hierarchy of Heaven, was the earliest to be created, as far as anyone knew. Abaddon didn't know when God created him, but he knew his place in the order.

Before Seraphim, Cherubim, and Thrones, he was. Before Dominions, Powers, and Authorities, he was.

Abaddon's first memory was kneeling before the Father, the Son, and the Holy Spirit. He couldn't remember whether there were others in the angelic realm, but he doubted it. Before the Hierarchies, he was the First of his Kind.

The Father handed him a massive sword; it was almost as tall as the angel.

"Your name is Abaddon, and We have made you with both joy and distress in Our hearts. We see every thread of every life We make, now and evermore. Every choice, every path, is open to Our vision. While We hope to never set you upon the path of your destiny, We must create you. You will not need to be trained in the ways of conflict, for you are War. You will not need to learn how to end life, for you are Death. It will not be necessary for Us to teach you obliteration, for you are the Destroyer. Watch, O Mighty Watcher. Learn, O Mighty Servant. Remember always, you are only Ours to command."

Everything unfolding in the Kingdom of Heaven thereafter came under Abaddon's thoughtful scrutiny. He watched as God created angels and Abaddon hovered over them as they trained. He listened as the Wisdoms debated laws, principles, morals, and judgments. Abaddon stood silent as a pillar, unnoticed, as Lucifer plotted the overthrow of God. He took no part in any of it, for God hadn't decreed he should. Abaddon understood his role better than any angel in Heaven. With him, there was no restraint or degrees of violence. He was the ultimate weapon of mass destruction.

It didn't surprise anyone Abaddon didn't fight, for or against God, when the War in Heaven broke out. Indeed, none of the Higher Hierarchies fought in the rebellion. Only the Lowest Hierarchy, being the Principalities, Archangels, and Angels, fought against each other. The other Hierarchies knew the truth. When the Holy Trinity sifted through the loyalties of the Lowest Hierarchies to His satisfaction, Yahweh would bring the conflict to an end.

When Jesus cast the fallen angels out of Heaven, He summoned Abaddon. The Destroyer, then clad in the brilliant white of the Lord's House, came forward, kneeled, and bowed his head before his Lord.

"I come, my Lord, as commanded. What is Your will?"

"Abaddon, My friend, We would have you go to the Abyss and mind what happens there. This is not a punishment, for you are welcome in the Kingdom of Heaven whenever you wish to return. You have freedom, Abaddon. The time will come when We shall call upon you and from the Abyss you will arise with power and vengeance."

"My Lord, I am your servant. May it be done to me as You command."

Abaddon did as the Lord instructed him. He watched as the fallen angels and archangels battled for power in the Abyss, but took no part. He observed as Satan descended further and further into narcissism, self-delusion, and madness. Abaddon didn't judge, for it wasn't his place to judge. He grew to love how the darkness wrapped around him like a cloak. No one trifled with him. Everyone stood back or took a different path when he walked through the desolate realm.

Satan caught him by surprise one day when the evil one approached Abaddon without permission or being summoned. By this time, Satan fully immersed himself in the delusion he was a god. It amused Abaddon to humor him, for he had nothing else to do.

When Satan commanded Abaddon to go to Spes Deserit to prepare the world for Satan and his minions by introducing War to the People, the Destroyer almost drove his sword through Satan's chest. Such presumption! The part of him understanding his role, however, merely let the moment pass.

He entered an artificial sphere the demons of Hell had constructed. The Team Lead, Glev'lac'sit, had been a brilliant angel specializing in the sciences before the Lord cast him out from Heaven. He had a better understanding of quantum space than anything else alive.

"Master Abaddon, you will feel a sensation of falling. You have no means of exiting the quantum bubble when I activate the field. Please be patient. We are sending you a great distance in a brief time."

Abaddon nodded his exasperation.

"Fine. Just get on with it."

The field activated, and the Abyss faded away. Quantum space was fascinating. Things existed there he had never seen while transiting Inter-Dimensional Space. He heard stars singing arias while they fled from black holes. He tasted the sound of their singing, which shouldn't have had a taste. It was confusing and exhilarating. He fell for a long while, yet didn't feel like he traveled anywhere. In fact, the strange and wondrous scenery before him didn't change as he transitioned. When he had enough of getting nowhere, he exerted the ethereal power of his wings on the bubble, hoping to see something move.

Something did. By exerting power on the quantum bubble, he altered the axis of the spin that kept time constant, relative to Earth. The spin controlling time ceased advancing at its programmed pace and reversed rapidly. When the bubble popped him onto the planet, he arrived thousands of years earlier than he should have. It felt no different to him and he didn't know he had slipped millennia behind the current time on Earth.

The quantum bubble collapsed.

Glev'lac'sit had programmed it to be synchronous with Earth time so he could monitor Abaddon and bring him back. The time discrepancy between Spes Deserit when Abaddon landed on it and Earth when he left overcame Glev'lac'sit's programming. The field collapsed, and it stranded Abaddon on Spes Deserit.

For an eternal being, the passing of a few thousand years is a trivial thing. He spent the first few decades watching people struggle with the overpopulation of the planet and the overconsumption of resources. He never intended to get involved with their quarrels, but was intrigued by the ripple effects war would have on an otherwise peaceful planet.

Abaddon took the form of a local merchant and

joined a local farmer over a pint one night. The farmer claimed bitterly about his neighbor and the unfairness of the greater amount of land the man possessed.

It was then he made the casual suggestion that a reduction in the surplus population could be beneficial to the entire world.

The resulting savagery staggered him. Abaddon never witnessed humans who took such delight in warfare and the development of new weapons to kill ever-increasing numbers.

At first, he enjoyed himself as the Fight flared and grew into a mania of death, lust, and destruction. Now, though, he was ready to go home.

It never occurred to him to reach out to God and ask for a ride.

An automaton flew up to the spire and levitated before him, breaking his reverie. Abaddon looked at the thing with distaste.

"What do you want?"

A harsh, guttural voice came out of the battle machine's speakers.

"The Council has ascended to consider Great Ron's complaint. We beg for the pleasure of your attendance, O Mighty One. We must have your wisdom, to ensure the Fight will never end."

Eleven other voices suddenly chimed in.

"The Fight must never end."

Abaddon looked at the machine with disgust. He was reaching the limits of his patience with the Combatants. Their persistent whining was grating on his nerves. He'd kill them all, but a part of him hoped Satan would find his way to this planet.

The world's residents would drive him over sanity's delicate edge in no time.

"Very well, I come."

Abaddon drew his sword and cut the metallic messenger into small pieces. It was unnecessary to do so, but it gave him satisfaction because of how much it annoyed the Combatants to see one of their precious machines destroyed. They were difficult to replace.

He cast one last glance at the human party winding its way through the streets below. They could wait.

No one escaped his gaze on this world.

Gwynver'insa's bolt hole proved to be a mansion by everyone else's standards. While cloaked in gray, it lacked some of the lunar dustiness pervading the city. She took them to the back of the palace and introduced them to a concealed doorway. It had been a long, hot, unnerving journey.

"Come inside," she said, her voice a barely heard whisper. "We dare not tarry when it becomes dark. The machines you saw outside the Garden hunt in the dark, for the Combatants equipped them with means to see our body heat."

"Thermal imagers," Tul'ran said to Darian and Johan's surprise. "Where we are from, we call such devices 'thermal imagers.'"

"As do we," Gwynver'insa said, beaming. "I am pleased our knowledge rivals yours. As we wind our way through this House, mark a path for yourselves. I have lived too long to have childish notions of immortality. Should they kill me, you will need to know how to leave this House and return to the Garden. When we get to the core of the House, I can turn on lights. The core is well-shielded from the outside and our presence here will be undetectable. This House is one of few not owned by a Combatant."

"A Combatant?" Johan asked.

"Yes, Lord Johan. In this world, there are only two types of human beings: Combatants and Victims. The Combatants control the weapons and continuously wage war against one another. Victims are those who want peace and fall to the weapons seeking living things upon which to quench their lust for death."

They marched down long corridors and passed huge gathering rooms. Only the light from the edges of Tul'ran's sword lit their way. The ceilings were so high, they couldn't see the uppermost height of the hallways. There was enough light to allow them to see the massive shutters bolted over all the windows. No light came in; no light exited.

The silence was so oppressive, even Gwynver'insa ceased her pleasant chatter. After what felt like hours, the group came into a large circular room with multiple beds and a tall, pentagon-shaped structure in the middle.

"This, my dear new friends, is the room called Last Stand. Within the walls behind each bed is a place where you may attend to your toiletries and physical needs. The conveniences in those closets will also clean your clothing and provide you with robes to wear while doing so. It is not safe to wander in this House beyond this room. I lived here for twenty years and scoured this place for weapons no one else had scavenged. While I found none, my knowledge of warfare and how to wage it are not as extensive as yours. I would hate to see you die in a place I swore safe."

Erianne glanced at Tul'ran; her eyebrows raised.

"We, too, would hate that, Lady Gwynver'insa. How are meals prepared, for I do not see larders in which you store food or ovens to cook them?"

Gwynver'insa laughed and twirled her way to the center of the room, like a girl pretending to be a Disney princess. She stopped at the pentagon-shaped spire.

"After the wars started, our technology developed at great speed. The Combatants killed all living things on this planet, including our food supplies. As people starved, and disease spread, the Combatants declared a ceasefire for two hundred years. During the Ceasefire, they invented tools such as this to bring in raw materials from the stars and prepare food from those materials. We no longer grow food. Ask and you shall receive whatever your stomach desires."

"It is a shame they found this technology so quickly. After two hundred years of peace, we had hoped the end of warfare would become permanent. Alas, our hopes ran unfulfilled. Not only was there enough food for everyone, but the Combatants also had a fresh supply of materials to create weapons. The fighting raged on as before the ceasefire, and with greater fervency."

Johan looked at her with his mouth open.

"Lady Gwynver'insa, do I understand from what

you have just said this device transports raw materials here from somewhere else in the cosmos?"

Gwynver'insa dimpled.

"You do, Lord Johan."

"I must confess, milady, this information flabbergasts me. By what means does this machine accomplish its task?"

The girl frowned.

"Do you know anything about physics, Lord Johan?"

He smiled.

"On my world, I have an advanced degree in physics. I have studied the universe and how it operates my entire life. Of my group, and I say this without meaning to boast, I am probably most conversant with physics."

Gwynver'insa clapped her hands.

"Excellent! Then you will have no difficulty understanding my explanation. The Food Maker searches the universe for the type of protein or plant you desire. As you know, Lord Johan, the probability of transmission of a wave packet through a barrier decreases exponentially with the barrier height, the barrier width, and the particle's mass."

"The device can only accomplish its goals with low-mass particles such as electrons or protons moving through microscopically narrow barriers. Transmission is readily manageable with barriers of thickness about one to three nanometers or smaller for electrons, and about zero-point one nanometer or smaller for heavier particles such as protons or hydrogen atoms."

"A nanometer is one billionth of a meter. An

average hair is about sixty thousand nanometers thick. Nanometers are used to measure wavelengths of light and distances between atoms in molecules," she said, the last words for the benefit of the non-physicists.

Tul'ran's face turned blank as he tried to process the strange unfamiliar words, while Erianne nodded knowingly. Darian just looked bored.

"Once the Food Maker finds the type of base for the meal you desire, it brings the base back to us one electron and proton at a time. Of course, since electrons and protons travel through the quantum realm, time has no meaning. The base particles were there, now they are here. Once the base particles arrive, the Food Maker reshapes them into the food you requested. The effect is to create healthy, nutritious food within a matter of seconds."

Johan's face was white. He looked at Erianne, awe flooding his distended pupils.

"Quantum tunneling. They use quantum mining to get raw materials from another world and reshape them into food here."

Gwynver'insa clapped her hands again.

"You have the right of it! Well done, Lord Johan! You must be specific about what you say to the Food Maker, for it will not assume any parameters. If your food is to be well-cooked and hot, you must say so. Try to describe what you want with as much detail as possible. The machine will keep making the food until the result satisfies you. Once you have proclaimed your satisfaction, you will only need to name the thing in the future and the Food Maker will create it for you."

"So," Darian said, slowly, "if I describe for the, um, Food Maker, how to prepare a steak with mashed potatoes and green beans, it will give me what I want?"

"Indeed, Mistress Darian! While I do not know what a steak and mashed potatoes with green beans are, I would beg you for an opportunity to sample your dish. I have not had a new dish since I separated from my family."

Darian moved her shoulders and tilted her head to the right side.

"Tell me, Lady Gwynver'insa, how is it you call everyone else in this group Lord or Lady, but I am merely Mistress Darian?"

Something changed in Gwynver'insa's face. She seemed taller, older; her gaze more piercing, as if she could see through bone, blood, and muscle into the gossamer strands of the soul. She stepped closer to Darian and stared deeply into the taller brunette's eyes.

"Lord Tul'ran, Lady Erianne, and Lord Johan have all pledged their hearts, minds, and souls to the King of Kings and Lord of Lords. They know Jesus as their Savior. By their proclamation of faith and belief in Him, Yahweh has adopted them into the family of God Himself. They are each a Prince or Princess of Heaven, though not yet ascended to their estate, and some day they shall reign with Him. I see the Light in their souls, Mistress, but I only see darkness in yours. You should change the status of your soul before it is too late."

"The only thing guaranteed on this planet is that you will die upon it soon."

CHAPTER THE SECOND:
RESIDUE

Mesopotamia, the twenty-third day of the fourth month, 2004 BC

They were a woeful bunch, the group standing in front of the house. He, a boy of eighteen years now, coming into manhood and given care of the house. She, a tall, slender girl of sixteen years, standing beside him. Next to her stood her frail sister, only two years younger, but so much smaller of bone and structure. Their mother hovered behind the girls, stockier than her daughters, but still pleasing to the eye. All three women shared similar lovely features and large brown eyes in an olive-skinned face. They carefully brushed their long, hazelnut hair and tied it back with bright ribbons.

A miasma of sadness hung over their heads like a dark fog fated to shade the light of the setting sun forever. They looked as if their lives, hopes, and dreams were saddling horses before them, not the three individuals busy preparing to leave.

Lamek Davis scanned the morose quartet in front of the house and shook his head. This would never do. He glanced at Heather Wu, who was checking the cinches on her ride. Tears filled her eyes. Coventry Quarterlaine was busy packing her horse, but Davis knew she wouldn't feel sad. After eight months stranded in Antiquity, she was finally going home.

Time to do something dramatic.

Davis slapped his horse on the neck and walked to the front of the House. His ever-curious neighbors had gathered round to watch their departure. Good. He wanted witnesses.

He smiled at Innanu, who was standing so close to Ro'gun's left side, their shoulders were touching.

"Innanu, as you favor me with your heart, extend your right arm, palm up."

Davis held her eyes as she complied.

"Having consideration for the abruptness of this moment, I now put to you this question: will you have Ro'gun as your husband, to have and to hold, in sickness and in health, until death shall part you? Will you love him well, care for his needs, support him in conflict and stand by his right side?"

Innanu blushed, but said, demurely, "I will."

Davis turned to Ro'gun; the whites of whose eyes were showing.

"Ro'gun, put out your left arm, palm down. Your left arm, son, not the right. Good man! Will you have Innanu as your wife, to have and to hold, in sickness and in health, until death shall part you? Will you love her well, protect her from all harm and every enemy, treat her with dignity and respect, and watch over her family as your own?"

Ro'gun's blush reached deeply into his hairline.

"I will."

Davis put their hands together and finger linked them. He raised his voice so his neighbors could hear him clearly.

"I, Lam'ek az Peregos, Son of Quil'ton az Peregos, Instructor to the Sword Himself, Head of my Line, eldest brother of Tul'ran the Sword, of the House az Nostrom, bond holder of Ro'gun az Amorain's life, now declare on my sword and with my blood Ro'gun and Innanu are bound as husband and wife. All who would seek to sever this marriage bond shall answer to me and to Tul'ran the Sword, the Prince of Death. Lady Omarosa."

Omarosa stepped forward, a delighted grin lighting her face. Davis had just promoted their status in front of the entire village. She curtsied.

"Milord az Peregos, I answer your call."

Davis answered her smile with a grin of his own.

"Milady Omarosa, on behalf of my brother, Tul'ran, who wanders far from hearth and home with his new bride, do I welcome you and your daughters into the House az Nostrom. As I have made Ro'gun my heir this very day, I also welcome you into the Line az Peregos. I charge you to watch over our children until my return, at which time we will hold a proper celebration of their wedding."

All of them were grinning widely now, and the neighbors murmured their approval.

Davis just made them the First Family of the village and secured their future solidly. He fervently hoped he hadn't committed a time fracture out of a desire to give this little family some hope.

Davis mounted his horse, joining Heather and Coventry on their steeds. All three were splendid horses and had cost a pretty penny. They would get them to Insertion Point without a problem. He squared his horse to the House az Peregos.

"We fare thee well. It may be some time before we return, but return we shall. We trust we will find the House az Peregos in order when we come back. Should anyone choose to harm anyone in my House, then by oath given on my blood, I shall set Tul'ran the Sword loose against the assailant and the assailant's House to the third generation. In such an event, may God have mercy on them, for the Taker of Souls shall not."

A murmur ran through the crowd. The Ballad of Tul'ran the Sword had grown in orders of magnitude since the village last saw him. Davis might as well have hung a sign over the door of the House that said, "Tul'ran Will Kill Ye, All Ye Who Bring Evil Here."

Davis sketched a salute and, with that, turned his horse away from a family he was certain he would never see again.

Denver, Colorado, August 30, 2097 AD
One year into the Tribulation

President Sylvia Oslo stared at the holo image in front of her, with her stomach dancing an acid mambo in her chest. She'd been dreading this call and knew it was only a matter of time before he made it. Eights months passed between the time of the nuclear attack on her country and Malchus Contradeum's reach out. He surprised her by taking this long.

"Good afternoon, Mr. President," she said, before he waved off her introductory remarks.

"President Oslo, you need to update your staff on proper protocols. I am to be referred to as Supreme Global Leader."

Great, Oslo thought. Another 'Supreme'. Why did men always need to call themselves a supreme something-or-other?

"My apologies, Supreme Global Leader. The last eight months have flown by so rapidly I haven't taken the time nor care to update myself with proper protocols. How fares the construction of the Global Capitol in Babylon?"

Contradeum smirked.

"It goes so well we have transitioned our government to the new city. Come visit us soon."

There was no mistaking the last statement for a polite invitation. It was a pure command, inviting only one response.

"Yes, sir."

"How goes the rebuilding of America? You opened your northern and southern borders completely to facilitate the transportation of builders and supplies. The convoys to the outward perimeters of the affected areas have been impressive. Who was your logistician?"

Like heck she was giving him the names of her

people.

"The responsibility for my country's recovery from the most hideous disaster in our history has fallen upon my poor shoulders, Supreme Global Leader. I must give much credit to the leaders of Canada and Mexico, who have been more than generous with their donations."

"But it's not enough."

Sylvia Oslo had been a four-star Admiral before she took over the office of President of the United States by introducing two forty-five-caliber bullets into the previous office holder's chest. Controlling the muscles of her face and the depths of her eyes to show no emotion was second nature. She took too long to answer the question, though, which was the same as screaming an affirmative.

"That is correct, Supreme Global Leader."

"Please allow me to state the obvious. The attack on your country couldn't have come at a worse time, weather wise. Strong prevailing winds drove radioactive fallout into your country's grain belt. Most of your freshwater supplies have also been affected. You couldn't seed much arable land this year. There are food shortages around the globe, so it will be difficult for you to purchase food for your people."

"The Second Cataclysm took out many of your doctors, nurses, health practitioners, first responders, and police. The levels of sickness in your country are increasing exponentially. Canada and Mexico are getting to where they can no longer sustain you. They may have trouble sustaining themselves this year. You are facing a long, frigid winter with a desperate starving populace. Have I over-exaggerated your plight, Oslo?"

So, she was no longer 'President'. Curse him for the son of a dog he was! She still had enough nukes to wipe the smirk off his face for all time. Enough nukes to force the rest of the world to give her whatever she wanted.

Her shoulders slumped. Could she do that? She served in the United States military for thirty-five years and earned the highest rank possible. Her peers respected her. Her family, what remained after the Second Cataclysm and the First Global Nuclear War, was very proud of her and told her so often. Could she really become a nuclear terrorist just to maintain the sovereignty of a country barely in existence? She was so tired. The weariness bled its way into the core of her bones. She lifted unhappy eyes towards Contradeum.

"What do you want?"

His eyebrows rose at the abruptness of her question.

"I want respect, Oslo, and I can command it. If you haven't heard, all the remaining nuclear countries have surrendered their arsenals to me. What used to be the United States of America is the last remaining holdout. I could let you and your people starve to death or continue to die of disease; it would be nothing at this point to sweep in and take over. Or we could start another nuclear war and kill millions of innocent men and women. There are no children left on Earth under the age of eleven years after the Second Cataclysm, so at least we don't have to be the monsters responsible for killing babies."

"The Rapture." Oslo said, too tired to care that she interrupted him. "At least call it what it is: Jesus Christ called his Church home and all those who believed in Him, placed their trust and faith in Him, flew away to live with Him in Heaven. If we're being honest with each other, at least call it like it is."

Contradeum's face was a study in rage.

"I am of half a mind to conduct a nuclear strike on what's left of your pitiful country based on your insolence alone."

Oslo stood up and removed her dress jacket and blouse, leaving only her bra on her upper body. She pointed to wires and devices implanted under her skin, leading from her heart to her brain.

"See all this gear? I had it implanted after the First Global Nuclear War. Command and Control of my country's nuclear weapons vest entirely with me. If I die, if my heart fails, if my brain ceases to function, these devices will launch everything I have left: nuclear bombers, ICBM's and SLBM's. One of their primary targets is that cozy little shop you have set up in Babylon. The commanders of my nuclear forces agree with me. You attack us and we will destroy the world. So, you petty little dictator, if you want your global reign to end in a big bang right now, go ahead. Pull the trigger. I dare you."

They glared at each other for long minutes. Finally, Contradeum nodded and gestured towards Oslo's chair. She sat down, not bothering to put her blouse and jacket back on.

"What do you want, Contradeum? And before you get huffy again, remember, I've nothing left to lose."

His jaws crunched back and forth as the hatred poured out of his eyes in an acid rain.

"I'm reorganizing the world into ten regions. I propose one of those regions to be all the Americas, North and South. You'll be its Regional Supervisor and you'll answer only to me. The world will rally to support all the nations affected by the nuclear war; we will feed you, clothe you and treat your wounded. In return, you'll turn your military over to Earth Forces. Including your nuclear weapons."

Oslo looked at him, her face impassive. On her orders, the military had already systematically stripped America's bombers and missile bases of the ability to conduct a nuclear strike. They fed all the missiles a special little virus directing it to launch against Babylon if Contradeum's overzealous people programmed the nukes to hit any target in what used to be North America. Oslo saw this day coming when the rest of the nuclear countries handed over their inventories. She was prepared to hand over her nuclear inventory, with one exception.

"You can have the bombers and land-based missiles, which you will remove from my Region. I keep my boomers, attack subs, submarine-launched nukes, bases, support, and maintenance. It's my insurance against you stabbing us in the back like you did last time."

"What are you talking about?" Contradeum said, his voice spluttering.

Oslo smiled. It was a dirty, mean smile.

"You have a leak in your office, Grand Supreme Highness. A leak who told me, in person, you started this war with some nano-bots and a vulnerable missile control officer. I have the informant's statement recorded, sealed, and locked away in several locations. An insurance policy against you deciding I've become too much of a pain in your rear. Maybe your brainwashed masses won't believe it, but it will plant a seed. Something as small as a mustard seed can grow into the size of a fifty-caliber bullet delivered to your brain by an angry American. I can think of about 159 million Americans willing to put one there right now. I'll go along with your plan, Supreme Global Leader, but I keep my boomers and attack subs."

There was a long silence. Maybe looks could kill, Oslo thought, as she felt her chest tighten against rising anxiety.

Contradeum stood up and favored her with one last glare.

"Fine," he snarled, and ended the connection.

Oslo leaned back in her chair, her heart hammering in her chest. She wondered if she was going to have a heart attack or a stroke. Not that it mattered in terms of her eternal destiny. Within weeks of the First Global Nuclear War, she accepted Jesus Christ as her Savior and started praying for the wounded, sick, dying, and starving in her country. At least Jesus took care of her eternity if her life ended this day. The rest of the world wouldn't be so lucky. Oslo lifted her wrist to her mouth.

"You heard?"

The male voice at the other end of the pickup answered immediately.

"I did."

"Keep all our nuclear forces at DEFCON ONE

until further order. If I die, you know what to do."

"I do, President Oslo."

She laughed bitterly.

"I guess that's Regional Supervisor Oslo, now."

Mesopotamia, the twenty-third day of the fourth month, 2004 BC

They left the village just as the sun made its final bow and ducked under the horizon. Coventry rode first, not dismayed by having the other two at her back. She was humming slightly, and a contented smile rested on her face. Davis nudged his horse forward until his horse came even with hers.

"How do we set up a quantum string connection out here?"

Coventry swept the horizon, back and front, with keen eyes.

"Once we're clear of the huts, we'll stop and set up the link. I need an undeveloped area. My device activates a quantum stream of two microns in diameter. It hunts through space and time until it contacts a satellite from our era. Once it connects to the servers on Atlantis, the stream widens to give us sufficient capacity to run a hologram."

Wu had pulled up to Coventry's other side.

"They can do that?"

Coventry nodded.

"Yes, it's astonishing. Any team with this device in the field can have instantaneous contact with Origin."

"What if the satellites go down?" Davis asked.

"It gets trickier. In such a case, I make the

connection through the Temporal Scepter at Insertion Point. If the Team has been in the field too long, they might need a Programmer to re-establish the connection."

"Except," Heather said, her voice quiet, "there are no Programmers left."

Coventry nodded somberly.

"You're the last one we have."

"Do the other Teams have a quantum string communications device?"

Coventry turned her face away so Heather couldn't see her.

"The one I have is the only one that exists. At least, such was the case when I transitioned here. Even if TTI could transition a device to the Teams in the field, we can't safely send an operator with the equipment. We can't just send a device. If the Team is dead, we'll have left futuristic equipment in the past. You know how many Directives we'd violate doing that."

After a few minutes of riding in the dark, Davis shifted in his saddle.

"Let's talk about the things you haven't told us."

Coventry dropped her chin to her chest and sighed.

"A little over eight months ago, the world engaged in a limited nuclear war."

"What?!" Davis and Heather said in chorus, spinning to face Coventry, who lifted her hand, palm out.

"I only found out before I came to your door. A lot has happened since you've been gone. We have a new world leader, a slimeball named Malchus

Contradeum. He dissolved the One World Legislature and calls himself the Supreme Global Leader. Before the attack on Atlantis, which my boss thinks he staged, he held an election. He only got fifty-two percent of approval, with the major detractors being America, Canada, Britain, and Russia. My boss thinks he suborned an American missile officer and supplied her with advanced nanotechnology. She introduced it into a missile silo and the nanotech launched a nuke at Moscow."

Davis closed his eyes.

"How in the nine shades of the afterworld did she get nanotech in a missile complex? They screen for them!"

Coventry sighed again.

"The missile officer was having an affair with the security chief. He just looked the other way. They both suicided after the launch."

Heather held her hand to her stomach, wishing it to stay in place.

"How many died? Are we going back to a nuclear winter?"

"Not yet to the last question. Five million dead in the first strike, a million and a half more in the last eight months. In terms of casualties, we have about three times the number in sickness and radiation injuries."

Davis frowned.

"So, the Russian nukes fizzled?"

Heather glared at him.

"Six and a half million dead and you think they fizzled?!"

Davis kept his voice soft.

"I'm upset, too, Heather, but you can't take the military out of me. Russian warheads are huge. If they launched everything and all of it hit their targets, the dead would be in the hundreds of millions. Nuclear war is a zero-sum game. No one survives it. Mutually Assured Destruction means exactly that."

"Davis is right, Heather. Our Anti-Ballistic Missile Defense Net did very well, eliminating 98.3 percent of incoming enemy warheads. Of the ones breaching our defenses, most of the warheads failed. The ones getting through took out Phoenix, Chicago, Dallas, Columbus, and Dayton. "

An icy grip of fear took a solid hold on Davis's guts.

"New San Diego?"

"New San Diego got lucky. None of the warheads targeting it made it through the Defense Net. The Net kept the West Coast safe. Prevailing winds moved the fallout away from the West Coast population surviving the First Cataclysm. The rest of America wasn't as lucky. Food production and freshwater supplies are suffering. Canada and Mexico came through like long-lost family with support after the strike, but it's still bad."

"So why do they need TTI, Coventry? It sounds like academic research is the last thing on anyone's mind right now."

The former Marine nodded slowly.

"You're right, Heather. We have bigger problems, like the shortage of food and medicine. TTI are looking for solutions in Antiquity. They're thinking of growing crops and harvesting them for the future."

Davis jerked his head up.

"Is it possible without messing up the timeline?"

Heather shook her head.

"It's possible, I guess, but a little doubtful right now. It would take time, materials, and a lot of money."

"How much time?" Coventry asked, her voice soft again.

"About six years to train the Programmers and organize everything."

Coventry bit her lips.

"I was afraid you were going to say that. We need a solution now. We don't have six years. If things keep going the way they are, the world only has five years left before it ends."

Atlantis, September 1, 2097 AD

Erasmus Hart jerked his head off his arms, folded on his desk, as his comm pad buzzed and flashed a steady red light. He wiped the sleep off his face and activated the pad, astonished to have a hologram of the American President sitting before him. As the hologram firmed up, the windows in his office darkened to a deep black and the audio dampeners whined into service.

His office turned into a SCIF, a Sensitive Compartmented Information Facility, in a matter of seconds. He couldn't remember the last time he received a secure, encrypted holocomm. Hart had never seen the Oval Office before, either.

President Oslo regarded him through hooded, somber eyes.

"Are you Erasmus Hart?"

"I am, President Oslo."

Oslo frowned at him.

"Your sheet says you were a police officer for twelve years in Chicago before you signed up with TTI. Do you have any family there?"

Hart shook his head, his eyes threatening to fill with tears.

"No, President. Most of my family died in the First Cataclysm. They lived in New York then. I lost some good friends eight months ago, but no family."

Oslo shuffled some papers and looked up at him.

"You have my deepest sympathies, sir. I lost six family members when the nukes fell. Do you keep up with the news, Mr. Hart?"

He nodded, alert and on guard.

"I do."

"All the Americas are now grouped into Global Region Ten under the new One World Government. I am Contradeum's Regional Supervisor. The Grand Poombah of the World now runs the United States. Does he gall you at all, Mr. Hart?"

Hart thought about it for a moment. This could be an elaborate loyalty test. The room was secure against anyone who tried to intercept the communication, so his comments would be confidential. It bothered him he had no ability to prevent Oslo from recording their conversation. If she was the Supreme Global Leader's Regional Supervisor, he had every reason to suspect the question.

"Before I answer that, President Oslo, I would be interested in hearing your comments."

She snorted.

"I was hoping you'd be more than just a sycophantic functionary, Mr. Hart. Are you just a sycophantic functionary? I need someone who has big brass ones between his legs to carry out a clandestine mission for me. Or did they take those off when you signed up for Atlantis?"

Hart bristled.

"I'm perfectly intact, thank you. I didn't live this long or survive this deeply in my career, rushing blindly into things. What do you want, President Oslo?"

She steepled her fingers in front of her.

"I want Heather Wu and Lamek Davis standing in front of me before your boss and her master can get their claws into them. My sources tell me they'll come back soon."

Her sources? She had sources on the island? Security looked more like a sieve than a pot these days.

"Your information is better than mine, President Oslo. I hadn't heard we found them in Antiquity."

Oslo regarded him for a long moment.

"Maybe you aren't the right person for this task." She leaned forward and Hart reached out to stop her from terminating the call.

"Wait, wait! Please understand why I'm being cautious. The world is in a volatile state, yes? It's being re-shaped into different geopolitical entities and if anyone is still loyal, to whom should they be loyal? Who do you trust, President?"

Oslo leaned back in her chair.

"Few, I admit. I'm trusting you with this call, am

I not?"

"Yes. But what do you ask from me beyond taking your call and keeping it between us?"

"I want you to scoop Wu and Davis off the Lens as soon as they materialize and throw them into the water. I'll take care of them from there."

Hart stared at her, uncomprehending.

"You want them dead?"

Oslo closed her eyes as if she desperately needed sleep.

"No! I want them to be alive. Just get them into the water. Unharmed. That's all. Can you do that without getting them or you killed, or involving your boss?"

Hart breathed into the silence.

"President Oslo, I am dedicated to the security of TTI and our missions here. You should know Supreme Global Leader Contradeum has visited Administrator Korhonen several times within the last eight months. TTI's primary mission may or may not continue. I know if I do what you ask, they'll probably feed me to the wonderful abundance of sharks regularly swimming around Atlantis looking for chum and those deemed as traitors. I've heard nothing from you encouraging me to risk my life."

Oslo's eyes resembled that of a shark, in this moment.

"Fair enough. America is dead, Mr. Hart. We signed up for this regional governance crap because we have no food, fuel, or clean water to get us through the winter. I made a deal with the devil and my scientists think we found a back channel out of the deal. Heather Wu is the key, but I can't very well interview her there. I just need a few minutes with her in the water, Mr. Hart, and you can have her back. You don't have to give me an answer right now. I'm sending you a secure link. If you decide not to help, at least send me their ETA. Oslo out."

The room lit up as the window screens dissolved. Hart sat still for a moment, then checked the recording equipment in his office. The recording showed him sleeping at his desk for the last 30 minutes. Someone slipped through their security protocols, accessed the holo recorders and tied in a loop of him sleeping during the entire time he was on the call with Oslo. They did it without tripping alarms or making anything look out of the ordinary. Only alphabet soup organizations like the NSA, CIA, or DIA had such cachet.

Hart looked down at his tablet and saw a new icon on the screen. They shaped it as an eagle. Someone was trying ridiculously hard to make it easy for him to make a decision potentially costing him his life. The only thing they couldn't do was make him press the icon.

Mesopotamia, the twenty-third day of the fourth month 2004 BC

Several hours later, the trio stopped their horses under a silver moon. The stars glowed in the dry desert air. The warm wind gently stirred the sand kicked up by their horses' hooves. It was a beautiful, romantic evening. At least, it would have been, had Coventry's news not trapped them in the horrors of their imaginations.

They dismounted from their horses, muscles stiff from prolonged travel on an ancient saddle not designed for comfort. Coventry took a bundle from her pack, caught Davis's eye and flicked a glance at Heather.

"I need to set up the string with classified equipment. Can you two give me a few minutes?"

"Of course," Davis said, before turning to Heather. "Let's hobble the horses and take a walk."

They busied themselves with their stock, making sure they comfortably cinched all straps and the horses' hooves were clean. Then the two of them linked hands and took a stroll on the dune. Heather snuck a glance behind her.

"Do you trust her, Mick?"

"Yeah, right. As 'bout as far as you could throw her."

Heather made sure Coventry wasn't watching them and slipped her hand into a concealed pocket. She showed Davis the two God Coins in her hand.

"I'm going to reprogram these once we get to Insertion Point. Keep her distracted for a few minutes if you can. I will program them to bring us back here fifty-eight weeks after we leave. Make sure your Coin is in your hand when we transition. If they cross us when we arrive, activate the Coin."

Davis looked at her with admiration.

"You think of everything. Good plan."

They walked in silence for a few minutes, then turned around. Coventry looked at them oddly as they edged closer to where she hunched over a console.

"The string is live." She touched her ear. "We're

ready, Administrator."

A clear holo image of Administrator Korhonen leaped into existence on the desert floor. Both Davis and Wu jumped, startled by the clarity of the image.

"Dr. Wu, I can't tell you how happy I am to see you. Protector Davis, I'm less happy to see you, but you kept Heather safe. You get points for that at least. Whose idea was the fake suicide?"

Heather gestured to herself.

"It was all mine, Administrator, but you and your team have probably figured it out. I'm not sure how long we can keep this quantum string live, so why don't you get to the point?"

Korhonen looked miffed at Wu's abrupt tone.

"Let's keep in mind I'm the one holding the cards. We found you in Antiquity, Dr. Wu. If you run, we can and will find you again. I'm here with an olive branch. If you don't accept it, Major Quarterlaine has instructions to kill you."

Davis glanced at Coventry's face, who met his gaze evenly. Coventry looked back at Korhonen.

"Administrator, you would be wise to stay away from threats. Davis is a formidable enemy, and I wouldn't put it past Heather to put a blade in me if I should attack them. They have been out here a lot longer than I have. I would be at a significant disadvantage in an armed conflict. I recommend we resolve this through peaceful means, unless you want me dead."

Korhonen sighed and sat down in a chair.

"I'm sorry. I'm beat. My conduct is inexcusable; please forgive me. Has Coventry filled you in on what's happened since you've been gone?"

Heather's eyes became teary.

"We heard, Administrator. I'm so sorry. Did you lose anyone?"

Korhonen closed her eyes for a long moment, her face drawn and pinched.

"We all lost someone, Heather. I'm tired of losing people. I have five teams trapped in Antiquity, counting Major Quarterlaine, that I'm on the verge of losing right now. We can't let that happen. I'm tired of presiding over funerals." She passed her hand over the surface of her desk. "I just sent a dataset through the stream. It grants you two complete immunities from prosecution, restores you to your positions, and provides for back pay. I need you to program a rescue mission to recover our Teams, Heather. Mr. Davis, I need you and Coventry to go get them."

Heather's eyes widened in alarm.

"I'm not sure I'm comfortable with you separating us, Administrator!"

Korhonen dropped her head slightly, weariness draining the vigor from her eyes.

"I can't help it, Heather. You're my last Programmer and way too valuable to send into the field. I know you have God Coins; no one is going to take them away from you. If you ever feel trapped, you can transition to whenever you've programmed it. Don't look so surprised. Credit me with some intelligence. It's what I would've done in your shoes. I need Davis in the field, but only to collect the other four Teams. After that, he can hang around your neck as much as you like. Those are the only terms I can offer you."

Davis and Wu looked at each other for a long moment. Duty and honor conflicted with desire. They were leaving relative peace and a reasonably good life for a world afflicted by nuclear war, starvation, and strife. Their world, their future, was dying. If they stayed, their consciences would suffer.

"We're at 30,000 feet and the ramp is open, Heather. What do you want to do?"

Her eyes were full of mourning. She lifted her hands to her face and rubbed her cheekbones, as if to urge her skin to life again.

"We jump, Mick. Let's hope it's not to our deaths."

Atlantis, September 2, 2097 AD

Hart watched the activity around the Lens with some interest. The engineers were happy to be back at work, and a sense of optimism filled the place. None of them should have the information Quarterlaine found Wu and Davis in Antiquity, but the island was too small to keep cheerful news suppressed for long. With everything happening in the world, good news was as welcome as a triple-bonus paycheck.

He pulled his personal device out of his hip pocket and studied the eagle icon on the screen. Any trust he had in any system of leadership was gone. Everyone was out for themselves, and he was nothing but shark-bait to the loser. Hart once believed in something. Maybe it was the American dream. Maybe it was the words used to feed men's minds with aspirations and their souls with purpose; words like 'honor', 'duty', and 'courage.'

What did those words mean anymore? He was a loyal man without a leader and without a country.

Hart was fifty-six years old. He knew he wouldn't live forever. The way things were going, he might not live another year, much less forever. He would die if he didn't have something or someone to believe in. Hart was that kind of man. For his life to have meaning, it had to have a means by which he could have honor.

Honor. He snorted. The things he had to do for Korhonen gave his soul acid indigestion. Take, for example, the traitorous Programmer Jacques Lavoie, who gave out the information resulting in the attack on Atlantis. He had a mother and father suffering from a treatable genetic disease. Someone plunged enormous funds into their bank account for the information leading to the attack on the Programmers' Complex. Korhonen told him to squeeze mom and dad dry of information by any means necessary, then kill them.

Hart had been a police officer, not a soldier. He had boarded the hypersonic stealth jet with his team and a lot of trepidations. No one trained him to extract information illegally, and he never beat a confession out of a suspect. He'd been a good cop. The flight to Lavoie's parents' address took no time at all. The reluctance of his heart to torture old folks made him wish the trip took decades instead of minutes.

When they arrived, local police had the house surrounded, and they had taped off the entrance ways. Hart approached a local police officer and flashed his credentials.

"What's going on?"

The officer, intrigued at being questioned by the Head of Special Projects for TTI, nodded to the house.

"Murder, suicide," he said. "Can you imagine? These people survive a nuclear war with a lot of money and many friends. They were generous and helped their neighbors whenever they could, for what little it did for them. We found them this morning. The husband shot the wife and then killed himself. No note, no motives, nothing. It's just a shame, that's all."

Hart had kept a straight face, but was enormously relieved. While they might never know who Lavoie's benefactor was, at least he wouldn't have to torture and kill anyone. On the flight back, he wondered if he could do such a thing. He also wondered why he was working for someone who could order it.

Hart glanced down at the eagle icon on his device. He stood for something once. His life wasn't over. He could make it stand for something again.

He caught the eye of his XO and gave her an imperceptible nod. Somewhere in the last thirty seconds, he decided, without really knowing how it happened. If he was going to die, it would be while doing the right thing.

Dying in bed was overrated, anyway.

Mesopotamia, the twenty-fourth day of the fourth month, 2004 BC

The rest of the trip to Insertion Point was uneventful. Carrion eaters had stripped the bodies of the Gutians to their bones. Only rusted weapons, tattered cloth, and hide shields marked the boney graveyard. At least the smell was gone.

As Davis asked Coventry to help him remove the tack from the horses, Wu discretely programmed the God Coins. When Davis returned, she surreptitiously slipped a God Coin into Davis's hand and he concealed it.

They had to sanitize Insertion Point, of course. Anything hinting of futuristic manufacture, they had to remove and bag to bring with them. It was the only way to prevent harm to the timeline. Davis arranged bundles around the locus of the Scepter's field. Coventry had packed the Scepter within a carrying case, which she was trying to juggle in her hands with three bags and her personal kit.

Wu smiled at her.

"If you drop the case, you're going to break a bone in your foot. Why don't you let me carry it?"

Coventry smiled gratefully.

"Thanks, Heather. Much appreciated. I still have to help Davis strip the MetaMaterials left in the canyon. Back in a sec."

When Davis and Coventry came back with bundles of latent MetaMaterials canvass, Heather was waiting in the center of the swag with the Time Scepter case in her hands.

Davis nodded at the large rectangular box.

"Will that thing work through the case?"

"It will," Heather reassured him. "I have a remote device which connects our Coins through the box's dampening field. Are you ready? Okay, three, two, one…"

The canyon faded away. Origin came into focus.

Men and women with automatic weapons surrounded the Lens, their guns pointed at the trio on the dais.

A man stepped forward dressed in black, with a black hood on his head.

"Lamek Davis, Heather Wu, you're under arrest for treason. We have termination authorization if you refuse to come with us."

CHAPTER THE THIRD:
CREATION

Spes Deserit, in the Year of Our Fight 2375
Mission Day One

By one accord, they separated into three groups and dispersed through the large circular chamber. Tul'ran drew Johan aside and asked the scientist to explain how food came from other worlds to this place. Erianne and Darian sought a more practical approach; they walked straight to the Food Maker and began strategizing instructions for preparing steak, mashed potatoes, and green vegetables.

Gwynver'insa danced around the room with a cloth she pulled out of a cabinet and was gaily dusting the meager pieces of furniture in the chamber.

Johan gave up trying to explain physics to a thoroughly frustrated Tul'ran just as Erianne and

Darian gave their last instructions to the machine working to create their meals.

Tul'ran shook his head, a small headache forming between his eyes. He knew he wasn't a stupid man, but the intelligence serving him well in his time helped him not at all here. The warrior was shrewd enough to know he wasn't short of aptitude; he lacked knowledge. Hundreds of years of knowledge. It was difficult to accept the impossible without feeling a trill of fear his lack of understanding could somehow jeopardize his life or the lives of the cohort he now commanded.

He turned to look for his bride and noticed Gwynver'insa standing off to one side. She cupped her right hand, palm up, and dropped her cupped left palm on top. A look of intense concentration crossed her face.

"What does she do?"

Tul'ran jumped a little, then blushed.

"You walk quietly, my lovely wife. I think you might have shaved a year from my life, so frightened was I by your stealthy approach."

Erianne grinned and squeezed the muscles in his left shoulder.

"Nice try. You aren't so weak, my man. What's going on?"

The sudden transition to the English language sent Tul'ran's mind into a twist, but after a moment, he responded in kind.

"Our host does something unusual."

Erianne and Tul'ran watched as Gwynver'insa continued to stare intensely at her hands. A golden light flashed out from between her fingers. An apple sat in her right palm and the slight woman squealed in delight.

Tul'ran felt Erianne's astonishment in his mind.

'Where did that come from?' was the silken question caressing his brain, speaking much as El Shaddai did. This was His gift to them: the ability to speak to one another mind to mind and heart to heart.

'I don't know. Her palm was empty and is now filled with an apple. Shall we go have a converse with our most unusual friend?'

They casually walked over to where the diminutive woman gleefully chomped down on her apple. Erianne gestured to the beautiful red fruit and smiled.

"Lady Gwynver'insa, my husband and I could not help but to notice the unusual means by which you conjured your fruit. Will you share with us how you did that?"

The smaller woman nodded eagerly.

"My talent works opposite to that of your husband's sword, milady. I cast my mind to the place where I would see something appear. I form the object in my mind, giving it shape, solidity, color, and, with my apple, taste. When I am finished picturing it in my mind, I give instruction to the emptiness between my palms and bid it appear."

She frowned into the ensuing silence. Johan had already bent and twisted Tul'ran's mind beyond comprehension; he was having trouble absorbing Gwynver'insa's explanation, and it showed on his face. It must have shown on Erianne's, as well.

"Have I done something amiss, milord and

milady?"

Erianne shook her head as if she was seeing the diminutive woman for the first time.

"Do you bring things from somewhere else, as does the Food Maker?"

Gwynver'insa grinned her delight, her smile extending full across her face and exposing her brilliant white teeth.

"Oh no, Lady Erianne! It would be wrong of me to take something from another place and bring it here. What if a person in the other place needed this apple to survive, whereas it is only a matter of want for me? No, no. I merely ask the apple to exist. My palms at the beginning seemed empty, but subatomic particles filled them. While the air between my palms looks devoid of construct, it is quite full on a molecular level. I instruct the molecules to take the shape of what my heart desires. It is simple, really."

Tul'ran looked at Erianne, even further lost by the words Gwynver'insa used to explain the miraculous. He turned back to Gwynver'insa and shook his head.

"Lady Gwynver'insa, please do not misinterpret our stunned silence and attribute it to disapproval. What you describe is something exceeding the limits of our abilities. Can you command any object into existence, or does your talent only extend to food?"

Gwynver'insa frowned, the lines barely creasing her pretty face.

"I must have the sense of it, Lord Tul'ran. The object I command into existence must be something I have experienced in my life. It would do no good for you to describe something beyond my ken and ask me to work it for your profit. Your people do not enjoy this ability?"

"You have the right of it," Erianne said. "I give you my truth, Lady Gwynver'insa, for it is only by honesty I suspect we will survive in this place. No one in the world from which we came can create something from nothing. I would wager my husband's sword no person in this world can do so, either. Your gift is wondrous, indeed. It is also dangerous. I do not think our friends saw you use your gift, nor should you display it wantonly. If word should pass beyond these walls that you can create substance from subatomic particles, then every person on this planet will seek you out for their selfish desires. You must protect your gift and we must protect your life at all costs."

Gwynver'insa's eyes widened.

"What do you mean when you say 'at all costs'?"

"It means," Tul'ran said, "we will lay our lives down for yours to ensure neither you nor your gift falls into your enemy's hands, permitting them to shape your gifts to an evil purpose. What did you mean when you said your gift works opposite from my sword, which my wife would apparently wager away as casually as a clay coin?"

Gwynver'insa laughed when he smacked Erianne on the shoulder; though, if the truth be told, it was more a love tap than an actual blow.

"May I see your mighty sword, Lord Tul'ran?"

Tul'ran drew Bloodwing over his head and held it out sideways in front of him.

"Be careful, Lady Gwynver'insa. I have it on good authority Yahweh created this sword for a powerful angel, and it is beyond sharp. Should you reach for it too casually, you might find a severed finger at your feet."

The sprite laughed, but came forward cautiously. She extended her right palm over the tip of the blade and ran it down to where the blade met the hilt. Her face paled and her large blue eyes swelled as she left her hand hovering over the blade.

"Yahweh has given you a dangerous gift and a mighty responsibility, milord. Should you use this sword for its intended purpose, it will uncreate anything. As long as the blade stays black, it operates as a sword. But see here, the fine blue light edging both sides of this majestic sword? This is not the same Blue Energy powering almost everything on this planet, including weapons. This light is different. Yahweh tied it to your soul and only your soul may command it."

"Should Lady Erianne pick up your sword to wield it, the light would disappear from it and it would just be another beautiful, deadly blade. You have found this sword will pass through any material, correct? Yes? The reason the blue line is so thin on your sword, Lord Tul'ran, is because it uncreates molecules in its path. There is no question it will pass through anything through which you swing it because everything in its path no longer exists when touched by this edge."

Tul'ran stood stiffly, the muscles in his forearm rigid.

"I must tell you, milady, your explanation frightens me to the end of my courage. It is a wonder I have not killed us all with Bloodwing."

Gwynver'insa shook her head.

"You need not fear, milord. You command it as surely as if you were a General and Bloodwing the Blade were your army. It does whatever you command, whenever you command it, by thought, word or deed. Yes, I am sincere. I believe it can hear your thoughts and take steps to defend you even without the wilful exercise of your body. Hence, the way it saved us when we arrived."

Bloodwing's surface suddenly glowed blue and wisps of blue light arose from the blade. The wisps danced as if forming from the top of a steaming hot beverage and then started angling toward Gwynver'insa's hand.

"Stop!" Tul'ran said, his voice cold and so possessed of command, both Gwynver'insa and Erianne stiffened. At once, the blue light on the blade disappeared, and the surface returned to its rich, silky black essence.

Gwynver'insa drew a shaky breath.

"Do you see, milord? For whatever reason, Bloodwing sensed a demonstration was in order, but obeyed your command to cease and desist the moment you gave it. You need not fear your blade, but you must also take caution. Every Combatant on this planet would give their souls to possess your sword. They do not know none of them could wield it, which makes their desire more dangerous. It seems we both have secrets we must not share beyond the silence of these walls."

The three of them jumped and turned at Darian's excited shriek. She held out a tray upon which sat five plates containing steak, mashed potatoes, and green beans.

"It worked! I hope it tastes as good as it looks. C'mon everybody, let's eat!"

Though they had all eaten in the Garden hours before, the stress of the attack upon them at the entrance to the Garden and the tension of walking through a combat zone left all of them famished. They dug into their plates. Johan, Darian, Tul'ran, and Erianne ate boisterously, being familiar with the dish. Gwynver'insa ate slowly, nibbling on each separate item on the plate at first, savoring the taste. When she finished, her face glowed with pure joy.

"It has been hundreds of years since I have enjoyed the taste of something new. My heart swells with gratitude, my friends. I am so grateful Yahweh sent you to join me on my quest to reclaim my planet from the Combatants. We must sleep now. There are still seven hours in this night and we must not journey forth until the sun rises. Once you choose a bed, say the word 'privacy' and the bed shall deflect light around it in such a way as to make it disappear. The shield, however, is not soundproof. I have devices for your ears if you find the ambient sound too great to support sleep."

Darian grinned at Tul'ran and Erianne, her smile containing a hint of malice on her curvaceous lips.

"No making out, you two. We may not see you, but we'll hear you. Johan and I don't want to have to rate your performance in the morning."

Tul'ran shook his head, offended that Darian should broach such a sensitive topic before everyone in the group. He opened his mouth to reply, but his wife's hand was on his arm and her plea for silence was in his mind.

"Don't worry, Darian. Tul'ran and I will behave ourselves. We should all get some rest. It's been a trying day."

The Council Chamber was old and ornate. Dust accumulated on every surface, but there were no cobwebs. All creatures who spun cobwebs died hundreds of years into the past. This was once the Council of Elders, containing 4,200 chairs. The chairs were portable workstations with the capability to access and display any fact desired by the occupant. The Chamber fell into disuse after the Fight began, and the Elders abandoned it within fifty years of the pitched battles that killed millions of humans. In the time of barbarism, diplomacy lost its voice.

The center of the Chamber hosted twelve chairs arranged in a circle. Each chair represented the last survivors of the Twelve Great Armies of Spes Deserit. These twelve chairs were the only ones still functional, and they programmed all to display the virtual presence of their occupiers. One by one, the chairs powered up and displayed the image of their owner. There were six female Combatants and six male Combatants, although their method of dress wouldn't have given a clue as to their gender. Each wore elaborate multi-layered uniforms, with rows of medals and awards on their uniform blouse. As gaudy as one seemed, her neighbor was much gaudier.

In human terms, each looked like a fifteen to sixteen-year-old teenager. They had the wisdom of one hundred years and the hormones of a juvenile.

Each of the Combatants in this world wasn't an adult or an original warrior. Clones, to be more precise, of young Combatants killed in action during the Fight and restored to bodily form by the machines. As soon as they attained the age of one hundred years and their diaries fully briefed them, they returned to the fight. Spes Deserit was no longer a world with vast armies and air forces. So many adults had died during the Fight, only their children now waged war.

As soon as a child entered the arena as a Combatant, the machines began growing a latest version of that Combatant. The life expectancy of a Combatant on Spes Deserit was only three hundred years, on average, and falling with each cloned batch. Every clone was less perfect than the previous, shortening each youth's life expectancy.

The Race of Combatants was dying. They knew it. They developed elaborate hiding places to avoid any confrontation leading to their physical deaths. All had access to immense armies of war machines and combat aircraft left to them by their descendants.

Machines repaired machines, but neither machine nor human built new weapons to replace the losses. All the weapons were ancient because weapon inventors no longer existed. Wherever possible, they avoided all-out conventional warfare. Such a clash would weaken the losers considerably, and the surviving Combatants would swoop over the battlefield, picking off the remnants. Conflict was sporadic and strategic, with limited engagements. They couldn't replace losses; therefore, losses had to be avoided.

Each Combatant was aware of the existence of the Victims, hiding somewhere in the world, but ignored them. Their job was to win the war; then they could find and enslave the Victims. Once they seized the Victims, they could conduct experiments to rejuvenate their bodies and re-establish their longevity. While they all suspected they knew of the geophysical location of the Victims, no one made a move to capture them. Such a move would invite global warfare on a grand scale and lead to their destruction.

To help sustain the Fight until one of them could seize ultimate control, they developed elaborate rules to ensure one Combatant wouldn't become so powerful they'd bring the Fight to a disastrous end. The Combatants wanted to win, but needed the Fight to justify their existence. Hence, the Rules.

One such Rule permitted a gathering of the Combatants, in simulated form, to discuss any grievances. They frequently sought Abaddon's advice in such meetings, for he had a unique way of resolving the problems while preserving the Fight. When the last Combatant took a chair, a bright light flared in the vast, darkened room, and Abaddon stepped into their mist.

"Who is the current designated meeting leader?" Great Ron asked, his voice harsh, guttural, deep and booming. The first name of each leader started with the letter from their current clone batch. They all came out of the batch designated as 'R', so all their names started with that letter.

"Shut off your voice encoder, Ron!" Great

Rhanda said with disgust. "We're the only ones here and you're not impressing anyone!"

Great Ron glared at the girl who addressed him so.

"I am Great Ron, not Ron to you! We have Rules, Great Rhanda!"

"You're both idiots," said Great Richard, as if trying to be helpful.

The three of them started screaming profanities and pounded on console tops thousands of miles from each other.

"Silence!" Abaddon roared.

The Chamber immediately fell quiet, although the protagonists all continued to glare at one another. Abaddon flicked razor-sharp feathers on his great wings.

"I tire of your bickering! What was so important to take me away from my work to attend this meeting?"

Great Ron waggled a finger at Great Raylene.

"I accuse the Great Raylene of the Southern Plains, whose pitiful little territory borders on my glorious lands, of developing new weapons of warfare and employing them without giving us forty-five-months' notice!"

The Chamber erupted, with Combatants demanding to know what weapons she developed, how she deployed them, and why they had no notice. Within a space of minutes, the conversation developed into another session of hurled profanities.

"Silence!" Abaddon roared again. He pointed at Great Ron. "Where is your evidence, Great Ron?"

Ron manipulated his board, and a three-dimensional image bloomed over the center of the table.

"I had parked a squadron of my finest war machines outside the Crystalline Wall. I was looking for a Victim who had been running around in the area making trouble. She came out from behind the Crystallines with four other Victims. Of course, I immediately tried to kill her."

The other eleven nodded their heads and murmured their approval. This one had been causing problems and was of no value to the Combatants as breeding stock. She had a volatile mind and lacked respect for the honors and prestige owed to a Combatant.

"Who were the other four?" Great Reed asked.

"I don't know," Great Ron admitted. "They just came out from behind the Crystallines. When I tried to kill them, all the stuff from my guns disappeared into the sword the shrimp was carrying. Now watch what happens."

All looked on with horror as streams of blue energy enveloped Great Ron's weapons and they vanished. This was a new tech indeed!

"What makes you think Great Raylene created this sword?" Great Reena asked.

"You girls always stick together," Great Ron said, his voice haughty. "That's why you're so weak. Great Raylene's territory is the closest to the Crystallines. My territory borders the rest of the Crystalline Wall. It's obvious she would make a play for my territory if she developed a new weapon. I accuse her!"

"Or," Great River said, while examining her nails. They were all brightly colored, but each one bore a different pigment. It was the newest fashion, she had decided. "The shrimp brought the sword with him from the place behind the Crystallines, and you are blaming Great Raylene as a play for her territory. We're not as stupid as you are, Great Dumb Ron."

An uproar again ensued, with the Combatants yelling, beating on the tables, and shouting profanities. Abaddon allowed the fracas to continue for a few minutes. Truly, he was tiring of this bunch. He knew where each of them lived. It would take no effort at all to kill them. The thought tempted him sorely. Kill them all and leave this love forsaken planet behind.

"The sword is mine."

Abaddon uttered the words in a soft voice, but their meaning finally glided past the harsh rhetoric into the ears of each Combatant.

"What did you say?" asked Great Ryan in the silence following the angel's statement.

"I said, the sword is mine. It is an angelic sword which does not belong in this realm. I will possess it and you cannot have it."

Great Ron raised himself up to look as indignant as a fifteen-year-old child might be. A three-hundred-year-old child who looked fifteen, Abaddon corrected himself.

"Why did you attack me, Great Abaddon?"

"I did not attack you, Great Ron. You attacked my sword, and it responded to defend itself. Had you reported the incursion of those individuals into this world, as I asked you hundreds of years ago, I would have taken care of the situation and you would still have your squadron. Be comforted; I have this situation at hand. This Council need not concern itself further with the girl or her friends. Is there anything else?"

"I'm owed compensation!" Great Ron said, his voice pitching into a squeaky yell. "Who's going to replace my squadron? You've left me at a disadvantage, Abaddon. Are you going to protect me if one of these jerks attack me? Huh? What're going to do for me, Abaddon?"

"Let me show you," Abaddon replied calmly. The back of the chair on which Great Ron sat suddenly shot thirty heavy metal spikes into and through Great Ron's body. The remaining Combatants gasped in horror, as blood spurted from Great Ron's mouth. His florid face pinched in pain as his eyes grew wide... then empty. Great Ron died. For now.

Abaddon turned to the remaining eleven.

"I've been on this planet for thousands of years. Each one of you hides in a place I know the location of consummately well. In every hide hole you have, I've emplaced weapons such as this. You're trying my patience, Combatants. The sword is mine. Pursue it at your peril. And do strive to remember I'm not your servant. Perhaps Great Ron's replacement will keep humility uppermost in his mind when he watches this diary."

In a flash, Abaddon was gone.

The other eleven remained frozen in their seats for a time. Their Rules forbade them from moving on Great Ron's territory until his clone assumed the Seat. None of them looked at Great Ron's corpse because they focused each of their minds on just one thing.

They had to have that sword.

Darian didn't move for several hours, well beyond the time when the surrounding sounds suggested people at sleep. After she activated her privacy screen, she remained in her clothing, waiting for the sounds of preparation and muted conversations to die down.

She was tired of being treated like some dumb brunette by the other members of her group. The recombinant physicians coded her DNA for intelligence, as well as perfect physical features. She may not have understood physics to the extent of Johan's knowledge, but she absorbed much more than the others gave her credit for.

Take Tul'ran's sword, for example. It absorbed elevated levels of energy without so much as weakening the metal. Once it absorbed significant amounts of energy, it redirected it to the source of the assault. There were no explosions when it contacted the machines attacking them. They just disappeared. Tul'ran existed four thousand years before her time. It was impossible for anyone to possess such technology in his era. She didn't know where he got the sword, but its characteristics were a matter of precious knowledge. It would be worth something to somebody.

Darian never wanted to come to this horrid planet. She curried favor with Tul'ran and the others after she flipped the bird at her previous master. As soon as she turned around in the Garden to find Erianne watching her, she knew she needed a new plan. Tul'ran and his group were the only game in town at that moment, and it had been apparent she wasn't going home. She fawned over them like they were royalty, and they sucked it up.

Her lips twisted in revulsion. They didn't disguise their distrust of her, either. Fine. They had no loyalty to her, so she could screw them over. She was angry enough to put a shaft in the back of the little tart they fawned over as well.

Maybe she could find someone in this world who would pay her the attention she deserved. During her entire life, she felt the stirrings of greatness within her mind. She could be a major big deal if someone gave her the chance. Every time she tried to climb, someone beat her down. She had enough. Now she was going to do it her way and take out anyone who tried to resist her.

Someone was in command of this world. She felt a presence when she arrived, which tasted like that of her old master, but different, in a safer way. If that someone was as powerful, or more powerful, than her master, perhaps he or she would send Darian home for, say, the location of Gwynver'insa and the properties of Tul'ran's sword?

Darian slipped out of her bed, which was way more comfortable than she expected, and commanded the privacy shield to shut. She stood still for several minutes, half expecting a challenge. None came. She glided out of the room on soft feet, heading back to the entrance, the path to which she had memorized on their way in.

She wasn't worried about being found by some roaming machine. Erianne had returned her gun. The tall, dark-skinned woman was an idiot to return

Darian's weapon. Undoubtedly, Erianne programed the Smart Projectiles to never target her party, but Darian didn't care. The gun had enough capability to fend off the machines, and she had combat training. Darian could take care of herself, just as she always had. She had had enough of Tul'ran's stuffy sense of honor, his constant glaring threats, and Johan's cloying infatuation. It was time to do it on her own.

Darian made it to the exit without incident. If opening the door set off any alarms, nothing prevented her from slipping out onto the street. She had extraordinary night vision, courtesy of the geneticists who programmed her. It was as good as night vision goggles in the dark night, which was barely lit by streetlamps. There was no need to worry about carrying food or water.

She expected to be found long before she needed sustenance.

Abaddon watched the brunette exit from Gwynver'insa's safe house and marveled at how stupid humans could be. Surely Gwynver'insa would've told her about the perils of this world. He would kill her to make the point after extracting some information from her. If she had none to give, she would die quickly.

The house from which she exited was one of the first built on this part of the planet. It had defeated his every effort to peel back the layers and expose its contents, having defenses defying all the current technology on Spes Deserit. The house was interesting, made even more so by Gwynver'insa taking up residence in it. While he could wait for as long as it took to kill Gwynver'insa as she left the place, he would prefer to go in and get her. And the sword. One must never forget about Bloodwing the Blade.

Abaddon considered the woman gingerly making her way through the streets. He'd deal with her using one of Satan's tactics. It would please him to use the evil one's strategies while thumbing his nose at Satan's ultimate goals. The woman was just a stupid human with raging hormones. He could seduce knowledge from her without having to lay a hand on her disgusting body.

With a casual thought, he reconstructed his body into a different configuration, and waited.

The silence was almost a weapon itself, cloying the mind with wafts of fear of what may lay hidden within its depths. Darian kept her hand close to her gun, straining with all her senses to strip hidden dangers from the night, to react to them before they got her. The air tasted like heavy metals and smelled like cordite. She strained her eyes to see as deeply into the city streets as she could manage, but still had difficulty identifying shapes, much less those that would do her harm.

Maybe this wasn't such a clever idea.

She was on the verge of going back, when a man stepped out of the gloom into the light of a streetlamp. Darian viciously clamped down on a fearful desire to run, and assessed the man standing, arms folded, in front of her. He was tall, dark-haired, and way too handsome. Her heart fluttered as she felt the power drifting from him in waves.

This man was one like her master, indeed.

The lines of his face were severe, otherworldly, and beautiful. She felt her heart stutter again and her body became aroused. Here was one worthy of her body, mind, heart, and soul. Whatever was pouring out of him tempted her to run up, throw herself into his arms and give him whatever he desired.

A portion of her brain to which she regularly listened sharply pointed out she hated men and how disgusting and invasive sex felt. It screamed at her, reminding her men never aroused her like this and she should flee. Her mind flashed to the times her father had raped her repeatedly, degrading her body in every way possible. It worked. The flare of arousal in her body burned out, leaving her sweaty and shaken. No one had such an effect on her before. She had to get a grip. There was no way she was going to be a love slave to some hell spawn on this planet.

She walked toward the stranger, while her hand discretely coded a Smart Projectile in the gun holstered on her right hip. He was a male, and they were not to be trusted, especially after what he had obviously projected at her. She stopped within six feet of him and bit back her irritation as he slowly scanned her up and down. It didn't matter what planet you traveled to; men were always the same. Pigs to the core.

"My name is Darian. What's yours?"

Abaddon didn't respond, nor did his face show any emotion at her introduction. He looked at her like she was a lab rat, which irritated her immensely.

"Before you get any ideas, big guy, I should warn

you of two things. I am well armed and I serve a powerful entity in my home world. An entity who would be pleased to do you great harm should you choose a course of action less than warm regard."

His eyebrows twitched.

"I know very well whom you serve, wench. I could smell Satan's stench off your soul as soon as you came within talking distance. Interesting. Are you here to check up on me?"

Anger at being called a wench danced with the shock of being recognized as one of *his* acolytes and flirted with opportunity.

"Of course. You haven't checked in for a long time, have you? See, you've been naughty. I've come to get a report of your progress, then you must send me back to Earth. I could wrangle a ride here with the fools in the house behind me, but I doubt they'll fall for my tactics again."

He regarded her with eyes as black as the surrounding night.

"You're lying," he said, drawing the words out slowly, almost in a drawl. Darian's heart skipped a few beats, and she fought to control the muscles in her face as he continued speaking. "I taste anger mixed with fear in your words, over which is laid a fine layer of deceit. You belong to Satan, so I expect such emotions. Very well. Let us assume for a moment he sent you here through duplicitous means for a full report. Perhaps I will give you one and send you on your way. Or, perhaps, I will kill you and claim you never arrived. Or, perhaps, you will give me what I want, and I will, in return, satisfy your desire to return to Earth. I have many options."

"If one of your options involves my body, you can kiss yourself to sleep, and we can part ways right now!"

Abaddon's eyebrows raised at her outburst.

"My, my, isn't that a touchy subject? I don't touch the bodies of human women, Darian, because I don't suffer under the chains of lust. I couldn't care less about your looks and curvature. Besides, I can smell Satan's lust for you off your skin. I would touch nothing the Beast desired, even if I were so inclined. You're safe from sexual assault on this world. At least from me," he corrected, as an afterthought.

Darian's anger twisted her face.

"He never touched me. Not like that, anyway. If you don't want my body, what do you want?"

"The sword," Abaddon said, his voice betraying a hint of eagerness. "The short male in your party carries a wondrous sword. I want it. Help me get it, and I will send you home."

Darian looked at him, distaste fouling her mouth like vomit.

"That's it? I help you get Bloodwing the Blade and you send me home? I would have thought you'd rather have Gwynver'insa."

Abaddon cocked his head to one side.

"Why would you think so, wench?"

Her voiced raced from her lips like a slap.

"Stop calling me that! You want my help, treat me with respect, or walk away!"

She didn't know how close she came to death then. Darian couldn't know the limits to which humans had tested Abaddon's patience over his years on Spes Deserit. Had she the ability to read his mind, she might've swooned with fear. She was spitting in the Destroyer's face. Fortunately for her, he needed her to get into the house.

"Very well. Darian. Why would you think I would rather have Gwynver'insa?"

Darian hesitated for a moment. It was one thing to give up the arrogant walking slab of meat and his stupid sword. It was another thing to give up a sister.

"I assumed she was the reason you were stalking her house."

Abaddon didn't answer for a moment, continuing to stare at her. He nodded.

"I find it fascinating how you wrap lies around truth so cleverly it's hard to distinguish one from the other. Yes, I'd like to have her. I suspect, however, I will need to get through the warriors of your party before I can have her. Two birds with one stone; is that not the phrase from your realm?"

Darian held out her hand.

"We have a deal?"

Abaddon didn't move, but a look of revulsion flashed across his face.

"I told you, Darian, I don't touch humans. Get me what I want and I'll return to Earth with you. You have my word."

Darian dropped her hand to her side and rubbed it against her pant leg.

"Fine. What's next?"

Abaddon smiled, but it wasn't friendly and there was no joy in it.

"Let's start by you telling me everything you know about that house."

CHAPTER THE FOURTH: "O, WHAT TANGLED WEBS WE WEAVE..."

Atlantis, September 2, 2097 AD

Eyes say so much. They convey conviction and strength of purpose, bound by a strong will and resolve. Eyes filled with mercy, love, and compassion could flare with murderous intent on spurious provocation. Those were the ones with which you had to take great care. The ones filled with purpose and deadly intent, like the eyes staring at Davis and Wu right now over the barrels of automatic weapons.

Davis was on the verge of activating his God Coin and bugging out, when the person standing closest to him whispered,

"At ease, Chief Davis. This is just for show. You

79

came back an hour earlier than TTI expects. That's why no one else is here. This charade is for the holo projectors. We need to take you to a meeting and the clock is ticking. Please come with us."

Davis looked at Heather, whose mouth still hung open from the shock of being surrounded by armed people pointing guns at her.

"Let's do what they say, Heather, okay? I have a feeling about this. Coventry knows what's going on."

Quarterlaine glanced at him guardedly as the three of them left the Lens to be quick-marched to the south exit.

"What makes you say so, Chief Davis?"

They walked through the exit and rapidly descended the metal stairs. This wasn't the usual exit from the TTI Main Building. These stairs led to the escape pods.

"You barely reacted to the people with guns, Major. You were expecting them. None of the dunnage came with us. Someone ordered the AI to return three living bodies and leave everything back in Antiquity. Not Standard Operating Procedure. I'd ask you where we're going, but I suspect you'll not give me a straight answer."

They left the building and the Security Unit hustled them into an orange, fully enclosed pod sitting over a monorail. As soon as the three travelers entered the pod and strapped in to the shock-absorbing padded seats; the leader of their escort punched some keys. The pod closed, and the unit plunged over the cliff.

It was a short, exhilarating, and terrifying ride. Within seconds, they plummeted into the ocean and the upthrust of the buoyancy force drove them back up. They were gyrating on the surface when a diver cracked the hatch and slid into the Pod.

The diver wore a dry suit with a conformal closed circuit underwater breathing apparatus molded into the suit. The suit was lighter and far less cumbersome than the old SCUBA tanks and BCDs, but custom-made for only one person. A diver with this rig could stay underwater for days, if they didn't descend below five atmospheres. The diver removed the full-face mask and smiled at the pod's occupants.

"Admiral Oslo?" Davis asked, incredulity pitching his voice higher than normal.

Her smile dimmed.

"We're going to have to get you a new roster, Master Chief. Admiral Oslo became the President of the United States before transitioning to Regional Supervisor of Global Region 10."

Oslo shook her head at Heather, whose mouth was shaping a query.

"Swallow it, Dr. Wu. I've no time for questions, and only a few minutes to bring you up to speed."

Oslo pulled a device from her side pack.

"In the meantime, Dr. Wu, please use this to reprogram your Coins to return to the Lens via IP Mesopotamia in forty minutes. That's your expected time of arrival. It will work with God Coins. It's my personal unit."

As Heather accepted the device and took the others' Coins, Oslo gave them a summary of what happened while they were gone. She briefed them on Contradeum's rise to power, the limited nuclear war, and the struggle after the war to feed, clothe, and shelter Americans.

"We're running out of life-enabling resources," she said, at the end of the horrific narrative. "The United States had to fold itself within the global community just to have food, fuel, and water to survive this winter. The situation is untenable. I have sources in the Israeli government who have agreed to provide me with samples of the microbes they used to turn their deserts into blooming crops. We're thinking of sending a team to a remote location about five thousand years into our past. The team will plant crops and harvest them in antiquity. We send the teams out today and tomorrow we transport back bushels of grain. Thoughts?"

Heather shook her head.

"It won't work, Regional Supervisor. Setting aside considerations of the potential impact on the timeline, which are not inconsequential, there are a lot of other problems. In no order of importance, TTI controls the Lens, Korhonen controls TTI, and Contradeum controls Korhonen. Programming a mission requires programmers, engineers, technicians, and travelers. Lots of travelers. You can't conduct such operations covertly. You would have to get the One Global Government to sign off on it."

"It's no longer the One Global Government," Oslo said sourly. "Contradeum changed it this morning. The world's government, headed by Contradeum, is now to be referred to as 'Global One Democracy'."

It was Davis's turn to look incredulous.

"GOD? He's calling himself GOD now?"

"Affirmative, Master Chief."

"President Oslo, I don't mean to contradict you, but I retired as an E-7, Chief Petty Officer. I got there in only eight years of service, largely because of an early promote. I made it to the goat locker faster than a lot of other guys, but not to an E-9."

Oslo smiled, and her voice softened.

"One of my last acts as President of the United States was to recall you to active duty and promote you to an E-9, Master Chief Petty Officer Davis. Didn't you get the memo?"

Davis was grinning from ear to ear.

"No, ma'am. I was a little too busy to check my email."

They laughed, some of the tension evaporating from the boat.

"Why were you put in a goat locker?" Heather asked, causing the sailors to crack up again.

"In Navy jargon, Dr. Wu, the goat locker is a lounge, sleeping area, and galley on board a naval vessel which is reserved for the exclusive use of chief petty officers. By tradition, all other personnel, including officers and even the commanding officer, must request permission to enter the goat locker. But enough of this; we're running out of time. What are the other problems, Dr. Wu?"

"Please, call me Heather. If you can get Korhonen to sign off on the mission, say, to resolve a humanitarian crisis, something for which Contradeum would probably love to take full credit, you need to train Programmers. A mission this size will need at least six, working around the clock."

"The current size of the Lens will accommodate

pallets weighing one ton; anything heavier will not translate and the Lens will abort the transition. I don't need to tell you how long it will take to feed America if you can only transport grain one ton at a time."

"The lens would have to be enlarged, which requires engineers and a tech team to design and build. You'd also have to build a bigger seaport, a commercial monorail from the TTI Main Building and the seaport, and increase security a hundredfold. These are just the problems I can think of from the top of my head. You need six years to make this work, Regional Supervisor. At a minimum."

Oslo visibly deflated.

"We don't have six years, Heather. We may only have five on the outside edge. Please work this problem when you have spare time. I can't suck on Contradeum's teats for the next five years; the humiliation alone may kill me. I'll see what I can work on at my end. Can you transition out of this life raft, or do we need to get you somewhere else?"

Lines crinkled across Heather's forehead.

"This boat is large enough to stand in, and I can calculate for the pitch of the waves. We are all going to be nauseated after we transition, but I can make it work. I'll need to keep the programming device."

"Heather once translated me into a corridor no bigger than I am, President Oslo. She's that good."

Oslo smiled at the reassurance and gestured in Coventry's direction.

"Major Quarterlaine will liaise with us, but please keep her involvement with me a secret. Loose lips and all that. Keep the programming device, but destroy it as soon as you can. This meeting never happened. Godspeed."

Oslo put on her face mask and Davis checked the seals and fittings on her suit. He gave her an 'okay' sign, which she returned. She slipped out of the life pod and into the water with barely a ripple.

"Very smooth," Davis said. "I'm impressed. She's pretty good in the water. How much time do we have left, Coventry?"

"We're scheduled to arrive in thirty minutes, Master Chief."

"Call me Mick, if you don't mind. It feels weird to be addressed by my Navy rank when I've been out of it for so long. At least it feels that way after spending over twenty years in Antiquity. Heather, can you transition us back into the TTI Main Building?"

Heather frowned.

"I can't. It's possible to translate us into the past, but we can't transition from the same spatial coordinates into a future thirty minutes from now. I know it's bizarre, but the quantum bubble doesn't allow us to travel into the future. Besides, none of the cargo is sitting on the Lens. Either we go back to Mesopotamia and collect everything, or we wait thirty minutes and get them to pick us up."

Davis shook his head.

"All this subterfuge was for nothing if we get caught out here, Heather. Someone's going to notice a life pod bobbing in the water and find us in it. How will we explain that? Security should've had a squad out here ten minutes ago. You're right, we need to go back to Mesopotamia."

"We can't go back there," Coventry said. "We pulled up the Temporal Scepter and brought it with us. The quantum bubble is closed."

"Not true," Heather replied. "The Scepter never came back with us, remember? It's probably still sitting on our stack of stuff. Besides, I have God Coins. They create their own micro quantum translation fields. It's why they're impossible to track; they don't need Temporal Scepters. What I just told you is classified, by the way. I can piggyback off our God Coins to send us back to where we came from because I know the coding. I just need a second. There."

Heather handed the Coins to Coventry and Davis.

"I've programmed them to transition back to IP Mesopotamia, with a translation returning us to Origin at the correct time. We're going to ride the vomit comet when we stop jumping around the quantum realm, but, hopefully, it'll be the least of our worries. This transition is going to be jerky because I haven't had enough time to program a smooth translation. I tied the translation to our God Coins, so this transition won't show up on the TTI mainframe. Ready? Okay, in 3, 2, 1…"

Seconds later, a security officer ripped open the pod's covering. It was wet inside, which was unusual, but otherwise, the pod was empty and secure. He keyed his radio.

"Samson here. It must've been an accidental launch. There's no one inside, and it looks like the pod's leaking. The launch or water impact may have damaged it, or it was flawed. Have the boat guys tow it up and check it out."

Samson looked around. He was flying a jet pack, which wasn't rated for underwater, and the surface of the ocean was rough enough and dark enough to not divulge what lay underneath. He shuddered. There were sharks down there and they had gained a taste for human flesh, from what he heard. He was sure as heck not getting wet just because a life pod slipped its moorings. They should test those things more often.

Mesopotamia, the twenty-fourth day of the fourth month, 2004 BC

The transition was brutal. Heather didn't know whether the pitch of the ocean in the bay had somehow inserted itself into the translation, but when they emerged at IP Mesopotamia, she immediately vomited. So did Coventry and Mick.

"Sorry, it was rough," Heather said, spitting the last sour taste out of her mouth. "Are you guys okay?"

Davis sat back and leaned against the canyon wall.

"That was worse than my most horrible bout of seasickness."

Coventry was lying on her side, resting her head on her arm.

"When's the canyon supposed to stop spinning? Can we stay here for a while?"

Heather nodded and immediately regretted moving her head.

"Yes. We're back in Antiquity. We could stay here for years, and it would make no difference to

Origin."

Davis rolled to his feet and staggered against vertigo to the bags laying in the middle of Insertion Point underneath the box housing the Temporal Scepter. He dug around until he found a water bladder and brought it back to the two women. Davis offered it to Heather first, who accepted it gratefully.

"Thanks, Mick," she said, after she took a swallow and passed the bladder to Quarterlaine. "What do we do now?"

Davis dropped his butt to the ground and put his head between his legs.

"Once the world stops spinning around my head, we can head back to Origin. Who are you working for, Coventry?"

Quarterlaine stopped drinking and side-glanced at Davis.

"What do you mean?"

"I'm in no mood to play games, Major. TTI sent you here, so you report to Korhonen. Oslo knew where to find us and you had to be talking to someone high in the chain to give orders to the AI and get us out of the Main Building on a life raft an hour before TTI scheduled us to arrive. You're obviously working with Oslo, as well. Anyone else? Do we need to worry about Contradeum, too?"

Coventry was too sick to her stomach to be indignant.

"My loyalties lie with the United States first and TTI second. President Jimenez seconded me to TTI Special Assignments because I was a pain in his butt. I never liked the idea of the good ol' U.S. of A.

having a President for Life and I made my objections plain. If my TTI orders don't conflict with my loyalties to America, I don't have a problem. Do you?"

Davis let out a ragged breath.

"Double agents give me heartburn, Coventry, but I can live with your divided loyalties if they don't put us in jeopardy. If you had counted Contradeum in your list, I would've left your body in a crevice somewhere."

Quarterlaine arched her eyebrows.

"Are you sure you could have, Master Chief? I have skills, too."

"Knock it off, you two," Heather said acidly. "You can measure your private parts on your own time. I feel too sick to listen to your chest thumping. You've already nearly killed us once today, Major. Are there any more surprises waiting for us?"

Coventry bobbed her head, her face suggesting she'd been taken aback.

"What do you mean, I already nearly killed us once today?"

Wu grimaced, anger dancing in her dark eyes.

"I programmed our Coins to take us back to TTI at the correct time, with our dunnage. Someone programmed a reroute in the TTI Main Frame to bring us there an hour earlier and leave our stuff behind. I thought you said I was the last remaining Programmer?"

Davis's eyes turned flinty.

"Yeah, how did you make that happen?"

Coventry rolled her head as nausea sent another wave through her body.

"It was Oslo. She had some people in the military work out a reroute solution. I've been in touch with her through a quantum string. One of her contacts stuck a nano patch onto the Main Frame and introduced the subroutine."

A string of profanity erupted out of Heather's mouth, sending Davis's eyebrows climbing.

"Amateurs! Nothing but freaking amateurs!" she said, at the end of the curse words. "You have no idea how close you came to killing us. Next time, include me in your plans, Coventry, unless you like the idea of a painful death. What else is Oslo going to do today?"

"Nothing of which I'm aware. President Oslo is desperate. She really hoped you'd find feasibility in her mission to plant grain in the past and bring it forward to feed Americans. Are you sure you're okay, Heather?"

Heather moaned and leaned forward into a series of retching, churning the stomachs of her companions.

Coventry looked at Davis and gave him a head jerk toward the canyon entrance. He nodded.

"I'd better recon the canyon entrance and make sure we have no incoming bad guys. Be back in two."

Heather waved feebly at him and went back to retching. When she stopped, she straightened up and accepted a hankie from Coventry to wipe her mouth.

"Thanks," she said, her voice weak.

"Glad to help. Do you mind if I ask you a personal question?"

Heather rolled her eyes.

"Does it have anything to do with seasickness,

nausea, or vomiting?"

Coventry barked a short laugh.

"Not today. Guarantee it."

Heather leaned back against the canyon wall and sighed.

"Okay, go ahead, I guess. Don't be surprised if I throw up in the middle of your question."

"Do you have something going on with Davis?"

Heather's eyes snapped open, and her eyelids narrowed.

"Why do you want to know?"

Coventry shrugged and positioned her body to sit, cross-legged, squarely in front of the smaller woman.

"OpSec. Operational Security. If something happens, will your first reaction be to protect him? Do you like him?"

Heather shook her body slightly.

"Of course, I like him. He saved my life and has kept me safe for eight months in a time in history where women were little more than property. How could I not like him?"

"That's not what I meant. Are you attracted to him? Are you two bumping uglies? Do you want to?"

Heather's face turned a darker shade, and her nostrils flared.

"Why, do you?"

"Nope. Not at all. I never will. I mean, he's a good-looking guy, and he has a smoking hot bod, but he's just not my type. Is he yours?"

The Programmer allowed a slight smile to touch her lips.

"Yeah, I think so. Not that he'll do anything, even

if I try to seduce him. He wants marriage before sex and I'm not ready for the altar yet. I've watched him train Ro'gun at our house in the village. Shirt off, sweaty muscles, and moving with dangerous intensity? I mean, who wouldn't want a taste of that?"

Coventry laughed.

"I concede the point, but he's still not for me. Thanks for telling me."

"Thanks for telling you what?"

Both women jerked around as Davis ambled back into the IP. His stride was firmer, and the gentle arrogance usually covering his shoulders was back.

Coventry stood awkwardly, her body still feeling the effects of a roller coaster transition.

"Heather says the trip back should be a lot gentler."

Davis cast his keen eyes back and forth between the two women.

"Heather, you look better. How's the nausea?"

Surprise fluttered across her face.

"It's gone!" She looked at Coventry, who took the smaller woman's hand and pulled her to her feet. "Coventry helped me through it. She's a bit of a sneak."

Davis cocked his head at the former Marine, who gazed back with a face giving him nothing.

"A sneak, huh? I'll not ask what you mean. So, smooth sailing from here in?"

Coventry shook her head in an emphatic 'no'.

"Not a chance, Mick. They'll welcome us home with open arms, but TTI is a mess. Our world is a mess, and it's just going to get worse."

Heather stood up and dusted off her trousers, giving Coventry a worried glance.

"What do you mean?"

Coventry inhaled and blew a large gust of air from her cheeks.

"I was an Army brat and a handful as a teenager. My parents made me read the Holy Bible, the New King James version, front to back when I turned thirteen. I have a photographic memory, so they figured if I ever smartened up, I'd always have God's word with me. I never looked at it until I was stuck in Mesopotamia for eight months. It was the only book I ever bothered to read front and back that wasn't *The Art of War* or the like."

"In the eight months when I was stuck in ancient history, the Bible opened my eyes. Jesus Christ became a real person to me and His sacrifice for my sins touched me in a way I never experienced. The day before I knocked on your door, I was hungry, tired, and scared. It was the lowest point in my life and that's when I gave my heart and soul to the Messiah."

Davis's face softened and he side-glanced at Heather.

"We recently had an experience that made Him real, too. I can relate. What does it have to do with what we're going back to?"

Coventry licked her lips a few times.

"I'm no pro with end times theology, but I'd bet my last coin the world is in the Tribulation period prophesied by the Bible. The Second Cataclysm had to have been the Rapture of the Church. Several times I read the Revelation to John, the Book of

Daniel, and other parts of the Bible dealing with the end times."

"I'm convinced Jesus has broken the first seal, which brought the Antichrist into power, and the second seal, which brought on the First Global Nuclear War. There are a bunch more seals, all of them worse than the one before. The world is going to get no peace for a few years. I'm nowhere near being an evangelist, but you two need to get your souls in order right now. A premature death is no longer a possibility in our future; it's an absolute certainty. If you die before you make a choice to accept Jesus as your Savior, then you've made a choice, and it isn't for God. Gets mighty hot where your soul is going to spend eternity."

Heather looked like she wanted to be sick again.

"I haven't thought much about religion. It never seemed important. My parents believed in living a good life and helping people where they could. I always thought it was enough."

"It isn't," Coventry said, her voice unwavering. "Jesus says He's the Son of God. It's a claim He made in the Bible. He also said He was the Way, the Truth, and the Life, and the only way to God and Heaven is through Him. There's no getting around His statement. If you believe in Him, if you accept Him as your personal Lord and Savior, you get Heaven. If you don't, you get Hell. End of story."

Silence fell in the Insertion Point. Davis finally nodded.

"Coventry, I need to tell you what happened to me and Heather before you knocked on our door."

Davis recounted his plan to save his Kelci's life

and how Heather volunteered to be part of it to save her husband, too. He told the hushed woman about how Jesus had stepped in at the last moment and changed everything. All three of them cried when Davis, in a choked voice, spoke of his last words with Kelci. The tears ran freely when Heather told Coventry of her last moments with her husband. After she finished, Davis spoke again.

"Does Jesus exist? Oh, yeah. He gave me a gift of saying goodbye to my wife before she died. I just never considered taking a step further and ask Him to forgive me for my wrongs. It's funny, He acted like my best friend even when I didn't know Him at all."

Coventry nodded.

"It's what He does, Mick. He loves us, takes care of us, does for us, even when we don't know Him. You never accepted Him as your Savior after He gave you a moment with Kelci, but it's not too late. And now's the time. Trust me. It's the only life insurance worth investing in anymore."

Davis's jaw worked back and forth as his eyes lingered on the canyon floor.

"I'm not a religious person either, Coventry, but I see the need. I won't speak for Heather, but I'm ready to commit."

Heather was crying, streaks of saltwater raining down her cheeks.

"Me, too. I can't deny who He is and what He did for me that night. What do we do?"

"Let's take a knee." When all three were kneeling on the canyon floor, Coventry took each of their hands. "Repeat after me. You can say this out loud or silently, praying from your hearts."

"Lord Jesus, I believe You are the Son of God, born of the Virgin Mary and made man. You lived a life without sinning. I believe you gave up your life as a sacrifice for my sins. They crucified You to death and buried You, but You rose from the dead on the third day. You ascended into Heaven and sit at the right hand of God the Father. Please come into my heart and soul and forgive me for my sins. Over the next number of days and years, open my heart to the ways I have sinned against You, so that I can confess them out of my heart and spirit. Lord Jesus, I am Yours."

Insertion Point-Mesopotamia was quiet, but in the Kingdom of Heaven, angels gave a mighty roar as two more souls found salvation. There would be a party among the saints, but the three people at the IP would only hear about it after their lives ended.

Davis stood first, still holding the hands of the other two women. He helped them up. All were smiling. Davis hugged Heather.

"No matter what happens now, we'll be together with everyone we love."

Heather squinted up at him.

"Let's just make the reunion later instead of sooner, okay?"

They laughed. Coventry tapped her wrist.

"Speaking of time, we need to make this happen. We have people dying in antiquity."

They brushed themselves off and checked the coordinates on the Coins. After getting an affirmatory nod from her travel mates, Heather activated the Temporal Scepter. With little fanfare,

IP Mesopotamia disappeared around them.

The Atlantic Ocean near Atlantis, September 2, 2097 AD

Sylvia Oslo waited patiently as the water drained from the submarine's dive trunk. Two female sailors helped her out of the trunk and stripped down her dry suit. Oslo climbed into navy blue coveralls and made her way out of the trunk to greet Captain Mike Willis, the commanding officer of the ballistic missile submarine in which she sailed to Atlantis.

The *USS South Carolina* (SSBN-838) was the last ballistic missile submarine of the Columbia class. America designed and built twelve of the *Columbia* (SSBN-826) class ballistic missile submarines to replace the Navy's Ohio-class subs. The Navy commissioned the *USS District of Columbia*, the first of her class, in 2031. Twenty-one years later, the *USS South Carolina* entered service.

Each SSBN in the Columbia class had sixteen missile tubes supporting the Trident II D5LE missile. The three-stage ballistic missile can travel 4,000 nautical miles and carry multiple independently targeted re-entry bodies. The 130,000-pound Trident II D5LE missile travels 20,000-feet per second. Each missile had four Mk-7 Re-entry Vehicles with 475 kiloton W93 warheads, or the equivalent of 475,000 tons of TNT. The independently targetable warheads had a spread covering a wide swath of a designated area.

The Navy designed the Columbia class for a forty-two-year expected service life. Unlike the Ohio-class design, which required a midlife nuclear refueling, they equipped the Columbia class with a nuclear fuel core capable of powering the ship for its entire expected service life.

They equipped the Columbia class with an electric-drive propulsion train, as opposed to the mechanical-drive propulsion train used on other Navy submarines. The electric-drive system was stealthier than a mechanical-drive system.

The old Ohio class boats had been the quietest submarines in the ocean. They were difficult to detect even for American Anti-Submarine Measures. An Ohio class sub could never compete with the *South Carolina* for stealth; the latter was an invisible ghost in any waters in which she wished to sail.

Thirteen years into the *South Carolina's* forty-two-year service life, the First Cataclysm struck. Long before the First Cataclysm bombarded the world with water, the Navy, in a secret study, determined a rise in ocean levels was inevitable. They upgraded Naval Base Kitsap, Washington and Naval Submarine Base Kings Bay, Georgia, to mitigate expected flooding. Those efforts resulted in both bases and the surrounding communities surviving the First Cataclysm intact.

The global environmental disaster ended production of any replacements for the Columbia class, but the *South Carolina* remained in excellent condition. She had to be. There were not a lot of boats in her class left.

Willis gave Oslo a casual salute, even though salutes were not required below decks, and she returned it graciously.

"Are we okay, Captain?"

Willis gestured towards the Command and Control Center.

"After you, Admiral. You came up in boomers, Ma'am. You know they can't find us unless we want them to know we're here. Do we want them to know we're here?"

Oslo glanced at him sharply and bit back her initial retort.

"I see where you're going with the question. It's tempting, Mike, it really is. I'd like to shake Contradeum up a little by showing him how close we can get to his precious island. My head says we need to keep our cards close to our chests. We don't have a lot of cards left."

The Captain nodded.

"You're the Admiral. Where do we go now, Ma'am?"

The radioman burst into the Control center.

"Captain! CRITIC traffic! We have a launch warning!"

Willis snatched the paper from the radioman's hands, scanned it, and handed it to Oslo.

"NORAD confirms a submarine ballistic missile launch from the Bering Sea. Track suggests three missiles are targeting Denver."

Oslo swore, immediately regretting the loss of her composure.

"Contradeum thinks I'm there. That son-of-a-bitch. Captain, I order you to launch a missile against New Babylon. Launch it and rig for ultra-quiet. We'll find out what happened to Denver when we can."

"Aye aye, Admiral. XO we have a launch order."

Willis unzipped his duty coverall and removed the

missile key hanging around his neck. Oslo raised an eyebrow, but said nothing. Proper procedure dictated the missile keys remain locked in a safe until the boomer received a launch order. The launch order contained the combination of the safes. At some point, someone sent the Captain and XO the combination for their individual safes and they hadn't bothered to put their keys back. The Executive Officer didn't surprise her when he pulled his missile key out of his coveralls, as well. It was a breach of protocol, but one for which Oslo was grateful. Without it, they'd have no ability to launch a strike.

Willis gave the orders to prep the missile for launch and the Navigation and Weapons Officers frantically programmed coordinates into the missile's four independent warheads. Once he received confirmation of readiness, Willis walked to the console. He inserted his key and nodded to his XO, who inserted his into a console six feet away. Together, they turned their keys, releasing the missile for launch. Willis turned to Oslo.

"Weapons are hot, Admiral. Do you confirm the launch order?"

"Captain, in my capacity as President of the United States and Chair of the Joint Chiefs of Staff, I confirm the launch order."

Willis turned to his Executive Officer.

"Lieutenant Commander, we have received a valid launch order. Do you confirm?"

The XO nodded, his black skin reflecting the red lights of General Quarters.

"Captain, I confirm we have received a valid

launch order."

"The launch order is confirmed. Launch, launch, launch."

The Weapons Officer acknowledged.

"Affirmative, Captain. Launch, launch, launch. Captain, we have ejected one missile from the tube. Attention, Captain, we have first stage ignition. Captain, we have a good launch."

Willis gestured to his XO.

"Rig for ultra-quiet."

"Aye aye, sir." The Executive Officer grabbed the all-ship for the announcement.

"Attention, all hands. Rig for ultra-quiet."

Oslo took a small step forward.

"Spread the word, Captain. If anyone so much as sneezes, I'll have them fired out of the torpedo tubes."

Willis smirked.

"Aye aye, Admiral."

Atlantis, September 2, 2097 AD

Davis, Wu, and Quarterlaine materialized with their cargo on the Lens to a standing ovation. Hundreds of people filled the Emergence Area of the TTI Building. Many of the cheering people were crying and hugging each other as the trio stepped off the lens and walked to the awaiting dignitaries.

It shocked Davis to see tears in Korhonen's eyes. The Administrator first grabbed Wu and gave the smaller woman a big hug.

"Dr. Wu, I can't tell you how happy I am to see you alive and well. I hope you're fit to start work right away. We have Teams in the field who have been away from home for far too long."

Heather smiled, her eyes tearing to the emotion in Marjatta's face.

"Yes, Administrator. I'll begin now. If someone could let me know which team is in the worst shape, I'll start my calculations immediately."

Marjatta hugged her again and gestured toward one of the nearby techs.

"Jonas will join you at your station and assist however he can. We have a Team in historic Canada on the verge of freezing to death. We need to get them out first."

Heather gave Davis a quick wave before Jonas rushed her off to her station. The TTI Building was a frenzy of activity now. They had a mission, and each person knew what had to be done to send off a Team and recover it. TTI was operational for the first time in months. The long days of boredom, fear, anger, and grief were now subsumed in purpose and professionalism.

Marjatta turned to shake hands with Davis and Quarterlaine.

"Thanks for bringing Heather home, you two. I know you'd like to get some good, hot food in you, and we'll make that happen. You probably have an hour before your next transition and where you're going is cold. We have people putting together winter gear for you; you'll want to check it before you leave. I'm sorry to rush you like this, but people are injured and dying in Antiquity, and I want them home."

Quarterlaine nodded and spoke for them, after

glancing at Davis.

"We'll go get them, Administrator."

Davis nodded. So far, no one had commented on his youthfulness. They must not have known he spent over twenty years in antiquity before having his youth restored by God. Davis shook his head. It was amazing what a person could get used to. It was one thing to believe in God, and another to have Him alter your age as easily as sipping on a cup of coffee.

"Coffee."

Marjatta and Coventry looked at him quizzically. Davis blushed.

"Sorry, Administrator. I just realized we were back in the land of coffee. As soon as the thought hit my head, every other neuron froze."

Marjatta laughed.

"Mr. Davis, you have my full sympathy and understanding." She turned to her aid, who always hovered at her right elbow when the Administrator was out of the office. "Winslow, please get Mr. Davis and Major Quarterlaine a couple of tall mugs of coffee. I'm afraid you'll have to drink it black. While our stores of coffee are still adequate, we ran out of such luxuries as milk, cream, and sugar a week ago."

Davis felt his forehead wrinkle.

"Please forgive me, Administrator, but when did milk, cream, and sugar become luxuries?"

Korhonen never answered. Sirens began wailing and security personnel started scurrying around, hands pressed to their ears and faces turning white. The new Head of Security ran over to Korhonen.

"Administrator, a submarine just launched a missile a thousand yards off the coast of Atlantis.

We've plotted a trajectory. It's headed towards New Babylon. Someone has launched a nuclear attack on the capital of the world!"

A steam cannon fired the missile out of the *South Carolina*'s missile tube six. The 'steam cannon' was an explosive charge that flash-vaporized a tank of water into steam. As the pressure of the expanding steam drove the missile out of its launch tube, it provided enough momentum for the weapon to clear the water's surface.

The missile slowed as it left the water, and gravity tried to pull it back down. Motion sensors in the missile monitoring the flight sensed the changes. The missile hung in the air for a moment until the first of the three rocket stages ignited.

The first stage rocket burned for 65 seconds and the missile extended its aerodynamic spike to smooth the airflow over the blunt-nosed cylinder. Without this spike, the missile couldn't survive its brief, high-speed transit through the atmosphere.

The Trident missile navigated with an inertial guidance system, based on a set of sensitive accelerometers measuring precisely how much the missile sped up and for how long. Its onboard computer used this data to calculate the speed and position of the missile.

Because of the internal guidance system's limits, the missile had a star sighting navigation system, as well. This sensor gets a location fix by measuring the position of the stars to provide fine detail correction.

The missile flew flawlessly. It ejected the first and second stages on time and as designed.

As the missile approached the Arabian Peninsula, it discharged four independent warheads with a large enough spread to cover the entire city of New Babylon. Each warhead had a yield of 475 kilotons—thirty times greater than the Hiroshima bomb. The missile's accuracy was less than 400 feet Circular Error Probable (CEP), meaning there was a fifty percent chance it would land less than 400 feet from the target.

New Babylon, the pride of the world, the shining new city destined to lead the shattered people of Earth into a new life, was dead.

It just didn't know it yet.

New Babylon, September 2, 2097 AD

Malchus Contradeum had been lounging in his office, shoes off, feet on his desk, when Jez Brandt burst in, screaming hysterically.

"Malchus, TTI has launched a nuke against us! We need to get out!"

Three burly men rammed into the room, unceremoniously picked Contradeum up and rushed him to a secure elevator. Within seconds, they were in the deepest levels of the Presidential Palace. A hyper-speed train waited for them, and when the first warhead hit New Babylon, Contradeum was so far away the train's sensors barely picked up the underground shockwave.

Contradeum had waited for the weekend to order a ballistic missile submarine to fire on Denver. He knew the city's missile defense net would likely intercept the warheads well away from the city, and didn't care. He designed the missile launch to remind Oslo of her manners and who was in charge.

America needed grain, medicine, and tons of supplies to get the nation through the next winter. Contradeum convinced himself Oslo would never launch a retaliatory strike, knowing he could starve North America. His belief assumed a logical, non-emotional response to what he'd done.

He was wrong.

Contradeum was enough of a realist to take precautions, of course. He had ordered his Cabinet, Advisors, and important employees away from New Babylon for the weekend, and all were clear of the slight possibility of retaliation. Twenty thousand people still lived and worked in the new city, but Contradeum didn't care about them. Most of them would survive, he thought. If they died, his Master would receive them with glee.

Contradeum never served in any military and didn't fully appreciate the martial capabilities of the United States, even as weakened as they were. His arrogance gave little significance to things he didn't understand or bother to learn.

Contradeum had been so sure Oslo wouldn't order retribution, he hadn't told Jez of his intention to attack America again.

He was also wrong about the capabilities of the defense net protecting the new North American capital city. Much to everyone's shock, the missiles evaded Denver's defense with an ease that left military experts flabbergasted. The devastation should have been apocalyptic.

It wasn't, but only because of one man's decision.

Captain Nikolai Borovsky commanded the *Vladimir Putin* (K-559), the formerly Russian ballistic missile submarine tasked to launch the missiles against Denver. Borovsky lost his entire family in the First Global Nuclear War. Contradeum thought it would be easy to pass him off as a bitter man seeking revenge for his losses, diverting any thought of the Supreme Global Leader's involvement in the attack.

Contradeum didn't know Nikolai had several friends who were well-placed in the Russian intelligence agency. Those who survived the First Global Nuclear War revealed to Nikolai Contradeum started the war, killing everyone he loved. Nikolai and his officers spent many an off shift sharing vodka and strategies on how best to kill the man who ruined the world and filled their lives with pain.

There were no records throughout the entire chain of command of Contradeum's order to attack Denver. Contradeum had ordered the Second Mate to shoot the Captain and First Mate of the *Putin* as soon as the boomer launched the missiles. The Second Mate had accumulated a large gambling debt, which she had barely kept secret from her commanding officers. She was running out of resources to pay the debt, and Contradeum thought her to be an easy target to compromise. He hadn't counted on a deep sense of loyalty born from her Russian roots. The Second Mate had gone to her Captain before the missile launch and revealed the Supreme Global Leader's intentions.

Yes, the missiles launched, but instead of the Captain and First Mate dying with most of the population of Denver, the boomer fell off the grid when the missiles left the launch tube. Every attempt to re-establish comms failed. Nikolai still had thirteen missiles, and he was planning to write Contradeum's name on all of them.

Contradeum couldn't have known Nikolai had ordered the detonation mechanisms to be disabled before the missiles launched. The Captain of the *Putin* fabricated duds, scaring the heck out of every Denver resident, but causing no loss of life. The warheads hit the ground, mowed down a few empty mansions and warehouses, and left the impact sights radioactive until cleanup crews could remove the debris. Dangerous duds, but duds all the same.

The missile flying from the *South Carolina* to New Babylon with deadly intent wasn't a dud.

When Contradeum planned to attack Denver, he expected the retaliation, if there was one, to target one of his missile bases. He was wrong again.

New Babylon was new; they had little time to test its defensive capabilities. The American warheads easily avoided the barrage of lasers, C-RAM projectiles, and anti-missile missiles. All four warheads detonated when they reached an altitude of one thousand feet above ground, as programmed. A nuclear explosion at altitude maximizes blast damage. Because its fireball never touches the ground, an air burst produces less radioactive fallout than a ground burst.

The heat, though, the heat was another thing. Each warhead produced ninety million degrees Fahrenheit of heat. The force of the explosion drove the heatwave into New Babylon's buildings. The developers constructed them to withstand high winds, earthquakes, and elemental disasters. They had no answer to the effects of a heat wave from a nuke.

Since thermal radiation travels at roughly the speed of light, the flash of light and heat preceded the blast wave by several seconds, just as one sees lighting before they hear thunder.

For air bursts at or near sea level, fifty to sixty percent of the explosion's energy goes into the blast wave. At fifty seconds after the explosion, when the fireball was no longer visible, the blast wave traveled twelve miles at about 784 miles per hour, which was slightly faster than the speed of sound at sea level. The heat and blast waves crushed and burned the buildings through which they passed, as if the developers made them of paper.

As the glare from the fission explosions dispersed, thousands of New Babylon residents lost their lives and many thousands more lay critically wounded.

For the rest of history, no one would ever live in a city called Babylon.

Contradeum's hands shook as he received the casualty figures. In his mind, there was a greater tragedy than the loss of lives. The souls of the people who worked in New Babylon belonged to Satan, and it would please his master to deny those souls to God.

The food, though, was a horrendous loss.

Contradeum had designed and built New Babylon to be a granary for the world. He had in mind the great famine recorded in biblical times, during which Egypt distributed, for a price, of course, vast amounts of grain to the countries surrounding it.

As a location, the new city was ideal. It was close to the expansive fields of Israel. Farmers shipped all the grains, meat, and vegetables grown in the non-devastated parts of the Earth to New Babylon for distribution. The Supreme Global Leader controlled the world's food supply, which meant he could dictate terms to anyone who lived on Earth. The critical food supply now burned or formed part of a radioactive slag.

There had been no backup plan because he didn't foresee the need for one. Surely, no one would attack the world's food supply.

Surely.

He wouldn't look at Jez. In Contradeum's last meeting with his master, *he* asked Malchus if the Supreme Global Leader intended to retaliate against Oslo's insolence. Malchus assured *him* he had no intention of taking any action, acknowledging his ego mattered little considering their overall goals.

Of course, Contradeum didn't believe his own words as they left his mouth. He worked the mission through many layers of cut-outs, with plausible deniability built within every layer. His deception, he thought, was secure. But now, not only did Babylon burn, Contradeum had to chase down an operational boomer with a mutinous crew.

The Supreme Global Leader feared the increase of Hell's population might please his master, but *he* would view Contradeum's actions as a massive blunder.

For the first time, he was right.

In the Kingdom of Heaven, thunder rolled. The masses of people and angels gathered around the throne became still. Jesus raised the scroll high in the air so that all could see.

This next seal was a terrible judgment on the Earth. Jesus had known hunger during His life there. For forty days and forty nights, He had fasted while Satan tempted Him mercilessly to give up His Crown in Heaven to serve Satan. Jesus knew what it was like to have hunger carve its way through His stomach and intestines, while His brain screamed for nourishment. The first three days of fasting had been bad enough because He transitioned from eating well to not eating at all. The remaining thirty-seven days had been a slow progression through hunger, pain, weight loss, depression, and desperation.

He wouldn't wish hunger on anyone and hated that even as the world developed, millions still starved. He and the Father made sure there was enough wealth and resources in the world to feed every human on the planet. Instead, billionaires hoarded their money. Leaders of the poorest nations lived as richly as the billionaires and bought guns instead of food to feed their poor. Satan made sure the wealth and resources given so generously by God never made it to the many hungry stomachs.

Satan. The Beast's time would end soon, and all those who believed in Jesus would live in peace, comfort, and joy for all eternity. Little comfort for those still alive on Earth.

Jesus's thumbs moved on the black seal and

snapped it in two. When the Lamb of God opened the third seal, the third living creature standing near the throne bellowed, "Come!"

For a moment, nothing happened. Then, slowly, a gaunt black horse staggered forward, looking as if it could barely move for lack of calories. The rider looked more emaciated than his poor horse. He held a pair of scales in his hand. A small amount of food on one scale balanced against a large amount of coin on the other.

The Third Horseman of the Apocalypse was Famine, and he was about to ride against the entire world.

CHAPTER THE FIFTH:
"... WHEN WE
PRACTICE TO
DECEIVE."

Spes Deserit, In the Year of Our Fight 2375
Mission Day Two

"We are betrayed."

The words, though softly spoken, rang harshly within the room and all scrambled upright, throwing back the warm, soft coverlets of their luxurious beds. What sleep they had wasn't enough, but the call to arms was clear in the soft-spoken tone.

Tul'ran and Erianne rose, dressing in their armor, finger-combing their hair, and rubbing sleep from their eyes. Erianne gave Tul'ran a lingering kiss and smiled at his scruffy face.

"Good morning, Tul'ran. Another shave is in order, milord husband. I near severed my lip in two when I kissed you just then. Even now I am sure my lifeblood streams from my face."

Tul'ran smiled and ran his fingertips over her dark-skinned cheek.

"And an exquisite face it is, milady wife. I shall lend you my cloak to stem the streams of blood. When you have done with your teasing, a shave would be most welcome. When time permits, of course."

Erianne disabled the privacy screen with a soft command, and they walked into the center of the room. Gwynver'insa and Johan waited for them, both looking apprehensive. Behind them, an enormous screen displayed the scene around the entrance they used the previous night. A vast array of humanoid robots and machines of war stood outside the large door. Of larger concern was Darian, standing in front of the army with a large man.

"What in the name of all things foul is Darian doing there?" Erianne said, anger tinging each word.

"She has betrayed us," Gwynver'insa said, still speaking in a soft tone. "Let not the smallness of the man next to her fool you. He is the angel Abaddon, also known as the Destroyer. In his true form, he is massive, with great black wings. His influence is why the people of this world are near extinction."

Tul'ran looked at the lifelike image on the screen. The man was very tall and his sizable shoulders were wider than Tul'ran's. Small man? How much larger would this angel become when he assumed his true form?

Abaddon's size would have worried him, but the newly discovered properties of Bloodwing the Blade made him feel much more confident about his chance at surviving a battle with this one. If the situation warranted combat. He closed his eyes and directed his mind towards a distant Heaven, sharing his thoughts with the beautiful woman who had miraculously pledged her heart to his.

'El Shaddai, King of Kings, Lord of Lords, is this Abaddon here by your instruction and to fulfill your designs?'

El Shaddai responded immediately to both his mind and Erianne's.

'He is not,' the Voice said, the words caressing with velvety smoothness. 'His purpose is yet to be revealed, though not on this planet. Avoid conflict with him if you can. If you must enter combat with him, you shall not kill him. I have yet a need for him elsewhere. You have precedence, Lord and Lady az Nostrom, and I have faith in your ability to overcome even with such restrictions shackling your wrists and against such odds as are now arrayed against you.'

"I don't believe this," Johan was babbling. "Why would she do that? What have we said or done that would make her want to bring an army here and kill us? How are we going to fight them?"

"We will not wage war against them here," Tul'ran said firmly. "We must retreat."

"Retreat where?" Johan looked at the diminutive blonde woman, who was sliding her hands over the wall beneath the screen. "Is there another way out, Lady Gwynver'insa?"

A faraway look crossed her tiny face.

"I... do not know. The House is speaking to me in ancient words and I am uncertain of their meaning. If I could have but a moment, gracious Lords and Lady, to focus my thoughts."

Johan looked up at the big screen, which displayed Darian, Abaddon, and the mechanical horde entering the building.

"With great respect, milady, a moment may be less than what we have."

Erianne put a hand on his shoulder and smiled into his anxious face.

"Be at peace, Johan. A way out will present itself. If it does not, well," she finished the last part of the sentence in English, "I currently hold to the theory Tul'ran and I are hell on wheels with air power in reserve."

Johan grudgingly smiled.

"I've seen the two of you in action. Theory confirmed. Okay, we wait."

They stood as patiently as possible while Gwynver'insa continued to run her hands along the wall. The minutes ticked by relentlessly and the woman who could create an apple from nothing moved with a slowness that ground the nerves of her companions. The screen kept giving them updates of the invader's progress through the halls of the House, while in the distance they could hear the clamor approaching.

Tul'ran looked at Erianne, and she raised her eyebrows at him, drawing Caligo. He nodded and removed Bloodwing from its scabbard.

"El Shaddai's restrictions will make the incoming

battle difficult, but possible, Erianne. The narrow halls will hamper the invaders much as the narrow canyon walls hamstrung the Gutians. If we must delay them to give Gwynver'insa time, 'tis better we do so before they enter this room."

Erianne nodded soberly.

"A wise strategy, milord husband. Shall we go and give them a quick death?"

"Wait!"

They all turned at Gwynver'insa's sharp command. It was the loudest they'd heard her speak in the fleeting time they'd known her. She was leaning against the wall with both hands, her forehead pressed into the smooth material.

"Wait, I beg of you," she whispered. "You must not shed blood in this place. Look, the House sends help."

On the main screen, a purple wall of energy suddenly appeared in the corridors in front of the invading army, which was now fifty strides away from the edge of the large room within which stood Gwynver'insa and her guests. The invading force came to a sudden stop. They watched on the large screen as Abaddon bent his head to Darian's face, and the two started an animated conversation. After what seemed an angry exchange, Abaddon reached out a hand towards the energy wall, then hastily withdrew it.

Tul'ran watched the conversation with interest. There appeared to be an inequality of balance in power between Darian and the man. From what he could see, each appeared to be jockeying for some position. He smiled. Their union was weak, and he was a master at exploiting weakness, usually to his enemy's certain demise. He turned to look at Gwynver'insa and jerked his head back.

Where once there was a massive wall next to the small woman, there was now a vast emptiness. The wall had disappeared, revealing another corridor sloping downwards. Gwynver'insa smiled, her face revealing tension and exhaustion from her efforts to communicate with the House.

"We must go there. This entrance will seal itself once we depart."

"Depart?" Johan asked. "We're going to leave Darian?"

Tul'ran walked over to face him squarely, cold eyes locking Johan's in place.

"It is apparent Darian has taken up arms against us, Johan. She stands with Abaddon the Destroyer, who does not look disposed to a friendly disposition. We must flee. She has set her feet on a path taking her away from the comfort of our arms and we shall honor her decision. Please, follow Lady Gwynver'insa into yonder maw."

Johan hesitated, but Tul'ran was in no mood to debate, and it was clear in his face. One does not dice with the Prince of Death. Johan shrugged his shoulders in resignation and followed Gwynver'insa into the hole in the wall. Erianne and Tul'ran sheathed their swords and followed in tandem, the taller woman reaching down to finger link her hands with his. After they passed through the maw, the wall reappeared as it was, solid and unyielding. Regardless of where the maw led, they had committed themselves and there was no going back.

The purple curtain hung before them, writhing luxuriously, winding from top to bottom in strands of fluctuating color. It was beautiful, but the song it sang bore warning of dire consequences should they be so foolish as to walk through its silky essence.

Abaddon tore his eyes from the power, weaving its delight sensuously before him, and looked at the brunette woman who had gained them entrance and little else.

"Take it down."

"What do you mean?" Darian asked, startled.

"I mean," the ancient angel said, striving for patience, "remove the barricade of energy before us so we may proceed into the House."

Darian glared at him.

"Why can't you take it down? I sense a power in you. You must be like Satan; I mean, you talk about him like you're brothers."

She shrank as he suddenly leaned toward her, fury dancing in his eyes.

"I am nothing like Satan! He's a demented fool who perceives himself as a god! I'm greater than he by every measurement you could ever know. Don't compare the two of us again. I can't remove this shield; purity is its foundation and only an innocent heart can take it down. Hmmm. I see your dilemma. You don't have an innocent heart, do you, Darian, pawn of Satan? Fine. I'm a creature of Heaven. I'll remove it."

Abaddon turned to the lavender wall and extended his left arm towards it. A hand span away; he stopped. The curtain sang to him and its song was dire. Should he seek to affect its existence, Abaddon himself might cease to exist.

It shook him to his core. He was Abaddon, created by God. He stood head and shoulders above every angel in Heaven. The Father told him They denied not even Heaven to him. He stepped back and looked at the walls with renewed interest, looking for what couldn't be seen by anyone who only saw into the physical realm. What he witnessed staggered him.

The walls were alive.

The House was alive. Not in the sense of breathing and feeding oxygen to a pumping heart, but living with the spiritual essence of the Holy Spirit. He could see the wraiths of Light pumping through the wall's interiors like blood through arteries. It was everywhere.

"What is it?" Darian dared to ask.

"This is not a House, Darian, it's a temple. This building once housed the Spirit of the Living God. I couldn't penetrate it because the House will only allow in those to whom it gives permission, and I never sought permission. Now that we've entered without invitation, the House will deny us further ingress."

He turned on her again.

"How did you, a slave of Satan, gain entrance into this place? What did you do, Darian?"

Abaddon could see fear dancing in her heart and skittering through her mind. She licked her lips, which confirmed his intuition. She was afraid, and she'd lied to him.

"I came in with the others. Gwynver'insa didn't seem to do anything special. She just opened the door and waved us in."

Abaddon closed his eyes. These foolish, foolish humans. They saw but couldn't see. They heard but didn't listen. Men and women thought but couldn't think. How much longer could he abide with them without slaughtering them all?

"Gwynver'insa didn't have to 'do anything special.' She was here at the invitation of God and extended her invitation to you. You gained entrance again because of your initial passage, but as soon as the House sensed our intentions, it sealed our way forward. You can't go forward and neither can I. We will leave."

Abaddon turned to give orders to the machines. Darian lunged forward and grabbed his arm.

"Now hold on! You said if I got you into the House, you'd send me home. I thought your word was sacred or something. Or were you just lying to me?"

The blow came without conscious decision or careful thought. With a speed rivaling light, Abaddon swung a backhand against the left side of Darian's face. The force of it threw her back so far, the right side of her face struck the unyielding wall. Darian fell unconscious to the floor within inches of the destructive curtain. Almost for a moment, a tug of compassion invited him to check to see how badly he damaged her. He shrugged it off. She was just another human, and what was another human death against the billions he had manipulated?

Abaddon's orders to his machines to withdraw were terse and laced with anger. He'd placed too much faith in the stupid human. He could no longer sense Bloodwing the Blade in the proximity. Somehow, the inhabitants of the House had fled from an unknown exit and were now far away. The trail was cold.

Abaddon looked once more at the crumpled form of the woman lying a distance away from him and glanced up at the curtain, troubled.

Why had the mantle denied him entrance?

Darian's world was one of blackness and pain. She struggled to consciousness, fighting against an ebon, wet blanket striving to keep her in the darkness of oblivion. The pain brought her to a semi-conscious state, but wasn't enough to get her past the last barrier into the light. It had been a long time since she felt such pain. Why was she in pain? Darian fought to open her eyes, but couldn't. She reached in front of her and her hand touched an indescribable warmth.

"Help me," she said, her voice a croaking whisper. "Please. Someone. Help me."

"Darian," a soft voice answered. "Who do you call?"

The ramp from the massive hole in the wall wound down for a considerable distance. Erianne couldn't estimate the time it took them to follow the spiraling path deeper into the bowels of the House. Eventually, they exited onto a large platform. She stopped, amazed. It was a subway. At least, the Spes Deserit version of a subway. A sleek, bullet-shaped train lay on its belly in front of them, giving the impression of a slick missile waiting patiently for release. It floated on air and didn't have wheels or rails. It looked like a dormant bullet.

Gwynver'insa stopped and froze in place, her mouth wide open.

"What is this?" she asked, her soft tones barely masking a tremor of fear. "I have never seen this machine. Are we in danger?"

Erianne walked up to the much smaller woman and put an arm around her slender shoulders.

"Fear not, Lady Gwynver'insa. This appears to be a mode of transport like what exists in my world."

"Yes, yes," Johan said, his voice rich with excitement. He ran up to the side of the train. "Look how someone preserved it. Even though the doors are wide open, there is no dust or garbage covering it."

Tul'ran shook his head.

"I tire of being the one who asks foolish questions in the face of indescribable machinations, but how does it work?"

Erianne smiled at him, her eyes warm.

"You lack knowledge, milord husband, not intelligence. This device appears to be one riding on a bed of air, though I cannot fathom the means of propulsion. It seems to lack power… or mayhap not," she finished, her eyebrows rising as the long tube suddenly powered up and lights came on.

"How did you do that, Erianne?" Tul'ran asked, astonished.

"'Twas not I, dear heart. The machine awoke of its own volition."

Johan was always a careful man, but he was no coward. He plunged forward, heedless of danger, and enthralled with discovery. He stepped into the interior of the train boldly and turned to face his fellow escapees. The entire body of the train was transparent; the other three had no difficulty seeing him.

"It does not seem to reject my presence, nor does it exhibit hostile intent, Lady Gwynver'insa. If we are to depart this place, this appears to be as good a mode of transport as any other."

Erianne looked at Tul'ran, who fidgeted beside her.

"This device troubles you, milord husband?"

He shrugged irritably.

"Since my first step upon this world, my love, I have faced wonders beyond my understanding. The only constant has been the enmity between metal and living flesh. I confess it makes me nervous to entomb myself in a machine and render myself defenseless."

Gwynver'insa stepped in front of him, stood on her tiptoes, and placed a palm on Tul'ran's cheek.

"Milord Tul'ran, are you afraid?"

Tul'ran smiled at her, affection shining in his eyes.

"Milady Gwynver'insa, fear has been my constant companion since the moment I took up steel and shed blood. It is through fear I have fought and with fear I have lived. Yes, I am afraid. It will not stop me from going into that machine, but I confess I will not like it."

Gwynver'insa smiled, her brilliant white teeth shining. She turned to stand between Erianne and Tul'ran and took both their hands with hers.

"Nor will I like it, milord. I confess I could do

none of this without the valor of you two stalwart warriors. You confess to fear, yet have Death eating from the palms of your hands. Would that I ever could bear fear in such a manner. Come, milord and milady, let us stride forward boldly. You shall bear me up in your mighty arms and I shall comfort you as I can."

She stepped forward and the other two followed, grinning at each other over the small woman's head.

'Now this is a woman with courage,' Tul'ran thought into Erianne's mind.

Erianne giggled, drawing a quizzical glance from Gwynver'insa.

'Indeed, milord. It goes to show even a titmouse can be brave.'

Tul'ran's lips twitched.

'And you were going to speak to me about diplomacy? How would our friend feel about being called a titmouse, I wonder?'

The four companions settled into the middle of a row of seats. Erianne and Tul'ran removed their swords and placed the tips of the scabbards on the floor in front of them, the length of the shaft between their legs. For a long while, nothing happened. Then, a soft, feminine voice spoke about their heads.

"We do not permit weapons on this conveyance."

Tul'ran glanced at Gwynver'insa.

"We are not leaving our weapons behind, Lady Gwynver'insa. You have seen what Bloodwing can do in the face of our metallic foes. If you were to convince me to abandon a sword El Shaddai gifted to me by one of His angels, which is unlikely in the extreme, I would have no other means by which to protect us."

She nodded.

"No one will ever ask you to part with your wondrous blade, milord Tul'ran. I would first cut out my tongue before even suggesting such a heinous act." She looked up at the ceiling. "Thank you, kind mistress of the wondrous conveyance. I fear our necessity demands the inclusion of our weapons in this transport, for our enemies pursue us and they are of far greater strength than our mere numbers."

"We do not permit weapons on this conveyance," the soft voice insisted.

Johan stood up.

"Well, that's it then. We have to find another way. We're not going anywhere without you two being armed, that's for sure."

Gwynver'insa cocked her head at the strange words spoken in English, as Erianne restrained Johan with one hand.

"Milady Gwynver'insa," Erianne said, "You have ensconced yourself in this House for some time in the past, have you not?"

She nodded, her long blonde hair cascading luxuriously with the gesture.

"Indeed, milady Erianne, I have."

"And when you returned after a long hiatus behind the Crystalline Wall, did the House offer you any challenge?"

"It did not."

"Then I would beg a favor of you, sweet Lady. Address this conveyance in the mode between master and servant, uttering the command, 'override'."

"As you say, Lady Erianne. Mistress of the Conveyance, hearken unto my command as it pertains to the weapons of my formidable colleagues. Override."

Silence ensued for a moment, then the voice returned.

"Override command accepted. Please remain still. This device will now apply a layer of entropy foam to immobilize you while we are in motion. This is for your protection and it will not harm you or your clothing. Such a safeguard is required, given the speed of our travel."

On cue, a yellow foam squeezed out of the seats around them and quickly covered all their bodies but their face. The foam was snug, but they found they could breathe with comfort. It felt like being wrapped in a thick, warm duvet. They were facing the nose of the conveyance, which was bulbous and transparent. The lights within the conveyance dimmed and the wall in front of the nose dilated opened. Slowly, the craft inched forward until the nose was almost touching another featureless wall. They could hear air rushing away from the outside of the craft.

"What transpires?" Gwynver'insa asked, anxiety tinging the edges of her words.

"The device is sucking air from outside the conveyance, so that between us and the walls there is no air. It is called a vacuum," Johan answered.

Gwynver'insa tried to shake her head, but the foam held it in place.

"Of course! What a silly I am today! If we travel

through a vacuum, there will be no air resistance against the frame of the conveyance. In this manner, we can travel at speeds beyond the sound barrier without the expenditure of copious amounts of heat and energy. The equations I see in my mind are most tantalizing. I am known, milords and milady, to have a passable singing voice. May I entertain you while we wait to begin our journey?"

"Of course!" came the response of her companions, amused at her sudden transition from an educated scholar with the equivalent of a postgraduate doctorate in physics to a playful youth.

Gwynver'insa opened her mouth to deliver a ballad, but never got to the first note. The wall in front of them swooshed open, and they were off. The conveyance dove into the tunnel like a peregrine falcon pursuing prey, building an incredible amount of speed in seconds. They sped up from sitting still to pulling seven gravities in ten heartbeats.

The foam covering their bodies did an exceptional job. It absorbed the acceleration and counter-pushed gee forces away from their body. The entropy foam covering their foreheads and necks generated enough force to keep the thrust's momentum from squeezing their faces. Even immobilized, the ride thrilled them.

The track followed the curvature of the planet and didn't dip or curve. It felt as if they were falling continuously, though there was no sense of down. Within minutes, the acceleration dropped and they could feel less force pushing against them as they coasted to a halt in front of another wall. It opened, and the conveyance glided in smoothly, stopping at the end of the chamber. This time, air flowed in as the surrounding tunnel pressurized the chamber.

The inner door cycled opened, and the conveyance sidled up to a platform nearby. All the yellow foam sizzled and evaporated from their bodies, leaving behind only a gentle smell of lilacs and no trace of its presence on their clothing or skin. The pleasant feminine voice was back.

"Welcome to the Hall of the Ancestors. May excellent results shape your destiny. Please enjoy your stay."

Please enjoy your stay.

They had just arrived and were already accursed.

Darian hung between life and death, her soul a gossamer veil flowing in the air like a long white gown under water. The sky was black, but edifices on the ground were strangely lit from within. There was no pain here, but nor was there peace, for joy eluded her grasp. She would float down to the surface, where she saw broken tombstones, burned crosses, and overgrown graves, before writhing and drifting into the inky night sky.

"Where am I?" she asked, not expecting an answer, her voice as wispy as her essence. When the answer didn't come, she refused to panic. She was here. The part of her anchoring her heartbeat to her life reassured her she wasn't dead, just... broken. She turned and saw an image glowing dimly in the sky. It was her parents, playing with her when she was six years old. They were oohing and awing as they caressed her dark brown hair. A lovely, happy family, until her mother put bright lipstick on her lips and her father got *that* look in his eyes. She shuddered and turned away.

In this image, she was in a park in Paris with Claude. It was summer; the leaves and grass were a brilliant green, and the flowers were magnificent in their array of colors. They walked finger linked along the quays of the Seine, a must for couples in love. They passed the Pont des Arts, the Louvre, the majestic Notre-Dame Cathedral and the Île Saint-Louis; sometimes kissing, sometimes looking deeply into each other's eyes, and always tasting joy in their hearts. Claude looked at her with such adoration, such devotion, but in the background Satan laughed at her and mocked her stupidity. Darian whipped her head away as a sharp pain lanced through her heart.

Is this what they meant by your life flashing before your eyes? A painful recollection of every horrible thing others did to her while pursuing their happiness? She pushed her will towards the images and asked for every moment in her life where someone directed love, true love, towards her. Show me the faces, her soul demanded, of the people who love me.

They appeared.

Claude's face was first, which shocked her. Was it possible? Could Johan have been right? Had Claude truly loved her and the video she watched of his betrayal, nothing but a well-constructed lie?

Johan's face followed next, looking forlorn, as he always did when he looked at her. The lovesick puppy really was infatuated with her.

She almost fell from the sky when she saw the next two faces. Tul'ran and Erianne smiled at her through her dream-haze, Erianne with her arm draped possessively around the warrior's massive shoulders, and Tul'ran's eyes lit with warmth as they regarded her. These two loved her? How was that possible? The Sword Himself looked like he always wanted to break her in two!

The last face was as impossible to her as the Warrior and the Beauty. It was Jay's face, the man who set them off on their journey from that impossible garden. She remembered him vividly; he wore a desert camo sweater over a tan t-shirt, which was tucked into black tactical pants. Amphibious tactical boots covered his feet. He must have seen battle somewhere; there were hideous scars on both his wrists. He was her height, with a brown hair and beard, and strangely luminescent eyes. Yes, that was him. Jay. How could he love her? He didn't even know her.

No other faces came. There must be more, she shouted, though no sound came from her lips. Surely, she sobbed, there must be more. There were none. Just the faces of Claude, Johan, Tul'ran, Erianne, and Jay. In all her thirty-two years, only five people on the entire planet had any feelings toward her of care, warmth, or unpolluted desire.

"Darian."

The voice was male, soft, and drifted toward her as if carried by the slightest breeze, although there was no wind in this place. She turned in mid-air, her long brunette hair and gossamer gown flowing this way and that, wrapping itself around her body and releasing like a dandelion seed.

"Who's there?"

"Darian. You must wake up. The place you rest in at this moment hovers between life and death, and it will close soon. When it does, if you do not awaken, you will die. The dark sky, broken gravestone, and charred wood represent the state of your soul. If you die, your life decisions will condemn you to never see the Light again. I have not lost hope for you, Darian. Will you lose all hope in yourself?"

'Who are you?' she asked without speaking.

"I am one who loves you, who has never stopped searching for you, who has left everything else behind to seek for and find you. If you want to know me, you must wake up."

Two doorways suddenly appeared, one to her right and the other to her left, hovering in mid-air. In the doorway to her left, Satan stood smiling, reaching for her, his eyes holding all the promises he made when she served him and loved him with all her heart.

In the doorway to her right lay a clay bowl holding a crude hammer, three large iron spikes, thorns braided into a circle, and the most beautiful red rose she had ever seen.

She looked at Satan, who had puffed himself out in his most handsome manner, oozing charisma, charm, and a strong masculine beauty.

To her right, she saw blood dripping from the thorn circle and the nails, but where they pooled, another beautiful, exotic rose took shape.

The temptation to go to Satan was so strong. She never believed all the horrible things people said about him. Until the whippings started.

She shuddered. How had she forgotten about those times? Vomit belching into her throat as she crawled through blood and gore to kneel at her master's feet. The cold metal rack pressing against her body as the whip bit into her flesh. Her blood racing to the floor almost as fast as her screams fled to the ceiling.

She pushed herself away from Satan's door, feeling the cycle of fear and self-loathing course through her mind at the sight of the corrupted angel inviting her to an eternity of misery and pain.

Life was harsh, unforgiving, and desperate. Why did she want an eternity of the same? What was the word the voice had used? Ah, yes. Hope. Was there hope for her yet?

Darian turned to the other doorway and stopped before she floated through the mantle. She reached down and scooped up the bowl and its contents. The second rose had only formed a gorgeous red head and a bit of stem. Darian tucked the half-formed rose behind her left ear.

She had chosen. She didn't know what she had chosen, yet, but she laid the cornerstone and could now build the rest of her life upon it if she continued down that path. To life then, and to hope, and to the people who loved her even though she deserved none of it. It would take a miracle to get them to forgive her.

Darian opened her eyes in the rotunda, which Gwynver'insa called Last Hope. She could barely see and moved her fingers to touch her eyes, but a hand gently restrained her.

"Not yet, Darian. Your head took a severe blow,

and both your eyes swelled shut. You had undisplaced fractures to the orbits of both eyes and a comminuted fracture of your left cheekbone where your attacker struck you. The force of the blow caused miniscule tears in your spinal column, and subarachnoid hemorrhaging in two areas of your brain. I repaired the bleeding and the tears to your neural and vascular networks. The fractures I healed without scarring, and the swelling will go down within a few days. You are very lucky I found you when I did. Had you stayed in the corridor, you would have died."

Darian lay still for a moment, absorbing everything he said.

"Thank you," she said, through lips that felt ten times their size. "Do I know you? What's your name?"

A hand caressed her forehead, gently to not cause her pain.

"I am a friend. You have nothing to fear from me. When your companions return, they will vouch for me."

She just about said they weren't her companions, and bit the words off her tongue. She was going to have to re-evaluate her opinions, emotions, and attitudes. At the very least, her attitudes. The dream-state was vivid in her mind, and she hoped it wouldn't fade. She had lessons to learn and foul habits to overcome. There was no guarantee she would get the time and patience she required from the others before they cast her out or killed her. The time to start on this fresh path was now.

"I appreciate it. I'm not afraid. Since we're going

to be stuck here together for a while, by the sounds of things, it would be nice to have a name to say when I want to talk to you."

She heard a soft chuckle and the hand once more gently caressed her forehead. This time it held a cool cloth. The sensation of it running over her battered face was divine. Darian felt her body ease into the hand's ministrations, and she started to doze. She barely caught his words before succumbing to the bliss of a healing sleep.

"E'thriel," he said in a whisper. "My name is E'thriel."

CHAPTER THE SIXTH:
THE GATHERING

Spes Deserit, In the Year of Our Fight 2375
Mission Day 2

Human senses amaze, delight, and impress. When one sense suffers loss, the others heighten in perception to appease the loss. Consider the sense of sight, for instance. When deprived of sight, the human mind grasps and enhances the senses of smelling, hearing, and tasting. Even now, while deprived of sight, the smell of frying bacon and wood smoke raised to mind's eye a vision of a pan over an open fire, with pieces of pork crisping in their own fat. The sound of the sparking flame, coupled with the sizzle of bacon fat, solidified the vision, and set the mouth to drooling. It was as if it were real.

Darian jerked awake, her body lunging upwards

on an opulent bed. She couldn't see. Her hands touched her face to find bandages wrapped tightly around her eyes. Panicked, she tried to rip them off, but a hand restrained hers.

"Gently, Darian. Please do not remove them just yet."

She took a deep, tremulous breath. The voice was familiar, friendly. The owner of this voice had saved her life.

"E'thriel?"

"Indeed, Darian. It is I. You have not suffered permanent damage to your eyes or your sight. The blow to your head swelled your brain a little and light will give you severe pain. Please be patient for just a while and I will remove the bandages when you fully heal."

Darian took some deep breaths.

"I had a dream before I woke up; I could smell bacon frying. It was so real. I can still hear it sizzling in the pan."

E'thriel chuckled. His hands smoothed the bandages over her eyes. He helped her swing her legs over the edge of the bed and find her feet.

"It is real. This House is not so much a dwelling as it is a Temple. This Temple has an interior Garden, complete with an artificial sun. I brought you to the Garden earlier this morning, after you lost consciousness. You slept for twelve hours and I thought you might be hungry when you woke up, so I made you breakfast."

Darian's mouth was salivating.

"Where did you get the bacon? I haven't had bacon since I was a child."

E'thriel guided her to a long bench in front of a table. Darian could feel the warmth of sunshine on her skin, while birds chirped in the background. The scents of flowers mingled with the smell of frying bacon and her senses swooned. E'thriel draped a light blanket over her legs.

"Rest here for a moment. The Garden supplies whatever the resident desires, Darian. I desired to feed you a breakfast of bacon, eggs, and hash browns. I was pleased to cook it for you. Will you have coffee?"

"Coffee?" Her voice keyed upwards. "You have coffee? I would love a coffee with two creams, please."

In a moment, Darian could smell the aroma of coffee wafting in her direction. She raised both hands in gleeful anticipation, and E'thriel rewarded her a moment later with a large cup of steaming brew. She smiled as she brought the mug to her lips, though opening her mouth to take a sip made her wince. Her face was sore, but the coffee helped take the pain away.

"This is the best cup of coffee I've had in a long time." She sighed. "Who are you, E'thriel? Are you from this planet?"

The angel smiled as he stirred the contents of the pan. He flexed his wings upward and outward, sixty feet spanning between their glowing white tips. They were clean again, unbroken, and empowered. He shot a heartfelt prayer of gratitude toward Heaven before answering her question.

"I am not from this planet, Darian. It would be best if we could defer the conversation regarding my identity until after we remove the wrapping from your eyes. My story will be incredible to you. I assure you; you are safe with me. You know nothing evil can come into this House; it is why the House stopped your entrance earlier."

Shame slashed through Darian's heart and she hung her head, the coffee momentarily forgotten. Tears forced their way from her eyes and wet the inside of the bandages. Without having regard for how the words would sound in his ears, she babbled out her confession.

"E'thriel, I'm an ungrateful, heartless witch. I turned on people who offered me a place with them and treated me well. Out of a selfish desire to go home, I turned my back on them and joined their enemy. I thought the man I met had power, like my Master on Earth, and such power could send me back to where I belong. The only thing mattering then was me and what I wanted. I'm so sorry. If you think I'm anything other than a miserable excuse for a human being, you should be aware I'm not. I'm certainly not worth the care you're giving me. I can see why the House decided I was evil and wouldn't let me in."

E'thriel left the pan for a moment and floated to her side. He reached down and lifted her chin.

"Darian, you made decisions you now regret. It is to your credit you regret them, which shows there is yet love in your heart. We will talk about your choices and where we go from here. This moment is a time for peace, not self-loathing. Breakfast is ready; I will dish it up."

She dropped her cheek to his hand and nodded,

feeling him move away from her.

"So, was the man I was with evil, too?"

E'thriel took the sizzling pan from the open fire and removed the bacon with his fingertips. He didn't feel pain and the simple heat couldn't burn his skin. He was eternal. Even if the hot bacon fat injured him, his body would rapidly heal. He placed a white towel under the warm plate and walked it to where Darian sat, crying. E'thriel gently removed the coffee mug from her hands and placed it on the table. He put the plate by the cup and placed a knife and fork in her hands.

"Here is your cutlery; the plate is in front of you. Careful, it's warm. It may take a few moments to become comfortable eating without sight. I know you are upset, but you must eat to make a full recovery. Please, Darian. Cry if you must, but please eat."

E'thriel sat down beside her, easing the bulk of his wings away from her body. Darian had to touch her food to find it on the plate and snatched her fingers away before the hot food burned them. Once she had a sense of where the food rested, she stabbed the tines of the fork through a piece of bacon.

"Who was the man I was with, E'thriel? Was he evil?"

E'thriel sighed at her persistence.

"The creature with whom you entered this dwelling is not a man; he is an incredibly powerful angel named Abaddon."

Darian stopped, her hand and the tantalizing strip of bacon inches from her lips.

"An angel? As in from Heaven? Angels are real?"

This drew a chuckle from her host, who shimmered his feathers.

"I guarantee you angels are very real. Abaddon was among the first angels, if not the first angel, created by God. He is powerful, perhaps the most powerful of all of God's servants, but the Father did not design him to be evil. His destiny is yet to be fulfilled. I guess you could say he is the Switzerland of angels, always neutral in his decisions and allegiances. He walks his destiny alone, with only God as his companion and friend. He should not be in this world, and his presence here shocks me. His neutrality should have guaranteed him entrance in this House. It surprised me Abaddon could not gain access to this place. Until I saw what he did to this world."

Darian moaned as she chewed and swallowed the piece of bacon.

"Oh my gosh, this is good. I forgot how wonderful bacon tastes. Can you guide my hand to a forkful of eggs?"

E'thriel complied, gently steering her right hand to a pile of scrambled eggs on her plate. He watched her delight as the eggs caressed her taste buds and incited them to joy.

"This is heavenly. Thank you so much, E'thriel. Heavenly. So Heaven is an actual place? It exists?"

E'thriel nodded and then chastised himself for forgetting she couldn't see the gesture.

"Yes, Darian, Heaven exists and is a proper place. There is a God in Heaven and He loves you."

Darian ate faster, becoming more comfortable feeding food onto her fork with her left hand and transporting it to her eager mouth with her right.

"How do you know that? Anyone who knows me can't possibly love me. How do you know so much about Abaddon?"

E'thriel smiled.

"In due time, Darian, I will answer all your questions. Do you want some juice to wash down your breakfast?"

She nodded and continued searching the plate for food.

"Yes, please. What kind do you have?"

"What kind do you want?"

"Coconut pineapple!"

She could feel the warmth of his smile and the transition as he moved away from the bench beside her.

"I will be but a moment."

Darian decided E'thriel, whoever he might be, was a good guy and a superb cook. The hash browns were crisp but not deep-fried, and he seasoned them perfectly. He flavored the eggs with dill and oregano, as well as salt and pepper, and they caressed her taste buds like lovers touch one another. E'thriel didn't know portions, though. As much as she ate, the plate never lacked for food. She felt the air beside her stir and the sound of a glass touching the table.

"Here is your juice," E'thriel said. "Let me guide your hand so you do not spill it."

To her surprise, E'thriel's touch didn't raise an acid reflux of revulsion in her stomach. His touch was warm and gentle as he moved her hand to the frosted glass.

"E'thriel, you are amazing," she said after she

drank several large mouthfuls. "The meal, the juice, it's all delicious."

"It pleases me you enjoyed it so. Have you had enough, Darian?"

She smiled, despite the reminder from the pain in her face such movement was to be frowned upon.

"More than enough, my friend."

Again, she felt the air around her stir.

"Bide here a moment, Darian, while I clean up. I will join you and we can talk, or you can sleep further, if you like. I am her to serve you until you recover fully."

Hmmm. Serve her until she recovered fully. She liked the sound of that. A contented feeling was threatening to creep into her mind, but the portion always condemning her into self-hatred wouldn't let it. She couldn't help but wonder, laden with guilt, where Gwynver'insa's party was and whether they were safe.

Where they were, who knew? The conveyance said they were at the Hall of the Ancestors; wherever that was. Tul'ran, Erianne, Gwynver'insa, and Johan exited the conveyance and paused on the platform. The only way out appeared to be an enormous marble staircase in front of them.

Tul'ran turned to Gwynver'insa, who hovered near Erianne. She had taken to his wife for protection; he noted with approval. His wife was fierce and she would safeguard Gwynver'insa well. Erianne also had a great deal of love and compassion, traits which Tul'ran lacked and the short blonde woman craved. He smiled at the diminutive woman with what he hoped was one bearing warmth and sincerity.

"Lady Gwynver'insa, to what course of action do you now bind us?"

She blinked and glanced around her, nervously.

"I know not, milord Tul'ran. If you must know it, I confess to being rash by engaging in this travel without full knowledge of my destination. One does not travel to the Hall of the Ancestors lightly. I have heard many stories of people who entered here and did not come out alive. I might have brought us into the clutches of our enemies." She raised a fist to her mouth, her eyes widening in horror. "What have I done, milords and milady? I might have brought us to the very pit of evil and our certain destruction!"

Johan stopped searching the large staging area and walked up to the much shorter woman.

"Lady Gwynver'insa," he said, smiling, "Please be at peace. You march with the Prince of Death and the Princess of Destruction. The people of this planet think they know war?" He snorted. "They are children compared to Lord and Lady az Nostrom. I doubt the House's conveyance would have sent us into the teeth of the enemy. If it did, those we encounter will not be our enemies for long. They will surrender themselves to us immediately or die. Fear not."

Gwynver'insa clapped her hands, delighted.

"Well said, Lord Johan! Well said, indeed! Yes, let us go forth with those assurances, knowing we walk in the shadow of this world's mightiest heroes. Come, Lord Johan, permit me to link my arm in yours as we ascend this majestic ramp."

Johan smiled and extended his elbow.

"It will be my honor, milady."

As they turned to the staircase, Tul'ran looked up at his wife and shook his head.

"How is it we have become so fearsome in Johan's eyes when we have known him for a short time and he has seen us in only two engagements? I worry he may mislead Gwynver'insa into an overabundance of confidence in our abilities."

Erianne linked her arm into the crook of his elbow and grinned down at him.

"If you must know, my darling husband, Johan has such faith in you because I sang to him portions of the Ballad of Tul'ran the Sword. I am thinking of making a recording and playing it on this world's airwaves. Surely we will have victory within minutes, then!"

Tul'ran's laughter boomed in the confines of the meeting space, causing Johan and Gwynver'insa to laugh. He allowed Erianne to guide him to a ramp rising upwards seemingly forever.

"I hope the day never comes, milady, that I should disappoint you in my feat of arms or bring to ruin the accuracy of my Ballad."

She squeezed his arm and laughed.

"I promise you the day will never come, Tul'ran. I own your heart and El Shaddai owns your arm. How could this world overcome such a combination?"

The warrior took the first of many steps upward and pondered her question. He had a feeling in the pit of his stomach this world intended to answer that query for him, and soon.

The lack of her sight was a nuisance, but Darian comforted herself with the knowledge it wouldn't be forever. After E'thriel cleaned up, he led her to a large divan. She lounged upon it like Cleopatra. He would probably feed her pomegranates, too, if she asked for them. She giggled as the thought momentarily tempted her to ask him to feed her grapes and wave a palm frond over her head.

"E'thriel, can I ask you a question?"

The angel removed sword and scabbard from the sash at his waist and laid it upon the grass, before collapsing on the ground in front of her.

"Of course."

"Is this your House?"

"It is not. The people of this planet created this House as a place for God the Holy Spirit to live when He visited their planet. It is a place of meeting, repose, and peace."

"Then why are you in this place? Gwynver'insa seemed to think no one else lived here for quite some time."

E'thriel shifted.

"I marvel at your intense curiosity, Darian. No, no, I do not avoid your question. My answer will make more sense if you tell me what vision you saw when you lay in an unconscious state."

Her head jerked towards him.

"How did you…? Never mind. I'll play. I saw two doorways. In one stood my old master, enticing me to come with him. In the other, I saw a rose, a clay bowl, a circle of thorns, a hammer, and three nails. Blood came out of the bowl and spilled on the ground, but where it touched the ground, another rose formed. It was coming to life right in front of my eyes and it was the most beautiful red rose I've ever seen. I knew what my master represented and no part of me wants a life with him. Not now. I decided on the doorway with the rose, even though I didn't know what those things were. Do you know what they meant?"

E'thriel blew out a soft gust of hair, so that it teased her hair. Darian giggled.

"The clay bowl represents Jesus Christ, the Son of God. The Holy Trinity formed the first man, Adam, out of clay. Jesus set aside His divinity and took on human flesh; He became the clay. The hammer was used to drive the three spikes into His hands and His feet when the centurions nailed Him to the cross. The moment of His crucifixion was the most horrible thing anyone has ever seen. God nailed to a cross by the people He created and loved. The Romans who crucified Him created a crown of thorns and pressed it upon His head because Jesus is the King of the Jews. The rose is a symbol of His love for you and all people. He shed his blood out of love for you. This is what the rose in your hair symbolizes; His love for you."

Darian threw her hand to her head and was astonished to find the flower tucked behind her left ear.

"It was real? I thought it was a dream. The flower's still in my hair."

"I wish you could see my smile," E'thriel said. "The flower is in your hair and you look beautiful."

Darian felt herself blush.

"Careful, Romeo. I have an adverse reaction to

men who hit on me. Don't make me not like you."

E'thriel ran his hand along the soft edges of the feathers on his right wing.

"Soon you will see why it is not possible for me to hit on you, Darian. For the time being, I assure you I am not and will never make advances toward you. The compliment was innocent and genuine. It related more to what I see in your spirit than what I see on your face."

Darian didn't know whether to be insulted or relieved.

"What are you, a eunuch?"

E'thriel's lips jerked upwards.

"In a manner of speaking. Getting back to our conversation, when you picked up the bowl and its contents in your unconscious state, a part of you decided. It was a decision towards God. I was in the House waiting for you to decide, for your decision was going to influence my next course of action. When a part of you made a choice for the Savior of the world, my path became certain. I am to help you heal and walk with you to your life's end, as your servant."

Darian sat still, a chill running down her arms and raising the tiny hairs on them.

"My servant? Until my life's end? I'm not sure I want a servant, E'thriel. I know I don't deserve one."

The angel sighed.

"You were born a child of God, Darian. Whether you will remain a child of God is a choice for you to make. I will answer your every question, with the hope you will decide for God and an eternity with Him. If you desire it, I will go away, for God will not impose my presence upon you against your will."

Darian ran her fingertips along her temples.

"I'm sorry, E'thriel, but my headache is coming back in spades. Could we defer the conversation about my soul for another time? If you stay, I want you to be a friend, not an evangelist, and not my pastor. Is it too much to ask? If it is, you can go."

E'thriel rose to his feet and moved to the divan, making noise as he walked so he wouldn't startle her.

"It is not too much to ask, Darian. I will be your friend until you sever our bond or until death finds you."

Darian allowed him to lead her back to her bed, while his last words bounced around the cages in her mind. She wasn't sure she was ready to have him as her friend. As for death finding her, she had escaped those dark clutches more than once. Why was he so sure death wouldn't find him first?

The cavern was gargantuan. They expected to find the dingy, dark air of the outdoors at the top of the steps, but the ramp opened to an underground cave with soaring ceilings and edges extending beyond the depths of their vision. It was as if the cave had housed an underground ocean no longer in existence. Lights on the ceiling illuminated the cavern well. It wasn't lit as if it were midday in a sunny world, but it was close.

A single, winding path stretched out before them, away from the staircase, bounded on each side by tall rock walls. The path was solid and smooth, suggesting manufacture rather than happenstance. The atmosphere was clean and dry, smelling like freshly mown grass. Temperature wise, it was pleasant. As far as caves go, it was nice.

Gwynver'insa stood still, her hands twitching and her eyes even larger than usual.

"I know this place," she whispered, her words laced with wonder. "This path leads to the Hall of Everlasting Joy. I thought it was a myth. Come, friends, quickly."

Gwynver'insa broke into a run. It took a moment for her startled companions to respond, but they leaped after her, shouting for her to slow down so they could catch up. They almost lost her when she took an abrupt right turn off the path onto a smaller one. So intent were they in their pursuit; they almost ran over her when she came to an abrupt halt.

They had run into a place of wonder. It resembled an amphitheater, with stone seats almost enclosing the entire arena into which they stopped. The seats stretched fifty or sixty tiers high and gave the impression of immeasurable age. It was so quiet; they could easily hear each other's rapid breathing from the exertion of racing through the cavern.

"There's no one here," Johan said into the silence.

Erianne gestured to the square boards lying on various seats, upon which some form of food seemed to be heaped. Even though they were far away, she could see steam rising from the platters.

"Don't be so sure." She moved her hand to Caligo's hilt, but Gwynver'insa restrained her arm.

"Be not hasty in drawing your weapon, Lady Erianne, I beg of you. Allow me to try something first."

Gwynver'insa stepped forward and the edges

outlining her body seemed to blur. She appeared to become taller, older, wiser. Her voice, when she called out, was bold and carried the weight of ancient authority.

"Attend me, people of the world once known as Hope. I am Gwynver'insa, She Who Creates From Nothing."

"Well, there goes Operational Security," Erianne muttered, look around for a reaction to her companion's loud proclamation.

"No one lives in the line of those who create from nothing," came a distant shout a minute later. "The last of them died twenty years ago, trying to make enough food to keep us alive. Go away!"

A look of forlorn loneliness crossed Gwynver'insa's face and her shoulders slumped momentarily. Erianne stepped forward and put a hand on her back. The shorter woman turned and flashed a sad smile at Erianne before straightening again. Gwynver'insa raised her arms, palms raised to the ceiling.

"I, Gwynver'insa, proclaim myself the last of her Kind. People of Spes, come forth! I am sent unto you by Yahweh, the Lord your God, with these people, your liberators."

"There is no God!" the distant voice yelled. "He's dead, or He abandoned us thousands of years ago. Go away, whoever you are."

Gwynver'insa's form flowed, and she seemed to become taller and more distinct in the appearance of ancient robes. An intricate crown appeared on her head, and her features glowed.

"Yahweh lives and even now reigns in the

Kingdom of Heaven. He did not abandon us. We abandoned Him when our people turned their hearts to hate and their hands to war. He has heard our cries over these thousands of years and has relented against His nature to leave us to the profit of our decisions. I come as His Prophet, with words of redemption and hope. Come forth, I implore you, and stand before me. Nay, I, Gwynver'insa, Empress of the World, command it!"

Tul'ran raised his eyebrows and looked at Erianne, who appeared to be as equally stunned. He looked at Gwynver'insa, whose form pulsated and morphed from the appearance of a diminutive elf to a tall Queen and back again.

"Do we ride in the company of royalty, milady Erianne?"

Erianne squinted at the hazy form of their friend, who seemed more fog than substance.

"As it would appear, milord husband. Our friend does not cease to amaze. She is more magician than Queen, I would warrant."

They watched with wonder as people slowly drifted into the amphitheater from the shadows. The People wore tattered gowns, though clean, and many of them looked as if they hadn't eaten for a long time. They tried to maintain their dignity, but times had been obviously harsh. All were about Tul'ran's height, which gave him a measure of satisfaction. He no longer felt like he was the shortest male on the planet.

As they came closer, surprised expressions crossed the faces of the People. Most bowed or curtsied to the woman standing in front of them before taking a place in the amphitheater.

One young girl came forward and solemnly offered a single potted flower to Gwynver'insa, who accepted it and held it like a scepter in one arm. She kissed the child on her forehead before shooing her to the stands.

To the surprise of Tul'ran, Erianne, and Johan, every seat filled. The People had designated spots, and they milled around for several minutes as they took their places. There was no outward emotion from them, but it was obvious they were guarded and scared. As they took their places, conversation increased in volume, from whispering to an indistinct murmur.

Gwynver'insa silenced their murmurings by beating her left fist on her chest. Thump. Thump-thump. Thump. Thump-thump. The people sitting around her began hitting their chests in the same manner until the entire chamber sounded like one giant heartbeat. They stopped when Gwynver'insa thrust her arms away from her.

It was so quiet, then; it felt as if they had gone deaf. No one moved. Even the children were completely still. Gwynver'insa lowered her hands to her side and took a step forward.

"People of Hope, Children of the Living God, I, Gwynver'insa, She Who Creates From Nothing, The Last of her Kind, Prophet of Yahweh, Empress of the World, call to order a Gathering. Listen and hear."

"We obey!" the crowd roared.

"For hundreds of years I have hidden away from you, appalled at the hunger in the hearts of the

People to kill, rape, and steal. With fear and trepidation, I watched as the Combatants tore our world apart and hunted those of us who despised sin and craved life instead of death. Powerless, I saw them tear our planet apart, leaving it desiccated and with skies filled with darkness. No more!"

"I announce the cessation of all wars and the recovery of this world into peace and joy. We, the one hundred and forty-four thousand, are the only people remaining in this world. Yahweh has heard your pleas, received your supplications, and He answers. The battle does not belong to you; you are not His warriors. Behold, Our Champions!"

Gwynver'insa stepped aside, turned, and swept her hands back to gather Tul'ran, Erianne, and Johan within her introduction. She beamed as the crowd leaped to their feet, screaming their greetings, approval, and gratitude. It was pandemonium.

Erianne moved her gaze around the hall full of people, many of whom were screaming and crying from joy. She looked at Gwynver'insa, who raised her hands and drew another roar of adulation from the crowd. It made her wonder. The part of her nature being always suspicious, which never quite trusted people to the fullest extent, was raising a tasteless question. Had this beautiful, gentle, lovely woman just set them up?

'There's going to be one heck of a celebration feast in here,' she thought at her husband, sensing a darkness in his thoughts, and tasting apprehension in her own.

'Indeed,' he thought back. 'And I fear we are to be served up as the main course.'

CHAPTER THE SEVENTH:
FAMINE

The main course. Food, glorious food.

In the depths of darkest night,
Long before the sun's good rise,
The dreams of those who once had hope
Fade to dust with dawn's fresh eyes.

How poetic suffering can be. Throughout history, authors, painters, and balladeers made a profit from reaching into the pits of human misery, caressing the agony of hearts in pain, and spreading their anguish to an adoring audience. It was art; until suffering became so acute, it left the realm of poetry and entered the kingdom of desperation.

People who once took covetous pride in the overabundance of their storage shelves now looked on with despair as their spouses scraped together the smallest of meals from the little they could scrounge.

Every day was the same. Wander the streets with items once considered too valuable to part with: gold, silver, art, and heirlooms in search of sustenance. People were eager to take their inheritance and trade it for food, any kind of food. Those who once looked upon famine with pity while they shifted to make their fattened stomachs more comfortable now watched their ribs bulge above their shrunken waists.

Hunger is its own kind of hell. It deprives the mind of dreams, nights of sleep, and days of joy.

If only one was speaking of Spes Deserit.

On Erianne's Earth, the world of the future, the world of her present, people starved.

Earth, August 23, 2098 AD
Almost three years into the Tribulation

Nuclear fallout and polluted rains stripped fertility from the heartland of North America, where fields once flourished with grain and farmers watched their stock get fat on the grasslands. Irradiated winds and rain didn't confine themselves to the parts of the world suffering nuclear strikes; they drifted everywhere, and soon extensive tracts of Europe also fell to infertility. Sterile lands meant no crops and no feed for livestock.

The only prospering country was Israel, the globe's new breadbasket. Vast fields of grain covered what was once desert sand. Cattle and sheep grazed on lush grazing lands. Israel shipped food as fast as it would grow, but it wasn't enough. The small supply of food grown around the Earth couldn't meet the increased demand.

Countries around the world begged for more production from Israel. As a concession, Israel's neighbors ceded land to the small country for the development of farmlands. Muslim countries even gave up the Dome of the Rock and Al-Aqsa Mosque on the Temple Mount in exchange for food. Israel celebrated when contractors bulldozed the site and the construction of the new Temple began. Yes, those were heady days for the beleaguered nation. It finally gained in territory and prominence what God had promised to Abraham.

The famine touched every country and every demographic. Giant food stores in the wealthier countries, which once threw food away for exceeding "Best By" dates, now offered empty shelves. People traded everything they had for a loaf of bread and canned preserves so far beyond their expiration dates they should've been sent to a landfill. No one cared. It was food, and they were starving.

The leaders of every country faced riots and lawlessness amidst the clamor for a meal.

Contradeum stared at the list of files hovering above his desk in his office in Rome with rising frustration. He counted at least fifty files glowing in red, screaming for his immediate attention.

"Jez, what am I supposed to do with all this? I'm the leader of the world! Why am I doing paperwork? Do we not have people to take care of all this garbage?"

Jez bit her lip to keep from saying what her mind wanted to blurt about his reference to garbage.

"Your people have tried to make as many decisions as possible to spare you, Supreme Global Leader. These are the requests they don't have the authority to answer. They're pleas for food and resources from your ten Regional Supervisors. You can only answer them."

Contradeum petulantly threw his tablet onto the desk.

"Supervisors! They're more like children! I want this, I want that, want, want, want. Where am I supposed to get what they want? I'll tell you what I want: a break from this incessant bleating."

Jez leaned in closer to Contradeum, her eyes narrowing to slits.

"What do you expect, Mal? You foolishly provoked Oslo into launching a nuke against us almost a year ago. At least we think it was Oslo. Our military still hasn't come to any conclusion about where the nuke came from because the rogue Russian sub is still out there, somewhere. They have friends who are fueling and arming them. And I warned you against stockpiling the world's food supply in one location. What did you think was going to happen when you ordered a missile strike against Denver?"

Contradeum jerked himself to his feet, glaring at the smaller woman, who refused to give ground.

"Nothing links me to the attack on Denver!"

"Nothing?" Jez mocked. "Not even our Master's servants who travel through unseen space and watch our every move? Do you think him stupid, Mal, or unaware? He has his agents and spies everywhere. He knows you ordered that attack to soothe your stupid male ego. Now we have a rogue boomer out there with thirteen unfired missiles and a big radioactive hole in the desert where our food used to be. All our command-and-control capabilities evaporated in a mushroom cloud because you couldn't sit on your arrogance for one more stinking minute. The Master wants to talk to you, Mal. In person. I hope I can watch."

Contradeum paled, and he sat down with a 'thud.'

"He wants to talk to me in person? When? I mean, it's going to have to wait." He picked up the tablet. "Look at all these requests. I have to find food for people before they starve to death. I'm happy to talk to the Master, Jez, but it'll have to wait until I get some of this done. Hungry people can't wait for a meal forever."

"Fine," Jez said, patting him on the shoulder as she walked by him. "I'll leave you to it then."

She glanced back before she exited his makeshift office in the building they confiscated in Rome. He was very busy now, sorting through the screens hovering about his desk. Jez Brandt smirked.

There was more than one way to motivate the man.

Their trip to Rome from Iraq had been dismal. The high-speed train delivered them to Baghdad within an hour of leaving New Babylon. They ran into the Presidential jet and were airborne within minutes, escorted by two fourships of advanced fighter jets heavily laden with missiles. The interior of the plane was opulent. It could cater to the Supreme Global Leader's every need.

Contradeum stomped into his private sleeping quarters and slammed the door. He didn't come out of the room for the entire nine-hour flight from Baghdad to Rome, leaving Jez Brandt to watch in horror alone, the newsfeed of the destruction of New Babylon. One bottom part of the screen kept a running total of the casualties.

The deaths.

Jez closed her eyes, remembering the faces of people she knew and worked with, and who now were radioactive ash sifted by the desert winds. Someone would pay for this, she had promised herself.

That was eleven months ago. Jez punched the buttons on the elevator at the end of the hallway to the Supreme Global Leader's office. The elevator descended to the lowest levels of the building, where they had created a new Situation Room. She stepped off the elevator and walked into the center of the room. General M'uoba, the Commander of Earth Forces, turned and saluted her.

"Good day, Second. How may we help you?"

Jez regarded the large man. He was six feet, seven inches tall and weighed three hundred pounds. M'uoba wore his black hair close cropped, in typical military fashion, but dressed in camouflage fatigues instead of the gaudy day uniform encouraged by Contradeum. She judged him to be a man who fashioned himself as a professional.

Everyone at Headquarters called her 'Second' because she was second in command behind Contradeum, even though she held no official title. She didn't mind it; a simple title suggested genuine power, unlike the medals Contradeum liked to hand out as if they were candy.

"Any updates, General?"

M'uoba shook his head.

"As you know, Second, we ruled out a nuclear strike by TTI on the day of the attack. They have military forces to maintain their security only and never had nuclear weapons in their inventory. The missile hitting New Babylon was a submarine-launched ballistic missile. We have accounted for all our boomers, most of which were in drydock being painted."

Jez grimaced. Contradeum had ordered all Earth Naval Forces ships to have his image painted somewhere near the bow of the boat. The narcissistic act was going to cost the Navy's budget about three billion bitcoins. Painting a ship not only took time and money, it took the ship out of service. At least it had made tracking their boomers easier.

"Okay, it wasn't one of ours. That leaves the Americans. Which boat?"

M'uoba shrugged.

"Pick one. For decades, the Americans have been geniuses at concealing the activities of their boomers. OpSec has never been so tight. We don't know when they leave their barns and return. How many are at sea right now? Don't know. How many are operational? Don't know. The one thing I know scares the life out of me."

Jez had been studying the tactical displays on the large video screens on one wall of the Situation Room. She whipped her body around at his last comment.

"What's that, General?"

"Their nuclear forces are on a snap count, Second. This means they don't need to go through the customary authorization sequence to launch a nuclear attack. The National Command Authority has released the missiles 'hot' to the boomer commander. He just needs a target and a launch order. It's how they responded so quickly to the attack on Denver. No sooner had the *Putin* launched its missiles than someone ordered a retaliatory strike on New Babylon. This is dangerous, Second, very dangerous. The Americans enhance exponentially the chances of an accidental global nuclear war if they have their nuclear forces on a hair trigger."

M'uoba's statements shook her. She had her fill of nuclear war and never wanted to see another mushroom cloud for as long as she lived.

"Who ordered the strike?"

M'uoba shrugged.

"Who is in command over there? For several days, no one knew. It took Regional Supervisor Oslo three days to appear on holo and denounce the attack on Denver. She never took responsibility for the attack on New Babylon and called it an 'unfortunate incident.' Unfortunate incident! Fifteen thousand, five hundred and eighty-seven people died in that 'unfortunate incident.' The rest are so severely injured they may yet die. The strike devastated food stores the world was relying upon. I would string her up for such a statement alone!"

Jez nodded thoughtfully.

"Where was she for three days, General?"

"We don't know. She wouldn't answer those

questions, claiming her absence from her office was a personal matter. Journalism is not what it once was, Second. There are no more investigative reporters. The media duly broadcasts whatever information authority figures give them and don't ask painful or embarrassing questions."

A thought trickled into Jez's mind, teasing her cerebral cortex, and inviting a theory.

"Would you say the boomer's response time was unusually fast, General?"

M'uoba regarded the older woman cautiously.

"I would."

Jez folded her arms across her slight breasts, her forehead wrinkling.

"Could it have been because Oslo was on the sub? It makes sense, doesn't it? NCA was right there. She was both, technically, President of the United States and Chair of the Joint Chiefs of Staff. Could she not authorize the strike from the boomer as soon as she heard about the attack on Denver?"

General M'uoba was a cautious man. He ascended to the rank of four-star General and Commander of Earth Forces by carefully testing the waters and paying close attention to shifting winds. The woman who stood before him didn't rank him, but she had the ear of the man who did. A man famous for his temper and petulance; both bad characteristics to have in someone who could end a career on a whim.

"I hadn't thought of that, Second. Your theory," he emphasized the word 'your,' "has merit. It would explain why Regional Supervisor Oslo was away from her desk for three days, and why the boomer attacked so quickly after the *Putin* launched her missiles. I suppose my question, if I am asked for a comment, is why Oslo was there? The boomer was within a nautical mile of Atlantis."

Jez tapped her fingertips against her folded arms as opportunities presented themselves behind her mind's eye.

"Why, indeed? What was happening on Atlantis eleven months ago?"

Atlantis, September 2, 2077 AD... eleven months earlier

Lamek Davis could have told Jez Brandt what he was doing eleven months earlier. He was sweating to death. At least, it felt like he was sweating to death. The Recovery Specialist stood on the Lens as TTI technicians fussed with a parcel lying next to him. They had dressed him in buckskin breeches, a coarse wool shirt, leather moccasins, and a humongous coat designed to look and feel like it came from some woodland creature called a buffalo. It fell from his chin down to his toes. The coat was hairy, huge, and hot. They also made his head covering of fur. It was cold where he was going. He'd be happy to be in this stuff in about ten minutes; they said. That was two hours ago.

Coventry Quarterlaine seemed even less happy, as she stood next to him. She was in a buckskin dress from chin to ankles, with a large *faux* buffalo wrap around her shoulders. She wore soft moccasins laced up the front with some white fur trim around the top of the calf-length boots. They had braided her hair on each side, but nothing covered her head.

Heather Wu walked over to them and offered

them hankies to wipe the sweat from their foreheads.

"Sorry about this," she said. "The packs had to be adjusted. The IP is at five thousand feet above sea level. In this location, at the time of the year to which you're traveling, the temperature hovers around minus ten Fahrenheit and there's a lot of snow. Our team's been there for eight months Antiquity Time, five months past their scheduled return."

"What year are we going back to?" Coventry asked while wiping sweat out of her eyes.

Heather smiled sympathetically.

"The Team traveled back to 1700 AD in a location in the mountains at the western edge of what we know as the province of Alberta, Canada. The current city in this location is Canmore, but, of course, nothing existed back then in terms of a settlement. As far as we know, the earliest European explorers reached the foothills of the Rocky Mountains about the middle of the eighteenth century. The first white man to set eyes on the Bow River was David Thompson, who visited the meeting of the Bow River and the Elbow River in 1767. Following the explorers came a slow trickle of fur traders, and following them came the missionaries."

"It wasn't until the 1870s that the first homesteader established a permanent farm in the Bow Valley area. The homesteader was John Glenn, an experienced farmer, trapper, and prospector, who had searched for gold in California and traveled through much of the West before going to the Bow River country."

"In 1877, the Blackfoot Confederacy, along with

the Sarcee and Stony tribes, signed a treaty with the federal government of Canada. By the terms of the agreement - Treaty No. 7, as it was called - the Indigenous people exchanged large tracts of land for cash payments and reserves of approximately one million acres. The government also agreed to teach the native people how to farm their land. The government later purchased John Glenn's homestead for $350, a cow and a calf. They wanted it as an instructional farm."

Davis snorted.

"Wow. Big money. I thought John Glenn was an American astronaut."

Heather laughed.

"Different John Glenn. You know there are other people in the world, not just Americans, right? Anyway, our Team wanted to study the Indigenous people before they encountered Europeans. It was the precursor to a comprehensive study of Indigenous culture and land rights."

"Why didn't they just come back after ninety days?" Coventry asked, irritably. "Your people programmed their Coins to bring them back."

A fleeting veil of sadness crossed Heather's face.

"You can thank Jacques Lavoie for that. He was the Programmer who sold us out to whoever bombed Atlantis. He was the only one in the TTI Main Building when the bombs fell. From what Security pieced together, his plan was to escape from the Island in the pandemonium. As insurance, he locked out all the Teams still in the fields and encoded the lockout with a 256-key passcode. He figured if he got caught, he could trade the passcode for his freedom. It took every bit of skill I had to break the code and unlock passage back to the Insertion Points."

"What would possess him to not unlock the Mainframe before killing himself?" Davis asked, scratching at the sweat dripping under his garments. "Was he so bitter?"

Heather shrugged.

"Who knows? Maybe he forgot? His note said he didn't know the Complex was going to be bombed, if you can believe that." She looked to her right, where a tech was giving her a thumbs-up signal. "Okay, here are your Coins for this mission. There's a reprogrammed Coin for each Team member. The pack has everything you need for field medical treatment for first aid and wounds. Treat the Team if you must in the Field, but put them on the Lens and get them here as soon as you can. Get in, get out. The Indigenous population, to this point in time, has never seen a European. Avoid contact with the local populace at all costs or risk a time fracture. Good luck."

Davis looked at Coventry and shook his head. They were going to need more than luck on this one.

The transition was smooth. TTI Main Frame disappeared, and they emerged in the middle of a rock formation with steep sides. Nine figures lay in the Insertion Point, which was covered in snow. An icy wind blew through the gaps in the rocks.

Davis and Quarterlaine slid in the snow to the figures on the ground. They had covered themselves with skins resembling Davis's coat, but there were no heater units anywhere near any of them.

Davis took off his mitts and winced as the cold bit into his hands. He felt under the layers of clothing and found a slow, steady pulse under the cold skin.

"This one's alive."

"So is this one," Coventry replied.

One by one, they checked each figure. Each had a pulse, but was clearly in the deepest stages of hypothermia.

"Are they all here?" Davis asked. He had put his mitts back on, but still felt the cold through them.

Coventry nodded.

"I checked their Coins. All present and accounted for. They have quite a trash heap in the far corner. It looks like their heating units failed a few days ago. They've been lighting fires to stay warm. From the skins and bones, it's clear they've been foraging off the land for weeks. Even with that, they're all skinny."

A worried look crossed Davis's face.

"They've been lighting fires?"

Coventry nodded.

"I know what you're thinking. Fires attract attention. We have to transition these people out right now, Mick, but we can't leave all this stuff here. If someone finds it, we cause a breach and maybe an anomaly."

Davis sighed.

"Here we go again. Okay, let's drag them to the center and activate their Coins. You're right, they have to get out of here right now to survive. I'll stay and start bundling the trash. Hurry back and give me a hand. It's going to be dark soon, and I'm already freezing off parts of me I want to keep."

Coventry was too cold to laugh. They struggled to drag the nine bodies to the center of the IP, near the Time Scepter. When they finished, they rested for a moment to catch their breaths.

"Move at least fifty yards away from the Scepter, Mick, or you're going to get sucked in with us. I'll count to sixty and activate the device."

"I'm gone," Mick said, and he worked his way out of the IP.

The Team had positioned the IP in a natural carve-out on the mountain's side. If you didn't know it was there, it would be easy to miss. Unless you were following plumes of wood smoke. The path downwards was traversable, but Davis took a lot of care. The rock was icy and the last thing he needed to do was break a leg. If this was winter in this part of the world, he wanted nothing to do with it.

Davis reached the bottom of the path, which ended at an iced over pond. It looked like it would have been a superb source of clean water. They had picked the IP well. He looked around the area beyond the pond. All he could see were trees, snow, mountains, and a beautiful blue sky. The part of his brain tracking such things reached sixty seconds in the countdown. Coventry should be gone. He waited a few more minutes just in case the cold had numbed that part of him, too.

Just as he was about to return up the slope, he heard a noise; it dropped him back into a crouch. He strained his eyes until they found what his ears heard. A group of men were making their way up the mountain. They were carrying spears and bows and were pushing hard against the deep snow. Davis counted eleven of them and sighed. He was no expert in Indigenous culture, but he knew a war party when he saw one.

Things were about to get interesting.

Jesus broke three Seals and three horsemen of the Apocalypse had ridden off the edge of Heaven to leave their marks on the Earth. Four Seal Judgments remained, as did Seven Trumpet Judgements and Seven Bowl Judgments.

Jesus looked down on the planet upon which His feet trod for thirty-three years. He had a deep love for the Earth and its people. In no other populated planet in the Universe, had the Messiah come. Were it not for Adam and Eve, it may never have been necessary for Him to assume human form.

Not that it was all bad. He had enjoyed the feeling of the sun on his skin, the wind in His hair, and cool water soothing aching muscles. He had enjoyed the love of family and friends, most of whom now lived with Him for all eternity. The Earth had carved a special place in His heart because He breathed her air and wiggled His toes in her grasses. But Adam and Eve brought sin into the world he loved and now the evil had to be cleansed.

The Lamb of God raised the scroll for all assembled to see and placed his thumbs over the fourth seal, colored ashen. He broke it, and a fourth Cherubim bellowed, "Come!"

The Fourth Horseman of the Apocalypse sat on a horse sickly, pale, and a yellow-green color, as if it were a decomposing corpse. The Fourth Horseman was Death and Hades followed behind him. Jesus stepped forward and addressed them both.

"I give you authority over a fourth of the remaining population on the Earth. You will kill them with sword and famine, with pestilence and plagues. You will release the wild beasts of the Earth upon them."

Death raised its sickle in salute and kicked his sickly looking horse into a trot. As the Fourth Horseman leaped off the edge of Heaven, Jesus reflected on how disease killed people on a far more massive scale than war. At least in warfare, the combatants suffered the most deaths. Disease was indiscriminate. It was a horrible punishment to inflict upon the Earth.

The Messiah turned away. He had hoped beyond hope the devastation being showered on the Earth would change the hearts of all the survivors to Him, so the pain could stop. The part of Him Seeing all things and knowing every future understood it would not be so. Some of them would continue in their evil ways and beliefs, against all pain, discomfort, and sorrow, until they drew their last breath. The Son of God drew a long breath as a tear fell from His eye. He looked up to see the Father gazing at Him with sorrow on His face. He understood His Son's heart and felt His pain.

There was just no other way.

There was no other way.

Davis had to distract the Indigenous warriors coming up the slope towards him. He knew they were expert trackers from the briefing packets. Human feet packed the trail from the IP to the pond.

It would take them no time to follow the trail back to the IP. If he bugged out, he would leave behind a treasure trove of highly advanced technology. He had to divert them from the pond and he had to do it now.

Somewhere from the deepest recesses of his mind came the word, 'Imoiitapi.' He remembered the word because it was an interesting story. The Blackfeet people had a legend about a 'hairy man'– that's what the word Imoiitapi meant–whom they had spotted in the Rocky Mountains. Later cultures would call the Imoiitapi by the name of 'Sasquatch.' Davis glanced down at himself, at the bulky, hairy coat covering him from head to toe. He grinned. This could work without causing an anomaly.

Davis took a deep breath and took off the coat. The icy cold grabbed at his breath and he shivered. He hated being cold, ever since his days in BUD/S. This assignment brought back memories of lying cold and wet in the frigid Pacific surf, his body shivering in a desperate attempt to get warm. He added a shudder to the shiver and drew his knife. Davis cut the back of the coat down the middle from the area where his thighs met his crotch. He stripped the laces from his moccasins and put the coat back on. With the laces, he tied the coat to his legs, so they appeared to be hairy appendages. He pulled the hat as far down on his face as it would go and grinned.

It was showtime.

Coventry transitioned back into the IP, expecting to find Davis busy working the site to clean it up for exfil. It was empty. Worried, she took a quick glance down the path from the exit, praying she wouldn't see his body crumpled at the foot of a ledge somewhere. As she panicked when she couldn't see him in her visual range, a loud, horrific moan floated up the mountain toward her. She froze, the hairs standing on her arms and the back of her neck.

She pulled out thermal imaging distance lenses and scanned the slope away from IP. The lenses caught Davis's outline. He was standing on his toes, facing down the mountain, hands raised high in the air, and uttering horrible moans. Confused, she swept the lenses down the mountainside and froze.

A group of Indigenous men were standing in the snow about twenty yards from Davis, their eyes wide and mouths hanging open. All carried weapons of some sort and had been advancing up the mountain to where Davis stood. Davis issued another moan and beat his chest. It was too much for the men. Hooting, they raced back down the mountainside, tumbling head over heels in the snow where feet didn't quite clear the deep drifts.

Coventry blew two breaths into her microphone and watched as Davis turned to look up the mountain.

"Retreat," she whispered.

"In ten," he whispered back.

Coventry watched as Davis broke the branch of a pine tree and swept it over the snow near the pond. She nodded. He was trying to cover their tracks in case the warriors came back. Not that it was likely. The mountains were getting dark.

There was a lot of work to do to make sure they cleaned the IP, in case curious thrill seekers made it to the hidden ledge. Coventry grinned and pressed the record button on the lenses three times in rapid succession. The lens would capture the last six minutes of video, as well as the audio. She could hardly wait to play it for their colleagues at dinner tonight. Davis's face was going to be a thing of art.

Earth, August 23, 2098 AD ... 11 months later
Almost three years into the Tribulation

Jez Brandt walked back to her office, a plan hatching within the depths of her brain from her conversation with the General. She had just settled into her chair when her assistant walked in unannounced. He never did that. Jez wasn't one to snap at her underlings, something they all appreciated, but his abrupt appearance sorely tempted her to snarl. She bit it back and nodded.

"Well?"

He swallowed and flicked his wrist at her holo screens. A map of the world snapped into being. Each continent had red dots on them, some larger than others and some expanding as she watched.

"What's this?" she asked, noting the existence of dots in each country and region on the map.

"It's a virus," he said, a sickly look on his face. "And it's a bad one. It's aerosol and spreads like a cold, but it's way worse. The virus goes right after the lungs. It's very hard on malnourished people. Without a ventilator, someone with severe affect will drown in their own mucus within days of infection. Those projections are brand new. It's already a global pandemic. We don't have a vaccine or medications to treat it because we don't even know what it is yet. Millions of people are going to get sick and die."

Jez put her head in her hands. She felt like weeping. The Master had told her their rise to power would be free of trouble. People would embrace Contradeum and the world would quickly transition to peace and security. The Master had promised them paradise on Earth, under his rule, and she believed every word. She had just taken a breath from their last nuclear skirmish, and now this.

She looked up with tired eyes and dismissed her assistant with a flick of her hands. Malchus was going to lose his stuff when he heard this. As usual, he would rant at her for an hour before they would get down to the business of the next steps. Unless she gave him a plan to focus on.

Jez looked at her image in the glass of her office. She looked old and haggard. No sleep and stress will do that for you, she figured. Oh, well. Her youth wasn't coming back soon. She got up from her desk and walked across the hall to Contradeum's office. She knocked and walked in when he gave her the nod.

"What's up?" he asked, his voice weary.

"This is bad, boss. My assistant just told me we're facing a deadly pandemic of unknown origin."

Contradeum threw his hands into the air.

"Of course we are! Why not? How many people are going to die, Jez?"

She shook her head slowly.

"I don't know. We don't have projections yet. It's going to be a lot, Mal. The virus is new, apparently, and we have no vaccine or cure."

Contradeum rose from his desk and walked to the large window in his office. It looked over the Via del Corso, the main street running through Rome. People engorged the street, buying and selling, or begging for food. The streets would get much thinner, soon. He crossed his arms behind his back.

"So, this is the world I get to inherit. War and death, plagues and pestilences. When's the glory supposed to start? I am the leader of the world and all people do is whine at me because they're hungry, cold, thirsty, or have no shelter. Like it's my fault. Do you have any good news for me, Jez?"

"As a matter of fact, I do. I have reasonable and probable grounds to believe Oslo was on the boomer which launched the attack on New Babylon and destroyed our food supply. I'm asking for your authorization to issue a warrant for her arrest for war crimes and crimes against humanity."

Contradeum's eyes brightened.

"I like it! But the Americans will never give her up. She's their hero."

Jez's smile was a grimace, but a smile all the same.

"They will if they want to eat. We still control the world's food supply. They'll give up Oslo or starve. We'll convict her and then we'll kill her for all the world to see."

CHAPTER THE EIGHTH: FEAST

Spes Deserit, in the Year of Our Fight 2375
Mission Day 25

The Hall of Everlasting Joy was massive, stretching throughout the entire cave. Torches lit the aisles and everywhere the smell of food permeated the nostrils and teased the senses. The air was festive and groups of people walked through the throngs, caroling. The joy of the People was palpable; a moving, living creature all on its own.

A gong sounded and reverberated through the air. Quietly, respectfully, the People took their assigned seats and waited.

Gwynver'insa entered the hall from a side opening and strode up to a podium set on a raised stage in the Hall's front, direct center. She carried a large ornate book bound in red leather and imbedded with runes in gold and silver. She placed the book on the podium and stood quietly for a moment, every inch the Queen.

Her attendants had piled her blonde hair on her head and slipped individual strands between the elegant weaving of a tall, ornate golden crown. She wore a red dress, trimmed with gold chains and medallions, which hugged her delicate form and plunged to her ankles. Tall shoes caressed her feet, tied with gold laces around her ankles and up her calves to the bottom of her knees.

Empress Gwynver'insa, the Last of Her Kind, opened the Book to a particular section and projected her voice into the vast Hall. The acoustics in the Hall were perfect. No one had to strain to hear her speak, even though one hundred and forty-four thousand pairs of ears hung on every word.

"A Reading from the Prophecy of Molodek'exsa, now ten thousand years past. Hearken unto me, children of Yahweh, God of all Life, Majesty of Majesties. Behold, there shall come to the world the Fight, upon the emergence of the Fight, war, and upon the emergence of war, death and starvation. The People shall take upon themselves the right of God to choose between Life and Death. They shall take from Yahweh the right to choose and become gods with power over life and death. Yahweh shall give them over to their unholy desires and allow them the cost of their choosing. And so, the Fight shall continue until the Day of Redemption."

"On the Day of Redemption, the Empress of the World, the Last of Her Kind, shall come upon the Judgment Seat from exile. She will call forth the

People from their hovels and the People shall come. Amid the one hundred and forty-four thousand, the Empress shall declare a Gathering. People who had no sustenance, those starved for food, shall once again eat in plenty the meat, the vegetables, and the fruit the land once offered abundantly but can provide no more. This day, the Day of Redemption, shall be a sign of the end of the Fight and the return of the People to Yahweh, their God. Thus sayeth the Lord through His prophet, Molodek'exsa."

Gwynver'insa closed the Book and stared at the People, who waited in anxious anticipation.

"I, Gwynver'insa, She Who Creates From Nothing, The Last of her Kind, Prophet of Yahweh, Empress of the World, proclaim today I fulfill these words in your sight."

The Hall erupted in a massive roar so voluminous it shook dust from the rock walls. Gwynver'insa raised her hand after a few moments and stilled the crowd.

"I, Gwynver'insa, She Who Creates From Nothing, The Last of her Kind, Prophet of Yahweh, Empress of the World, proclaim today to be the Day of Redemption."

The cheers erupted again, louder this time, and the shouts of joy mingled with tears as hearts sobbed out their relief. After Gwynver'insa called the assembly to order again, she gestured to her right.

"Behold, People of Hope, our Champions, who will go into this world and end all wars, strife and killing. The blood of their enemies shall flow like water at their feet and the Houses of War shall be no more. Rise and greet Lord Tul'ran az Nostrom,

Prince of Death, Lady Erianne az Nostrom, Princess of Destruction, and Lord Johan, Prince of Sciences and Philosophy."

There was no cheering as the trio walked into the hall; instead, the assembly stood and waited until the trio took their place behind Gwynver'insa. Solemnly, the assembly, as one person, bowed deeply and held their bow for a five count before standing up. Then they beat on their chests until the hall was once more filled with the sound of a giant heart, beating its lifeblood in the souls of the People. When they finished, the assembly knelt and pressed their faces to the ground.

Gwynver'insa turned to the trio, knelt, and pressed her head to the ground.

"Lord Tul'ran, Lady Erianne, Lord Johan. We, the People of Hope, pass to you our claim for justice and our desire for peace. On this, our Day of Redemption, we disavow war, violence, hatred, and deception. We repent of our sins and return our hearts, minds, and souls to Yahweh, our God. We charge you to deliver this world from evil, Warriors of God, and pledge you our prayers in support. May it be so."

"May it ever be so," the assembly said; the words a hollow boom within the Hall.

Gwynver'insa stood. She turned to the People kneeling before her and raised her hands to the ceiling.

"Yahweh, we thank you for sending your Warriors to our aid. We disavow war, violence, hatred, and deception. We repent of our sins and return our hearts, minds, and souls to you, our God.

Please bless our Warriors as they go into the world to rid it of evil. Bless the food you have set before us for our body's use and grant us your peace. May it be so."

"May it ever be so," the assembly intoned.

Gwynver'insa smiled.

"Now, let us feast!"

The assembly roared their approval and took their seats again, chattering with excitement. The Food Makers on each table dispensed plates of hot cuisine, which were distributed to all the members of the table before they dug into their meals with gusto.

Gwynver'insa's attendants had placed a small table on the raised stage. She sat in the middle of the table, with Johan on her right, Erianne to her left, and Tul'ran at the end of the table. The Empress leaned over and whispered something into Johan's ear and he laughed. Tul'ran took that moment to direct a thought into his wife's mind.

'It is official, my love. The Empress has proclaimed us the Liberators of this world. The three of us, only two of whom are warriors, against tens of thousands of war machines and a scattering of minds bent upon our destruction. Do you have a thought about how we will accomplish this impossible task?'

Erianne turned to look at him and smiled. Gwynver'insa had given each of them crowns for the feast, and the gold metal shone against her black hair. Her green eyes sparked and danced against her mahogany brown skin, as her white teeth lit up her face.

'Fear not, milord husband. You'll think of something.'

He'll think of something. Right. Tul'ran looked at the immense crowd wolfing down food, laughing and enjoying merriment for the first time in hundreds, if not thousands, of years. Their Empress had placed all their lives in his hands. He felt his stomach lurch and closed his eyes.

He could enjoy this more, he knew, if it wasn't for the prophecy Gwynver'insa pronounced three weeks earlier.

Mission Day 4... three weeks before the Gathering

It had been a difficult three weeks leading up to the feast. With Johan's help, Gwynver'insa had created a Food Maker in a private alcove near the hall. The first one had taken seventeen hours to create, during which the diminutive woman didn't eat, sleep or rest. When she finished it, she was too weak to move.

Erianne ordered a bowl of chicken noodle soup from the unit, over which Gwynver'insa swooned. Erianne carried her to a thick bed of furs in a corner of the same room, where the Empress of the World slept for a full twelve hours under the careful eyes of her warriors.

Tul'ran, Erianne, and Johan took turns watching over her as she worked and when she slept.

"Why do we need to worry about her here?" Johan had asked near the twelfth hour of her rest. "Is she not among her People? She must be safe here!"

Tul'ran and Erianne shook their heads in unison.

"No, Johan, she's not," Erianne said. "She announced herself as She Who Creates From

Nothing. If the Combatants have spies among the People, they will certainly come for her. We can't allow evil access to the power to create something from nothing. It would spell the end of this world."

Tul'ran stared at the Food Maker sitting in the room's corner.

"How is this possible, Johan? From what you told me, this device is a thing of scientific wonder far beyond the technology of your time. How could Gwynver'insa create this thing with the exercise of her mind?"

Johan shrugged.

"My friend, you ask for wisdom from the dust mote riding the hair sitting upon the wrist of God. I barely understand the science behind how this device works, much less the manner of its construction. If you asked me to build one, I could not. I couldn't even design the schematics for someone else to build it. Not only does our lovely Empress comprehend the workings of the Food Maker, the science behind it, and the schematics of its design, she can recreate it with the force of her mind. She is beyond a genius. There is no mind like hers on Earth. All I can say is that she did it, it works, and I would marry her tomorrow, if she would have me."

A sleepy voice rose from the depths of the pile of furs on the ground of the alcove.

"Be careful what you promise, Lord Johan. I find you most pleasing to the eye and delightful to the mind. You may find wishes answered in this world."

Gwynver'insa sat up and yawned delicately into one hand. Erianne shook her head.

"You have arisen from twelve hours of sleep,

Your Imperial Majesty, and you look as if you had spent all those hours before a mirror making ready for the day. Truly, I am jealous."

Gwynver'insa giggled and bounded out of bed. She ran up to Erianne and embraced her in a tight bear hug.

"You are one to talk, sister. Every day I look upon your tall, slender form, gaze into the depths of your beautiful green eyes and wonder how such beauty can exist. Truly, God is an Artist. And when we are alone, all of you must call me Gwynver'insa, or Gwyn in the short form. There should be no titles between us, for we are family, and family should not be so formal."

She let Erianne go and curtsied to Tul'ran.

"As long as that meets with your approval, Warrior Lord. I would wish to do nothing to bring the wrath of the Sword Himself upon my shoulders. Horror of horrors if such a day should come." She turned the curtsy into a deep, sweeping bow.

Tul'ran grinned.

"Imp. You have learned some of my wife's mischief, little sister. And how does it come to pass you address me in a title I have not spoken in this world?" He cocked a sardonic eyebrow at Erianne, who was trying very hard to look innocent. "Hmmm?"

"Milord husband, it may have come to pass, by some off chance, that while our regal sister was in the course of her labors, I sang to her all one hundred fifty stanzas of the Ballad of Tul'ran the Sword."

A look of horror swept over Tul'ran's face.

"You did not!"

Gwynver'insa burst into giggles.

"She most certainly did! I was in the seventh hour of my labor. You and Johan had gone out, as you said to him, 'to check the perimeter.' By this I understood you to mean the two of you would search out any weak points in the security of the Hall of Ancestors and take steps to safeguard against intrusion."

"My lovely sister stood watch over me, hand ever close to her blade, to deal death to any who sought to harm me. I called out to her and bade her entertain me so I would not lose focus on my task. Erianne asked if she should sing your Ballad, milord Tul'ran, and I begged her for a recital. I most appreciated the stanzas of how the two of you met and fell in love." She twirled around the room three times, clasped her hands together, looked at the blushing warrior, and sighed. "So romantic."

Tul'ran shot a mock glare at Erianne.

"We will speak of this later, traitorous wife."

Erianne glided up to him, wrapped her arms around his neck, and widened her eyes.

"Ooo, I perceive a threat. Will you punish me, milord husband? What form will it take, I wonder, hmmm? Should I have our sweet Empress create a pillow for my backside before this evening's meal?"

Tul'ran's face became redder, and he disentangled himself from Erianne's arms.

"Nothing is outside the realm of possibilities, milady. Should we attend to our toiletries and break our fast?"

"Indeed, we must!" Gwynver'insa exclaimed. "I

will show you the way to the baths, where you may refresh yourselves. When you are done, we shall come back to this place and you shall entertain me with new dishes for my repast." She stood on her tiptoes and waved her right forefinger in the air as if it were a wand. "I command it."

They laughed and executed awkward bows.

"Yes, Your Imperial Majesty," they said, in unison.

"What about the Food Maker?" Johan asked when they finished laughing. "Is it safe to leave here?"

Gwynver'insa smiled at him and squeezed his left biceps.

"Ever the cautious one, Johan. No, no, do not look sheepish. It is one of the many qualities I admire in you." She turned to the Food Maker and frowned. The unit shimmered for a moment, then vanished. "There, I have hidden it behind a curtain that bends light around it. Should anyone come into this place, they will see an empty alcove. Come, let us bathe!"

She skipped out of the room, grabbing Erianne's hand and pulling the laughing woman behind her. Johan looked at Tul'ran and shook his head.

"Just like that, she creates a privacy screen. We have to be careful with our words in her presence, Tul'ran. A careless slip of the tongue and you may wonder how you're going to get rid of a giraffe."

Johan followed the women out of the room, and Tul'ran raised his eyes to the ceiling.

"Here I am again, the one with the least knowledge in the room. Tell me, El Shaddai, what's a giraffe?"

Darian woke up to birds singing and the sun warming her body. The bed upon which she lay was the most comfortable she had enjoyed. The combination of the firm mattress and the soft coverings made her feel like she slept on a cloud. She didn't know how long she slept, but felt energy coursing through her body.

She rolled to the edge of the bed and sat up, swinging her legs over. Darian touched the bandages covering her eyes, which obscured her vision in darkness.

"E'thriel?"

The answer came with satisfying immediacy.

"I am here, Darian. Welcome to a new day. You are looking much better. There is still a lot of bruising on your face, but it is healing. As is your brain. The swelling has gone down in the fourteen hours in which you slept."

"Fourteen hours! No wonder I have to, uh, um, use the facilities so badly."

She felt the warmth of his smile, even though she couldn't see his face.

"If you will take my arm, Darian, I will lead you to the facilities where you can have your privacy and refresh yourself."

She stepped off the bed, tucking her arm behind his elbow. It surprised her how high she had to reach up to take the crook of his arm. Whoever E'thriel was, he was very tall. They walked together for a few minutes before E'thriel took her arm and placed against the door of her washroom.

"Here we are, Darian. Call out when you have finished, and I will take you back. Please do not take off your bandages. The light in the room is dazzling and I remain concerned about the response of your brain from exposure to it."

She patted his arm.

"Don't worry, E'thriel, I'll behave. I have a bit of a headache and I don't want to make it worse." She bit her lip. "When I'm finished in here, can we talk about my nightmares?"

"Of course, Darian. I am here for you in whatever capacity you require."

She smiled and moved into the facilities. When she finished her toiletries and splashed water on her body, she moved to the door and stopped. The urge to peek out from under the bandages swathing her eyes was strong. A part of her desperately needed to know she wasn't blind. Darian set her lips into a firm line. This was the new her, she reminded herself. The new her was going to live up to her word and listen to good advice.

She opened the door and called out in a soft voice, "Finished."

Darian felt a stirring to her right and heard a strange rustle, as if a bird had snapped its wings. That was odd.

"I am here, Darian. Come, take my arm. We go to the garden, where I have prepared for you a breakfast of French toast, drizzled with cinnamon and maple syrup."

Her eyebrows shot up.

"French toast, cinnamon, and maple syrup! Are we rich then, my friend, to afford such a luxury?"

E'thriel chuckled.

"This House yields whatever you ask of it,

remember? I thought you might enjoy a decadent breakfast. How long has it been since you have had a breakfast like this?"

Pain lanced through Darian's head as she struggled to remember. She put her fingertips to her temple.

"Ouch! I can't remember, E'thriel, and when I try to, it hurts."

"Then do not," he said. "You are still recovering, Darian. Do not stress yourself, or apply your mind to arduous tasks. I promise you will make a full recovery. Be at peace, if you can."

They were back in the garden. She could feel the sun on her skin and smell flowers and grass, and food! Her stomach lurched and demanded sustenance. Now! She laughed.

"I'm starving. Let's eat."

They took their time eating breakfast, chatting about nothing. Darian asked him to describe the garden for her mind's eye and E'thriel complied with descriptive detail so complete she had a beautiful vision of where they sat. When they finished, he cleaned up their plates, and they returned to the divan.

"You wanted to talk about nightmares," he prompted, when she finished making herself comfortable.

Darian hesitated.

"Forgive me, E'thriel, but this is hard for me. I don't know you. You're a man and I don't trust men because, well, because men haven't been kind to me. But you're kind. I mean, I'm not saying bad things about you. It's just hard because I don't know you

well enough to trust you and anyone I've ever trusted
has let me down."

E'thriel sat cross-legged in front of her and
fanned his wings so it would create a gentle breeze
across her body. She wore a shift that covered her
from head to ankles, with bare arms, and the breeze
was pleasant against her skin.

"Let's consider your statement, Darian. In the
time you have known Johan, Erianne, and Tul'ran,
have they let you down?"

Darian rubbed her fingertips over the bandages
covering her eyes and thought about his question.

"Well, Johan tried to walk away from me a few
times, but he always came back, especially if I asked
him to. Looking back on my times with him, I was
mean to him and he took it, mostly. Sure, he snapped
back sometimes, which means he has some self-
respect, but he didn't stay angry at me for long.
Usually, he just followed me around like a lovesick
puppy and tried to do pleasant things for me." She
was quiet for a few minutes as she realized she
missed him.

"Tul'ran, well, there's a hard nut. In my vision,
while I was unconscious, I asked to be shown the
faces of those who loved me. Johan's face, I
expected, but Tul'ran's face just about knocked me
off my perch. I always had the impression he would
rather kill me and feed me to his horse than hug me
and call me a friend."

E'thriel chuckled.

"Horses don't eat meat."

Darian laughed, a sharp bark.

"I know that! It's an allegory of how fierce I

consider both to be. Tul'ran's protected me, along with everyone else, so I guess I can believe he's cared for me. And no, he's never let me down. I'm not sure how he'd feel about me after I've stabbed him in the back."

E'thriel reached behind him and grabbed a bowl from the table. He put the bowl in her hands. She reached in, pulled at the fruit, and popped one into her mouth.

"Grapes! E'thriel, you sneak. How did you know I was thinking about grapes yesterday?"

He chuckled.

"When you were lounging on this white divan in your white smock, I thought you looked like Cleopatra. I supplied grapes and fans today."

They laughed for a minute, and Darian dipped her fingers back into the bowl.

"What about Erianne?"

Darian popped a grape into her mouth and smiled.

"Erianne's a sweetheart. It's easy to move her to a tear. Oh, don't mistake me, she's tough! I'll never forget the look on her face when she had her sword at my throat. That girl can cook! She was vicious on the battlefield against those soldiers on horseback. If she ever fought Tul'ran, I'm not sure which of the two of them would win."

"Erianne would," E'thriel said, "because Tul'ran could never bring himself to hurt her."

Darian nodded thoughtfully.

"Yeah, I can see that. They are so in love with one another. Makes me kinda jealous."

E'thriel allowed a few minutes of silence to pass

before he spoke again.

"So, tell me about your nightmares, Darian."

A shudder rippled through her body.

"It's always the same dream. I'm back in the corridor, standing in front of the purple energy curtain. Abaddon is sneering at me, telling me I'm just a bug he could squash. I go down on my knees and beg him to send me home. He laughs, contemptuously, and says, 'Oh, I'll send you home, alright. You don't have to worry about that. I'll send you home in a body bag.' Then he hits me in the face. I'm laying there, crying, but he keeps hitting me in the face and asking me what color I want my body bag to be."

Tears were rolling down her cheeks.

E'thriel moved to sit at her side and wrapped a massive arm around her shoulders.

"Peace, little one, peace. Abaddon cannot threaten you here, nor would he do so in my presence. The Lord gave me primacy, and Abaddon is subject to my will as it concerns you."

Darian was sobbing.

"What does it mean, E'thriel? Am I going to die? Is he going to kill me? Will I never get off this planet?"

"May I suggest," he answered gently, "you ask the wrong question? Everyone dies, Darian; it's inevitable. The question you need to ask is, what happens after you die? Trust me, it's the only question worth asking."

Darian pulled away and looked toward his voice.

"What do you mean? I always thought when you die, that's just it. It's over. There's nothing else."

"Do you believe in angels, Darian?"

She shrugged.

"You could fit what I know about angels into a teaspoon and have room to spare. I always thought they were a good luck charm, or something you pray to for riches. Girl angels with tiny wings who strummed hearts and decorated calendars, or baby angels who shot arrows into people to make them fall in love. I never took them seriously."

"Would you like me to tell you the story of how angels came to be?"

Darian sat back and leaned into his chest, marveling at the warmth of his body.

"Sure, go ahead. That sounds fine."

So, he did, describing his creation in the third person and the creation of the universe and humankind. He was a wonderful storyteller, making the details spring to life in her mind. It took hours, and at the end of it he filled her brain with images of Heaven, and angels, and God.

"Is what you said true? It's all real?"

"It is, Darian. I give you my word."

She sighed and closed her eyes.

"I like your story, E'thriel. A nap right now would be good. I'm going to try to dream your story."

Just like that, she fell asleep, nestled in the arms of her angel, in a garden where the sun shone, and birds sang, and she dreamed of flying through Heaven on vast white wings.

Abaddon was back on his perch, on top of the tallest spire facing the House of the Lord. He had sat brooding there since he took the mechanized infantry out of the House and dispatched them back to their masters. One question had been gnawing at his mind like a starving dog on a bone.

Why had the House refused him entrance?

Had the Father Himself not told Abaddon before he left for the Abyss Abaddon was always welcome in the Kingdom of Heaven? Was the House not an extension of Heaven? Why had it turned him away with dire warnings if he should attempt to enter again?

He could always ask the Holy Spirit. Every angel had an intimate, direct connection to the Holy Spirit. He tried to remember the last time he communed with the Holy Trinity and was stunned by the answer shining in his mind. That long? He had been here that long?

What was he doing here?

More importantly, what had he done here?

The answers came. Answers he had been hiding in the deepest recesses of his mind because they convicted him of shameful things. He wasn't here because Yahweh, the Most High God, sent him here. Abaddon was on Spes Deserit because Satan told him to come, and the Abyss had bored Abaddon enough to accept what he considered a welcome diversion.

Who told him to tempt the People? Yahweh had not granted him permission to test their faith and obedience, as he had permitted Lucifer to tempt Adam and Eve. Abaddon had posed one question to a simple farmer, which anyone could construe as innocent. Was it his fault the humans leaped to the answer of war and pursued it like an addict? They loved the Fight in all its glory, with warfare, bloodshed, pain, and misery. He did nothing to promote their love for violence.

But he didn't dissuade them from it, either, did he? In fact, as the years fled, he turned from advising the Combatants on more lethal means of killing, to stepping in and slaughtering thousands by his own hand. To balance the scales, of course, so there never would be one outright winner. An outright winner would end the Fight.

Abaddon looked at his massive right hand. This hand had once belonged to God. It sickened him to think he had unwittingly committed it to Satan's service. He might have not actively encouraged evil on this planet, but he steeped himself in evil once it flourished. He winced as he thought about the girl whose face he smashed and left to die in the House. Why should she bother him so? Except, she was a creature of pain, made so by Satan, and he leaped in to further that pain. He looked at his hand again.

What had he become?

CHAPTER THE NINTH:

PROPHECY...

The baths were luxurious. The bathers had their own separate grotto with three individual pools, each warmer than the other. They were large enough for the bather to stretch out full length and have the waters caress all pain, stiffness, and care away.

Erianne straddled the thighs of her husband, the water lapping around her slender waist, and smiled as she ran her left hand over his massive chest, indulging in the feel of his muscles under her fingertips. She leaned her naked body into his and planted a gentle kiss on his lips. As she kissed him, softly, sensuously, her right hand fished a dagger out of her armor piled up behind him.

He stiffened slightly as he felt the kiss of the sharp edge of the knife against his neck. She raised her head and grinned.

"You promised I could shave you, remember?" she said, in English.

He laughed, replying in her language.

"Good grief, Erianne. You could pick a better way to let me know what you're going to do. I just about had a heart attack!"

She grinned; her teeth were brilliant against her dark brown skin.

"Suck it up, buttercup. You should be used to me by now."

He cocked his eyebrows at her.

"You know, you're right. We've been married for what, months now? How do I not know you?"

Erianne made herself comfortable over his hips, which, she saw to her delight, aroused him. She was determined to tease a hard bounce out of him before they left their grotto. Erianne splashed some warm water on Tul'ran's face and rubbed it with her left palm.

"Gird yourself with courage, covenant-husband, for your wife, the Princess of Destruction, rides with a vengeance against the scurrilous growth sweeping across your firm jowls."

It sounded some much better in the Tongue than 'now I'm going to shave you.'

She ran the killing edges of her knife across his face, expertly scraping away his thick stubble. It was the sixth time she shaved him since they met, and she was becoming adept at cleaving hair from skin without the slightest loss of blood.

As always, he leaned back and closed his eyes, enjoying the feeling of the blade dancing on his weathered skin.

"Don't fall asleep," she admonished him. "You'll either drown or I'll cut your throat."

He chuckled without moving the muscles of his face. She made the last pass across his jawline and admired her handiwork. Erianne cocked her eyebrow at her grinning husband.

"Nice and smooth. Now you can't do any damage to my tender skin."

She moved in a way he understood to be an invitation, and their bath took on a dance all lovers know, as their skin glowed under torchlight, and somewhere distant blooms filled the cavern air with sensuous smells of tuberose, jasmine, gardenias, and orange blossoms.

Gwynver'insa, Empress of the World, leaned back against the stone wall of the alcove and belched loudly. She threw her hand to her mouth and her face turned bright red as her companions burst out laughing.

"I am so sorry! How uncouth!"

Erianne leaned over and gave her a gentle rub on the knee.

"In some cultures in my world, sweet sister, they would consider such a burp a compliment. Did you enjoy your breakfast?"

Gwynver'insa smiled dreamily and leaned her head back against the wall again.

"Oh, my goodness, yes! The eggs benedict was amazing, as were the huevos rancheros. And bacon!

Bacon should be its own food group. I have not had such tastes in thousands of years. When this war is over, I will give all of you thrones and make you reign with me forever."

Tul'ran smiled, but its edges were grim.

"We have not the length of your years, Gwyn, and El Shaddai may yet have other contests for us elsewhere. Provided we win this one, of which there is no guarantee."

The Empress's eyes lit up, and she sat up, ramrod straight. Her voice deepened, and her face momentarily gained the age and wisdom of her years. When she spoke, the words seemed to come from the depths of eternity, and not her slender throat.

"You shall prevail, Tul'ran az Nostrom, Prince of Death, for I have Seen it. You shall rage against this world, and it shall fall before your wrath in panic and fear. I See the blood of your prey dripping from your fingertips, and you shall write your name in their blood over the graves of your enemies. This campaign will cause you pain, Lord Tul'ran and loss, but your grief shall bind your arm to the greatest victory in the history of this world."

The light left her eyes, and the gentle face of their friend was back.

"Why do you all look at me like that? Do I have egg on my face?"

Tul'ran lowered his eyebrows from the altitude at which they threatened to leap from his forehead.

"What you just said startled us, dear sister."

Gwynver'insa looked bewildered.

"It startled you when I asked if I had egg on my face?"

Erianne's lips twitched.

"No, silly elf. It startled us when you told us Tul'ran would conquer this world in rage and sorrow."

Gwynver'insa became still and some of the color left her face.

"When was it I said such a thing?"

Johan sat down beside her, taking her hand in his.

"Gwyn, only a moment ago, you said those very words. How is it you do not remember them?"

The diminutive woman closed her eyes. When she opened them, fear shone within.

"It was a prophecy," she whispered. "This is the way of the prophets in this world. We speak so others should hear the words of Yahweh, but we cannot recall the words once spoken. I do not know what it is I said."

Johan looked at Tul'ran and Erianne, who seemed as awestruck as he felt. He repeated what Gwynver'insa said, word for word.

"How should we interpret your prophecy, Gwyn?"

She shook her head and pursed her lips.

"I do not know, Johan. I cannot interpret my own words. It is not how prophecy works." She looked up at Tul'ran. "You will prevail, milord, but I fear the cost to you will be immense." Tears dotted the corner of her eyes as she looked at Erianne. "I pray you will not be the source of his grief, my darling sister."

Silence descended like a lead curtain over the atmosphere of the room. Finally, Erianne jumped to her feet and swiftly drew Caligo from her sheath.

"I, for one, did not hear words suggesting I cause my husband's world-conquering rage. And if I do, so what? Are any of us here immortal? Do we not do the bidding of El Shaddai? Has he promised us a long life? If I cause my husband's sorrow, it will be because I found my death swinging Caligo at the heads of my enemies while fighting at my husband's right hand. I promise you more will perish at my hands than the one life my enemies may take!"

Tul'ran stood, a wide smile on his lips.

"Bravo, my love. We knew from the beginning of this venture, Gwyn, that El Shaddai promised neither of us victory nor survival. We shall go to war together and win it or die. Now, put away your sword, my love. You are frightening the children."

They laughed, and Erianne returned Caligo to her sheath.

"How do you not fear death?" Gwynver'insa asked, with wonder in her voice.

Erianne reached out a hand to help the smaller woman to her feet.

"Because we know two things, my sister. The first is that we will someday die. The second is that El Shaddai promised me and Tul'ran we would wear our swords in Heaven when we pass to the next life, so all who walk past us will know the deeds we carried out in His name. Pain of sorrow would be a heavy burden for either of us, because we love each other so, but our love for El Shaddai and fulfilling His will shall always come first."

Johan stood up and brushed dust from his pants.

"Well spoken, Erianne, but can we drop this conversation? I'm getting depressed. Aren't we supposed to be getting ready for this Gathering Gwyn called?"

Gwyn clapped her hands and smiled brightly.

"Yes! The People expect the Gathering to be a Feast of epic proportions. It could only be successful if we have a Food Maker on each table. One hundred and forty-four thousand will gather for this feast, which is 7,200 tables of twenty people."

Erianne's eyes widened.

"You have to create 7,200 Food Makers? Gwyn, my love, it took you seventeen hours to make one. It would take 122,400 hours to make enough Food Makers. That's 5,100 days or fourteen years. It's not possible."

Gwynver'insa looked at her somberly.

"Erianne, I have called a Gathering. By law, we must convene it within thirty days of the Call or I will lose my right to rule."

Erianne threw her arms up.

"That's insane! Do you mean to tell me when there were billions of people on this planet, the ruler would have to feed them all within thirty days of the Call?"

"Yes, my darling sister, it is exactly as you have said. Recall, however, when my ancestors created the law, they divided the world into sub-regencies. The sub-regents sold lands to vassals, who sold them to their people. At each point in the pyramid, the sub-holder had responsibility for the holder below them, down to the smallest village. When a Gathering was called, the holders of the land organized themselves at every level to ensure each person attended the local Gathering and would enjoy a feast before the

Emperor broadcast the business of the Gathering for the People's vote. If the Emperor, or incoming Emperor, enjoyed the good favor of the people, the Gathering would go smoothly. If the Gathering broke, then we deemed the people to have spoken, and the Emperor graciously declined the throne."

Johan was wincing as if his head suffered the pain of colliding thoughts.

"Allow me to summarize, Gwyn, and tell me if I'm correct. The Emperor owned the lands. He sold his lands, to whatever extent he wished, to kings and queens. The kings and queens sold portions of their holdings to nobles, who would sell to the People in plots of decreasing sizes, to the extent each could afford."

"Yes!" Gwynver'insa said, clapping her hands sharply together. "Until the Gathering. Every one hundred years, the system reset and the land all returned to the Emperor. A king today could be the village priest one hundred years hence. The People would elect every position, including that of Emperor or Empress, who would then allocate and appoint titles under the popular vote and according to the principle of equity."

"If someone served as a collector of garbage, he or she could never serve in that capacity again and had to be allocated another role in successive Gatherings. In this way, no one was ever too rich or too poor. Every person lived with humility, charity, and grace ever foremost in their hearts, for one never knew the role into which the next Gathering would thrust them."

"If I may," Erianne said, "are you saying every one hundred years you would have the equivalent of a global election for every position and place of responsibility around the world?"

"Yes!" Gwynver'insa beamed. "Truly, my brothers and sisters are wise!"

"Leave me out of their company," Tul'ran said, bemused. "I do not understand what you say about the ruling structure, and I am content to remain in my ignorance. Answer me this Gwyn, as you favor me with your love. How did you come to be Empress of the World?"

"I am not the Empress of the World."

Tul'ran shook his head.

"I am confused. Did you not command the People to come forth on your authority as Empress of the World?"

"I did, but I am not the Empress unless I hold a successful Gathering. When we ascended to the top of the staircase, my brother, I saw what could only have been the Place of the Judgment Seat. The theater into which I ran was the Judgment Seat, and it only holds one hundred and forty-four thousand Judges. Anyone who enters the amphitheater exposes themselves to judgment and is bound by the decision of the Judges. It is why the People could find refuge here; any Combatant who entered this place would, by law and tradition, expose all their deeds to judgment."

"I know the Prophecies of Molodek'exsa. I am the last of my line, for only my ancestors have the gift of creating from nothing and none of my family now lives. Hence, I would fulfill that part of the prophecy. The prophecy foretold the population of the world would not be more than one hundred and forty-four thousand when the Empress came who would bring an end to the Fight. I was in a chamber that held one hundred and forty-four thousand people. So, I took a chance. I called the People forward by laying claim to the throne as Empress. You cannot imagine my relief when the People filled every seat."

Johan shook his head.

"Remind me, Your Imperial Majesty, to never dice against you. With nerves like yours, I would fear for my every throw. How long has it been since the world has had a regent?"

Gwynver'insa's face became downcast.

"We have not had an Emperor or Empress for over two thousand years. As soon as someone would try to call a Gathering, the Combatants would kill them. The quickest way to die on this planet is to declare yourself for the throne."

Johan cleared his throat in the ensuing silence.

"Then why did you take this risk, Gwyn?"

Gwynver'insa smiled and pointed at Tul'ran and Erianne.

"Because of them. When I fled to the Garden, I prayed to Yahweh for someone to come and deliver my world from the Fight. For such a long time, I prayed and waited. Each time I walked with Yahweh in the Garden, He assured me the time would come when he would send two warriors, a husband and a wife, to end the killing. When the three of you stepped into the Garden, I knew Yahweh had answered my prayers."

"This world used to be one with law and order. I can only reclaim it through law and order. For my fearsome brother and sister to prevail, they must have the authority to act. The only way I can allow them to act is if I am Empress of the World. So, here we are. We must do within thirty days what it should take fourteen years to accomplish, or we forfeit all."

This silence lasted a lot longer. Tul'ran shuffled his feet.

"I know I am not the wisest of you, but I wonder if I might ask a question?"

"Ask!" the other three said together.

"Do you, at this Gathering, need to have thousands of individual machines serving the people whatever their hearts desired? Or would it be enough to only make a machine serving a set amount and type of food? I seek a shortcut through time and effort, if one exists."

Gwynver'insa leaped into his arms and planted a kiss on his cheek.

"My brother, your brilliance matches your feat of arms!"

Erianne leaned in from the other side of him, planted a kiss on his other cheek and grinned at Gwynver'insa.

"A menu! We only need to give them a set menu. It can be a platter of the best hot food they have had in a while. Would that help you, my beautiful sister?"

Gwynver'insa answered by twirling about the room as she did when overcome with joy.

"Indeed, indeed, indeed. We will program this unit to create the food. I will then make receivers for this unit, which will take much less time, and we will place the receivers on each table. Each copy can serve only one dish, but it will be enough to satisfy the Law of the Gathering. We will find people to help us with the lifting." She stopped, her mind working feverishly. "Twenty-one days! We can have this done in twenty-one days! Now, what shall we serve them?"

Spes Deserit, in the Year of Our Fight 2375
Mission Day 25... The Gathering

Tul'ran looked out over the multitudes, who were gulping down their meals with gusto. He looked down at his platter and marveled at it. A generous slab of roast beef joined mashed potatoes, gravy, green beans, mushrooms, kidney beans, and a generous portion of bread. No one would be hungry, and all ate food they had never seen in this world. Every bite was a novel experience, and the People loved every morsel.

The Empress had churned out receiving units of the Food Maker at a ferocious rate once they set the menu and pronounced the food delicious. They had no difficulty finding people to carry the Food Makers to the tables constructed by other volunteers. Other citizens gathered materials and gold to make the new Empress's dress and crown. Out of the joy of their hearts, they also made crowns for Tul'ran, Erianne, and Johan.

Tul'ran had expected some grumbling about the demanding work the People were doing for Gwynver'insa's Gathering, but the opposite was true. The People were so overjoyed at the prospect of having an Empress who would end the Fight; they did everything in their power to make the Gathering a success. And it was.

He looked over at his table where Gwyn alternated between entertaining Johan and Erianne with amusing stories, and they laughed without a care in the world. A lump suddenly closed his throat and his eyes momentarily misted.

If Gwyn's prophecy was accurate, one of them would die to restore peace.

One of them could be his wife.

E'thriel uttered the words Darian had been dying to hear for three weeks.

"It's time to remove your dressings."

She held her breath as he gently removed the wrapping from around her head.

"Please keep your eyes closed, Darian, after I take the dressing off. Even with your eyes closed, the light will seem dazzling. Give your eyes a second to adjust. Then you can open them."

She complied. He was right. When the dressing came off, it was bright behind her eyelids, which gushed a wellspring of relief and gratitude from her heart. It was one thing to be told you wouldn't be blind, and another to feel the light on the other side of your eyeballs.

She opened her eyelids slowly and felt a rush of relief again. The colors of the garden were breathtaking, even brighter and more beautiful than she had imagined. There was the bed upon which she had lain for three weeks and a few days, much smaller than it felt when she lay in it. Close to it was the table where she dined and the divan on which she reclined. But where was…?

"Behind you," E'thriel said softly.

Darian turned and froze.

"E'thriel?!"

He sketched a bow, smiling. Darian closed her eyes and opened them again. He was ten feet tall, and his fantastic white wings extended sixteen feet from either side of his body. His robe was brilliantly white and she could see the outline of a halo above his head. His hair was long, blond, and straight, but there was no hair on his face and arms. He had tucked a massive sword into his belt. He was the most beautiful and dangerous thing she had ever seen.

"You're an…"

"Angel," he finished when she could not complete the sentence. "More specifically, I am your guardian angel."

Darian told herself to breathe before she passed out.

"How did I deserve a guardian angel?"

E'thriel grinned.

"God the Son assigned me to you when you picked up the bowl, Darian. He told me to protect you until you made a choice."

Darian's head was swimming.

"A choice? What choice?"

"Whether to accept Him as your savior. Picking up the bowl was a good first start, Darian, but there are other things you would have to believe and accept before you take the next step."

Darian raised her hand.

"Can you give me a minute, E'thriel? You've just proven to me in the most fantastic way possible everything you've said about God and angels and Heaven is true. I need a little time to absorb it."

He smiled.

"Of course, Darian. Just call my name and I will be here." With that, there was a flash, and he disappeared.

"E'thriel!" she called out, panic rising in her chest in an acidic wave.

Another flash and the grinning angel once more stood in front of her.

"Yes?"

Darian smiled, relieved.

"Nothing, just don't go too far away, okay? I might need a giant-sized pillow for my next nap."

The angel laughed and shimmered his feathers.

"Fear not, Darian. I am always with you and only a word away."

With that, he was gone. Darian picked up the dressing from the table, where he had folded and gently placed it. It smelled like rain. She kissed the cloth and wrapped it around her hand.

She wondered if she was smart enough to recognize a second chance when someone handed it to her on a silver platter. Darian searched her heart and found neutrality in its emotional spaces. She'd heard what he said, every word. There was a final choice to be made. It would be for God or against Him, and it would have eternal consequences.

Darian sighed and raised the dressing to her lips again. Why did she have to make everything so difficult?

When would a choice ever be so obvious that she could make it without endlessly weighing pros against cons, benefits against costs… good against evil? She shuddered. That's what it came down to: good against evil. Like the being she once called her master. He was Satan, the evil angel who rebelled against God and whom God cast out of Heaven. She owed him nothing, and it repulsed her she once offered him her life and her soul.

Darian wandered around the garden, smelling the flowers and marveling at their beauty. Birds of many varieties and colors flittered from tree to tree, adding their individual songs to the orchestra of tranquility. She could see how a God of love would make such a place. This was a God she could love.

It was time to meet God at the center of her heart, with the hope He would accept her and forgive her. Okay, she thought, how do I do this?

"You can start by turning around."

Darian lifted her face to the sky, tears welling in her eyes. She knew the voice. It belonged to the man to whom Tul'ran, Erianne, and Johan had bent their knees in the Garden of Eden. After E'thriel's stories, it could only belong to one man. Someone Who was man and God, and who introduced Himself to her by name. She turned and her face lit up in a dazzling smile as she sank to her knees, arms out and palms up.

"Hello, Jesus."

CHAPTER THE TENTH:
...FULFILLED

Denver, Colorado, November 11, 2098 AD
Three years into the Tribulation

Sylvia Oslo wanted to scream. The data holos hovering over her desk glowed red, and the numbers were worse than depressing. North America was out of food. Worse, a pandemic was circulating through her Region like a California wildfire, and she had neither the medicine nor medical personnel to treat it. She dug her nails into her palms until they threatened to draw blood.

One out of three people had died from the plague. It attacked the lungs, drowning them in their own mucus. The victims suffered for seven days fighting to get air into their lungs, struggling for every molecule of oxygen, and then they died.

There were not enough doctors, hospitals, medical clinics, or nursing stations to treat them. They died in their homes, hotels, malls, and in the streets. Medical personnel had to bulldoze ditches and then push the corpses into them. It was the worst horror Oslo had ever witnessed, and she did, every night, in graphic 3D on the news holocasts.

She had tapped every resource possible to feed the people of Canada, Mexico, the United States, and the South American nations. Federal forces combed through every warehouse, storage facility, and granary to gather and distribute food to starving people. The government bought food on the black market to feed its citizens. Cartels and criminal organizations abandoned selling drugs; there was only a market for food, which they sold at outrageous prices.

There were regions where people were killing their farm animals and pets to feed their families and neighbors. She had heard rumors some parts of her Region resorted to cannibalism to survive. Oslo shuddered. She prayed those rumors were not true, but feared such an atrocity was now happening on her watch.

Oslo tapped a screen for the Strategic National Stockpile. The AI primly informed her the SNS didn't contain food reserves. It told her the Federal Emergency Management Agency stockpiles food, water, generators, and other resources across eight distribution centers in the United States and its territories. Oslo snorted. FEMA had exhausted its reserves seven weeks ago.

The Regional Supervisor dropped her head into

her arms. She caused this mess. Had she only known Contradeum launched duds at Denver in some bizarre parts-measuring threat, the world would still have a large food supply and her people would have meals on their tables. Damn her stupid pride! Oslo knew anger, fatigue, and fear had played into her decision to nuke New Babylon, but it was no excuse.

The system of checks and balances broke down when America devolved to a single leader with no Cabinet. It further eroded when she assumed power while retaining her position as Chair of the Joint Chiefs. Too much power had coalesced into her hands and while her intent had not been evil, the result certainly was.

She heard a knock on her door and lifted her head. "Enter," she said, crisply.

Her Chief of Staff entered the room, looking like he lost his wife, best friend, and dog. Oslo smiled.

"You look like a walking country western song, Ed."

He didn't return the smile.

"President Oslo, you need to turn on your news holo. It's shocking news, ma'am. I'm sorry to have to bring it to you."

Oslo activated the news holo, which covered one wall of the Oval Office. A banner ran under the image of a microphone set on a podium, advising the world of an urgent message from the Supreme Global Leader. A few minutes later, Contradeum walked up to the podium, looking stern. He had on a navy-blue suit, was clean shaven, and impeccable in appearance. He didn't look like he was suffering from a lack of sustenance.

Contradeum faced the holo projector.

"People of the world, I must bring you distressing information. As you know, someone attacked me with a nuclear missile while I served you in the city of New Babylon. Many thousands of people died in that attack. Equally distressing was the loss of our Strategic Food Reserve. The missile destroyed millions of tons of food ready to be distributed to all of you. I am doing the best I can to restore shipments of food to you, my people, but the process has been slow."

"We were all devastated by the loss of life and the devastation of our resources. I know this is hardly compensation for such losses, but we have now identified the person who is responsible."

It horrified Oslo to see her photo pop up on a side holo screen.

"The person responsible for the attack on New Babylon is Regional Supervisor Sylvia Oslo. I have instructed the Government of Democracy Judiciary to issue a warrant for her arrest. She is to be tried for war crimes and crimes against humanity. The Judiciary will also issue an Order seizing any military forces still in the possession of Region Ten, including any remaining nuclear forces. Never again will someone be able to launch a nuclear attack against anyone in the world."

"I warn the people of Region Ten to surrender Regional Supervisor Oslo into custody and deliver her to the GoD Judiciary immediately. GoD will ship no food to Region Ten until she is in our custody. I hate to take such a severe measure, but we cannot permit Oslo's atrocities to go unpunished. Your

Supreme Global Leader will now turn you over to the Goddess's Chief Priest for evening prayers."

Oslo canceled the screen and stared at her security detail. No one said anything, but the words were screaming in the room. Sylvia Oslo was out of options, and she knew it. She could no more let people starve to preserve her freedom than she could put a gun to their heads and blow their brains out. The guilt at having been responsible for taking so many innocent lives had been chewing at her stomach and shortening her sleep ever since she launched the nuke. She knew there would be blowback; it had been a matter of time.

Part of her felt relieved it was over for her. She knew what the outcome of the trial would be: a short-lived stance in front of a firing squad. She had made her peace with Jesus and already begged forgiveness for her sins. Many times over, in fact, since that horrific day. She knew there was nothing He could not forgive. The rest of the world might never absolve her, but she would stand in front of the Lord and give an account for her life, and He would forgive her. That's what He promised in the Bible and it was the only promise left to give her any hope.

Regional Supervisor Sylvia Oslo stood up and rearranged her uniform. She looked at the Secret Service team leader and gave him a thin-lipped smile.

"Better get your cuffs out, Murph. We have a plane to catch."

Origin came into focus, and Lamek Davis slumped to his knees, cradling the Temporal Scepter in his hands. He was exhausted. TTI had bounced him through time and space so often in the last few months, he could barely remember his name. They had hoped to recover the missing Teams within forty-eight hours of their return, but the system blipped.

The minute they returned from the ancient Canada rescue, the mainframe went down, hard. Weeks passed, and they waited in agony as TTI searched the world for parts to repair the machine. War, starvation, and epidemics had ground global manufacturing to a halt. You couldn't just order stuff off Amazon; Amazon was gone.

It was a blessing to live on a remote island in the Atlantic. As soon as the first word reached them of the new epidemic, Korhonen shut Atlantis down hard. Robotics handled all freight to Atlantis and androids chemically sterilized the freight before a human touched it. No one on a ship or a plane could leave the vessel. The stern measures kept anyone from dying on the island, but they all watched with horror as the global casualty figure jumped into the hundreds of millions.

They got parts for the machine, eventually, but some of them had to be retrofitted or redesigned. Finally, after months of waiting, they resumed rescue operations.

Which had become recovery operations at the very end. Davis glanced at the two black body bags sitting on the lens beside him. At least he was in better shape than those poor souls. Davis let his chin drop to his chest as technicians came running up to remove the body bags and crates of garbage from the

Lens. He knew he should get up and prepare a report for Korhonen, but he couldn't care less about protocol and the demands of his job. He turned over the Scepter to a technician, but couldn't bring himself to get up. Davis was done.

A heavy hand fell on his left shoulder and a deep voice said,

"Get up, sailor. The only easy day was yesterday."

Davis jerked his head up and stared into Michael Sullivan's grinning face. He jumped to his feet and grabbed the bigger man into a bear hug.

"Sully! You're alive! How did you get here?"

The two of them disengaged, and Sully shook him by the shoulders.

"You didn't think you'd get rid of me that easily, did you? You've got stories to tell, my man. Heather already warned me I'd find you much younger than the last time I saw you. Still can't believe what I'm seeing. She won't tell me the how of it; just said you'd tell me when you're ready."

Davis darted a glance around the busy room.

"Where's Heather? She's usually here to greet me when I get back."

"She's with my wife, Jeannie. The two of them hit it right off. We'll join them later. In the meantime, I've gotta check you out medically and get you in shape to debrief the skipper."

As Sullivan guided him off the platform, Davis glanced at his friend's body.

"You're a lot skinnier than the last time I saw you, man. You okay?"

Sully grimaced.

"Yeah, I just skipped some meals here and there,

that's all. Jeannie and I survived everything, Mick. I never thought I'd live through a nuclear war. Remember the shed I treated Heather in? There was a whole sub level where I had a two years' supply of dry goods, canned goods, and dried meat. Jeannie and I were lucky because we had a well on our property the fallout didn't contaminate. We rationed as carefully as we could, but we were down to our last week of food when Korhonen called."

"When you started bringing back injured people, all TTI had left for a physician was Dr. Payton Dumont, but she's a trauma surgeon. Heather convinced TTI they needed my skills as an ER doc. Since my wife, Jeannie, is a trauma nurse, we were the medical team TTI needed to help Dr. Dumont and fill in the gaps. Korhonen jumped all over it. She has some kind of pull, Mick. Within hours of the call, we had a TTI hypersonic stealth jet on our property and a handful of people loading our stuff to move here. We were a lot luckier than most."

The men walked into a medical bay next to the Emergence Field. Sully had Davis strip down to his underwear and pasted some probes to his chest and legs.

"This will give me a complete diagnostic. You look like you lost some weight, too, *hermano*. Do you want some coffee while we wait for the readouts?"

Davis grinned; a smile tinged with sadness.

"We ran out of coffee weeks ago, Sully, although I'd love one. I'd also love peace on earth and goodwill towards men. I'm not likely to get any of that soon."

A twinkle lit Sully's eye. He lifted his wrist

chronometer to his mouth and said,

"He's ready for you, darlin'."

The sickbay door opened, and Heather walked in with a tray. Behind her strode a short Mexican woman with long black hair and a cheerful, round face. She wore surgical scrubs and walked with a slight limp. She stretched out an arm and shook Davis's hand with a firm grip.

"It's nice to meet you, Mick. I'm Jeannie Sullivan. Michael has told me a lot about you in the last couple of days. Some of it was even complimentary."

Davis laughed and disengaged his hand to grab a steaming hot cup of coffee off the tray.

"It's nice to meet you, too, Jeannie. Everything Sully said about you was wonderful. Hi, Heather. I missed seeing you on the platform."

Heather put down the tray and leaned over to kiss him on the forehead.

"I would've been there, but Jeannie thought bringing you a cup of coffee would be a nicer touch and better for morale. You've had a rough few days, Mick. You brought them all home. Thank you."

A lump found its way into Davis's throat.

"Not all of them are alive, though."

Heather ruffled his hair, her eyes misting.

"You still brought them home, Mick. You had to do the last mission alone after Coventry damaged her knee in jolly old England. I'm just glad to have you back for good."

Sully was busy tapping the holographic screens above the bed and then nodded, satisfied.

"You're in reasonably good health, Mick. A few days' rest and some extra calories will make these numbers look even better."

Davis took a long sip of his coffee and sighed.

"You never told me how come I'm drinking coffee right now."

Jeannie laughed.

"Your brother from a different mother is quite the miser. Over the last two years, he restricted us to one cup of coffee a day. The decision almost ended his life a few times. When TTI picked us up, we still had twenty pounds of quality dark roast left. We donated nineteen pounds to TTI, and they allowed us to keep a pound for ourselves. We splurged today and made a pot, since there's no alcohol to celebrate your return. Sorry that we have no sugar or milk substitute left."

Davis raised the mug in salute.

"I'm just grateful to drink coffee again. Thank you. Can I stay a while, Sully, or do I have to go right now?"

Sullivan took an exaggeratedly long look at the screens.

"In my professional opinion, you need to rest for at least one hour and consume some liquids before I can release you for a debrief. Sorry, Brother, but I can't do better than that. You only brought two bodies back and Korhonen will need to know why. You and Quarterlaine recovered everyone else alive, so you set yourself some lofty standards for rescue missions."

Davis shook his head.

"This last one was bad. TTI tasked the Team to study the Casarabe society in the Amazon during 1220 AD and they were only planning to stay in-country for ninety days. The Casarabe inhabited about 4,500 square miles of annually flooded savannah. They were advanced for their time. The city structures were impressive. They built sixty-six-foot conical pyramids covering roughly the size of thirty soccer fields. According to my infil packet, they developed the city between AD 500 to 1400. They had tall ceremonial structures, moats, the whole ten yards."

"Whoever planned this mission didn't do it well. They planted the Insertion Point in an alcove off a river. They selected a suitable spot with a small, freshwater stream nearby, but there was no easy access to a food supply."

"When Recall didn't work, they tried to make the best of it. I took a quick look at their journal entries when I entered the IP because no one was there. I found two bodies by the river. Some kind of animal had attacked them while they were fishing. It was gruesome because whatever attacked them partly ate their bodies. They had been dead long enough for their TIRADs to dissolve."

Sully crossed his arms in front of his chest.

"Why do you say they poorly planned it?"

"Inadequate site survey. Piranha polluted the river, and they were voracious. There were no fruit trees within easy walking distance and the jungle was a mess. They lost seven Team members to piranha, snake bites, spider bites, and a strange flu or a virus not covered by their pre-insertion inoculations. Some of their losses were early in the fifteen months they had to stay past Recall. Their journal said they dumped their dead into the river after stripping off their clothing and dog tags, and let the fish take care of the remains. It might sound cold, but it was a smart thing to do. Burying the bodies could have caused an anomaly. I brought the last two home, as well as all the dog tags and equipment."

After Davis found the bodies, he had sent a message via a quantum string to Korhonen that there were no survivors. He could barely keep his stomach contents when he had to bag the bodies by the river. Davis was wearing a suit made of MetaMaterials, so he was invisible to anyone who might've seen two black bags being dragged through the jungle to the IP. Korhonen allowed him to stay in antiquity for five days to search for evidence of other survivors.

Unlike the First Team, Davis had prepared well for an extended stay. He brought enough field rations for thirty days and had inoculations for any conceivable bug. He wore jungle gear under the MetaMaterials and had two combat knives secreted upon his body.

On the first day, he conducted a multi-layered radius search pattern of about one mile around the IP, hacking through the jungle with the First Team's machete while keeping a careful eye out for snakes, spiders, ants, and anything else with teeth or fangs interested in chewing on him. It was hot, exhausting work. He didn't sleep well at night because Coventry couldn't transition with him and he had no one to take watch.

Before the Casarabe mission, he and Coventry had traveled to northern Britain - inhabited by Brythonic-speaking Celts - in 499 AD looking for the Team who traveled in search of a mythical king called Arthur Pendragon. They located the IP within a circle of stones. The Team overlaid their camp with MetaMaterials, which bent light around the camp and made it look as if the middle of the stone circle was an empty field of grass.

This Team was smart. The IP was at the top of a hill surrounded by meadows. When Recall came and passed, they built a fire oven five hundred yards away from the IP and concealed it with the MetaMaterials canvass. When they ran out of food, they hunted rabbit and deer for protein and found edible plants for roughage. The IP had an underground stream right next to the stone circle.

Davis and Coventry shocked them by suddenly appearing in their midst. It overjoyed the Team when they learned they could go home. They were in such good shape they helped Coventry and Davis sanitize the IP and oven area. Coventry was near the oven area gathering the MetaMaterials canvass when she spotted a group of Celts emerging from the treeline about eight hundred yards away. She almost made it back to the IP when an errant root caught her foot and twisted her knee, tearing her medial collateral ligaments. She hobbled back to the IP before the Celts spotted her, but Medical gave her an immediate down check when they triumphantly returned with the survivors.

Seven hours after they brought Team Britain home, Davis was in the Amazon, lacking a shipmate and a lot of valuable help.

On the second day in the Amazon, Mick followed the map left by the Team, bringing him to the Casarabe city. He spent four days scanning the city from different vantages, looking in vain for anyone who didn't seem to be part of the era. The Team's logs didn't suggest anyone had gone missing or native, but Davis had to be sure. Once the five days were up, he was as confident as he could be Team Casarabe had not survived their mission.

Sully topped up his coffee.

"Don't be too hard on yourself, Mick. It wasn't your fault those Teams overstayed in antiquity. You brought home twenty-seven people who are going to live and have stories to tell. Better casualty results than combat, my man."

Davis took another grateful sip.

"Yeah, I know you're right, but I feel for those people who didn't make it. Eight historians and one Protector. Their Protector died one hundred days into the mission when a poisonous snake got her."

Sully shuddered.

"I hate snakes."

"So do I," Jeannie chimed in. "Nasty little buggers. Some of them can kill you within hours if you don't have an anti-venom and the death is painful. One of the selling points for coming to Atlantis was Korhonen's promise there were no snakes."

After laughing, Davis finished his story.

"When the Protector died, she left eight Historians to fend for themselves. None of them had survival training, which I find shocking. Like I said, they made a good go of it, but time and inexperience just caught up with them. They must have been terrified. Worse, they would never know why TTI abandoned them. I'll give them credit for this: I doubt very much they did anything to damage the timeline. Professional to the end. That's what my report will say."

"Which I should have received in my office, I might add."

Everyone jumped as Marjatta Korhonen walked into the sickbay. She walked over to the pot of coffee, looked around the sickbay, and spotted a beaker near the sink. She grinned at Sully.

"Can I use this for the last of the coffee, or does it contain a microbe that will kill me ten minutes from now?"

Sully laughed.

"Cleaned and sanitized, Administrator. Please, help yourself."

Korhonen poured a beaker full of coffee and turned to face Davis. Her voice softened.

"Sully's right, Mick. Don't beat yourself up. You did a fantastic job out there, especially since you were alone. Our AAR, After Action Report for your benefit, Heather and Jeannie, will contain a lot of recommendations about the composition of future Teams and the training they will need. If there are future Teams."

Davis raised his eyebrows.

"I didn't realize time travel was in question."

Korhonen nodded.

"The world's a mess, Mick. You've been so busy saving lives someone hasn't fully briefed you on all of it. We're a little sheltered out here in the middle of the ocean, but the disasters the world encountering are coming for us, too. We may have to design future missions to help the world out of a horrible hole, but I doubt they'll ever be for research again. I confess I ran down here as soon as I heard you came back and eavesdropped the whole time. You might as well tell us about the China mission, and we'll be up to date. It'll save you a walk up the stairs."

Davis smiled. Korhonen had mellowed a lot since he joined TTI. He might even start liking her.

"The China mission was the most successful of all. The China Team transited history to 1500 AD to study the Ming Dynasty. When they first transitioned there, they found an abandoned hut a half a mile outside Beijing. It was secluded and far off any roads or paths. They put the IP right inside the hut."

"When they missed Recall, they just carried on. The Team built a garden and bought some pigs and chickens from locals. They kept to themselves and kept recording everything they did. We not only brought them back, healthy and well, but with a treasure trove of historical data. They get as much credit for their save as Coventry and I do."

Korhonen looked up at the ceiling.

"At least that went right. I'm putting a commendation on your record, Master Chief Petty Officer Davis. Don't look so surprised. I know about your promotion and it's good here too. You turned out to be a good news story, Mick, although I'm keeping most of it classified. I'm going to head back to my office and let you catch up. Just a warning for all of you. It's going to sound strange coming from me, but heed it. Don't trust anyone around here, not even me. Loyalties are shifting every day, and this world is getting darker by the minute. Keep everything close-held. Thanks for the coffee."

Marjatta saluted them with her beaker and walked jauntily out of the sickbay, grateful for the living and silently mourning the dead. There would be time for tears later. Her eyes filled with moisture, blurring her vision, and she sped up her pace. Or maybe now.

Maybe it was time for tears now.

The Hague, November 25, 2098 AD

"Order in court. All rise."

Sylvia Oslo rose to her feet unsteadily. Her jailers heavily shackled her wrists and attached them to a waist chain, as they also did with her ankles. She was wearing a bright orange jumpsuit and ached from the beating the Global Peace Forces administrated when they took her into custody.

Her last fourteen days had been one of nightmare. When she left the Oval Office, she didn't proceed directly to her hyper jet. First, she sought General Lester Rozinski, the USSTRATCOM Commander, and briefed him about her situation. She directed him to order the boomers and attack subs to port, with the further instruction all remaining nuclear warheads were to be dismantled or rendered inoperable without significant overhaul.

If the United States was going to lose their nuclear arsenal, she would make sure Contradeum could never use it against them.

She also ordered Rozinski to inform the Supreme Global Leader the United States would surrender her as requested.

"I'm not inclined to obey that order, President

Oslo," Rosinski had said, his jaw firmly clenched.

Oslo smiled wanly.

"You're a good man, Les. If I hadn't knee-jerked a nuke into New Babylon, I wouldn't be in this mess. I'll be fine. Thanks to the Church you helped to build after the War, my future is secure. Don't lose faith, brother. If what Pastor Ross has been saying in his sermons comes true, the future looks grim for this world. I'm amazed by how many people have become Christians since the Tribulation period started. It's in the millions now. And appalled how many have died and gone to Hell because they didn't."

He looked at her, his eyes pleading.

"All the more reason to fight this, Syl. We need strong leadership to get us through the next three and something years."

She had slapped him on the shoulder and tried, without success, for a carefree grin.

"And they'll have it in you. Seriously, Les, what choice do I have? If I keep our nukes and thumb my nose at Contradeum, what does that get us? Another nuclear war? We can't sell the nukes for food, and we can't use them to make food. Our people are starving. I can't stand another video image on the evening news of people barbecuing their pet dogs because they have no other protein source. Make sure you trade me for lots of supplies."

Oslo then promoted Rozinski to Chief of the Joint Staff and acting President of the United States. After she took his final salute, she checked herself into a hospital and directed the removal of the devices she had implanted after the First Global

Nuclear War, which gave her full command and control of America's nuclear forces. It would not do to have those devices fall into the hands of their enemies. The procedure required a significant amount of neurosurgery and laid her up in bed for a full week after the surgeons completed the procedure.

She watched from her hospital bed as Rozinski informed the world he had taken Regional Supervisor Oslo into custody and would deliver her to Global Peace Forces once container ships with food and supplies entered American ports. Oslo smiled.

She had heard that Contradeum called Rozinski to congratulate him for America's cooperation and Rozinski told him where the Supreme Global Leader could shove his communicator. It was enough to ensure the next Regional Supervisor of the Region Ten would come from somewhere else on the globe. Oslo shook her head. Rozinski always was a stubborn old goat. She was going to miss him.

The day after the hospital released her, she stood at the Denver airport in the full, gaudy dress uniform assigned to her as Regional Supervisor. She wouldn't taint the uniform of the United States of America by allowing herself to be taken into custody wearing it. The media were present in droves when Global Peace Forces stepped off their hyper jet and politely escorted her onto the plane.

When the media was no longer watching, they tore off her uniform, raped her, and beat her body. They kept the blows away from her face, so the bruises would not show up on the holos. Oslo had not expected the sexual assaults, which came very close to breaking her spirit. Regardless of what she had done, she didn't deserve that. She knew Contradeum instructed the "Peace" Forces to abuse her. It was his ultimate act of one upmanship before they put her on trial.

When she stood in front of the Chief Justice of Earth for her trial, she still felt horribly wounded, emotionally and physically, from her treatment. Oslo resolved to face her trial with dignity and prayed she could confront her death honorably. She had no delusions about how the case would go. It was only out of respect for Rozinski she pled not guilty to the charges.

'One last fight,' she thought. 'Then I get to go home.'

The clerk, dressed almost as gaudy as the Chief Justice, stood and faced her.

"Sylvia Oslo, you are charged you ordered a nuclear strike against the city of New Babylon, with the resulting death and destruction of the said city and its residents, and did, thereby, commit war crimes and crimes against humanity. Sylvia Oslo, how do you plead: guilty or not guilty?"

"Well, of course she pleads not guilty," said a cheerful voice in an English accent as a short man sauntered into the courtroom and walked up to one table near the front. "For the record, I am Sir Edmund Rolle, King's Counsel, Barrister for the Accused."

The Chief Justice turned red in the face.

"What are you doing here, Edmund? We listed no one as lawyer of record for the Accused. She's self-represented."

"Hello, Charles," Rolle responded cheerfully. "You look well. No shortage of food in the court cafeteria, I see, judging by your waistline."

The Chief Justice sputtered, but no sound came out of his mouth. Rolle put a stack of papers on the counsel table and walked up to Oslo. He was about 5 feet, 6 inches tall and looked stocky in his jet-black jacket and robes. In the tradition of the British legal system, he wore a powdered white wig on his head. He had warm brown eyes and when he grinned, it looked like he had a coat hanger stuck from one side of his mouth to the other.

"The King of England sends his regards, Regional Supervisor Oslo. He has retained me to represent you, if you will accept my services."

Oslo returned his grin.

"Gladly, Sir Edmund. I'm not sure how much you can help, but I would be pleased to have your wise counsel."

"Jolly good!" Rolle returned to the counsel table. "I spoke to my client, Your Worship, and she confirms my representation. Shall we get on with it, then?"

To Oslo, it looked as if the Chief Justice was about to blow an artery.

"You cannot represent this woman. The Court has declined her legal representation."

Rolle widened his eyes.

"Charles, surely you jest! Why, the provision of legal services to provide full answer and defense to criminal charges has been the cornerstone of every justice system since the Magna Carta. By whose authority do you deny Regional Supervisor Oslo the right to legal counsel?"

"You will address me as 'Your Excellency' and the prisoner as 'the Accused'!" the Chief Justice snarled, banging his gavel on the table.

"Oh, Charles, don't be such a snot. You really should watch your blood pressure, old chap. But I shall play along with your customs, of course. Surely, Your Excellency, this court would not deny my client one of the fundamental rights of every human being on this planet: the right to legal counsel to assist her with her defense. If it is your intention to do so, then I demand to know by what instruction or operation of law do you proceed in such a fashion? Is this not a court of law? Is this not the highest trial court in the world? Surely it is bound by the principles of natural justice and the fundamental rights of human beings!"

Chief Justice of the World, Charles Figley III, glared down from his high perch and said nothing.

"Come, Your Excellency, shall I infer from your silence it was the Supreme Global Leader himself who instructed you to deny Regional Supervisor Oslo a fair trial by disallowing her a right to counsel?"

"I never said so," the Chief Justice said primly, after casting a nervous glance at the dozens of holo cameras in the courtroom.

Rolle grinned his coat hanger smile and arranged his robes to sit at the table.

"Excellent, I'm glad we resolved it then. Does the Prosecutor wish to call its first witness, or should we break for tea?"

Oslo expected the trial to be a glorified kangaroo court, but Rolle exposed it as a farce. The prosecutor called as her first witness a woman from the Global Aviation Authority, who testified three days before the missile strike on New Babylon she tracked a plane from Denver to the city of St. Mary's in Camden County, Georgia. Naval Submarine Base Kings Bay is next to the city, she testified. Two days after the missile strike, another plane traveled from St. Mary's to Denver. The prosecutor presented this evidence as proof positive Oslo was on board the nuclear submarine launching the missile.

Rolle shredded the witness in cross-examination. He had her admit after the First Cataclysm, during which flooding devastated Jacksonville, St. Mary's became a central distribution point for relief supplies in the Florida area. It wasn't unusual, therefore, to see planes fly from Denver to St. Mary's. Rolle produced flight records for twenty-two such flights in the five-day period in question. He also had the witness admit she could not produce any flight manifests showing Oslo or anyone from her security team on board any of those twenty-two flights.

"Really, Your Excellency," he said after the teary-eyed witness left the stand, "I do hope the Prosecution will adduce better evidence than this. For all I know, it was Your Excellency on board the submarine. Were you not in Denver during the same five-day period at an international judicial conference?"

The gallery tittered, and Figley slammed his gavel on the bench.

"Silence," he roared. "Counsel, I caution you to

take these proceedings seriously. If you cannot do so, I will cite you in contempt."

"Yes, yes, of course," Rolle murmured, pretending to be chastised. "I will give this court the respect it so richly deserves."

The next witness for the Prosecution was no better. The witness, a French submarine commander, testified the submarine launching the missile must have been an American submarine because they had accounted for all other boomers. Rolle looked like a hungry dog licking his chops when the time for cross-examination came.

"You said, sir, your office accounted for all other nuclear missile submarines at the time of this unfortunate incident?"

"Yes," the officer replied warily.

"Does your statement include the *Putin*, whom the Supreme Global Leader himself has announced became rogue on the same day?"

The officer hesitated.

"We didn't know the *Putin* went rogue until after the submarine commander launched his missiles at Denver," he said after a few moments.

"Indeed, indeed. Did you know where the *Putin* was before it assumed the mantle of a rogue?"

The officer licked his lips and glanced at the holo cameras.

"We had a general idea of her patrol pattern, but under no circumstances was the *Putin* ordered to fire missiles at Denver."

Rolle paused to look thoughtful.

"I see. So you are telling us the *Putin* launched nuclear missiles at Denver without the authorization or knowledge of the Supreme Global Leader or any of the commanders of the Global Armed Forces? Is that correct?"

The French officer looked relieved.

"Yes, that's correct."

Rolle smiled.

"If we accept as plausible that the *Putin's* commander could have launched a nuclear strike without the authorization or knowledge of anyone superior to him in the chain of command, then it is equally plausible an American submarine commander could have gone rogue and launched a nuclear missile against New Babylon. Would you agree?"

Oslo could see the French officer knew Rolle had trapped him. His jaw moved back and forth for a few moments as his eyes scanned the holo cameras. After several long seconds, he nodded reluctantly.

"Yes, it is plausible the American submarine commander went rogue and fired the missile without authorization."

Raleigh sketched a half bow.

"Thank you, sir." He moved as if to sit down and then stood up again. "Dash it. I almost forgot to ask my last question. The passage of years and all that. Tell us, sir, which American submarine was it again firing the missile?"

The French officer turned red in the face.

"We don't know. The movements of American nuclear missile submarines are so secretive and kept under such tight security there is no way of knowing which submarine fired the missile. We cannot track them and we do not know at any moment which submarines are docked and which are at sea."

Rollie widened his eyes in mock horror.

"Do you mean to suggest, sir, the very missile submarine with its rogue and likely insane commander who fired a nuclear missile on New Babylon even now patrols the high seas in search of its next target? Are any of us safe, sir?"

The French officer had no reply. He sat there, embarrassed, until Rolle said he had no further questions and sat down. Figley looked as if he wanted to step off the Bench and strangle the sixty-four-year-old defense lawyer with his bare hands. Oslo smiled. Rolle was ruining his pet trial and the Chief Justice was ready to blow a gasket because of it.

The Prosecutor's last witness shocked the entire courtroom. He was a skinny man with beady eyes and a scabby mop of brown hair. His testimony concerned his observations of Oslo attending a new Christian church in Denver, where the pastor preached from the book of Revelation and other books in the Bible prophesying the End Times. He described in graphic detail how the pastor announced Babylon would end its existence in flames.

The witness spoke of the horrific details forming the basis of sermons on the Seal, Trumpet, and Bowl judgments predicted in the Bible. In his opinion, Oslo's Christian beliefs, the judgmental nature of her faith, and the church's intolerance directly led to the bombing of New Babylon.

Rolle strenuously objected to the witness's evidence, arguing it was inflammatory and prejudicial. Figley blithely overruled the objections and Oslo fumed. The decision to launch the nuke had been hers, and hers alone. It had nothing to do with Pastor Ross, who was only teaching the truth to new Christians about what they could expect from the Tribulation. She wanted to testify to that effect, but Rolle shot her down.

"I have not asked you, Regional Supervisor, whether you were on the boat or ordered the launch, nor do I intend to do so. My job is to raise a reasonable doubt and I cannot do so if I put you on the stand. While I don't know what your evidence would be, I know you would tell the truth. I will not have your truth, whatever it may be, torpedo my defense. No pun intended. Apologies."

Legal argument took two days after the Prosecutor closed her case and Rolle declined to call evidence. Figley only deliberated for two hours before returning a guilty verdict. They spent two more days arguing about sentencing, but the result was inevitable and everyone knew it.

When the Court convened for sentencing, Chief Justice of the World Charles Figley the Third puffed himself up and smirked at Oslo.

"Having considered the arguments of counsel and relevant judicial authority, and having found you guilty of the offenses with which you are charged, I sentence you, Sylvia Oslo, to death by firing squad. May the Goddess have mercy upon your soul."

"Your Goddess can shove her mercy up her hindquarters," Oslo snapped, to the immediate uproar of the Gallery.

Figley kept pounding at the table and screaming

for order, while the Prosecutor looked horrified, and the guards scurried to maintain proper decorum.

Before they took her away in shackles, Rolle came up and shook her hand.

"Bravo, President Oslo. Ten years earlier, in any courtroom in the world, we would've won this case. I hope you know that. You are a brave woman and you have my respect. I will pray for you."

She smiled at him bitterly.

"Thank you, Sir Edmund. You fought the good fight and I am proud to have had you in my corner. My time on this Earth is almost done. It is you who will need the prayers, my friend. If you haven't already done so, please seek Jesus in your heart and accept Him as your Savior. The time to do that is running out."

Rolle smiled at her, bowed, and turned away. He would remind her of this conversation someday when the two of them lunched in Heaven and recounted the story of their last attempt at a fair trial the world would ever see. As a Christian man who found Jesus after the nuclear war devastated his country, he could hardly do less than treat her to a glass of wine after all she would go through.

In the Kingdom of Heaven

The Fifth Seal was the color of arterial blood. The blood represented the deaths of all those who came to know the Lamb of God as Lord and Savior during the Tribulation period. While He was sorry they had suffered and died because of His word and the testimony they maintained, He was grateful they found salvation before they drew their last breath.

The breaking of this Seal marked the mid-point of the Tribulation period and recognized the sacrifice of the martyrs throughout all of Earth's history. It also recognized the people who died for the faith during the Tribulation.

Jesus raised the scroll again for all to see. He placed his thumbs over the Fifth Seal and bore down on it. When it snapped, a sound echoed throughout Heaven as if someone rolled large bleachers out into an auditorium.

A staircase appeared at the edge of Heaven and a large string of people stepped up into Paradise. The enormous crowds in front of the throne parted for them, and the martyrs made their way to an altar at the foot of the Throne of God. Their clothes were bloodied and torn, and some showed the aftereffects of the violence of their deaths.

Once they made their way to the feet of Jesus, they kneeled. One of them raised his hands, made bloody by his clothing, looked up at Jesus with pleading eyes and said,

"How long, O Lord, holy and true, will You refrain from judging and avenging our blood on those who dwell on the earth?"

Jesus smiled and turned to His angels.

"Bring to each of these, My good and faithful servants, a white robe."

He turned to the assembled martyrs.

"Welcome to the place I have prepared for you. You followed Me even in the face of the vilest persecution. When you were told to abandon your faith and deny Me, you did not. Come into My rest and bide a while longer until the number of your fellow servants, brothers and sisters, who are to be killed as you have been, is completed."

The martyrs accepted their robes and angels took them where they could change, meet loved ones, and feast as Heaven's guests of honor.

Jesus looked at the Earth and wept. The evil infecting the Earth would soon martyr and bring many more of His servants home.

The Hague, November 27, 2098 AD

Sylvia Oslo stood straight under a clear blue sky and enjoyed the warmth on her skin. It was very brave of her to say she would die for her faith, but when today was the day, her courage quivered. She opened her eyes and faced the twelve men and women who stood at attention before her. Oslo had hoped to see some compassion in their eyes, some sympathy on their faces, but they looked at her with cold, dead expressions.

Her heart quailed. She was about to die. She felt too young to die, like she hadn't had enough time with her faith and the Bible. If only she could have done more to help people, instead of murdering them. A tear leaked from her eye. The media thought she wept for herself, but the tear was for the poor people who died in a nuclear conflagration with unsaved souls. They now suffered for an eternity in the place reserved for the devil and his angels.

Malchus Contradeum strutted into the parade square wearing long black robes over black pants and a black shirt. He looked grim as he walked up to a podium ringed with microphones.

"Sylvia Oslo, you have betrayed our trust and the trust of all the people of Earth. The Supreme Court of Earth found you guilty of war crimes and crimes against humanity. Do you have any last words?"

Sylvia shook her head in the negative, not trusting herself to speak. She was glad they tied her to a post; she wasn't sure her knees would have kept her up.

"Sylvia, this world worships a benevolent Goddess who loves every person. She is Mother Earth, who welcomes all her children into her bosom. Since she is a kind and generous Goddess, I offer you this one chance at mercy. Deny your foolish Christian beliefs and accept the Goddess as your lifesaving Mistress. If you swear by the Earth, the Moon, and the Stars you will never present a threat to the world again, the Goddess will forgive you and we will set you free."

The scared part of her screamed in her mind the offer was generous, and she could yet live. Yes, she reminded her terrified self, but for how long? And then what, an eternity of boiling oil? No thanks.

Again, she shook her head in the negative, willing her traitorous lips to stay firmly sealed.

Contradeum did his best to look sad.

"Suit yourself. We have offered you mercy, and you have declined it. Sergeant-at-Arms, do your duty."

The Sergeant-at-Arms marched forward, his back ramrod straight. He stopped, lifting his right knee and slamming his foot to the ground, sword held at the ready in his right hand. He spun to face her.

"Sylvia Oslo, we condemn you to die by firing

squad. Do you have any last wishes?"

Again, a head shake.

"Do you want a blindfold?"

That was an easy one.

"No," she said, her voice unsteady.

"As you wish." He spun back on his heel.

"Company, ready arms!"

The twelve soldiers raised their rifles into a ready position, and twelve safeties came off.

"Aim."

Twelve rifles raised to point at Sylvia's body.

"Fire!"

Sylvia Oslo was free.

Contradeum turned to the holo cameras after the medic pronounced Oslo dead and they wrapped her body for cremation. There would be no funeral service. Contradeum had ordered her ashes to be thrown into the ocean.

"My dear subjects, you see the price of this woman's vile and traitorous conduct. Let this be a lesson to anyone else tempted to rebel against us. You heard the testimony in this woman's trial; how she was a member of the cult called Christianity. The words of her so-called pastor pushed her over the edge to commit her nefarious deeds."

"For centuries, we have known Christianity to be an exclusive religion. How many times have you heard them say the only way to God was through their Messiah? You and I are a superior breed of humans who believe in acceptance and inclusivity. There is no room in this world for an intolerant religion."

"From this moment, we declare Christianity to be an anathema, an illegal religion presenting a clear and present danger to the peace and harmony of your world. I not only ban it, not only make it illegal, but I appoint you to be the judge and executioner of all people who profess to be Christians. You heard me correctly. From this moment, it is legal to hunt and kill Christians. You must give them a chance before you kill them to accept the worship of your Goddess and renounce their Christian beliefs. If they do so, you must spare their lives. If they do not, kill them using whatever means you feel to be right."

"In fact, I give you *carte blanche* to torture and kill them in the most atrocious ways possible. Doing so will denounce their beliefs and deter others from following their ridiculous faith. If you torture and kill them, you are conducting acts of love because their deaths may lead others to faith in the Goddess. How blessed are you who follow these commands!"

"Soon, I will reveal my grand master plan for the revitalization of our world. It will be a glorious place, with peace, prosperity, and justice for all. Serve us and we will allow you your every desire."

"Go now, and may the peace of the Goddess be upon you."

Lester Rozinski shut off the hologram and stared at the wall, offering a prayer of thanks to the Lord that Sylvia died well. After a moment, he removed the four stars from his uniform.

It was over. America was dead. The new Regional Supervisor could come in and try to do something with this mess.

Rozinski and the members of his church were the walking dead. As soon as Peterson had testified against Sylvia, his pastor had convened an urgent remote meeting with his parishioners. He exhorted them to flee into hiding, leaving no trace of their lives behind. No one knew how many others their Judas had identified to the authorities.

Rozinski had stayed in office out of a sense of duty to Sylvia. He stayed until she died, but with Contradeum's pronouncement, it was no longer an option. It would be harder to reach people now and convince them Jesus Christ was the only eternal way out of the disaster the Earth had become. Being a missionary had become a death sentence. He set his mouth into a grim line. If Sylvia Oslo could die well, then so could he. Bringing just one person to faith in the Messiah would be worth what remained of his life.

It shocked him he could walk right out of the New White House and onto the street. The pronouncement was too new, and unreal, to take effect. That would change. Soon, the haters would load their weapons to start the thrill of hunting Christians. It would be the persecution of all persecutions.

As he walked into his new life as a fugitive, Rozinski reflected on one final thought.

There would be no stopping the Antichrist now.

CHAPTER THE ELEVENTH:
REDEMPTION

Spes Deserit, in the Year of Our Fight 2375
Mission Day 45

Abaddon sat in the back of the Council Chamber, wrapped in his black wings, and brooded. An air of gloom hung over him like an iron cloak. The Combatants were all aflutter by the return of the Great Ron, now the Great Sean, the first of their new genetic batch. They had abstained from combat, playing by the rules, and looked forward to the return of their twelfth member so they could continue the Fight.

The holo image of Great Sean swooped into the Chamber with a flourish, his brightly colored uniform encased in a long red robe trailing behind him. He entered to a standing ovation from the rest of the Combatants, nodded at them with a genial expression on his face, and took his place.

Great Robert was the most senior of the group, so he spoke first, as was his right.

"Great Sean, we, the Combatants of Spes Deserit, welcome you back to the War Council. May you find success in your every campaign."

Abaddon frowned. Such hypocrisy had become commonplace with this bunch. They would congratulate each other on campaign successes while seething over the losses they suffered. Too often in the past they had followed such congratulatory messages delivered in person with a knife to the throat or poison pellets concealed in wine. It was only one reason the group could no longer meet in person. Too much of a chance someone would die.

Great Sean nodded his gratitude.

"I return with delight. Having carefully studied the Diaries, particularly the most recent entries, I assure you it will be more difficult to keep me from the pleasure of the company of this august body in the future." He stared at Abaddon as he made the remark. "I also took the time to comb my headquarters and removed from it all devices having the potential to kill me without warning."

Abaddon regarded him without expression. It would do the whelp good to think he was safe. So cocky, so arrogant. They professed to learn from their errors, then committed the same ones repeatedly. Usually, at this juncture of the meeting, Abaddon would become frustrated with them. Today, he sat in silence as questions circulated within his mind like a vast whirlpool.

The meeting progressed without rancor and

didn't devolve into shouting matches and uttered profanities. It was the quietest meeting between the Combatants in centuries. After discussing minor agenda items, the Combatants stood up and saluted each other.

"To the Fight, until death do us part," they said, in unison, and disbanded.

Great Raylene of the Southern Plains lingered after the remaining Combatants turned off their holos. She turned to Abaddon and contemplated him for a moment.

"What troubles you, Great Abaddon?"

He shrugged his irritation.

"What makes you think I am troubled?"

Great Raylene smiled.

"You weren't your usual boisterous self during this meeting. Normally, you'd offer words of encouragement, advice, or some sarcastic comment on the stupidity of one of my peers. Today, you sat far away from us and said nothing."

Abaddon stood up and spread his immense black wings wide.

"Perhaps I am questioning the utility of my presence here. I see no further purpose in my involvement in the Fight. I have taught the Combatants everything they need to know and now consider the next step in my journey."

Great Raylene raised her hand in alarm.

"You can't leave us, Great Abaddon. You must not leave us! Were it not for you, the Fight would have ended centuries ago. What would we have done then?"

Her statement froze him in place.

"How would the fight have ended centuries ago? I never saw willingness by the Combatants to desist from warring with one another."

She looked at him oddly.

"Do you not remember, Great Abaddon? During the two hundred years of peace, when we had to develop technology to bring food and materials from other planets for our survival, there was talk among the Combatants of making peace permanent. It was you who raised the question of who would control the distribution of food. You said the Combatant who controlled the food supply owned the world. The Fight flared into existence immediately after you posed the question. Over twenty million Combatants and Victims died over the ensuing forty days. You taught us victory need not only come from force of arms and battles in the field. It could also come from other things important to our survival."

Great Raylene bowed deeply.

"Were it not for you, I wouldn't stand here today ready to take up the Fight with my enemies for the glory of ultimate victory and eternal acclaim. All hail, Abaddon!"

Her holo blinked out of existence and she left the shaken angel alone in the dismal chamber. There had been billions of God's children on this planet before he came. He had asked two questions in the thousands of years he had been on Spes Deserit. Those questions had wiped out the entire population of this world. Almost the entire population.

Why was he here? What motivated him to spill blood so rapaciously on the obliterated ground of this world?

He knew the surface answer; Satan sent him here to soften up the planet for his ultimate rule. Why did he play that megalomaniac's game, though? He had nothing in common with Satan's brood. Their attempts to make themselves into gods would fail, according to God's prophets. The prophets were never wrong.

These questions had plagued him ever since the House denied his entrance and warned him away. These people had done him no ill. Why did he wage war against them?

The answer finally bloomed as brilliantly in his mind as the sun looking up over the edge of the horizon at dawn.

He hated humans.

Humans had killed Jesus. Abaddon despised all humans and wanted them to suffer like Jesus suffered at their hands.

When Mary and Joseph took Jesus to Nazareth to raise Him there, God the Father had taken Abaddon aside.

"You have seen, Abaddon, the angelic guard with which I have surrounded My Son to this time?"

Abaddon's feathers shimmered in delight at having a private audience with Yahweh. Such a privilege was rare.

"Indeed, I have, Majesty."

The Father nodded.

"My Son is now two years old, and it is time for Him to have the life of a boy growing into an adult. My angels are fervent in their desire to protect Him and will not let Him stumble over a stone for fear of bruising His knee. This is not the way My Son must mature. He must experience everything humans do, including pain from minor mishaps, the sorrow of a broken heart, and the joy of haphazard play. I will shortly withdraw My angelic army from His protection, but He will not entirely be alone. I send you to Him, Abaddon, with these instructions: do not hover over Him as a mother hovers over a child. Be near and see that Satan and his demons do not kill and maim Him. In all other things, let Him live His life and learn from His experiences."

A thrill of joy and awe coursed through Abaddon. What an immense honor this was!

"By your command, Father, I will do all that you say."

For thirty-one years, Abaddon never left Jesus's side. He watched as Jesus grew from a child into a boy into a teenager and then into a man. Abaddon observed as the Messiah laughed and cried, ran and slept, ate and felt nurtured in His mother's arms, healed the sick and raised people from the dead.

He recalled the time when Jesus was six years old and sitting quietly by a small stream. Abaddon sat near him in Inter-Dimensional Space. Suddenly, Jesus turned and looked right at the massive angel.

"What's your name?"

Startled, Abaddon looked around until he realized Jesus was addressing him.

"My name is Abaddon," he said.

"Are you my friend?" Jesus asked. "You've been with me since I was two years old, but you never talk to me."

Abaddon wasn't sure what he should do. The Father had ordered him to protect His Son but left vague any details of how he might interact with the future Messiah of the world. This was God the Son, He who created the universe with the Father. Jesus was still his Lord, even if he was a six-year-old human. Abaddon nodded gravely.

"I am your servant and it would honor me to be Your friend. Your Father in Heaven sent me here to walk through life with You and protect You from grave danger. You are the only one who can see me and You should probably not tell others I am here."

Jesus nodded.

"I thought so. You're too big to miss. That's how I knew no one else saw you. It's nice to meet you, Abaddon."

Abaddon felt a rush of warmth course through his body.

"It's nice to meet you too, Lord Jesus. I think you should go home now. Your parents will start worrying about you soon."

Jesus jumped to his feet.

"Okay. I'll race you!" He said and took off running.

It was the first of many quiet encounters Abaddon had with Jesus throughout His life. Most encounters were only short sentences, spoken from time to time, when they were alone and no one was in earshot. Abaddon loved and admired Jesus. He was a dutiful son, a compassionate man, obedient to His parents, and gracious to anyone He met. He had a quick laugh and joy never left His eyes.

Until the garden of Gethsemane. Abaddon closed his eyes, as if trying to squeeze the memory burned into his brain. He was with Jesus in the garden of

Gethsemane when the Lord had blood pouring from his forehead like sweat, so distressed was He. Abaddon heard Jesus praying for the Father to take the cup of sorrow away from Him but finished His prayer with a pledge to do His Father's will.

When He finished praying, Abaddon ministered to Him.

"Lord God, I will obey your every direction. I know there are things about this situation I do not understand, and I do not question Your will. Know I am here for You to the very end. I do not say this to tempt You, but only to remind You that You have but to give the word and I shall come to Your rescue. I am the Destroyer, and I will lay waste to Your enemies."

Jesus smiled and touched Abaddon's face.

"Abaddon, you have been My good and faithful servant. No, more than that, you have been My friend. I must ask you now to endure the most painful task you will ever bear. You must stand aside and take no action for My protection. This will be brutal for you, but you must not permit yourself to interfere. At the beginning of time, the Father and I designed what happens next. Stand by Me, faithful servant, but do nothing, as I carry out Our strategy for the redemption of all humankind. You will suffer with Me, Abaddon, but you must not interfere."

Abaddon didn't like the sound of that at all, but he meekly bowed his head.

"By Your command, my Lord."

Abaddon turned and smashed his fist into the wall of the Council Chamber, pounding an immense hole in the shale.

He had stood by, shaking like a kitchen boy, and watched as Roman soldiers stripped off his Lord's clothing and scourged Him with whips having metal objects embedded at their ends to rip flesh from bone. Every agonized scream from Jesus's lips was an agonized scream in Abaddon's soul. Abaddon did nothing as the soldiers created a crown of thorns and jammed it on Jesus's head, while mocking Him and pretending to worship Him. The thorns dug into His flesh and blood dribbled down His face as His eyes wept in agony.

Abaddon walked with Jesus as He struggled up the hill to Golgotha; the crossbar of His cross hanging on His battered, bleeding back. Abaddon looked on in anguish as the Roman soldiers laid Jesus on the rough wooden cross and then drove a spike into each of Jesus's wrists. They folded one of the Son of God's feet over the other and drove a spike through Jesus's feet into the wood underneath as the Lord screamed from the pain of the rusted spikes piercing His flesh.

The helpless angel almost ripped his own chest apart when they raised the cross and crucified his Lord.

It was at this moment, Abaddon felt hatred.

When he saw the Roman soldiers laughing and casting lots for Jesus's clothing, he realized how much he wanted them to suffer and die. He hated them with such an intensity he would have gladly taken out his sword and killed every human being on the cursed hill and in the entire city of Jerusalem. He remembered raising his hand to the hilt of the sword, but catching Jesus's eyes before he could draw it.

The Lord could barely hold himself upright and catch his breath, but the meaning in His eyes was clear.

Don't. All things must come to pass.

Abaddon tried to rub the horror of those images from his eyes. He translated himself out of the Council Chamber and into the sky above the magnificent wood doors leading to the Judgment Seat on Spes Deserit. He had known for hundreds of years the remnants of the Victims hid at that location. Abaddon had planned to draw them out and shed their blood on the broken streets of the city surrounding the Judgment Seat.

Why? These people were not the ones who crucified his Lord.

The better question was why he had forgotten what Jesus had done for every human being. He died for them to redeem and save them. What gave Abaddon the right to slaughter them? The question haunting him for the last several weeks suddenly became words spoken in the air.

"Abaddon, why are you here?"

Abaddon whirled and fell to his knees while hovering in the air, covering his face with his great black wings. Standing before him was the Holy Spirit of God in all his splendor. He stood in the shape of a man, but tendrils of holy energy constantly swirled through and around His body.

"Lord!"

"Abaddon," the Holy Spirit persisted, "why are you here?"

Abaddon felt shame course through his soul.

"I'm here because Satan sent me."

The Holy Spirit contemplated him for a moment.

"Did We give you into Satan's hands and bind you to follow the will of the evil one?"

Abaddon's body shook with tremors of fear.

"You did not, Lord."

"Did We give these people into your hands for judgment and punishment?"

The shaking increased in intensity.

"You did not, Lord. Satan suggested I come here, and I was bored. I had spent too much time in the Abyss with Satan and his foul beasts. Before I came, I didn't think to ask for Your permission. I didn't think to question my motives. I have committed a great evil here, Lord, and served Satan instead of You. Will You strike me down in judgment?"

The Holy Spirit looked at Abaddon and shook his head. There was sadness in His eyes.

"We must not judge you yet, for you have a service to perform for Us on Earth. You will do one more thing for Us here and then I will take you to the Abyss, where you will wait in chains for your time to come."

A great weariness came over Abaddon. He was to become a prisoner in the gateway to Hell, chained and abused by Satan and his minions, until it came time for Abaddon to fulfill his purpose. Greatness felled by pride. He knew the moral of that story, did he not? How had he ever allowed himself to forget it? He hung his head and answered his God.

"By your command."

The Great Sean keyed the final sequence and sat back, satisfied. The android's eyes opened and Sean stared at the mirror image of his face. It was perfect, down to the last detail. His mechanical doppelgänger could go anywhere, and Sean would see everything through the android's eyes.

"What's your name?"

The android considered for a moment.

"I have no name."

"What's your purpose?"

"My purpose is to proceed to the ancient city of Kai'ku, find the human male with the sword of destruction, kill the human male, and bring back the sword."

"Correct. What priority do you assign to this mission?"

"Highest. This unit shall achieve its mission or perish."

"What weapons will you use?"

"You have prohibited the use of energy weapons. I am equipped with a solid metal spear, which I will use to strike the male in the heart or the brain. As soon as I incapacitate the male, I will seize the sword and fly to the pre-assigned destination."

Sean smiled and patted the android on the arm.

"Very good. I designate you Unit One. You shall speak to no one of your mission, except me, and if they capture you, you shall self-destruct. Confirm."

"Unit One shall speak to no one of the mission, except you, and if captured, shall self-destruct."

Sean activated the wireless connection and put on a virtual reality headset, allowing him to see, in three dimensions, and hear everything experienced by the android.

"Execute."

She closed her eyes and let her thoughts melt into the languid pool in which she soaked. Her desire flowed like mercury from the deep recesses of her mind, down through her throat and into her heart. All the catacombs of her heart, where once there dwelt a darkness of the vilest nature, now gleamed with the crystal tendrils of glittering joy. Her heart sparkled while somewhere a harp led her soul into songs of thanksgiving.

"Are you well, Darian?"

She opened her eyes to see Jesus kneeling before her dressed in black tactical pants, black amphibious boots, and a desert camouflage sweater. She marveled at how his eyes glowed from the Light within and smiled.

"I just remembered where I'd seen you before. When I was at Insertion Point-Mesopotamia, you were in the locus with Tul'ran and Erianne. You dressed in a white robe tied around Your waist and wore sandals on Your feet. I guess it's why I never recognized You in the Garden."

Jesus smiled, his teeth dazzling against His olive skin.

"I watched Johan dance like a monkey to stop you from firing your weapon." He paused as Darian laughed. "I took you out of Dimensional Space when you tried to assassinate My warriors. I stood behind you the whole time. Does it distress you to know it?"

"No, Lord," she said, pleased the answer was true. "Life hurt me badly before then, and evil twisted my soul into a tight knot into which the Light couldn't shine. I'm better, now, Lord, than I've ever been."

The last twenty days had been incredible. Once

she accepted speaking face-to-face with Jesus Christ Himself, the Savior of the world, the Creator of the universe, she opened up to Him. They talked about her life, her pain, and every shard of self-hatred Satan had carefully planted in her mind. They talked, shared meals, laughed at each other's jokes, and she healed.

When she had enough of hearing herself talk, Jesus spoke of His life, His friendships, and His ministry. She sobbed for hours when He described the day of His crucifixion and cried for joy when He spoke of the experience of His resurrection.

When there were no words left, she kneeled before Him, palms up, confessing her sins and begging Him for His mercy. After she accepted Him as her Savior, she could feel the flow of the Holy Spirit into her soul, and she rejoiced.

She didn't miss how He dressed himself today.

"I guess this is it, huh? You look like you're off to war, Lord. Where does that leave me?"

He sat down on the grass in front of her, cross-legged.

"I'm afraid your options aren't very good, Darian. I know how badly you want to go home to Denver, but your inheritance is no longer available to you. While you were here, a submarine launched three nuclear missiles at Denver. The warheads didn't detonate, but one of them landed on top of your parents' mansion. Not only did it destroy the house, it left radioactive shards all around your estate. It was so bad, the authorities sealed off the house and the grounds and declared them off-limits until the radiation subsides. I'm so sorry."

Darian wondered how she had any liquid left in her body to pour tears down her cheeks after the last twenty days. She looked up at Him through blurred vision.

"If anyone else told me this, I wouldn't believe them. This is the story of my life, one train wreck after another. Do I have any other options, or am I stuck in this House as long as I live?"

Jesus smiled and reached out to hold her hand.

"This House was once a place of celebration. People would come here from all around the world to commune with Us. You could hear the laughter and singing blocks away. There are many rooms here, which you haven't yet seen, which would make you happy as long as your heart beats. However, you should know your companions are preparing for the last conflict in this world."

Darian looked down and bit her lip.

"I was their Judas Iscariot, Lord. I sold them out so fast they must've heard the sonic boom as I left. Tul'ran will kill me the second he sees me."

Jesus laughed softly.

"While My son is fierce, he is as equally just. He wouldn't strike you down before he gave you an opportunity to tell your side of the story. Besides, you have one major advantage. Deep within his heart, he loves you."

That surprised her.

"How could he love me? I've done nothing but irritate him since the moment I met him. You should've seen the twisted look on his face when he saw me for the first time."

Jesus spread his arms wide.

"I did. I was there. Omnipotent, omniscient, and omnipresent, remember?"

Darian giggled.

"Forgive me, Lord. You look so, um, normal and You're so easy to talk to I forget who You are sometimes. If his look wasn't one of hatred, then what was it?"

"It was one of painful recognition. You resemble a slightly older version of Tul'ran's second-youngest sister. If the two of you stood side by side, you would look like twins. Evann'ya was Tul'ran's fiercest champion. More than once she stood between Tul'ran, when he was a young boy, and his father, when his father was drunk and wanted to beat him. When she couldn't stop him from being beaten, she'd hold Tul'ran's head on her lap, wash his face with a cool cloth, and sing to him."

"Despite the favor Tul'ran's father heaped upon the heads and shoulders of his daughters, Tul'ran loved all his sisters. He practically worshipped Evann'ya. I know he recognized his sister when he saw you and felt the recognition deep within his heart. My son can't help but to love you. Evann'ya ingrained it in his soul."

Darian looked deeply into her Lord's eyes. She could see sadness behind the Light.

"Do I want to know what happened to Evann'ya?"

The Lord looked away.

"Marauders raped and killed her when Tul'ran was twelve years old. They did the same to his mother and youngest sister. Tul'ran watched the whole thing. I'd like to tell you I've healed the scars of that day, but those wounds run to the core of his spirit. Tul'ran washed their bodies, wrapped them in clean linen, and set them on a funeral pyre. It was the day he first met Me, and it has bonded us ever since."

Darian moaned.

"Is there no one in the world whom rape hasn't touched? How is it so prevalent?"

"It's how evil works, Darian. It picks an act so destructive it carves deep trenches into the psyche of the victim and those who know the victim. Evil encourages people who don't know Me to carry out heinous acts against their fellow humans. It destroys the victim. It also harms the attacker, burying them so deep in sin it's difficult for them to open their hearts to Me and seek forgiveness."

Darian snapped her head up.

"You forgive rapists?!"

Jesus pulled up his sleeves to show her the ugly scars on his wrists.

"I didn't incur these wounds for people who only cheat on their taxes. No sin is worse than any other sin. All sins, no matter how minor they might seem to the sinner, fall short of Our perfection. Even one sin falling short of the perfection of God will cause Us to cast the sinner into the outer darkness. Tell me, as a former servant of Satan, how were your sins better than those of a rapist?"

Darian felt her cheeks turn hot.

"That was harsh."

Jesus once again took her hand.

"I'm sorry, Darian. The truth is sometimes harsh, but it doesn't lose its character as the truth. I'll forgive anyone who comes to Me in genuine faith, with remorse in their hearts, and confess their sins to Me. My Father sent Me into the world so whoever believes in Me will have eternal life."

Darian sat still for a moment and considered His words. She nodded.

"I guess a part of me victimized by sexual assailants wants them to burn forever."

"You must forgive them, Darian. Forgiveness acts as medication for your spiritual, emotional, and psychological wounds, healing them and bringing you peace when the pain is gone."

"Did Tul'ran forgive the men who raped and killed his mother and sisters?"

Jesus shook his head.

"Tul'ran is a special case. When he called out to Me as a tortured twelve-year-old boy, I felt deeply for him. I offered to make him a Judge in his era. It was the only way to preserve his sanity. I spoke to his mind and gave him missions to carry out in My name. He judged his family's rapists and murderers with My approval and executed them."

Darian closed her eyes. She tried to imagine herself as a twelve-year-old boy having to watch the women he loved being sexually abused and killed. Her stomach twisted within her body, and she felt a warmth in her heart for him.

"Thank you for telling me his story. It explains a lot. I'm not sure we got to my option."

"If it's your desire, I'll have E'thriel take you to your friends to reunite you with them. If you choose to go, I must warn you they all face a grave danger. I can't guarantee your safety if you choose to join them."

Darian's face lit up with her dazzling smile.

"You already have. You've blessed me with three weeks of conversation with my Creator and Savior. I know if anything happens to me, I'll be in Heaven with You."

Jesus matched her smile.

"You will. You have my promise."

Darian swirled the water in the pool.

"Then this is goodbye until I see you again. I'm not able to hug you at the moment. Thank you, thank you, thank you, from the bottom of my heart. It'll be my joy to tell this story to my friends. Now, where's my beautiful angel?"

Tul'ran's beautiful angel found him at the well, poking the water with his fingertips and watching the ripples fan across its smooth face. Erianne watched him for a few moments before she walked over and flopped down beside him.

"Is there a lack of work in this place, I wonder, such that I should find my husband reposing by a pool of water, contemplating the vicissitudes of life?"

He smiled at her and flicked the back of his hand against the surface of the well.

"Though I am not as learned as you and our friends, I proclaim, with great confidence, this hardly qualifies a pool of water."

Erianne giggled.

"I concede the point. What holds you in your doldrums, milord husband?"

Tul'ran wouldn't answer her. She took his chin in her hand and raised his head to look into his eyes.

"I'm your wife," she whispered. "You've no secrets from me, my love. Spill it," she finished in English.

"You may find this cowardly, Erianne, but I cannot divorce my mind from our sister's prophecy. I spoke with brave words when she foretold my future, but my heart quails at the thought of your death in the upcoming warfare. I do not know how I will fare if El Shaddai takes you from me. You have invested my heart with love, my soul with peace, and my thoughts of a future where we are old and must have our grandchildren bring us our blades. How am I to carry on without you?"

She leaned in and kissed him on the forehead.

"My love, you mourn me, and I am not yet dead. Recall, if you will, our sister's mind often scatters like dandelion seeds. She did not name me directly as being the source of your grief. Have you so quickly forgotten the Massacre at the Pass, as they sing it in verses one hundred and forty-two to one hundred and fifty in your Ballad? Apparently, we fought like angels of God against not just men, but hounds from Hell leading demons on chains forged from the bones of sinners."

Tul'ran's loud laugh echoed off the walls of the water chamber.

"Not having heard those stanzas recently, the ferocity with which we fought the Gutians seems to have slipped my mind."

Erianne stood up and offered him her hand.

"Then we remedy your memory at once. Come with me. I have a plan."

She led him to the Judgment Seat and turned in a

circle, gesturing at all the empty seats.

"Behold, the training arena. Cross swords with me, Tul'ran az Nostrom, and we shall see if you can match your wife for skill and speed with the blade."

He grinned his wolf's grin at her.

"And what shall we do for practice swords, covenant-wife? It would hardly do my mood much good were I to cleave you in half with Bloodwing."

Erianne drew Caligo from her sheath.

"You are so wonderfully overconfident. Our many conversations about the qualities of Bloodwing the Blade led me to thinking. What if our eternal swords are more than sharp-edged tools by which we separate head from neck? Behold, my discovery."

She extended her sword away from her body on a horizontal line and passed her hand over it from the hilt to the tip.

"Practice blade," she commanded, her voice having an odd, otherworldly undertone. The edges of the sword immediately lost their shine and the metal of the sword dulled considerably. She walked to one seat and tapped it with Caligo's edge. It didn't make a dent in the stone.

Tul'ran felt his eyebrows leap to the top of his forehead. He drew Bloodwing and held it out in front of him, passing his right hand over the blade from the hilt to the tip.

"Practice blade," he commanded, in the same tone by which one would command angels. His sword immediately assumed the appearance of a dull iron sword. The weight and balance remained, but he could not cut the edge of his fingertip when he ran it down the blade.

Tul'ran whipped Bloodwing around his body in several quick turns and nodded his satisfaction.

"Now it is my wife's turn to receive the spanking she alluded to earlier in our sojourn here."

Erianne grinned.

"Big talk from the pool boy. Let's see if you remember any of your skills."

She lunged, and he as quickly parried, turning it into a counter stroke from which she spun away with the speed and agility he so often admired. They started slowly, checking each other's defenses. After fifteen minutes of gentle sparring, the fighting became more intense. Soon, they became a blur of action in the center of the arena, cutting, spinning, kicking, and dancing through movements that would have left anyone else less skilled lying bleeding in the dust.

They moved as one, yet disparate in their attacks, defenses, and counterattacks. One would see an opening and thrust to it, only to have it close and be turned into a counter. It was too fast to strategize, to think, or plan. Everything was instinct and skill.

Dust whipped up around their feet as they battled in the center of the Judgment Seat, their breathing rushing in and out of overtaxed lungs as they sparred in a frenzy.

They fought until sweat ran from their foreheads into their eyes and their clothing clung to them, drenched. Finally, they stopped, panting, neither one of them successful in reaching past the other's guard to touch skin and make a point.

As they eyed each other in the center of the dusty

amphitheater, they realized at the same time the import of what had just taken place. Tul'ran had finally met his equal in the lithe body and supple wrists of his lifemate.

The Judgment Seat erupted into a tsunami of applause and cheers. Stunned, they looked around to see the People filling every seat in the chamber. During their seventy-five-minute bout, word had spread of the activity in the arena and people had flooded into the Judgment Seat to the oblivious disregard of the combatants. Now they stood and cheered as Tul'ran and Erianne blushed and tried to regain their composure.

Gwynver'insa walked into the amphitheater, proud and regal, with Johan ever-present on her arm. She stepped away from the Historian and walked in between Erianne and Tul'ran. The crowd immediately fell silent. Her voice was loud and echoed off the chamber walls.

"In the tradition of the Judgment Seat, I call upon you to judge. I present to you Lord Tul'ran az Nostrom, Prince of Death, and Lady Erianne az Nostrom, Princess of Death. If there are any among you who judge them unfit to be Our Champions, then speak now or forever hold your peace."

The arena became so silent, Erianne thought she had gone deaf.

Gwynver'insa let the silence hang for several minutes. She then took the hands of her friends and raised them high in the air.

"This is my brother, and here is my sister. They came into the Judgment Seat voluntarily, without fanfare. By seeking judgment from you, they have solidified their legal claim against the Combatants. In the name of Yahweh, I proclaim them free of punishment for the things they will do to liberate this world for us and pardon them from any violence they may carry out in our name. Behold, Our Champions!" she shouted and the whole chamber dissolved into a pandemonium of cheers, whistles, tears, and screams.

After the bedlam subsided, and people started filing out, Erianne caught Gwynver'insa's attention.

"What was that all about, sister, if I may be so bold to ask?"

Gwynver'insa became serious.

"My brave sister, you gave me no quarter. When you and my courageous brother stepped into this chamber and began your dance, the two of you presented yourself for judgment. No one comes into the Judgment Seat unless they intend to state a case and receive a decision from the People. I am grateful the two of you did so well. Had the People found against you, I would have had no choice but to put you two to death. Thank you, my brother and my sister. You have wrought mightily for me today by giving legitimacy to my Throne and my decision to commit you to war in our stead."

Gwynver'insa walked away, leaving the mouths of her friends hanging open.

"Please tell me, beloved wife, you knew of these conditions before you led me to this place?"

Erianne shook her head.

"No, milord husband, but do you see how nothing in the world can wager against us? Even when we unwittingly dice with Fate, we emerge victorious. You should fear less for me than for the destiny of this world. I sense our Empress will soon cry havoc and let slip the dogs of war. We are the wolves straining at the edge of her leash. May God have mercy on the souls of those she releases us against."

The world hovered in front of them, slowly rotating. They had gathered in the small room in which Gwynver'insa made the original Food Maker after giving Tul'ran and Erianne time for a much-needed bath. It did not escape her notice they glowed from the aftereffects of spent lust, as well, but refrained from commenting.

The rotating planet was a holographic image, so the dark fog wrapped around the globe didn't obscure the ground. Tul'ran's eyebrows kept dancing on his head as Spes Deserit turned before him.

"Is this planet just one desolate city? Where are the fields, the forests, and the lakes?"

Sadness made Gwynver'insa's large blue eyes wet. She had convened this meeting because she felt the urgency of it in her bones. Something was coming. Some course of action needed to be planned, and so she convened her Peace Council.

"The Combatants sucked the lakes dry during their frenzy to manufacture war machines. Early in our history of conflict, they burned the forests to run their furnaces to melt the metals they strip mined from the fields. Everything living, they sacrificed to make dead things that killed. When war is your god, you will sacrifice everything to make war. Yes, my Brother, this planet now is just one desolate city. Win the war for me, Tul'ran, and I shall turn this planet into the jewel of the universe."

He shook his head and sidled a glance at Erianne.

"You ask much, my darling sister. It is my hope and desire to deliver this world to you, but I cannot make you any promises."

Erianne leaned down and kissed him.

"You must understand, sister Empress, we come from another world in the cosmos. Sometimes our words do not translate into the meaning we would otherwise give them. What my husband meant to say is he will cast the war machines into the furnaces of despair and bring the Combatants to their knees. They shall kneel before you at the Judgment Seat and beg for your mercy."

Johan grinned.

"Milady Erianne, I hear the ring of prophecy in your voice. Do you aspire to the status of the Second Prophet of Spes Deserit?"

Erianne widened her eyes.

"Why ever would I do so? Is the position of First Prophet closed for application?"

Gwynver'insa giggled, walked up to the taller woman, and folded herself into Erianne's arms for a hug.

"You may have the title of Empress as well, should you desire it, my dear. I miss my days of study and quiet contemplation in the Garden. I would retire to it with joy and leave you to the bedlam of ruling."

Erianne kissed the top of her forehead.

"Keep your titles, dearest sister. I have my hands full trying to keep my husband out of trouble, a task which occupies my every second."

Tul'ran snorted.

"Perhaps we should discuss again how you and I came to stand in judgment before the population of this world."

Erianne opened her mouth for her retort, but never finished it. An excited man ran into the room.

"The lights have come on at the conveyance station. Someone comes!"

Erianne cast her eyes to the ceiling and whipped Caligo from its sheath in a blur of motion.

"Finally! It's about time we saw some action! To the ramparts!"

Tul'ran shook his head as she lunged out the door and drew Bloodwing. He looked at Johan.

"Take Gwynver'insa and keep her safe. Her life has precedence because she is the salvation of this world."

Johan gave him a firm nod.

"I'll protect her with my life."

Tul'ran grinned at him and ran after his wife. He had noticed how close Gwynver'insa and Johan had become. Their growing relationship was the subject of much delighted talk among the People. Tul'ran knew Johan would take great care of her, indeed.

It took him a few minutes to catch up with Erianne because her long legs made her faster in a sprint than him. They arrived at the station just as the bullet-shaped conveyance pulled in. Tul'ran noted with interest a thin layer of frost covering the conveyance's entire exterior. He didn't remember that to have happened when they came to this place, but then he hadn't been paying attention.

The conveyance was brilliantly lit from within, as if it had transported the sun. As the doors opened, a fog rolled out, obscuring their sight of the being strolling through the doorway. The moment of confusion dissipated when the fog disappeared.

"E'thriel!"

Erianne sheathed Caligo and ran up to grab the angel in a bear hug. Tul'ran put Bloodwing away and strode up to the eternal being, holding out his right forearm to be grasped by the angel.

"E'thriel, I am pleased to see you. Does your presence here mean a successful completion of your last mission?"

E'thriel beamed.

"I am delighted to report, Lord Tul'ran, I delivered Katja and her brothers to Heaven, where they kneeled before the Judgment Seat of Christ. Jesus found the names of all four written in the Lamb's Book of Life. Even now, they repose in Heaven waiting for you and Erianne to join them. They are safe for all eternity."

Tul'ran exhaled a large gust of air. A weight he didn't know existed lifted from his shoulders and his eyes misted. He offered a silent prayer of gratitude to El Shaddai. Erianne gave up her grip on the angel and squeezed Tul'ran into her body, tears running down her cheeks.

"You saved them, milord husband."

He shook his head.

"I deserve and take no credit, my love. It was El Shaddai who heard their confession and forgave them their transgressions."

"They weren't the only ones."

E'thriel stepped aside and Darian stepped out onto the platform, leaving Tul'ran and Erianne in stunned silence. She wore a mint green long jacket sweeping like a cloak from her neck to the back of her ankles. Under the jacket, she had on a royal blue short-sleeved shirt falling below her waist. Matching pants completed the rest of her ensemble, though her boots denied the impression she just stopped off a fashion runway. She wore black amphibious combat boots extending just above her ankles.

Her long, brown hair hung loose, and it cascaded over her shoulders and fell over her breasts. Darian's face glowed, and the sparkle in her blue eyes was breathtaking. Joy radiated from her in waves.

Darian walked up to Tul'ran, dropped to her knees, and bent forward. She pulled her long brunette hair up and away, exposing her slender neck.

"Lord Tul'ran, Lady Erianne, I've sinned against you by thought, word, and deed. I betrayed you to evil and exposed you to harm through my selfish desires. Know I've confessed my sins to El Shaddai, and He has forgiven me. I beg you to accept my confession and forgive me for my trespasses against you. Should you not accept my plea for mercy, then I beg you to strike quickly and end my life."

The silence stretched for a long moment. Tul'ran kneeled before Darian, and he took her face in the palms of his hands. He looked deeply into her eyes and then kissed her forehead as he had seen Erianne do to Gwynver'insa.

"Do you think me comparable to the Lord our God? I am the dirt He rubs off his feet before He ascends His Throne. I see peace in your eyes I haven't observed before. The light within you could only have come from El Shaddai. If He forgives you, I accept his judgment, forgive you from the depths of my heart, and greet you with joy."

Tears leaped to Darian's eyes.

"Are we now friends?"

Tul'ran smiled wistfully.

"We're more than friends, Darian. You're my sister. If I didn't know better, I would swear you to be my second-youngest sister, Evann'ya. The two of you could've been born as twins from the same womb. You are my joy."

Tul'ran helped Darian to her feet, and Erianne drew her into a hug before kissing her on both cheeks.

"What's with you, Darian? Do you always have to take the longest road home?"

Darian laughed and wiped tears from her face.

"I'm kinda stubborn that way. Hello, beautiful. Killed anybody today?"

Erianne giggled.

"It's been a slow day, but there's twelve hours left in it. You never can tell what might happen."

Darian looked around the platform.

"I have a few more apologies to make. Where's Johan?"

There was an awkward silence while Tul'ran cocked an eyebrow at Erianne.

"Why should it be me?" Erianne asked him.

"What do you mean, why should it be you? What are you not telling me? Erianne, is Johan okay? Did he get hurt?"

Erianne glared at her husband, who steadfastly kept his lips firmly pressed together.

"Johan is good, Darian. It's just, well, you may find him a less attentive toward you than he has been in the past."

Darian stared at her for a long moment before realization dawned.

"Wow, it didn't take long for him to get over me. Who's he in love with now, Gwynver'insa?"

Tul'ran nodded.

"Yes. When we arrived here, we found one hundred and forty-four thousand of the People hiding in this place and slowly starving to death. With Johan's help, the Empress created a Food Maker to feed her People."

Darian's face turned blank.

"Which Empress is that?"

Erianne looked at Tul'ran and grimaced.

"The People of Spes Deserit have acclaimed Gwynver'insa as their Empress."

Darian's eyes grew slightly larger.

"Boy, Johan really traded up. He went from pining after a rebel without a pause to the ruler of an entire planet." She smiled. "Good for him. I was a real jerk towards him and he deserved better than me every day of the week. Are they engaged or anything?"

Erianne laughed.

"The boy moves fast, but not so fast. No one is thinking along those lines until the war is over. No, the two of them have just been very close. When they created the first Food Maker, it could only serve one dish. Johan figured out a way to give the Master

Food Maker many menu options, and how to transmit the final product to seventy-two hundred copies in the Hall. The People now have a chef who creates daily dishes for them. They eat something unique every day, even though they all eat the same dish. No one's complaining. The food is delicious and they're better nourished than they've ever been."

"He's helped the Empress in other ways," Tul'ran chimed in. "Johan has a good head for government and has been advising Gwynver'insa how to structure her Empire to govern the People fairly. He never decides she ought to decide, but is ever-present to guide her in the right direction. The People recognize them, informally, as governing as if they were one ruler and show him almost as much deference as they do the Empress."

"Okay, I get it," Darian said. "Honestly, I'm happy for them. After Jesus forgave me for my sins and healed me from my pain, I have a completely different attitude towards people in general, and men in particular. You don't have to worry about me. I'll behave myself when I meet them."

"We know you will, and we'll be right beside you," Erianne said as she placed her right arm around Darian's shoulders and guided her toward the staircase. To Tul'ran's surprise, Darian reached back and wiggled her fingers until he wrapped them in his massive hand. Darian squeezed his hand and smiled.

"I feel like Dorothy going off to see the Wizard."

"Who's Dorothy?" Tul'ran asked after a few seconds of silence, to their roars of laughter.

CHAPTER THE TWELFTH: DESECRATION

Rome, May 11, 2099 AD... midway through the Tribulation

His day of glorification had finally come. He smoothed the long white robes wrapped around his body and admired himself in the mirror. They died his hair a rich brown color, and he had grown a short, cropped beard. The sandals on his feet were designer-made, and the designer wove gold strands throughout the leather. He had let his hair grow out, so it ran in waves down to his shoulders. He raised his arms outward, the long sleeves falling from his arms. This is how a messiah should look.

Malchus Contradeum turned to the twelve people who had dressed him, prepared his hair, and applied cosmetics for the holo cameras. He waved his hand toward the door.

"You've done your job. It's now our time. Let us

meet our servants."

It was summer in Rome, and the day was beautiful. Contradeum walked through the halls of what Roman Catholics once knew as the Vatican, but the building was now known as the Center of All Religion. For the last three-and-a-half years, the worship of the Mother Goddess Earth flowed from this building outward to the masses. This religion incorporated the most permissive values of all religions, except Christianity.

Christianity was extinct. It existed only in underground churches run by secret networks. The mere admission a person is a follower of Jesus Christ warranted an immediate summary execution or prolonged torture. Contradeum smiled. The draconian measures he had put in place to deal with Christianity had worked very well to bring faithful devotees to the Mother Goddess. It helped the Mother's worship services always incorporated consumption of wine, ingestion of narcotics, and orgies. Satisfying the flesh was an excellent method of recruitment.

Contradeum waited impatiently in the hallway next to the balcony on which the Chief Priest would anoint him in front of his subjects. Jezebel Brandt approached him, elegantly dressed in a tuxedo. She smoothed the robes around his shoulders and grinned her delight.

"Supreme Global Leader, I can't tell you how excited I am that this day has finally arrived. I've been waiting for it for such a long time, I was afraid it wouldn't come to pass."

Contradeum left a condescending smirk on his

handsome face.

"Thank you, Jez. I'll fulfill my destiny today. Can you explain to me why a Chief Priest is anointing me and not a Chief Priestess? One would think the head of a religion worshiping Mother Earth would be a woman, not a man."

Jez's smile wavered slightly.

"It was the Master's decision. You know that Mal." Her smile brightened. "This is a momentous day; let's not spoil it by quibbling over minor details. Go stand in front of those people and accept your adulation. I'll watch every moment with more excitement than you'll ever imagine."

Marjatta Korhonen smiled as she watched the interplay between Contradeum and Brandt. He had gone above and beyond to make himself look like the prophesied messiah. The only thing missing in his ensemble was the blood accompanying the messiah's sacrifice for sinners. Well, she could help him with that. Korhonen fingered the pendant dangling between her small breasts. Her security people made it of silver and the pendant contained a double-edged, thin dagger with edges dipped in poison. She never forgot the humiliation she endured at this pompous buffoon's hands. The TTI Administrator always wondered what Contradeum would look like with a knife in his chest. Maybe today it was her turn to become the leader of the world.

As Contradeum and Brandt walked through the curtained exit onto the balcony, Korhonen found her place within the order established for the dignitaries. Her cheeks still burned with the memory of how condescending Contradeum had been when he extended her invitation. Like he expected her to wash his feet or something. Her fingers wanted to go to the Pendant again, but she stilled them. They were now in the open and there were holo cameras everywhere. Best not to tip off Security.

Contradeum squared his shoulders as the announcer finished a long and exuberant introduction of him. He walked to the edge of the balcony and the tens of thousands of people in the square below roared their screams of approval. He raised his arms and basked in the glow of their adoration, counting it as his due. After a while, he motioned to the Chief Priest.

In contradiction to Contradeum's simple attire in a white robe, the Chief Priest's investments were gaudy to the extreme. They were multicolored and incorporated every trinket and symbol known to every religion in the world. Thick gold chains carried the symbols of every religion. The short, heavily bearded man was sweating profusely. The sun was blistering, and his vestments didn't breathe. Fortunately, the ceremony was brief.

"Do you, Malchus Contradeum, accept the position of Supreme Global Leader? Will you rule the people of this planet Earth to make everyone rich beyond their wildest dreams and bring peace to a tortured world, while allowing them every pleasure of the flesh?"

"I will," Contradeum said to the cheers of the people below.

The Chief Priest raised his hands in benediction and traced an arbitrary symbol in the air over

Malchus's head.

"Then by the power vested in me by the Goddess, I grant you the supreme power to rule the world and bring peace and prosperity to every person in every nation."

The Chief Priest reached behind him and produced an intricate, heavily jeweled crown and placed it on Contradeum's head. He then took a golden scepter, the head of which appeared to have a snake wrapped around a tree, and placed it in Contradeum's hands. The Chief Priest turned to the square and shouted,

"Behold, your King!"

The people screamed until they were hoarse. Contradeum turned to accept the congratulations of his ten Regional Supervisors and other dignitaries assembled behind him on the balcony.

One by one, each of the Regional Supervisors bowed low to him and kissed the ring on Contradeum's left hand. He shook their hands, pouring out words of gratitude for their support for him during the first three-and-a-half years of his reign. It was a sham, of course. He appointed all of them and they owed him for every luxury, every item of food, and every bit of crypto currency they owned. He made them, and they knew he could unmake them in a moment of unbridled fury.

Contradeum stopped in surprise in front of the last person standing at rigid attention at the end of the line of dignitaries. The crowd below him sang and chanted as nude servants walked through the gathering with narcotics. People were opening expensive bottles of champagne and pouring it on one another. Others were indulging in body shots.

Somewhere, an orchestra was playing an ancient symphony while people mocked them and made obscene gestures in their direction. Contradeum took hold of himself. He wouldn't let this unwelcome visitor ruin a perfect day.

"General Rozinski, I'm surprised to see you here. In full dress uniform, no less. You were absent from our service without leave for quite some time. Have you now come to your senses? Will you kiss the ring of your commander?"

Rozinski bowed low and kissed the ring on Contradeum's extended hand before he straightened.

"I spent the time away from my duties in prayer and fasting, seeking an answer about what role I should perform in these unusual times. When I had a revelation of what steps I should take, I wept for hours. I'm very grateful to be here, Supreme Global Leader. Will you do me the honor of shaking my hand?"

Contradeum grinned.

"Of course! Am I not the most merciful man in the world's history? There has been no one else like me. I'm grateful you've seen the light and come to worship the Goddess."

Contradeum extended his right hand to accept a handshake, and Rozinski lifted his as well. The General's right hand kept rising, though, and his left hand suddenly clenched. A spring in the General's right sleeve activated, and a dagger leaped out from the cuff. Rozinski drove the knife into and through Contradeum's heart. Contradeum's eyes widened with shock as he stared stupidly at the blade extruding from his chest.

Rozinski grinned savagely as bullets fired by Contradeum's security team pounded into his back. Before he fell, tearing the blade out of the Supreme Global Leader's chest, he ground out the words,

"Sylvia Oslo sends her regards."

The Sullivans and Davis and Wu had lounged in Heather's quarters since they were the largest. They made an evening of it by preparing dinner and snacks. Davis would have watched anything other than Contradeum's coronation, but nothing else was on the holos. As usual, Contradeum made sure he was the only game in town.

The three hours of fanfare leading up to Contradeum's acclamation as Supreme Global Leader were nauseating. Exuberant broadcasters belabored Contradeum's contributions to peace and the steps he was taking to rid the world of famine and disease. Every person they interviewed tried to top the other with their praises.

"Another hour of this," Davis said, "and my chicken wings are going to find themselves in the toilet."

"Hey, look at that!" Sully said, pointing to the three-dimensional image hovering in front of their eyes.

They watched General Lester Rozinski march onto the balcony and take up a position on the far-right side. He had decked himself out in full dress uniform, medals and all.

"Isn't that the General who took over for Oslo

and then disappeared?" Heather asked.

Sully nodded.

"Yeah, I'm confused. After President Oslo's execution, he just fell off the map. Contradeum's military was on the verge of issuing an arrest warrant for him, claiming he was AWOL. No one's heard from him since the day he walked. Look at his face, Mick."

Davis nodded.

"I know the look. I've seen it on dozens of special operators' faces over the years we served. He's on a mission, people."

"What kind of mission?" Jeannie asked.

"Don't know. I wonder why they would let him be part of this if he's been AWOL? He should be in chains in the brig. Here comes Contradeum. Look how he's dressed up. He's doing everything he can to look like Jesus."

They watched as Contradeum took his oath, then walked around to accept the fawning adulation of the assembled dignitaries. Contradeum finally stood face-to-face with Rozinski. After they jawed at each other, they went to shake hands.

Sully exploded out of his chair.

"Holy smokes!" he yelled. "Did you see that? Roz just put a knife into Contradeum's chest!"

They watched, unbelieving, as bullets pounded into Rozinski's body before he fell. The audio pickups were very good, and they heard his last words as he died.

"Revenge," Heather said in a hushed tone. "He killed Contradeum to avenge Sylvia Oslo's execution."

Davis shook his head.

"It goes deeper than that. I read somewhere the Christians believe Contradeum is the Antichrist. We are three-and-a-half years into a seven-year Tribulation period, according to them. If Contradeum dies, what happens to the last half? Do they call it for lack of opposition?"

Heather picked up on Davis's cue.

"I read the same article, Mick. Here's where my photographic memory comes in handy. The article referred to Revelation 13, which they said is a major chapter about the Beast, also known as the Antichrist, and the False Prophet. Clearly, the man with all the religious trappings is the False Prophet. Verse 3 says Contradeum will suffer a fatal wound and it will get healed. The False Prophet makes everyone worship the Antichrist, whose fatal wound gets healed. Revelation 13 suggests the Antichrist will come back from the dead. When he does, Satan will indwell him. He will deceive people into believing he is a god by performing grand signs, even making fire come down out of heaven to the earth in the presence of men."

Davis nodded; grateful she was so quick on the uptake.

"I guess it means Satan and Contradeum are trying to recreate what happened to Jesus. They kill their messiah, leave him dead for three days, and then resurrect him somehow. Maybe they're faking his death."

Sully was squinting at the holo, watching the replay as Rozinski fell and ripped the knife out of Contradeum's chest.

"That's a hard kill, Mick. Contradeum better have a miracle tucked under his armpit if he's going to come back from that hit."

Pandemonium reigned. So wrapped up in their debaucheries, the crowd in the square didn't even notice their leader sink to his knees with blood pouring out of his chest. The Regional Supervisors and the dignitaries were all screaming and shouting for medical aid, adding to the riotous atmosphere.

Jez stood back, trying hard to conceal the smile on her face. Security carefully searched and screened every person before they came to this heavily guarded zone. As Second, she was the one who cleared Rozinski for entrance into the celebration. She concealed the dagger and spring apparatus in the men's water closet, where her agents instructed Rozinski to look. She had taken great delight in executing this part of the Master's plan to kill Contradeum with a knife thrust to the heart.

For what seemed to be the thousandth time, she thought about how much of a fool Contradeum was. Sure, he had the looks and charisma to woo people to him and sway their decisions. Physically, he was the perfect man to be the Ruler of the World. Spiritually, mentally, and emotionally, he left a lot to be desired.

She wanted Contradeum's job from the very beginning, and it offended her when the Master gave it to Malchus. The Master showed her scriptures from the Holy Bible as to the role Contradeum would play and then she understood why the leader of the world had to be a man.

When her Master told her a week ago, someone would assassinate this narcissistic, misogynistic cretin today, Jez became wildly drunk. She hadn't lied when she told Contradeum how anxious she had been for this day to come.

The paramedics worked feverishly on Contradeum for some time after dragging him inside from the balcony, but it was no use. General Rozinski had been with the United States Army Special Forces. He knew where to put a knife to kill a man. The paramedics looked at her and shook their heads.

Malchus Contradeum, Supreme Global Leader of the Government of Democracy, was dead.

It took a long time to get the attention of the people in the square. After soldiers fired several shots in the air to stop the revelry, Jez stepped to the edge of the balcony. Tears etched lines down her cheeks. How was the crowd to know they were tears of joy, not sorrow?

"You have seen a great deal of frantic action on this balcony in the last few minutes. I regret to inform you we had a traitor in our midst. Former General Rozinski, who had abandoned his post and was Away Without Leave, slipped into this ceremony uninvited and drove a knife into the Supreme Global Leader's chest. Moments ago, despite the valiant efforts of our paramedics, they declared Malchus Contradeum dead."

The crowd became so silent, you could hear the wind blowing empty cocaine packets around the vast square. After Jez made a hand gesture, the technical people replayed repeatedly, from several angles, the attack on the giant holographic screens surrounding the squares.

People began crying hysterically and stampeding away from the square. Jez smiled in delight. Hundreds of people would die in the stampede and thousands more would become injured. She could hardly wait to see the casualty reports on the daily news.

Speaking of which, news drones suddenly appeared, hovering in the air before her. Each drone cast a hologram of the reporter associated with the drone. They all screamed questions until she raised her hand.

"People of the world, you have witnessed the hideous assassination of our beloved Leader. Until we appoint a new leader, I'll run the administrative duties of the Government of Democracy. We will not appoint a new leader, according to our Constitution, until our great and wonderful Supreme Global Leader has lain in state for thirty days. Once we prepare his body, Malchus Contradeum will lie in state at the main entrance of this building so you can come and pay your respects."

"Will there be an investigation?" one reporter shouted.

Jez nodded.

"An investigation has started, and I already have some preliminary details for you. The person who stabbed our glorious Leader in the chest was none other than former General Lester Rozinski from Region Ten. It shocks us that such a loyal and well-respected military man would assassinate the cherished Ruler of the World. It will not surprise you to know the renegade Christian sect twisted his mind into believing our Leader was the Antichrist. They encouraged him to assassinate our beautiful Supreme Global Leader because of their foolish doctrine."

"Did Rozinski survive the attack?" another reporter yelled.

Jez made a negative slashing motion with her right hand.

"He didn't. Our security forces shot and killed him at once, but not quickly enough to save our glorious Leader's life. It is unfortunate Rozinski didn't survive. Just as the Romans crucified villains and bandits at the start of the first millennium, it would have been our choice to crucify Rozinski for this heinous act. An ancient society crucified the man the Christians serve. While I can't set policy and make such decisions, I urge all local leaders to crucify every Christian they find. If that's what they worship, let them experience it for themselves."

The people who remained in the square cheered wildly at her last statement. Jez dismissed the reporting drones and turned back into the building. Tonight, she would dine with the Master, and they would celebrate his success. The Plan was finally coming together. Satan would be the world's god and he would rule on Earth. Jezebel Brandt would finally realize her lifelong lust for ultimate power.

After all, he promised her she would rule with him, didn't he?

Satan had one pleasurable task to perform before he joined Jez for dinner. He normally didn't take part in removing the souls of sinners from the physical realm into the spiritual realm after they died. The Angel of Death attended to such duties. The angel appointed by God the Father to guide people from their physical bodies to the Kingdom of Heaven was a kind and gentle spirit. His duty was to make the transition from life to death an easy one for the deceased.

Satan hated humans and couldn't care less how savagely he treated their souls. On this day, Satan asked for and God permitted him to remove Contradeum's soul to the Abyss to wait there until it was time for Contradeum's judgment.

The moment Contradeum's heart beat for the last time, Satan seized his soul and pulled the bewildered spirit from the corpse. They stood there for a few minutes while Contradeum tried to recover from his daze. He was stunned by the amount of mayhem surrounding them. Dignitaries were screaming and one had fallen into a faint. Two celebrities hovered over the dignitary, fanning his face to bring him back to consciousness. Paramedics frantically ripped clothes off Contradeum's body and attached med sensors to the bared skin. Blood no longer poured out of his chest and the pallor of death was upon his face. The body's eyes were fixed open and dilated wide.

Contradeum looked up and saw the holo screens depicting the scene of Rozinski slamming the blade into his heart before Security shot and killed the General.

"What happened? Is that me? Am I dead? How is this possible? I am the Supreme Global Leader of the Earth. You promised me I would rule this world with you!"

Satan sneered at him.

"How many times did I tell you to read the chapters of the Bible concerning you, foolish human? Had you done so, you would have known this day was coming. I am now going to rule in your body, but you can't be in it with me. Your time on this Earth is done, slave. I'm sending you to your new home."

A portal opened. Satan grabbed the horrified soul by his throat and cast the screaming spirit into the black hole before jumping in after him, laughing hysterically.

Rome, May 13, 2099 AD

The lines were very long, and the throngs waited patiently in the summer heat for a chance to see Contradeum's body. All who walked by his glass sarcophagus commented on how wonderfully they had cleaned his body and clothed it for burial. The sarcophagus was completely transparent and surrounded by black roses. His body lay on a bed of white silk; they had dressed him in blazing white satin. They left his crown on his head and the scepter of his office in his hands. He was the king the traitor betrayed, the savior who died, and the hope of the world sacrificed for the many.

Every hour, a priestess of the Mother Goddess would take off her vestments and lay down with Contradeum, naked, as if to warm the body laying in the coldness of death. The men and women walking by to pay their respects nodded in approval.

Later, all the priestesses who did this last service to the Supreme Global Leader would take part in a globally televised orgy with those mourners who showed the most grief while passing through the rotunda. After passing by the body, mourners signed up for the orgy and the organizers handed them thirty grams of marijuana to smother their pain and to give them the opportunity to enjoy their day.

Everyone agreed this was a grand way to kick off thirty days of mourning.

Contradeum felt like he had been falling for a hundred years through an inky blackness so thick it was like oil passing over his skin. As he fell, Contradeum's body solidified around him and grew strong. He saw a light in the distance, towards which he was dropping incredibly fast. Before he could react, he slammed into the rocks at the base of a circle of torches, shattering eight ribs in his chest and his left collarbone. Contradeum screamed in agony and choked off the scream when the pain of taking a breath burned through his torso.

Tears flooded his eyes as he encountered pain more severe than anything he felt before. He heard a gravelly laugh and looked up to see a massive angel carrying a large gray chain walking towards him.

"What do we have here?" G'shnet'el said. "Could this be His Magnificence, the Supreme Global Leader of Earth?" He sketched a sardonic bow. "Truly you honor us to have such eminence grace our presence."

G'shnet'el walked to a wood fire burning within a circle of rocks into which he had thrust iron rods. He pulled one rod out of the fire, the tip of which glowed red hot. The foul angel walked over to where Contradeum lay moaning and jabbed the rod into Contradeum's upper thigh. Malchus screamed again as his flesh burned and sizzled under the hot metal, then wrapped his arms around his ribs to stop the pain.

"Why are you doing this? We serve the same master. I sold my soul to him decades ago for his promise I'd rule the world with him. He promised!"

Satan wandered into the circle of light with a wide smile splitting his face. He gave G'shnet'el a hearty nod and turned his attention to the man laying in front of them, whose eternal body rapidly repaired itself.

"Do you feel deceived, Malchus? Did I ever give you the impression you were dealing with anyone other than the Prince of Evil? When did I give you the belief you could trust the truthfulness of my words? Had you ever read the Good Book, you would've seen my enemies call me the Prince of Lies. You deceived yourself by ever believing you could rely on anything coming out of my mouth." Satan laughed, and G'shnet'el joined in.

"Master," Contradeum said, begging, "I've been your faithful servant. All I want to do is reign with you. I'll do anything for you. Allow me to show my love to you. Tell me what I can do."

The smile on Satan's face was diabolical.

"I'm so impressed by your desire to serve me. Do you truly wish to show your devotion to me?"

"I am," Contradeum said, eagerness in his voice. "I'll do anything."

Satan clapped his hands.

"Excellent! Go to the fire and take out one of the iron rods that has been sitting in there for many hours."

Contradeum scrambled to his feet and ran over to the fire, pulling a rod out from the hot coals.

"Now," Satan said, his smile widening. "Press the hot tip against your stomach until I tell you to stop."

Contradeum's face took on a distinctly sickly look.

"Master, this will cause me great agony."

"I thought you wanted to rule with me?" Satan said, mocking him. "How can I trust you if you're not prepared to suffer for me as I have suffered for you?"

A man in his rational mind might have asked how Satan ever suffered for him. Contradeum was far from thinking intelligently. Only minutes ago, he was basking in the glory of being crowned the king of the world. Now he stood in a place surrounded by the darkest depths of night, being tormented by the god he worshipped.

His forehead broke into a sweat as agony shredded the fine edges of his sanity. Contradeum swept his gaze back and forth between Satan and G'shnet'el, both of whom obviously enjoyed his pain. G'shnet'el's arm suddenly moved and razor-sharp metals embedded in the tips of his whip sliced into Contradeum's chest and ripped the flesh away. Contradeum screamed.

"Do as the Master commands, or I'll do it for you after I've flayed every ounce of flesh from your skeleton."

Contradeum stared around the Abyss frantically, looking for an escape, looking for a rescue, but there was none.

Pain.

This was his new life. His eternity. Pain.

He swallowed hard and then screamed as he pressed the hot tip of the iron into his own flesh.

Jez Brandt paced the atrium of the vestibule where Contradeum's body lay in state. This was the tricky part. She had subtly leaked information to the media, suggesting something miraculous was going to happen today. Social media was buzzing with understated tidbits her team had been posting in the last two days. She could feel herself sweating through her blouse underneath her red velvet jacket. Jez rubbed her palms together and tried to calm herself.

Today was the riskiest day of the entire operation. The Master assured her many times this would work without deception, CGI, or any other form of graphic manipulation.

"This is something more in the domain of magic than science," he said. "Just as you've had faith in me throughout your life, you must have faith in me now. Did I not give you a highly successful political life? Did I not make you rich beyond your parents' dreams? You have done well by me, Jezebel Brandt. Be patient."

She snorted. Well, and good for him to say that. She was the face of the Government of Democracy right now. If things spun sideways, there would be a brutal internal fight for control of the world. Jez knew the military barely tolerated her.

She knew she didn't have their support. She could be the next one lying on the ground with blood pouring out of her chest. Jez shuddered. Unlike Contradeum, she had full knowledge of whom she served. She needed to extend her life on Earth for as long as possible and make her master as happy as possible, so things would go well for her in the afterlife.

It was time. The sun peeked in through a window from which the building attendants had removed the shutters and slowly traced its way across the atrium floor. Her team established a small perimeter around the sarcophagus, and Contradeum's body was all alone within it. She instructed the removal of the transparent cover of the sarcophagus to expose the body to the air.

As soon as the sunlight touched the feet of the sarcophagus, an unworldly wail reverberated through the vestibule. It was enough to make every hair on her body stand up. The harmonic continued and grew louder as the sun crept its way up the sarcophagus towards the head.

A group of priestesses came into the atrium singing an aria in high soprano voices. They dressed in long white gowns, but they had handcuffs on their wrists attached by chains to metal collars around their necks. Each priestess chained herself to the neck collar of the woman in front of her and each one of the thirteen carried a long white tapered lit candle. It was a beautiful symbolism of their devotion, Jez thought. It wasn't for Jez Brandt personally; she was never the submissive type.

The priestesses surrounded the sarcophagus just

as the sunbeam fell on Contradeum's face. They swayed and their aria turned into a low, guttural moan. Suddenly, they gasped and fell silent. Everyone in the atrium heard a deep draw of breath. Then another. After a few seconds, Contradeum bolted upright and opened his eyes. Everyone in the vestibule screamed or gasped and fell to the ground, shocked and awed.

After three days, Contradeum had risen from the dead!

Except it wasn't Contradeum. Oh yes, the body was that of the former Supreme Global Leader, but the essences of what made someone a person, the spirit and the soul, had long passed from the flesh. As the sunlight was playing its way across the sarcophagus, Satan had stood in Inter-Dimensional Space over Contradeum's body. When it was time, he leaned over and breathed into Contradeum's nostrils in a mockery of what God did to place His spirit into Adam. From Satan's breath, his very essence flowed into the body and took possession of the corpse that had once been Malchus Contradeum.

Satan inserted his ethereal body into his former servant's physical one with great care. It was a difficult and tricky process. He had to assume possession of every cell. Until this day, he didn't know how to create life from death. He had to grovel before God the Father for the knowledge, which angered him. His humiliation was worth it, though; soon he would rule the earth in a physical body and finally become the only worshipped god on the planet.

Once inside, he used the technique taught to him

by God to repair any cells, flesh, or tissue that had degenerated in the three days since Contradeum's death. He reconnected all synapses in the brain and made them viable. Finally, he enervated the heart to start it beating and drew his first breath as a human being.

The world would now glorify him as their messiah and their living god.

The Antichrist leveraged his body out of the sarcophagus and spread his arms wide before the frightened people scrabbling about on the floor and groaning their fear.

"People of the world, be at peace. Fear not. I died and now I have risen. Look at me. Come and touch my flesh. Feel the warmth of my skin. I died as a human being. I have risen as your god."

Jez could barely contain her joy. She walked over as slowly as she could, making sure the media focused their cameras on her. She prostrated herself before the Antichrist and pressed her forehead to the floor.

"Master, I acknowledge you as my god and I worship you as the savior of the world. Please bless me and let me serve you to the end of my life."

The Antichrist beamed.

"My good and faithful servant, come and kneel behind me. I accept you as my acolyte and I look forward to your worship. I have come so that you could revere me, honor me, and serve me as I deserve."

Jez knew her master now lived in the body of Malchus Contradeum. Power radiated from him, and his attractiveness was extremely seductive. Just looking at him made her weak in the knees. The others in the building felt the same way. Slowly, they came up to the Antichrist, their mouths open in disbelief. He grasped their arms, smiling benevolently, and they all fell to his feet, worshiping him. He had an aura of power so profound it even affected everyone watching on their holos at home.

Lamek Davis couldn't tear his eyes off the screen. He and Sully had dissected from every angle the knife thrust killing Contradeum and agreed it was a perfect kill stroke. The knife slid into the center of Contradeum's heart. When Rozinski fell, he deliberately tore the knife sideways, ripping the heart open in the chest wall. To see the man standing, breathing, and greeting people after lying dead for three days was beyond belief.

"Can you feel it?" Heather whispered. Her eyes were wide and her skin looked flushed.

"I can," Jeannie said, the words cloaked with awe.

"Feel what? I felt nothing," Sully said. "What am I supposed to feel?"

"The charisma," his wife said. "It's oozing out of him. I can feel it from here. He's incredible!"

Sully snorted.

"After laying dead for three days, I bet it's not the only thing oozing out of him."

Lamek laughed out loud as the women glared at Sully.

"You two need to get a grip. Are we forgetting who this man is? According to the Dark Web, Contradeum is now the Antichrist. Do you know what the Antichrist is? He's Satan inhabiting the body of a man who Rozinski killed with a knife and Satan resurrected back to life. Instead of drooling over him, check your insurance policies. This is not good."

Heather glared at him.

"You're disgusting. I'm not talking about bedding him. I'm just saying he has an incredibly powerful aura, and I can see how someone could get drawn into it."

"Just be careful you're not," Davis snapped. "The world is going to burn because of this guy and he's going to take as many people down with him as possible."

Sully was looking at him oddly.

"What kind of stuff have you been reading on the Dark Web?" he said.

Davis bit the inside of his lip, and Heather cast a worried glance at him. They had given their souls to Jesus Christ, which was now the equivalent of a death sentence. Neither of them had discussed their faith in Jesus with the Sullivans because they didn't know where their friends stood in the spiritual realm. Heather slightly jerked her head back and forth, but Davis ignored it. Judging by what he had just seen on the holo, there were no more tomorrows in which to have this talk.

"I've been reading things. They make sense and explain everything happening so far. The things to happen now are going to make what we've been through look like a birthday party for three-year-olds. It's kinda hard to talk about."

"Is it classified?" Jeannie said.

Sullivan smiled at her.

"Not if it's on the Dark Web, honey." He side-glanced at Davis. "But it's dangerous to look at anything on the Dark Web. I'm going to need to know you're talking about, Mick."

Davis said nothing for a few minutes, rubbing the back of his left hand with his right. An ugly scar reminded him of how close he came to losing his hand. Heck, he came close to losing his life.

"Do you remember the time in Africa, Sully?"

Sully's eyebrows raised.

"You mean the time in Africa when you saved my life with a bullet-shattered left hand, and you took two rounds in your back dragging me to the helo? Is that the time you mean? This must be seriously messed up crap if you find it necessary to remind me what a hero you were."

Davis cocked his head to one side.

"What I'm about to tell you could cost me my life. Heather's, too. Jeannie, I don't know you, but I know Sully. He wouldn't marry a woman who wasn't worthy of him in every sense of the word. So, I'm going to trust both of you with this." He paused. "I'm a Christian, Sully. I've been reading commentaries on the Dark Web authored by Christians who are trying to focus people on what's coming next by reviewing biblical prophecy."

"Me, too. I'm a Christian," Heather chimed in, defiance in her voice.

Jeannie laughed softly, while Sully just looked relieved.

"*Chica*, my husband and I became Christ followers on the night nukes rained down from the sky. My parents were devout Roman Catholics. Even after they disappeared during the Second Cataclysm, I refused to believe the events of the Bible were coming true. I had spent so many years denying God in my life, it was hard to see Him working right in front of my eyes."

"But when the bombs fell," her eyes welled up with tears. "When the bombs fell, I ran to Jesus like he was my Papa. Michael was harder to convince, but we had little to do in our shelter while we waited for word whether it was safe to rejoin the world. I had a Bible my Mama gave me and we started reading it together. When we finished it, we both committed our lives to Jesus and asked for His forgiveness. Mick, you're singing to the choir."

Davis blew a big gust of air out of his lungs.

"Thank God! I had no idea how I was going to bring this up. Hey!"

Davis rubbed the back of his head where Sully had slapped him.

"That hurt!"

"You deserved it, you dumb SOB. I'm angry you'd think I'd turn a Brother into the authorities for any reason, even if I wasn't a believer. We might never agree on anything again for the rest of our lives, but I'd still always have your six. Jerk."

Davis rubbed the back of his head ruefully.

"I'll remember this lesson for a while. What did you hit me with, a wrench?"

They came in droves. In streams. Dignitaries, politicians, and celebrities. He was a bright star, shining in the gray skies of endless fog and rain. They orbited around him like asteroids swinging around the sun. His aura consumed them and flooded their senses, overpowering their sensibilities. It wasn't rational, but everyone who left his presence felt like they met God.

He didn't woo them with words or promises; he fed off the darkness in their souls like a vampire, leaving them weak and light-headed and giggly. Five minutes was all he needed to turn a hard-hearted cynic into an ardent supporter.

Word came to him after Israel finished building the Temple in Jerusalem; they wanted him present during the opening ceremonies. It was recognition for his negotiation of permanent peace in the Middle East. Perfect. He could make a statement cementing his status and affirming his destiny in a place where the entire world would see it and know the truth.

"Jez."

The door to his private study swung open and Jezebel Brandt crawled into the room on her hands and knees, wearing very little clothing. He had permanently affixed a solid gold slave collar to her neck and called her his slave-bride. Her mind was in a state of permanent glow, a constant erogenous high. A week ago, she would have flown into a rage if he tried to put her in a submissive costume and treated her like a slave. That personality, that Jez Brandt, no longer existed. She no longer knew her own thoughts and didn't care. She existed to serve him, her Master, and it was enough.

"Yes, my Master."

"See to it the C5 Galaxy carrying the special item precedes us to Jerusalem. We must put it in place before I arrive."

Jez bowed her head and put her palms together.

"I will, my Master. Is there anything else I can do for you? Anything at all?"

He gifted her with his benevolent smile, and the warmth of it offered to melt her into the thick carpet.

"I know what you ask, Jez, but it's not possible. There is no possibility of a physical relationship with you. It's not personal. I must not have congress with any woman. You must be content with worshiping me from afar."

Disappointed, Jez pushed her forehead into the carpet.

"Your will be done, my Master."

The Antichrist smiled as she left the room. Those words were the strongest narcotic in the universe. 'Your will be done.' Soon, every tongue on Earth would speak those words and worship him from their hearts.

In the transformation into human flesh, he seemed to have forgotten some very important details. He forgot the clock, ticking, in the hallowed halls of Heaven, limiting his time as a being worshipped by others. The millennia of planning and preparation had come to such glorious fruition; the prospect of an ending was completely outside reality. Earth was finally his and its people would only know *him* forevermore as their god.

Their arrival in Jerusalem was the epitome of pomp and circumstance. The host nation treated them to the largest gun salute in the history of humankind. Besides food, Israel grew flowers, and it seemed the people threw every exotic bloom cultivated in the country at his sandaled feet as he walked off the plane to his motorcade. Others waved palm branches as he walked to his electric limousine.

When they arrived at the Temple Mount, security had to fight to keep the enormous crowd away from the Most Important Person. The crowd chanted his name and sang songs to his glory. It swelled his chest and fed fuel to his pride. This is what he waited for. This is what he deserved.

The Temple building faced eastward. It was oblong and comprised three rooms of equal width: the porch, or vestibule; the main room of religious service, or Holy Place; and the Holy of Holies, the sacred room in which the Ark of the Covenant historically rested. A storehouse surrounded the Temple except on its front side.

The Temple had five altars: one at the entrance of the Holy of Holies, two others within the building, a large bronze one before the porch, and a large, tiered altar in the courtyard. The Jewish people considered the Holy of Holies, the innermost sanctuary, as the dwelling place of the Divine Presence, the Shekinah. Only the High Priest could enter it, and only on the Day of Atonement, or Yom Kippur.

He Who Was Not Contradeum entered the Temple, and the media sensed something was amiss. The Antichrist didn't stop in the outer courtyards where gathered the gentiles and tourists. He and his entourage walked straight through into the inner courtyard. Someone should have protested. Someone should have stopped him. Yet no one stood in his way as he walked to the floor-to-ceiling curtain barring entrance to the Holy of Holies.

When the Antichrist arrived at the entrance to the

Holy of Holies, he turned to face the crowd following him.

"People of Israel and people of the world. Legend has it God made His presence known to you through pillars of fire or clouds or a wooden ark. Who among you has seen Him? We have read accounts of Moses meeting with God, but God hid His face from Moses. What kind of God hides His face from the people who worship Him, sacrifice to Him, and pray to Him?"

The Antichrist reached down and ran his fingers through the hair of a young girl before accepting a bouquet from her.

"When in all of history did you see God touch a girl's hair and take flowers from her hand? I tell you the truth, it never happened. It never happened because I only arrived this day."

A startled murmur rumbled through the crowd.

"Every religion has its prophecies regarding the coming of the messiah. Many believed the messiah's enemies would kill him and three days later, he would rise from the dead. Did you not watch a knife stab through my heart? You saw, did you not, as the paramedics proclaimed me dead? Will you ever forget where you were when I sat up in my sarcophagus and invited people to touch my living flesh? You have been waiting for me and I am here to accept your worship."

He reached his right hand to the cloudless blue sky and turned his wrist. Lightning ripped down and tore the curtain to the Holy of Holies in two. Many of the people screamed and pushed away, but his voice mesmerized them into immobility.

"Fear not! We need the screen no longer. The curtain separated you from the truth of what religious leaders have hidden from you for centuries, waiting for this day. Behold, the truth!"

The Antichrist's acolytes pulled away the curtain, and the collective gasp from those assembled could be heard a block away. Standing in the middle of the Holy of Holies was a twenty-foot-high statue of Malchus Contradeum. It was perfect in every detail, including coloration. The Antichrist took a wooden staff from one priest, standing and gaping in disbelief at the statue.

"People of the world, we all know how compelling holograms can be. They are so lifelike, so real. But can they do this?"

He took a mighty swing and shattered the staff against the shinbone of the statue. People fell silent, completely powerless to work against the spell he spun with his voice and his charisma.

He raised his arms.

"I am your god. You will worship me. You will have no other god but me. Worshiping other gods will cause your deaths; therefore, disobey me at your peril. I am a jealous god, and I will tolerate no one who will not worship me. Soon, all of you will accept a small tattoo on your temple or wrist that will identify you to everyone else as my faithful servant. Do not resist taking this tattoo. It is a symbol of your love for me and a guarantee of protection. Without it, you cannot buy or sell goods. Restaurants, supermarkets, and all vendors will not sell to you. Refuse my mark and you will surely die."

One priest had enough.

"No! This is not right! This is an abomination and a desolation of all our beliefs and our entire history! You have desecrated this temple by your blasphemy, and I will not have it. Begone, evil one."

Human resiliency is astonishing. The mind can accept almost anything and achieve results many would consider miraculous. It can also shut down in the face of something so overwhelming, the nature of it defies reason and understanding.

The statue came to life.

"How dare you question me, your god," it said in a deep, rumbling voice. The statue reached up to the sky and turned his massive hand. The priest screamed as a stream of fire streaked down from the sky and torched him.

Everyone in the crowd fainted. They all fell unconscious at the feet of the Antichrist and his statue. A few minutes later, each awoke to the grizzly scene of the blackened body of the priest lying in the open hand of the statue, blood dripping between the statue's fingers.

The Antichrist smiled.

"It was so kind of this rebellious man to offer the first blood sacrifice to me. He has established how you shall make offerings to me, your god. You shall bring anyone who worships a god other than me to this place and cut their throats in the hands of my statue. Sacrifice anyone who breaks my laws on this altar. If you have a grievance with your neighbor, come to this place; my statue will select the offender and end the grievance. Worship me and obey me and you will live in peace and prosperity. I am a kind and generous god who will make each and everyone of you rich and will bring peace to this world. All you have to do is offer me your souls."

The assembled crowd sank to their knees and prostrated themselves before him. Jez softly began a chant of 'Messiah, Messiah, Messiah' and the crowd eagerly followed her. The Antichrist beamed. He dipped his hands in the blood of the dead priest and started walking through the assembly.

The Antichrist asked each person present if they would give their soul to him and all said they would. He drew a vertical line of blood on the forehead of each of his newly gained disciples. Someone started singing a song of praise to him and he gesticulated with his arms as if he were a director and they were his choir. Fear gave way to adulation and the more they worshipped him, the more he poured out his mesmerizing essence into the gathering.

When he marked each person, the Man Who Was Not Contradeum, the Antichrist, walked back to the Holy of Holies and stood in front of his statue. He raised his hands, and the crowd fell silent.

"I declare the God of the Bible to be a fraud and anyone who follows Him is an intolerant fool."

There was a subdued gasp.

"I pronounce the God of the Torah to be a hoax."

The people were eyeing the statue, which had glared at some people who had gasped. They firmly pressed their lips together, mindful of the cost of disrespect.

"I proclaim the God of the Koran to be a deception and not worthy of worship."

The Antichrist insulted every religion, declaring their gods to be frauds. When he finished, he began calling those deities every sickening, despicable name of which he could think. It was blasphemy to the millionth power and shocking in its vile nature.

In one scant hour, all the world's religions fell.

The shockwave from the Antichrist's vilification of the world's religions ripped around the entire globe. Riots erupted in the surviving cities. Police and military locked themselves within their stations and barracks and refused to go out into the streets. People raped and killed and stole and murdered and satisfied every evil desire laws had shuttered in their hearts. News drones stayed hundreds of feet above the streets to avoid being destroyed and the holo images sent into the airwaves were the wickedest anyone had ever seen.

Mick, Heather, Jeannie, and Sully sat in Mick's quarters, numbly watching the Antichrist's usurpation of the world's religions and the destruction unleashed by his declaration. His statement rendered invalid every law based on some form of religious teaching and the people embraced the new destructive chaos passionately.

"Is this the end of the world?" Jeannie said, tears streaming down her face.

Davis shook his head.

"No, we're only halfway through the Tribulation. According to what I've been reading, the next three-and-a-half years are going to be hell on earth. It will be the stuff of nightmares."

"What kind of nightmares?" Jeannie asked.

Davis retrieved his personal device and opened a file.

"For starters, listen to this. I think this is coming

next:

> I looked when He broke the sixth seal, and
> there was a great earthquake; and the sun
> became black as sackcloth made of hair, and
> the whole moon became like blood; and the
> stars of the sky fell to the earth, as a fig tree
> casts its unripe figs when shaken by a great
> wind. The sky was split apart like a scroll
> when it is rolled up, and every mountain and
> island were moved out of their places. Then
> the kings of the earth and the great men and
> the commanders and the rich and the strong
> and every slave and free man hid themselves
> in the caves and among the rocks of the
> mountains; and they said to the mountains
> and to the rocks, 'Fall on us and hide us from
> the presence of Him who sits on the throne,
> and from the wrath of the Lamb; for the
> great day of their wrath has come, and who
> is able to stand?"

Davis searched the faces of his friends.

"What I just read to you is from the Holy Bible,
in the book called Revelation. Chapter six, verses
twelve through seventeen, if you want to read it
yourself. We may not understand all of it yet, but you
can count on one thing. We're in for it now."

Sully took a deep breath.

"So, what's our exit strategy?"

Davis looked at him dumbly.

"What do you mean?"

Sully reached out and squeezed Davis's shoulder.

"Come on, Mick. How long have we known each
other? No matter who was Team Leader, we always

knew we could count on you to pull us out when things got FUBAR. Well, it sure looks to me like things are FUBAR now." He gestured to the three-dimensional holographic display hovering at the front of the room. "It won't take long for this mess to come here. We need a plan, Master Chief, and we need it now."

Davis shook his head glumly.

"I don't know what to tell you, Sully. Where do we go? This world has become a microscopic place. What's happening out there is going to come here, probably sooner than later. I'm open to suggestions."

"Why do we have to go to a place?" Heather asked in a timid voice.

"Explain," Jeannie said.

Heather opened her palms where two God Coins glistened under the ambient light.

"We could go to a when and leave all this behind."

Davis could see Jeannie and Sully perk up. He hated to be the bucket of ice water.

"We pulled up the Time Scepter, Heather. The quantum bubble back to Mesopotamia is gone. We couldn't go back if we wanted to."

Heather pursed her lips.

"Who brought the Scepter back, Mick?"

He frowned.

"I thought Coventry brought it back."

"Coventry had a lot of things on the go, and I offered to carry the Time Scepter. When she handed me the case, I removed the Scepter and hid it in the canyon wall, and covered with MetaMaterials. I couldn't bear the thought of never seeing our

Mesopotamian family again. The case I came back with is empty. I carried it to the storage room. No one was going to stop the last Programmer from performing her duties. That's how I got away with locking up an empty case."

Jeannie's eyes lit up.

"Then we're safe? We can escape all this by going back in time?"

"Whoa," Davis said, holding up his hands. "Let's rein this one in for a second. If we go back and stay there, we could cause a temporal loop or a rift. We would take ourselves out of this timeline completely. Can you tell us, Heather, we won't cause a time disruption by doing that?"

Wu shook her head, frustrated.

"I don't know, Mick. Look at all the garbage the terrorists pulled by going back and forth to the same IP without causing a temporal distortion. It's like the timeline is a living thing. If you do something like what Dr. Weinstein tried to pull, it pushes back. We can't go into the future. How do we know the four of us didn't disappear forever tonight?"

Sully rubbed his forehead.

"So if we escape to the past, we could fulfill our present destiny of disappearing from the timeline by escaping to the past? How does that make sense? Isn't it the very definition of a temporal loop? I'm not saying we shouldn't do it, but we need to think this through carefully."

There was a knock on the door, and Davis held up one finger.

"Hold that thought," he said as he crossed over to the entryway. His quarters didn't have the fancy door access system once enjoyed by the Programmers. It was just a door and didn't show him who was on the other side. Not that it mattered. He no longer had enemies in the present.

Davis swung the door open and froze. Erasmus Hart stood on the other side of the doorway with a large caliber handgun pointed two feet away from Davis's head. Beads of sweat formed above Hart's eyebrows and he looked stressed. The hand holding the gun trembled slightly, but Hart kept the muzzle locked on Davis's forehead. Hart's eyes were wild and kept darting from the Master Chief's face to over his shoulder into the quarters. When he spoke, his voice shook.

"I'm here to ask you a question, Mr. Davis. Your life depends on the answer. Are you a Christian?"

CHAPTER THE THIRTEENTH: ARMAGEDDON

Spes Deserit, in the Year of Our Fight 2375
Mission Day 45

They had waited. In silence, they waited, having placed their trust in the ones who would go before them and stand in harm's way. It was astonishing how quickly they gathered and how quietly they stayed. The whispers had flown from mouth-to-mouth like swallows darting about in the crisp air of Spring. Something was happening, but all they could offer was their silent support. So, they lined up and waited.

When Tul'ran, Erianne, and Darian walked up the ramp from the conveyance station, they were stunned to see a solid row of people on either side of them, not moving or speaking, just standing and watching. Even as they walked past the People, no one made a sound. The People simply fell in behind them, like a wedding procession, as the path wound its way to the Hall.

Darian took two long strides in front of Tul'ran and Erianne, and they closed in ranks behind her. Her body language made her intentions clear. She would go before the Empress and stand judgment without the aid of Her Imperial Majesty's Warriors.

Tul'ran found his heart swelling. Her courage once more reminded him of his beloved sister, Evann'ya. She would've been like this, striding forward with purpose, head held high and determined to meet her fate with valor. He hadn't seen these parts of Darian's personality in the past; they were a pleasant surprise and a painful reminder of what he had lost those many years ago.

At the end of the path, Gwynver'insa stood as tall as her five-foot two-inch body permitted. She wore the long red dress of her station. The sleeveless gown hugged her frame from her neck to her ankles. Her attendants clipped a train to her shoulders on either side of her neck and played it out fifteen feet behind her. The delicate interwoven gold crown sat high on her head. There was no question of her position; here was the Empress waiting for her warriors to return from their investigation of the disturbance that brought the People from their labors to the conveyance station.

Johan stood behind and to the right of Gwynver'insa; his face was impassive, but his cheekbones flushed. Darian gave no sign she noticed him. She walked up and stopped ten feet shy of where Gwynver'insa stood. She dropped into a deep, respectful curtsy. Though it must have been awkward, she stayed in the curtsy as she spoke.

"Your Imperial Majesty, I have come in peace to beg your forgiveness. I've sinned against you by thought, word, and deed. I betrayed you to evil and exposed you to harm through my selfish desires. When last I saw you, I brought your enemy to your door. In doing so, I placed you in grave jeopardy. I have seen the error of my ways and the destructiveness of my path. El Shaddai has heard my confession and granted me absolution, but yet I come before you, for it was also you whom I wronged. I beg for your mercy and for my life. Should you not accept my plea for mercy, then I beg you to strike quickly and end my life."

Gwynver'insa glided to where Darian stood. She reached down with her right hand and lifted Darian's chin before grasping her shoulders and encouraging her to stand. The Empress stared into Darian's eyes for a moment, before extending up and placing her hands on either side of the taller woman's face. Gwynver'insa pulled Darian's head down and kissed her on the forehead.

"Sister," she said, her words wrapped with awe. "I See you. Where once there was nothing but darkness, now your soul glows with white fire. Yahweh's spirit flows in and around you like a silken cloak. Who am I to deny Yahweh His judgment? As He forgave you for your wrongdoings, so do I forgive you."

Gwynver'insa took Darian's arm and turned her toward the People, as a tear leaked down Darian's cheek.

"Hearken to my words. Here is Lady Darian Angelica Ostrowski, beloved of me and the Lord your God. As you love me, so shall you love her and treat her as if she were my very sister."

Tul'ran flinched involuntarily as the People behind him roared their approval, and he gave Erianne a sheepish grin when she cocked an eyebrow at him.

"Whereof so skittish, milord husband? No danger lurks as far as the eye can see."

He grinned.

"Forgive me, my love. So caught up was I in Gwynver'insa's gracious greeting, the exuberance of the People nigh made me fill my trousers."

Erianne giggled and looped her left arm within his right elbow.

"Grateful I am, you have more control of your bowels than your words suggest. Look now, this should be interesting. Darian goes to renew her acquaintance with Johan."

Gwynver'insa had pulled Darian's arm under her elbow and led her to where Johan stood, his body rigid. They stopped short and Gwynver'insa turned to face Darian.

"Long have I known of Johan's interest in you, Lady Darian. As you may have already heard, he and I have begun a dance which may lead to the melding of our lives before an altar. These are the things I know. In the order of things I do not know is whether you have a claim to his heart. If you do, will you relinquish it, sister?"

Darian smiled and, to the shock of everyone present, leaned down to give Gwynver'insa a kiss on the lips.

"Sister, not only do I relinquish any claim Johan may have had on my heart, but it would also delight me to the end of my life if you would allow me to stand with you as you drag Lord Johan to the altar."

Johan's face became redder.

"Hi, Darian. I don't think anyone is talking about marriage just yet. It's nice to see you again."

Darian grinned at him and addressed Gwynver'insa.

"Your Majesty, it strikes me you have not apprised your consort of the entirety of his duties. If it is your desire, it would please me to brief him."

Gwynver'insa giggled and gave Darian a bump with her hip.

"Stop it, sister. See how he blushes! I fear you will cause him to collapse. Come, Johan, take my other arm and put your anxieties to rest. We shall dine tonight at peace and partake in wine." She gave Darian a coy side glance. "Then I will tell you how you are to propose marriage to me."

She and Darian couldn't stop giggling as they led the hapless physicist from the Hall.

The chef outdid himself at the banquet that night. The food was bountiful, and the People oohed and aahed over each course. Gwynver'insa sat in the center of the table on the dais, Johan seated to her right in his usual place of honor and Darian on her left. She entertained Darian with stories of what she missed after they fled the House, while Tul'ran and Erianne enjoyed the rare solitude of each other's company at the end of the table.

Then the Empress stood, and the Hall fell silent. "Rise."

The People stood as one. Gwynver'insa raised her arms, palms faced to the sky.

"Hearken, my People, to my words. Bind my words to your memories, for we write a new chapter in our history as I speak. No sooner had the alarm been raised when our steadfast warriors drew their swords and leaped into action. They did not know what waited for them at the trail's end. Did they hesitate in the absence of knowledge of what awaited them? Nay! Did they send another to bait their foe and assess the strength of their enemy before wading into the fray? Nay! Was it necessary for anyone of us to face violence or a threat to our person? Never! Though this action led to the joyous reunification with my sister; their courage drove them to action without consideration of the consequence to their lives or safety."

Gwynver'insa turned to face Tul'ran and Erianne.

"Lord Tul'ran and Lady Erianne, we are in your debt."

The Empress of Spes Deserit executed a deep bow, and the People followed suit. Tul'ran and Erianne goggled at their response and struggled to keep their faces straight.

'Love of my life,' Tul'ran cast into her mind, 'see how they honor us when we rush off and return with the long-lost, without bloodshed. What will they do if we ever fight a battle?'

Erianne stifled a shudder.

'I know not. Let us hope they do not choose to cast us in bronze while we yet draw breath.'

Tul'ran coughed to cover a startled laugh while everyone resumed their seats. He stood up and walked behind the table to lean over and whisper in Gwynver'insa's ear, intent on conveying their desire to not be cast in bronze while they lived. Erianne reached over to take Darian's left hand. Darian looked over and smiled, then saw the seriousness of Erianne's eyes.

"What is it, Erianne?"

"Sister, I must ask you for a heart favor."

Darian's eyes widened, and she matched Erianne's muffled voice.

"For you, anything. What's wrong, sister?"

Erianne glanced over to make sure Tul'ran was still engaged in conversation with Gwynver'insa.

"There is a prophecy uttered by Gwynver'insa's lips that Tul'ran will suffer a horrifying loss. As the prophecy goes, in the rage arising from his grief, he will go out and conquer the world for Gwynver'insa. Only the death of one person could cause him to fly into an anger like that: mine."

Darian tightened her grip on Erianne's hand.

"No! I refuse to believe it! The Lord wouldn't have brought you here for you to die and leave Tul'ran with a shattered heart."

Erianne shushed her with her left hand.

"Peace, sister. Quietly. I don't think the prophecy specifically points to me. I'm not so arrogant to believe it couldn't. If it does, I want you to make me a promise."

Darian was shaking her head from side to side.

"I don't like this conversation. Not one bit. But, like I said, I'll do anything for you. What do you want me to promise?"

Erianne looked up at her husband, who was laughing boisterously as Gwynver'insa covered her mouth and giggled. She looked back into Darian's eyes.

"I want you to promise me if I die, you'll take care of my husband. When his first wife died, it destroyed him. I don't know how bad it'll break him if he loses me, but I know darkness still clings to his bones like iron. I fear his response more than I fear my death. My biggest fear is he couldn't live without me."

Tears leaked from the corner of Darian's eyes and threatened to spill down her cheeks.

"I promise," she whispered, as she reached over to draw Erianne into a hug. "I'll take care of him. But if you die, I'll bring you back from the dead and kill you myself."

Spes Deserit, in the Year of Our Fight 2375
Mission Day 46

Abaddon knelt before the Holy Spirit, his massive black wings covering his head. He remained in supplication during the night, while he confessed his sins to the Holy Spirit. He finished just as the sky barely lightened with dawn. The Holy Spirit peered down through the grimy environment to the massive doors leading to the Judgment Seat.

"It is time. Beat your wings, Abaddon. Move the filth obscuring the sun from those doors so the People will once more see the morning sun. Keep the rays shining upon those doors until we leave this place for the last time."

"By your command."

Beating his wings wouldn't have achieved the desired result on their own, but his wings imposed gravity upon the detritus surrounding him and removed it from the sun's path.

For the first time in three hundred years, the sun shone on the doors to the Hall of the Ancestors in the City of Kai'ku.

Tul'ran and Erianne heard the screams long before they saw the two people racing down the path toward them.

"Now what?" Erianne said, her voice cross. She had had too much wine to drink the night before and, not being used to the consumption of alcohol, was feeling the aftereffects.

"I know not," Tul'ran said, "but their faces suggest joy and excitement, not fear. They are so overcome with their news, they forget themselves and tug on the hands of their Empress like school children. We to her side."

Just as Tul'ran and Erianne came up behind Gwynver'insa, Darian came into the room from the other entrance.

"What's going on?" she asked Erianne.

"Don't know. I think we're about to find out."

Gwynver'insa turned to them, her face filled with wonder.

"The sun has reappeared in our sky for the first time in hundreds of years. Come, let us go see this miracle."

The Empress lunged into a sprint towards the ramp, running up to the surface. Erianne rolled her eyes and she, Tul'ran and Darian, raced after the impulsive Regent. The ramp spiraled upwards and ended before two of the largest doors Tul'ran had ever seen. He didn't know how they opened because there appeared to be no mechanism controlling the doors. He need not have worried. Gwynver'insa made a casual, imperious gesture, and the massive doors groaned and shuddered as they opened outwards. She and Tul'ran ran through and stopped, the brightness of the sun momentarily blinding them.

It was almost as if they were in the eye of a hurricane. All around them swirled the bleak darkness of the airborne trash, while in the center of the miasma, the sun peered down through a beautiful blue sky. Gwynver'insa was twirling on the empty street, her face raised to the sun as she giggled. Tul'ran smiled. If ever there was someone who defied a label, it was their Empress.

One never knew when the regal leader would transform into a joyous girl before changing into a prophet of doom.

The android didn't feel emotions, even though it looked convincingly human. If he could feel emotions, it would have been satisfaction. It had waited for hours for the opportunity to satisfy its directive. The target now stood before him; with the coveted sword strapped to his waist. The android dashed forward, its infrared vision finding the target's heart through the leather armor.

This kill would be too easy.

It embarrassed her how puffed out the run up the spiral ramp had made her. In the past, she would have left everyone else behind her without a significant rise in her heart rate. It looked like cardio training was in order.

She just cleared the doorway when a movement caught the corner of her eye. In that instance, time slowed to a crawl. She saw the android moving forward quickly and silently, raising an ugly-looking spear pointed at Tul'ran's back. Tul'ran didn't see the attack coming. There was no time for thought or consideration of options. She lunged forward and pushed Tul'ran as hard as she could while screaming, "No!"

The spear entering her back was a burning shaft of agony. It thrust past her heart and wedged in her ribs, cutting her left main coronary artery. She sank to her knees while the android jerked at the spear to pull it out of her body. After the head of the spear had passed through her rib cage, it had twisted and was now jammed against her chest wall. She wanted to scream, but the force of the blow had knocked the air out of her lungs. Panicked surged within her mind.

In that instant, she knew. The prophecy was going to come true, after all.

She was going to die.

Tul'ran staggered from the blow at his back, quickly regained his balance, and drew his sword. His reactions were blindingly fast and the first swing of Bloodwing severed the head from the android. The next swing cut off the android's arms.

The last swing severed the torso from the legs. He whirled, looking around for another enemy, but there was none. Then he saw the woman kneeling on the ground with a spear through her back and his heart dove into his mouth. His breath rushed in with a gasp, but he couldn't breathe.

No, not this. Not again. Please, El Shaddai, not this.

Tul'ran took two long steps, turned, and knelt in front of Darian. Her eyes were full of pain, and she struggled to draw breath. Blood covered her right hand where she had touched the tip of the spear protruding from her chest. She looked at Tul'ran, at the horror in his face. She reached out with her hand and pressed it against his cheek, leaving a streak of blood where her fingertips touched. As her hand fell away, a vertical stripe of blood ran from his cheekbone under his left eye to the edge of his mouth.

"Kill them all, dear brother. I love you," she said with a gasp. She looked at Erianne, who had run over to her and kneeled at her side, tears streaming from her eyes. Darian opened her mouth to say it was going to be okay, that she felt no pain, but the words wouldn't come out.

Darian Angelica Ostrowski died.

Or did she? Darian looked down at her body, at her friends who bowed down before her, sobbing, at Gwynver'insa, who had fallen to her knees, her fists clenched, her face to the sky, screaming, and couldn't believe it. Then Jesus stepped up to her right side and E'thriel put his arm around her on her left.

She looked at Jesus, bewildered.

"I'm dead? I'm the one who was supposed to die?"

Jesus smiled at her.

"Your physical body is dead. You saved Tul'ran's life, Darian. Greater love has no one than this: to lay down their life for their friends. I said it thousands of years ago and my disciples faithfully recorded it for the world to read. Your soul lives on for eternity. In the kingdom of Heaven, I will give you a new body, which will be much better than this one. You will never again feel pain, sorrow, or fear. Your eternal body cannot die and even if it were to become injured, you would heal rapidly and without pain. It is more accurate to say you have just been born into your second life."

Darian shook her head from side to side rapidly.

"I don't understand. Did I not just come to accept you as my Lord and Savior? I haven't had an opportunity to do anything with that yet. Jesus, I wanted to tell people about my story, about what you did for me and how you saved my soul. I'm so young. Why did I have to die now?"

Jesus put a hand on her shoulder.

"My Father and I set this moment as the date and time for your death. It would not have mattered whether you were on this planet or on Earth. We noticed when the geneticists manipulated your DNA to imbue certain characteristics in you. Darian, you had the potential to become the most powerful person on Earth. Satan saw this from the beginning, which is why he worked so hard to ravage your life early, to bring you under his dominion, and to suppress you. When you were born, the Father and I could not take a chance you would follow the string of your future that would lead you into dominating the world. For this reason, we set today as the time of your death."

Darian trembled.

"So You destined me to come to this planet in order to be killed?"

Jesus turned her to face Him.

"No! We destined you to die this day, but it need not have been in this way. Your death in this place was just one strand in the millions of futures made by your choices. In another thread, Satan killed you after over exuberantly punishing you. Pluck another thread and you died on a raid in Antiquity. Or you died when an assassin replaced you as the leader of the world. On Spes Deserit, you died as the Catalyst."

Darian looked at E'thriel.

"Did you know? When you pulled me out of the corridor and nursed me back to health, did you know I was going to die today?"

E'thriel swept his head from side to side, his long hair swirling as if he was underwater.

"The Lord sent me to Spes Deserit to collect your soul and escort you to Heaven for judgment. I did not know the exact date and time of your death, nor did I know whether your judgment would keep you in Heaven or send you to Hell. When I saw your choice to pick up the clay bowl as you floated in the place between life and death, I rejoiced. It was then I knew there was a chance yet for you to choose the Lord."

His words shook Darian to her core. She looked at Jesus, her eyes wide.

"It was that close? I was that close to spending eternity in Hell?"

Jesus nodded.

"We tried to give you as many opportunities as possible to accept Me before this date came. The choice you made in your unconscious state opened the door for Me to enter and plead for you one last time. I tell you the truth, Darian; there was much rejoicing in Heaven when you decided on Me. You had devoted yourself to Satan, and many thought you lost to Us forever. Yes, it was that close. It is that close for every human being. No one can say 'I will put off whether to follow Jesus later, when I come to the end of my life' because no one knows when the end of their life will come."

Darian blew a big puff of air through her cheeks. How near she came to an eternity in agony frightened her to the depths of her soul.

"I'm sorry to be so obstinate, but can I ask you one more question?"

Jesus laughed and drew her into a quick hug.

"Of course," He said, after releasing her. "All Our knowledge is now available to you. Ask and We shall answer. Seek and you shall find."

Darian gestured to where Erianne was running her hands over Darian's face, tears streaming from her eyes. Her chest caught a sob as she saw how deeply Erianne was mourning over her death.

"You said I was the Catalyst. What does that mean? How is my death going to push Tul'ran into conquering the world?"

Jesus grimaced.

"Watch, my darling daughter, and you will see. Your death has frozen him in time. Soon, he will make decisions affecting his eternal destiny. In the life of every person there comes a pivotal moment splitting their paths to Us or away from Us. Such trials are necessary, and people enduring such trials shall be acquitted or condemned."

"The trial of Tul'ran az Nostrom has now begun."

Tul'ran stared at Darian's face, but he didn't see her. He was back in Mesopotamia, in his family's courtyard, watching between the slats of the shed as the Gutians raped and murdered his mother and sisters. Evann'ya was staring at the shed, screaming as the barbarians viciously assaulted her body. He could see she was trying hard to not let her attackers know her brother sat trapped inside the wooden structure, but she couldn't tear her eyes away from where he watched. Even in her death, she protected him. She protected her little brother. For the last time, she had saved him.

The rage welled up in him like a tsunami. The hatred of those who would take away from him someone he loved stirred the cold, hard darkness living in his spirit and brought it to a boil. He stood, the bones of the knuckles in his right hand turning white around the hilt of Bloodwing.

The Blade glowed a bright blue and tendrils of the energy of uncreation ascended from its surface. They danced in the air for a moment before turning and plunging into Tul'ran's right arm. The energy coursed through his body, enervating powers the warrior never knew he possessed. It reached his dark eyes, which suddenly blossomed with the same bright blue as Bloodwing the Blade.

Erianne looked at him and gasped. She slowly stood up.

"Milord husband, what's happening?"

He looked at her with those shining blue eyes, but the voice that came out of his mouth carried none of the warmth she associated with her lover and best friend. It was cold, icy cold; the kind of cold layering the depths of space, which never saw the warmth of a star.

"I will kill them all."

A fear-filled resolve lit her eyes.

"Then I will go with you to protect your back."

His face never changed.

"You will not. Take Gwynver'insa below and safeguard her in case they dare to bring arms against the Hall of the Ancestors. Her life has precedence because she is the salvation of this world."

He turned to look at Gwynver'insa, who shriveled under his stare.

"Do you have a conveyance by which I can traverse the surface of this world?"

"I do, Lord Tul'ran," she said, as she bowed her body low to the ground, "but the filth in the skies will not allow the engine to run."

Tul'ran bared his teeth, and the surrounding air turned to ice.

"We will see about that."

Tul'ran looked down at Bloodwing and spoke words in a language none of them could understand. E'thriel could. It was the language of the angels, spoken before Time ran its course in the universe.

A ball of light, about the size of Tul'ran's fist, rose from the Blade and floated in front of his face. Tul'ran spoke to the ball of light in the strange language, and it rose like a helium-filled balloon to the edge of the curtain where the sun shone, and the darkness fought against it.

The ball bobbed innocently in the open sky until it met the edge of the rubbish littering the atmosphere of Spes Deserit. Suddenly, it flared into a sheet of brilliant blue flame extending from the ground into the upper reaches of the stratosphere, moving away from them in all directions at the speed of light. Before they could catch their breath, the brilliant blue sheet was behind them, roaring its defiance against the polluted sky and then burning out in a last explosion of brilliance.

Everywhere, the sky was clean. The sun shone on the dilapidated, burned-out buildings of the city, casting a glare for the first time in hundreds of years on the way the Combatants had ravaged the planet. Even the shadows were more brightly lit that daylight had been on this world.

Tul'ran turned to Gwynver'insa again.

"I have removed the impediment. Bring me the conveyance and get below."

Gwynver'insa bowed deeply and uttered some sharp commands to the People standing near the doors. Tul'ran walked over to the android and picked up its artificial skull. He laid Bloodwing against it and the Blade turned black, with brilliant gold lines on it.

"What does he do?" Gwynver'insa asked Erianne. She was shivering.

Erianne rubbed tears from her face and then put her arms around her Empress.

"I know not, sister. When I studied history on my planet, I remember seeing pictographs of things called computer motherboards. The gold inlay on Bloodwing suggests such a design. The sword is as much a mystery to me as it is to you, Gwyn."

Gwynver'insa pulled out of the hug and tugged at Erianne's arm.

"Whatever he does, it is no longer our concern. Help me gather up Darian and take her inside. We will wash our beloved sister and prepare her body for burial. I am glad you are here, sister, for I could not bear to grieve alone."

Erianne turned on the diminutive woman, her eyes wild.

"My husband goes to war, and I must go with him!"

"No, you must not," Gwynver'insa said, in her strongest command voice. "Look at him, sister. I can feel the presence of your husband within that shell, but the man who examines the head of that villainous device is a berserker. He is about to vent the full extent of his fury upon this world." She shuddered. "If you go with him, you will put yourself in harm's way. He might kill you without meaning to do so. The part of him that is still your husband, the man who loves you, knows this. It is why he ordered you to stay."

Erianne turned to look at Tul'ran, her heart cut with shards of agony. He had the face of a berserker.

Gwynver'insa was right. She no longer recognized the man she loved under the mask of fury.

He was Death, and he was about to ride against the world.

The conveyance was a replica of the train that brought him to the Judgment Seat. Abandoned streets of the global city sped past him in a blur as the conveyance twisted and turned through its desiccated skeleton. The remains were a sad testament to the ravages of war, but Tul'ran felt no emotion other than an all-consuming fury. Never again would these foolish creatures take the life of an innocent. He was Tul'ran the Uncreator, and he would rid the world of the blood shedders and vermin who fought for pleasure.

The conveyance stopped at the Fortress of the Great Sean. Bloodwing had cracked the cryptography protecting the android's software with an ease which would have made the Great Sean weep. Everything known to the Great Sean's AI was now known to Bloodwing. This was the first of twelve people who would realize Tul'ran's wrath before the sun set on this day.

Armageddon had come to Spes Deserit.

Tul'ran raised his voice to the sky and Bloodwing opened a channel so everyone in the world could hear his words.

"Great Sean, I am Tul'ran az Nostrom, the Sword Himself, Prince of Death, He Who Is The Uncreator. You have taken the life of my sister, who did you no harm and offered you no insult. For her murder, I condemn you to death. I give you sixty seconds to plead for mercy from Yahweh and seek His forgiveness, but make no mistake. He will not save you from death. I come as His Judge, and I adjudge that on this day you die."

Sean responded with violence. Machines surrounding the Fortress lunged forward and began pouring energy at him. The bolts simply evaporated without coming close to Tul'ran. He raised Bloodwing and sent a massive shaft of sizzling energy towards the machines, which disintegrated them into nothingness. A tower to Tul'ran's left fired missiles at him. Tul'ran gestured at the tower, negligently, and the tower and its missiles exploded in a shower of blue sparks before evaporating. A cloaked android lunged at him from beneath a pile of rubble; Tul'ran caught him with his left hand, and the energy of uncreation flowing through his veins undid the vile thing with less than a passing thought.

When is a battle nothing more than a rout? When one force is overwhelmingly superior. Nothing on Spes Deserit was superior to the power in the man who had not been born in this world, but would gladly end it.

Within minutes, there were no more war machines anywhere near the Fortress. Tul'ran's blazing azure eyes searched through the Fortress, seeing through layers of structure as if Sean made them of glass, and he gestured again with his left hand. A shocked young man strapped into a monstrous chair suddenly appeared before Tul'ran. He had been called, and the call transported him before the warrior who would end his war.

"Time's up," Tul'ran growled, and he ran Bloodwing through Sean's chest. Sean's mouth gaped open and his face turned white. He struggled to say something, but his body was already dead, and his soul was already in Abaddon's hands. The same Abaddon who counseled him about better ways to make war would escort his soul to the Abyss.

All around the world, Combatants and Victims alike stared with shock at the abruptness of the attack and how quickly the Great Sean fell.

Tul'ran investigated the Fortress with his ethereal vision and Saw the comprehensive collection of vats holding Sean's clones in various stages of creation. Tul'ran pushed his palm towards the Fortress, fingers spread. He hesitated for a moment, setting the parameters of the nothingness to follow, and made a fist.

The Fortress was gone. As easily as the wind moved through the sky, the forces enveloping the body of the Sword Himself cast the obscenely monumental structure into nothingness. The Uncreation was complete. Never again would a Combatant formerly known as Sean inhabit the world. Tul'ran removed Sean's DNA from the gene pool on Spes Deserit as casually as a man picked food from his teeth.

It was time for the second course.

The Great Raylene had not paid attention to the battle against Sean's Fortress. As soon as Tul'ran uttered his global announcement, she mobilized her forces. She had carefully invaded Sean's territory while he prepared to take the Chair. It was against the Rules, but when the Victim's amazing sword came into play, she threw out the Rules. It was everyone for themselves.

She directed her machines to attack the strange warrior from the rear with as much violence as she could muster. She was so confident of the success of her attack she had paid no attention to the screens playing Sean's execution for the world's consumption.

It was a fatal mistake, but few people see those coming.

The Great Rhanda had monitored the Great Raylene's incursion into the Great Sean's territory. While admiring her opponent's temerity, she wasn't about to allow the Great Raylene an advantage. She surreptitiously committed her entire force to a flanking maneuver designed to sweep over whatever of her enemy's forces remained after the stranger defended against her attack.

The Great Rhanda had very little respect for her opponents. To her, they were stumbling blocks to world domination. She had such confidence in her abilities; it didn't concern her that the stranger's power seemed to be immense. He would be so occupied fighting Raylene he wouldn't see her coming.

She was wrong.

Tul'ran grimly cut through the machines arrayed against him, his fury growing with every blue bolt sent to kill him. He was Death. Why did they not fear him? How were they not bowing at his feet, wiping his boots with their tears, and begging for their lives?

It infuriated him they would keep coming, even knowing the inevitability of the outcome. Soon, there would be no more war machines on the ground or in the sky. There was no encompassing gloom in which to hide or use as a cover for an ambush. They were not prepared to fight in the light, and in the light, he destroyed them.

When the last machines faded into oblivion, Tul'ran gestured again. Two shocked young women sat before him, strapped into their combat consoles. He sent a blaze of electricity crashing into their chairs. They screamed their way into death as millions of volts electrocuted them. Two more souls fell into Abaddon's waiting hands.

The bolts of energy followed the wireless connections back to each of the Combatant's fortresses. The bolts flared and what was, now was not. Tul'ran removed their clones from the planet's gene pool as casually as taking a sip of water.

It became quiet.

Tul'ran the Uncreator looked around him at the broken city filling his vision and felt disgust. With his supernatural eyes, he could see how the city covered the planet like a blight, an infestation. There was no value to it. The city could not worship him. Its hollow bones impeded the gathering of the People, who would worship him as their god.

At his command, blue vapors danced on Bloodwing's surface. He carefully set the parameters of his desires. He would make sure his command would affect nothing in which a human lived.

The Uncreator pressed the tip of the Blade into the ground before him. At first, nothing happened. Then the buildings started to shimmer and sway until they faded from existence. The city didn't fall. It simply no longer was. Around the world, except in structures where humans lived, only black dirt remained where buildings, lights, vehicles, and other things once sat. Tul'ran the Uncreator felt satisfaction course through him. Spes Deserit was clean again. Soon, he would remake it in his image.

A gong sounded. A frightened voice resounded in the surrounding air.

"This is the Great Rhalla, speaking to Lord Tul'ran az Nostrom, the Uncreator. I surrender. I will send you the coordinates to my fortress. You may destroy my machines, my clones, and my fortress. I beg you to spare my life for the Judgment Seat."

One by one, the remaining eight Combatants announced their surrender on the same terms. Tul'ran pondered it. Why should he not kill them all? What were they to him? He vaguely remembered their arrogant continuation of a meaningless war cost him the life of his sister. She said, 'Kill them all.' Should her brother deny his beloved sister's last wish?

He would save the other humans to be his slaves, but the nine seeking his mercy would surely die.

"Who are you?"

The Voice in his mind startled him. He knew the Voice. He had known it all his life. There was a Name associated with the Voice, and there was power in His Name.

"Who are you?" the Voice insisted.

Who was he? What an odd question. He was Tul'ran the Uncreator, the destroyer of this world and its new god. He would have compassion for the living who were innocent, but the bringers of death would feel nothing but his wrath. The living would become his slaves and they would celebrate his victory over this world every day.

"Who were you when you first heard My Voice?"

The memory drove a shaft of pain through his heart. He knew very well who he was back then, although his newfound godhead tried to shunt the memory aside. He had been a helpless twelve-year-old boy.

"Yes, you were a helpless twelve-year-old boy when I met you. Who am I?"

His mind refused to obey him. The dark memories wouldn't be pushed away. His father had locked him in a shed, helpless, terrified. His mother and sisters bled out before him, while his father did nothing but shriek. He had called out for a god back then, and someone answered. What did He call himself, the god who spoke to him in a small, still voice? Ah, yes. El Shaddai.

"What are you to Me?"

Tul'ran pondered on that, and his eyes lost some of the blue brilliance which allowed him to See everything on the planet, all at once. The power of the Uncreation was a force beyond his wildest imaginings. It wanted him all for itself, yet the Voice drew him back to a semblance of mortality. He recalled. He was El Shaddai's Judge.

The Voice calmed him, caressed his mind, and soothed his rage.

"Who commands you?"

The memories came flooding back. El Shaddai. Erianne. Johan. Gwynver'insa. Darian. Another stab of pain. He took a deep, ragged breath as the pain threatened to stop his heart.

"You do, my Lord. You are El Shaddai, the God Who Protects Me. What is your command?"

The Voice purred in his mind.

"Those who have surrendered shall be subject to judgment by the populace of Spes. You shall wipe out the clones and the means by which they may make more copies of themselves. You shall cast the war machines into oblivion and bring the remaining Combatants to the Hall of the Ancestors. They shall kneel before the Empress at the Judgment Seat and beg for her mercy. You have done well, Tul'ran, but the time for killing is no more."

The part of him loving the power coursing through his veins, lusting for more, wanted to ignore these commands, for he knew now what it felt like to be a god. He struggled. His eyes flared back into a glowing blue flame.

The temptation to resist El Shaddai and become the god of this world was strong. The power left a taste in his mind more delicious than the finest wine, the softest haunch of beef, the sweetest kiss. With his sword, he could command things out of existence. The puny humans on Spes Deserit could never stand against him. He could take this planet and all who lived on it would have to worship him. His time had come. Never more would he know the pain of loss. Forever, he would live and rule on this planet. All who displeased him would die.

'Tul'ran?'

He knew her voice, too; it was a shock to the conceit within him wanting to be a god.

'Milord husband, do you hear my voice?'

No, the god-being screamed. No, it whimpered. I want to live. I want to rule.

Her voice was firmer now. The language she used was the one he learned in his youth. It called forth deep roots to customs wrapped in the blood flowing through his arteries.

'Tul'ran az Nostrom, the Sword Himself, Master of Bloodwing the Blade, Sword of Judgment, Deliverer of Death, hearken to my words. I am Erianne de mi Corazon, Lady az Nostrom. You entered a covenant with me while kneeling on the desert sands of Mesopotamia. By your oath, you lent your sword and your life to my cause. You promised my enemies would be your enemies until you laid to rest all strife, or until one of us should die. You swore this on your honor and your sword. I command you to return your heart to me, your covenant-mistress, by the oath you have sworn, and the blood spilled between us!'

Tul'ran blinked his eyes as his head swam. The darkness of the color of his eyes returned, pushing away the power of the Uncreation. He looked down at Bloodwing, which faded into the dark black sheen he had always known. The covenant. How had he forgotten about the covenant binding his life to hers in blood and iron?

'Erianne?'

Erianne heaved a tremendous sigh of relief and she clutched her chest as if to still her hammering heart. She smiled at Gwynver'insa, who had been holding her breath, her fists clenched so hard the knuckles were bone white.

"Rejoice, my darling sister. Your brother was lost, but now he is found. He faded to death, but lives again."

Gwynver'insa laughed, tears flooding her large blue eyes.

"Praise Yahweh! Bring him home, sister. Bring him home."

It took longer than they would have liked. Tul'ran drove the conveyance to where each of the remaining Combatants kneeled on the ground, their fingers linked behind their heads. Tul'ran found chains on the conveyance and chained them all together. They were so intimidated by him; they didn't even squabble amongst themselves when he threw them into the conveyance. He bounced their bodies off the conveyance floor, and it hurt, but they kept quiet. At the hands of the Prince of Death, it had been gently done.

The Fight was over. There was no desire for battle left in them, for something greater than them had come and they didn't know how to war against it.

The power flooding every cell in Tul'ran's body was gone, but it remained in Bloodwing. He could no longer uncreate with a gesture, so it took longer to cast the Blade's rays over the war machines and fortresses to make them disappear for all time.

As the sun made its last wave of farewell in the evening sky, the first observable sunset in centuries, Tul'ran pulled the conveyance up to the Hall of the Ancestors. Erianne and Gwynver'insa waited for him in front of the massive doors. Members of the

People came forward to escort the Combatants to the Judgment Seat, while the two women lingered to greet Tul'ran.

He pulled himself out of the conveyance and wearily walked to where Erianne and Gwynver'insa stood. It annoyed him a little that they didn't run up to him and smother him with hugs and kisses.

"What ails you?" he asked, a gruff tone carrying the words from parched lips.

Erianne walked to him, her eyes brimming with tears. She reached *up* to touch his face, then ran her fingers through his hair.

"Your body has changed, milord husband. You are now my height, and your hair…"

He touched his head, running his fingers through the long, thick strands.

"What of my hair, my love?"

She smiled tentatively.

"It's pure white, Tul'ran, with a jet-black crown surrounding the top like a halo."

She kissed him, but there was a hint of sadness on her sweet lips. She pulled back, her fingers still in his hair, weaving enchantments through it.

"Death itself has crowned you and named you as its heir, milord husband."

CHAPTER THE FOURTEENTH:
A FAINT HOPE,
A FALSE PEACE

Tul'ran and Erianne held each other close, trying desperately to pass the love in their hearts into each other's bodies, through their lips and hands and sighs. Their loss of each other almost came from something other than death; a temptation to grasp ultimate power had nearly pulled them apart forever. They would have stayed in their embrace for many minutes longer, but Gwynver'insa's gasp startled them.

"It's still there!"

Tul'ran and Erianne jerked their bodies toward her, hands leaping to the hilts of their swords. She was pointing into the sky, her mouth rounded in an 'o'. Her warriors flung their eyes to the sky and froze in wonder.

A field of billions of stars stretched out before them, so close, it seemed, one could touch them. Multicolored gaseous structures wove between them, adding a delightful shawl to the diamonds shining in the sky. The major attraction, though, was the moon. It occupied the horizon, an emerald green orb shining as a beacon against a cloak of stars. Clouds danced across its face and it reached out to them, promising adventure.

Gwynver'insa laughed and danced around Tul'ran and Erianne. She grabbed their hands and pulled them into her pirouettes, and they stumbled as they tried to keep up with her exuberance.

When they stopped, breathless, Erianne hugged Gwynver'insa to her.

"Why does your moon give you such happiness, Gwyn?"

Gwynver'insa looked up at her with wild joy radiating from her tiny face.

"In over one thousand years, these eyes have not looked upon our moon. As the Combatants demolished this planet, so, too, had I believed our moon torn apart. It is a planet, much like this one, but smaller. It has an atmosphere, gardens, and life. We always wanted to go there, but a ring of ice surrounds our world at the very edge of space. Our greatest fear was the damage it would cause to our world if we tried to punch through the ice to go to our moon."

She laughed bitterly, remembering the image in her mind of Tul'ran wiping the planet clean of broken buildings and machines.

"Perhaps it would have been better for us if we

347

tried."

Tul'ran smiled at her.

"Do you want me to send the ice away?"

Gwynver'insa raised delicate eyebrows over widened eyes.

"You can do that?"

Tul'ran lifted Bloodwing, and a tongue of blue flame ignited on its surface.

"With this sword, I can remove anything from existence, sister. But ruminate on it. El Shaddai may have placed the layer of ice there with purpose; you should determine His will before you set my sword's power against it."

She drew him into her arms and hugged him, reaching around to bring Erianne into her embrace.

"I will seek His will, my powerful brother. But first, let us just stand here and enjoy this view for a few moments longer. We have onerous tasks to perform in the next few days, my beloved friends. Let us take a moment to enjoy the beauty of this night sky."

A banished angel and three disconsolate souls entered the Abyss with little fanfare. The Holy Spirit walked before them, and the spirits of the Abyss shrieked and hid themselves in the darkest confines of the liquid blackness.

"G'shnet'el," He called out, softly.

G'shnet'el slinked in from the darkness, his wings covering his face against the glare of the Light. The presence of the Holy Spirit burned his flesh, and His purity was agonizing. He knelt before the Holy Spirit.

"I come. How may I serve you, Lord?"

The Holy Spirit took Abaddon by the shoulder and brought him forward.

"You will chain this one to the Rock of Humility. But be careful, G'shnet'el, not to mock or torment him. One day, We shall set him free against the Earth to do Our will there. On that day, We will give him complete authority over you and all the demons in the Abyss. He will make you pay for your torment. I shall watch you, G'shnet'el. If you disobey these instructions, I will take it upon Myself to render your punishment."

G'shnet'el shuddered.

"I hear and obey, my Lord. We will treat Abaddon respectfully and well, even as we chain him and ever thereafter."

The Holy Spirit turned to Abaddon, an aura of sadness dancing around his brilliantly lit form.

"Go with them, Abaddon, for we can no longer trust the exercise of your discretion. Some day We will set you free to do Our will."

Abaddon hung his head and walked away, dragging his massive black wings on the ground behind him. Three other fallen angels fell in beside and behind him, but not coming too close. Defeated, he may be, disconsolate he was, but Abaddon remained the most powerful angel ever created and they were not inclined to forget it.

"What about these three?" G'shnet'el said, gesturing at the obviously frightened Sean, Raylene, and Rhanda. They huddled together, whimpering, darting fearful glances around the gloom that tried to wrap its tendrils around them.

The Holy Spirit looked at them sadly.

"We do not know them, and we do not claim authority over them in this place. You should know, G'shnet'el, We see everything you do here. Some day, you will stand before Us in judgment, and We shall consider the pain you have inflicted on Our children. We already have four of Our children in Heaven who will testify as to the cruelty of their treatment at your hands. You will pay for every shred of pain you inflicted, even on those condemned by their choice away from Us."

Fear raced through the fallen angel like mercury, burning like liquid nitrogen. He didn't know They would judge him for the things he did in Hell. G'shnet'el cursed Satan. The decision to follow that megalomaniac was going to cost G'shnet'el more than he could have ever imagined.

Spes Deserit, in the Year of Our Peace 0001
Mission Day 48

A little girl marched down the long aisle, dressed in green, the color of Spring. Her parents wrapped her long red hair up in a crown on her head. Tears misted her eyes and fell, glistening on her cheeks. She cast black rose petals in front of her as she walked down the empty aisle. The Empress's attendants sang a low dirge, and she measured her pace against the cadence of their song.

Behind her walked Darkshadow, delivered to Spes Deserit by God Himself at Tul'ran's request. The massive warhorse pulled a cart painted red and decorated with gold.

In all his life, Darkshadow had resisted traces and harness, choosing to express his displeasure with sharp teeth and deadly hooves. This service, though, was for his master. Darkshadow would have done anything for Tul'ran, including the indignity of pulling this contraption.

On the cart lay the coffin. Gwynver'insa had outdone herself when creating Darian's last resting place. She made it from a rich mahogany wood. The lid was solid gold and Gwynver'insa molded it in an exact replication of Darian's face and form. Black ribbons decorated the handles of the coffin and the edges of the cart. It was sadly beautiful.

Behind the cart, the Empress rode Destiny's Edge, with Johan following her on foot. She fought to keep her face regal, but tears bloomed from her eyes and stained her cheeks whenever she looked down at the coffin. She wore a gold dress; the train fell from the horse's rump and trailed behind her on the ground. Her attendants intertwined black ribbons through her crown. They had been very nervous about her riding into the Judgment Seat for the ceremony on this strange beast, but she demurred.

"If my sister had the courage to sacrifice her life to save Spes, then I can muster the courage to ride Lady Erianne's horse," she told them. "The subject is closed."

They bowed, acknowledging her will and wishing sometimes their Empress were a little less impetuous.

Tul'ran and Erianne were not in the procession. They stood in the entrance to the Judgment Seat, dressed in their black armor, swords drawn. Their faces were grim, and no one would meet their gaze.

All noticed the physical changes in Tul'ran's body. He was taller and the bright silver of his hair offset the black halo stripe around his skull. The People gave him wide berth and never failed to bow as he walked by. Fear tempered their admiration for him. Everyone had watched the Battle for Hope so many times, they'd committed it to memory. Death wasn't a murky thought or shadowy figure; it walked among them and acknowledged their bows with what Tul'ran intended as a gentle smile but was never that.

The little girl, however, had the nerves of a true warrior. She marched up to them and sketched a bow. Erianne wanted to smile, but knew the circumstances wouldn't permit any display of humor or pleasure.

"Who passes?" She asked the young girl, her tone severe.

"The dead," the young girl answered, according to the ritual.

"Who dares to bring the dead into the Judgment Seat?" Tul'ran roared, flicking the tip of his sword as he issued the challenge.

Gwynver'insa nudged Destiny's Edge around the cart to come between Tul'ran and the young girl.

"I dare. I am Gwynver'insa, She Who Creates From Nothing, The Last of her Kind, Prophet of Yahweh, Empress of the World. This woman died in the service of our planet. With courage, she gave her life so we could live. With love, she sacrificed herself for another. She was the Catalyst for the redemption of our People from the Fight. We bring her here to honor her and proclaim her a Hero of Spes, the world of Hope."

"The dead shall pass," Erianne said, her voice choking on the lump in her throat.

Tul'ran and Erianne raised their swords in front of them in salute, turned, and led the procession into the Judgment Seat. The People had assembled and waited patiently. Off to one side, the nine Combatants kneeled in the dirt, dressed in long gray gowns. Members of the People chained the necks and hands of the Nine in front of them and clipped the chains to rungs in the dirt. This was to be no mere funeral. While Darian was being honored, the Nine were to be judged for their crimes.

The People gasped as Darkshadow stepped into the Judgment Seat, whinnying loudly as he pulled Darian's body into their presence. The war horse walked proudly, tossing his head and snorting at the awed crowd. He enthralled them, many of them having not seen a horse for over a thousand years, and he was enjoying their attention.

Darkshadow stopped before a raised dais and looked at Tul'ran, his ears flickering. Their reunion had been one of pure joy. No sooner had the Crystalline Wall allowed Darkshadow and Destiny's Edge through, than Erianne and Tul'ran were galloping their steeds on the bare plains of the newly cleared world.

Both had wondered how their horses would endure a ride on the train to the Judgment Seat, but the train's AI understood what it carried and gave them a slow, smooth transport. Their horses acted as if the novel experience was unworthy of notice. After all, they had been at the epicenter of stoppages in Time. What was a mere train?

Tul'ran walked over to his horse and release him from the traces, patting his neck, and whispering, "Good boy." He led Darkshadow to stand next to him in the ceremony. Erianne helped Gwynver'insa dismount, then she brought Destiny's Edge to stand next to Darkshadow.

They had spent the better part of two days giving children rides on the horses while Gwynver'insa and Johan prepared Darian's body and planned her funeral. It was no wonder the horses were so popular.

When Gwynver'insa and Johan took their place on the stand, a gong resounded through the Judgment Seat.

"Who comes?" the Empress Gwynver'insa said, her voice deep and resonant.

The little girl had climbed up on the cart, mindful of tearing her dress, and stood at the head of the coffin.

"I come!" She proclaimed in a loud soprano voice, her voice screaming outrage and defiance. "I am the voice of Lady Darian Angelica Ostrowski, who came to this world to save it from the enemies of the People and to end the Fight."

"Why do you come?"

The little girl turned and pointed at the Nine.

"I died at the hands of the Nine and I accuse them of my murder. Honor me, Your Imperial Majesty. Revenge the death of your sister who loved you and whom you loved by heaping honor upon me to their shame."

She scrambled down from the cart with as much dignity as she could muster.

A cube lit up in the middle of the vast ceiling of the Judgment Seat, situated so that every eye could watch. The cube replayed the moment of Darian's death and the People gasped with horror. They cried as Erianne and Gwynver'insa attended her body, while Tul'ran prepared to take his vengeance into the world. The cube reran Armageddon, and the People sat as if enchanted. Finally, it played the confession of each of the Nine as they summarized their role in the ongoing Fight.

The cube disappeared. Gwynver'insa spread her hands out, palms down, as if to cover the coffin with them.

"People of Spes, world of Hope, hearken to my words. Behold Lady Darian Angelic Ostrowski. She was born thirty-two years ago in a distant world. In pain, she was born and in pain she lived. Others saw her beauty and broke her body out of their jealousy of her. Her parents abused her and corrupted their love for her. They pleasured themselves with her body and destroyed her mind."

"We despise them."

"Her parents sold her into the service of evil. I saw the scars from the whippings the evil one laid on her tender back."

"We despise him."

The crowd sighed. Such evil was far beyond their understanding and their hearts rent apart at the thoughts of how those she loved badly damaged this beautiful woman.

"Then she met Lord Tul'ran az Nostrom and

Lady Erianne az Nostrom. They gathered Lady Darian within their powerful arms and crossed swords before her face, separating her from evil. Our Warriors loved her and invited her to this world, which she accepted gladly. I knew her for only a fleeting time, but I testify that in her last days, Lady Darian's soul glowed like the sun with Yahweh's spirit. She died a servant of the Lord and as my beloved sister."

"People of Spes, the world of Hope, I put forward to you, my sister, Princess Darian of Terra, for your consideration of the honor of Hero of Spes. All who judge her worthy stand now. Those who would judge her unworthy and face my wrath and the wrath of the Warriors of the Lord, speak now or forever hold your peace."

All the People rose swiftly, in silence. Gwynver'insa drew out the moment, casting her glance around the Chamber and nodded. She descended from the dais and walked to the cart. Her attendants placed a short staircase at the base of the conveyance. The Empress ascended the steps and climbed near the head of the coffin. At her hand gesture, the attendants lifted the gold lid from the coffin.

Darian lay in repose, her brown hair arrayed down the sides of her face and over her breasts. They clothed her in battle leathers, colored black, in the design worn by Erianne and Tul'ran. Johan had cleaned the spear that took her life, cut it in two so it would fit in the coffin, and placed it in her right hand. Gwynver'insa had created a gold crown and fitted it gently on her head. In her left hand, Darian held a smaller replica of Gwynver'insa's scepter.

An attendant walked forward with a heavy gold chain, at the end of which shone a massive ruby, and gave it to her Empress. Tears poured from Gwynver'insa's eyes as she tried to hold back a sob. Gwynver'insa held the chain high and showed it to the people before draping the chain around Darian's neck. She leaned down and kissed her sister's lips. When she straightened, she turned to the People.

"Behold, Princess Darian of Terra, Hero of Spes. We will bury her in our field and her statue will stand tall over the People, so no one will forget her sacrifice. We will mourn for thirty-two days, one day for each year of her life. I proclaim this day to be a global holiday. Every year we will pause in our labor to pay her tribute. All honor to her."

"All honor to her," the People rumbled, the harmonic of their words echoing through the vast chamber. The People wept, their eyes welling to the heartbreak of Darian's death and their beloved Empress's grief.

Gwynver'insa stepped down and Johan stepped up to place a rose on Darian's chest. Tears streaked his face. He bent over and whispered,

"You were a pain in my butt, Darian, but I loved you anyway. Try not to give Jesus too hard of a time." He kissed her forehead and stepped down.

Erianne had such a powerful grip on Tul'ran's forearm, he could feel her nails biting into his arm. Their backs were ramrod straight as they walked to the head of the coffin and ascended the stairs. Tul'ran set his face as if he carved it in granite, and he couldn't bring himself to look at Darian.

It wouldn't be good for the People of Spes to watch their deliverer collapse into a puddle of tears. Erianne had no such qualms. She put her forehead on Darian's and sobbed. Darian had so few chances to know pure love in her life. If only she had lived long enough to realize how well her new brothers and sisters could love and care for her. Erianne straightened and put a red rose on Darian's chest.

"We love you, sister. Be safe in the hands of the Lord. We will see you in Glory some day and our joy will know no end."

They stepped down, and the attendants closed the coffin lid. Twelve women stepped up to the cart. Erianne was training them to be Gwynver'insa's security detail. All wore swords created by their Empress and dressed in black leather combat clothing. They slid the coffin off the cart and placed it on their shoulders. They slow-marched their Princess out of the Judgment Seat as the People thumped the rhythm of a heartbeat on their chests.

The Princess Darian Guard would carry her two miles outside and place her body into the grave they carved out from the soil. A monument would stand over her grave, but Gwynver'insa had not created it yet.

Erianne laid her head against Tul'ran's. She still wasn't used to his new height, and it felt strange to not bend her head to his. She sighed. So many changes. So much sorrow.

Tul'ran kissed her head at the hairline.

"You mourn, my love," he whispered.

"I mourn, my love," she whispered back. "I hope El Shaddai will forgive me, but I half expected He would raise Darian from the dead just for us."

Tul'ran put his arm around his wife's waist.

"The Prophet of Spes, who speaks to El Shaddai daily, has assured us that Heaven holds a banquet this day for our sister. She is at peace, and He showers His love upon her. I would not bring her back to the misery of this universe only because of our heartbreak and our loss."

Erianne snuggled into his hug.

"I know, my love. All honor to her."

"All honor to her," Tul'ran replied, tears clouding his vision of the coffin bearing the body of the woman who had looked so much like Evann'ya. His heart ached knowing that it could be years before he would see either Evann'ya or Darian again. He could wait, but while the pain of their passing would dull, he knew it would never end.

The trial was a foregone conclusion, but the People divided on sentence. Some came forward and argued for death.

"Let Lord Tul'ran finish his task," one said. "He came to rid us of their menace. We owe it to the Prince of Death to allow him to complete his mission."

Another stood and shook her head.

"Have we not laid enough of this grisly task at the feet of Lord Tul'ran and Lady Erianne? When have we shown them peace? We point them to the crises we created by our complacency and tell them to attack. How are we better than the Combatants? I say, show the Nine mercy. Educate them. Never give them a chance to wage war again, but let us not take their lives."

The debate raged on for hours, with no consensus in sight. Gwynver'insa gestured, and Tul'ran ambled to her side.

"Lord Tul'ran, I am of a mind to exile the Nine," she said to him in a faint voice. "Yahweh has dissuaded me from removing the ice shield surrounding this planet. Doing so would shorten our lives and cause damage to this world. He may allow us to travel to our moon by other means someday, but the time is not now. El Shaddai said if we chose exile, you would deliver the Nine to a destination where they will never again pose a threat to our world. What say you, milord?"

Tul'ran looked at her with mournful eyes.

"I need time to answer, Your Imperial Majesty, for my heart is considerably distressed that I have lost your love."

Gwynver'insa looked startled.

"In what way have you lost my love, dear brother?"

Tul'ran smiled.

"Why, in the way you have addressed me so formally and inferred I would not comply with your every desire."

Gwynver'insa giggled, and some lines around her eyes smoothed out.

"I forget how precocious you can be. You get it from Erianne, I think, who is the biggest tease I have ever met. When El Shaddai needs you elsewhere, beloved brother, will you take these wretches with you?"

Tul'ran grinned from ear to ear.

"By your command."

Gwynver'insa gestured him away, fighting to keep a smile off her face. She stood up, and the People fell silent.

"I render judgment."

Whispers floated through the chamber. This was new. No one ever rendered judgment if the Judges weren't unanimous. History spoke of some cases taking years to resolve, while the Judges cajoled each other into a unanimous verdict.

"This world has seen enough death, and I am sickened by it. Let life bloom again as we seek to rebuild a better place. We cannot imprison the Nine, for we have no such facilities, nor will I create them. Spes will be a peaceful world complying with Yahweh's laws. We all desire this after thousands of years of hatred and conflict. We have sinned by our complacence and allowed evil to root itself into our souls. Yahweh has disclosed to me His laws, which I shall place on every device. Weekly, we shall gather and discuss His laws and pledge ourselves to His service. Never again shall we kill."

"Therefore, I adjudge we shall place the Nine in the custody of Lord and Lady az Nostrom, who will deliver them into exile in another world. Until then, they shall remain chained in the Lower Rooms, fed, given facilities, and treated with respect. This is my judgment. If you agree, rise now. If you disagree, remain seated or forever hold your peace."

All one hundred and forty-four thousand People stood, and their applause echoed through the Chamber for a long time.

Spes Deserit, in the Year of Our Peace 0001
Mission Day 93

The little girl marched down the long aisle, dressed in green, the color of Spring. Her parents wrapped her long red hair up in a crown on her head. Her eyes glittered and a wide smile split her cheeks. She cast red rose petals in front of her as she walked down an aisle surrounded on both sides by the People in their best holiday dress. The Empress's attendants sang an aria of joy, and she measured her pace against the cadence of their song. Forty-five days had passed since the People of Spes had laid their beloved Princess Darian to rest.

Behind the little girl rode the Empress of the World, the First of Her Line, on the monster of the beast the People knew and loved as the war horse, Darkshadow. Her attendants dressed the Empress Gwynver'insa all in white; even the scabbard housing the sword at her side was white. Her crown sat high on her head, and white ribbons swam among the delicate spires of gold.

Johan rode next to her on Destiny's Edge, dressed in a chestnut brown suit and looking every inch the Emperor Consort. He, too, wore a crown, though it wasn't nearly as ostentatious as the one belonging to the woman who would be his bride. He had insisted on that. It was the only thing for which he got his way that day.

Tul'ran and Erianne marched behind the horses, leading the Princess Darian Guard. Gwynver'insa had created armor of red leather for them, to enforce their status as hero warriors.

Erianne put her long, black hair up and wove into it the sheer scarf Tul'ran bought for her in Ur and placed on her head on their wedding day. It set off her brilliant green eyes, which danced with unrestrained glee.

The People had lined up on each side of the path, and as the wedding party passed them by, they all fell in behind. This, truly, was a wedding procession. They sang and danced as they followed the bride and groom to the Hall of Everlasting Joy.

Tul'ran leaned over to whisper in his wife's ear.

"How is this marriage to work, milady wife? Johan is young now, but Gwynver'insa will yet live for a thousand years. How soon will it be before she mourns his death?"

Erianne jabbed him in the ribs with her elbow.

"Trust you to bring up such a morose thought on this festive day. Lay your heart to rest, milord husband. With Johan's consent, she altered the very cells of his body and the building blocks within those cells to extend his life for thousands of years."

Tul'ran's eyebrows threatened to jump off his head.

"She can do that?"

Erianne giggled.

"She can, and she did. Gwynver'insa asked if I wanted her to do that for us, but I declined."

He looked at her, astonished.

"You declined? Why ever for?"

Erianne couldn't stop giggling.

"I told her she would understand after living with her husband smelling like a goat for five hundred years."

Laughter exploded from Tul'ran, who blushed as red as his leathers when Gwynver'insa and Johan turned around to smile at him. The rest of the procession went without interruption, and they soon stopped in front of an altar in the main hall. Tul'ran and Erianne helped the bride and groom dismount and led the horses to one side, where two lads grasped the reins.

Johan and Gwynver'insa took up a position facing the altar, their backs to the People. Tul'ran and Erianne stood behind them, standing as the equivalent of Best Man and Matron of Honor.

Erianne looked around.

"Who did they get to officiate the wedding? I don't see anyone stepping forward."

Nothing happened for several minutes, and the People grew restless. Suddenly, a brilliant light flared on the dais and E'thriel stepped out from the light. He spread his wings wide, and the People gasped with delight. E'thriel caught Tul'ran and Erianne's eyes and grinned. He loved surprises, but loved delivering them even more. The angel stood to one side.

Darian the Eternal stood behind him, her glorified body shining as brightly as the angel. She wore a fitted white gown from her neck to her toes and her hair glowed. Her smile blazed as brightly as her gown. She was beautiful and her aura sent waves of happiness throughout the People.

Darian smiled into their shocked faces.

"People of Spes, world of Hope, I bring you greetings from Yahweh, the Lord your God. He is well pleased with you. So much so when I pleaded with him to allow me to descend from the Kingdom of Heaven briefly to officiate this wedding, He consented, though it is far beyond the pale."

Darian the Eternal took a step forward and directed her smile at the beaming bride and the shocked groom.

"Empress Gwynver'insa, the First of Your Line, do you take this man, Johan Weinstein, to be your husband? Will you love him for as long as you both shall live, honor him as your Consort, and remain faithful to him, always?"

Gwynver'insa's face shone almost as brightly as Darian's. She had begged Yahweh for the chance to be married by Darian and He had agreed, being whimsically inclined Himself.

"I will, my Princess."

E'thriel handed Darian a simple-looking metallic stick. She passed it over Gwynver'insa's right wrist, and it drew a metallic gold band around her wrist, tight to the skin. It resembled a tattoo, but the ink was made of gold. No one could remove it once Darian sealed it. The People of Spes married for life.

Darian turned to Johan.

"Emperor Consort Johan Weinstein, do you take this woman, Empress Gwynver'insa, the First of Her Line, to be your wife? Will you love her for as long as you both shall live, honor her as your Queen, and remain faithful to her, always?"

Johan was still trying to get over seeing Darian standing in front of him, officiating at their wedding. Gwynver'insa gave him a slight tap on his leg, bringing him back into the moment.

"I will, my Princess."

Darian passed the stick over Johan's left wrist, drawing the gold band around it. When she finished, she motioned for them to put their wrists together. When they did, the bands locked in place, as if they were heavily magnetized. The bands would join them like this until they retired to their bed to consummate their marriage, which would happen before the wedding feast. When the bride and groom returned to the feast, their wrists unhinged, then the People would know the ceremony was complete.

Darian raised her hands, palms up.

"Then by the power invested in me by the Lord your God, I bind you in holy matrimony. What God has put together, let no one try to separate. People of Spes, I present to you this husband and wife. All honor to them!"

"All honor to them!" the people roared and burst into a loud round of applause. As they shouted and yelled their happiness, Darian leaned down and whispered in Gwynver'insa's ear.

"Didn't I say I would stand with you when you dragged Johan to the altar, sister?"

Spes Deserit, in the Year of Our Peace 0001
Mission Day 95

It was the third day of the marriage celebration. Tul'ran stepped outside for a breath of fresh air, the moon glowing in the sky above him. Gwynver'insa had graciously created a bench for them to sit on and enjoy the view of the universe. Tul'ran loved Spes' night sky. He and Erianne came up here often to sit beneath the stars, tease each other and snuggle. He would miss this world when it came time to leave.

It had been a shock to see Darian appear with E'thriel to officiate the wedding. When the ceremony was over, he wanted to hug her, but she held up a hand before he could reach her.

"Beloved brother, you must not touch me, for I am in my glorified body. Someday, when you and my favorite sister come to join me here, we can hug for centuries. Know that I love you, Tul'ran, and I look forward to that time with an ecstatic heart."

He nodded, restraining the urge to touch her.

"I understand. Thank you for saving my life, Darian."

Her smile widened, and her eyes shone with love.

"I promised Erianne I would take care of you, Tul'ran. When I saw the android advancing on you with the spear, I kept my oath and placed my body between you and your enemy. I would do it again a thousand times over."

Tears fell from his cheeks.

"I look forward to our reunion, Darian."

Darian gestured Erianne forward, and they talked. Both were laughing at the end of the conversation, and Tul'ran shook his head. He knew he was the subject of their humor and it bothered him not one whit. For the first time in his life, he felt peace.

A figure stepped out of the nighttime and came to sit beside him under the emerald moon. Tul'ran tried to rise, but the man put a hand on his shoulder.

"To what do I owe this honor, El Shaddai?"

The Lord smiled.

"Is it not enough to say I wish to enjoy the company of one of My favorite sons beneath the sky of My creation?"

Tul'ran laughed softly.

"Were I not your Judge, the bearer of a sword giving me infinite destructive powers, I'd fully believe it." He cast a glance at Jesus's face. "How did you know, Lord, I wouldn't succumb to temptation and take on the mantle of a god?"

"I didn't," Jesus said soberly. "The choice was yours, Tul'ran. I gave you every reason to choose Me and My path, but until you declined the power, I didn't know which way your decisions would take you."

Tul'ran drew a sharp breath.

"Was it not a terrible risk to take, Lord?"

Jesus smiled.

"It was. It is the risk We have taken with every human being since the day We created Adam and Eve. Since the day We created every version of Adam and Eve in the Universe. We didn't create humans to be robots, obeying Our every whim. The Father and I wanted companions, friends, people who would walk with Us through eternity."

Tul'ran looked over the fields in front of him. Gwynver'insa had already created crops and orchards for her people. Soon, she would cover the entire world with fields, trees, lakes, and streams. Many creatures would walk the land and swim in the planet's waters.

She and Johan discussed a new system of governance to include some small measures for population control. Both learned the lessons from the history of Spes Deserit and were loath to repeat the mistakes leading to Tul'ran leveling the world.

"And when You have fully enjoyed the company of one of Your favorite sons, El Shaddai, what then?"

Jesus gestured upwards into the stars.

"We have begun unraveling the influence of evil in the universe, Tul'ran. While we have thus far focused Our efforts on the planet of your birth, there are many places out there still needing the might of the Prince and Princess of Death. Go to the Crystalline Wall with the Nine. We will send you out on our next assignment."

They sat in silence for a moment. Tul'ran looked over at his Savior and smiled.

"Yes, but not tonight, right, Lord?"

Jesus laughed and settled back onto the bench. Gwynver'insa had constructed it to be very comfortable. He might have to take the design back to Heaven with Him.

"Yes, My son, not tonight. When you are ready to leave this place, take the Nine to the Garden and I will meet you there. Look, here comes your Lady."

Erianne glided over and took one knee in front of her King.

"Lord. Do I interrupt?"

Jesus slid over on the bench to give her room to sit with her husband.

"You do not. I was just telling Tul'ran your time here must soon end."

Erianne lifted Tul'ran's arm and snuggled into the crook.

"Excellent. Another mission. I hate to say it, but I'm getting a little bored."

Tul'ran's eyebrows sought escape from his

forehead, and Jesus's laughter boomed into the night. He stood up and stretched before turning to face them.

"You have done well, my Judges. I can give you a few more weeks of sanctuary before I make life more exciting for you. Enjoy the view, and the harmony, while you can."

He was gone.

A husband and his wife sat quietly beneath a beautiful night sky, while a comet raced through the cosmos far away, framed by the brilliance of a tapestry of stars, webbed by the gossamer strands of nebulae, through which plunged an emerald green moon. Behind the massive doors behind them, they could hear laughter and revelry as the People celebrated the marriage of their Empress. Somewhere birds, created by the bride for this occasion, cooed and sang their arias.

Soon, their Empress would tearfully kiss them goodbye as they set off on their next dangerous mission and make them swear they would return to visit. They would accept her promise that when they came back, they would find a world of beauty, peace, and prosperity. Tul'ran and Erianne would leave behind the physicist their world thought dead and the body of a cherished sister whom their world never knew.

But not tonight.

Tonight was for the moon and the stars, and the love burning in their hearts as their lips met under the joy-filled eyes of their loved ones in Heaven.

CHAPTER THE FIFTEENTH: SHE WHO WAS NOT

She Who Was Not hovered over Spes, watching the scene play out before her. The world's darkness didn't hinder her, for she was in a pure energy state. She was both of the physical world and not, for no being could detect her in her energy state unless she revealed herself.

Jesus's presence captivated her. It wasn't like God to visit a planet outside the Garden, especially so far from home. The Holy Trinity mostly concentrated their efforts on the miserable, insignificant planet called Earth by its human inhabitants. Such an unimaginative group of creatures. To find Him in this region of the cosmos, thousands of light years from Earth, was intriguing.

She Who Was Not had very few emotions left after millennia of existence. Curiosity was one of them, but she knew to be careful. Her curiosity once blew apart an entire planet, the aftermath of which significantly damaged the atmosphere of another. It wouldn't do to be so careless. The destruction of the planet had incurred God's wrath, and she had no desire to do so again until she increased her power to where she could oppose Him.

There was only room for one God in this universe, she decided. She Who Was Not was determined to be it. Then she could annihilate whatever she wanted without consequence.

Now, that would be bliss.

She Who Was Not withdrew her sight from Spes and considered her options. It was impossible to act while in a pure energy state. She would withdraw to her world and reclaim her physical body. She had the means to deliver her physical body to Spes Deserit within a matter of only a few sunrises and sunsets. It was necessary to make sure her body was ready to undertake physical activity. It had been many years since she reclaimed her physical form.

She Who Was Not had witnessed the last conflict in the world below with growing excitement. She watched in awe as a human wielded the Sword of Uncreation. How lucky was he! She was astonished when the human stepped back from godhood and poured all his power back into the sword. It presented him with the ability to take a world as his own and bend the humans on it to his bidding, and he refused it. What a fool! If ever such an opportunity was presented to her, well...

She paused. The sword had the power, not the man. If she possessed the sword, the power would be hers. There was no chance she would turn down the opportunity to have whatever powers the sword offered to her. This was her moment. After thousands of years, she would finally have her revenge.

She would have to kill the man and the woman who ran with him, but she didn't care. They were mere humans and unworthy of consideration. What was their deaths to her?

She looked back down at Spes, where the two humans held each other within their arms and stared placidly at the stars. If she were in her physical body, she would have felt ill. How cute. They were in love. What a farce. She knew from painful experience love was nothing more than a yoke, shackling the freedom of one person to another's goals and dreams. It was better to be independent and strong. She would teach them this lesson as well.

She Who Was Not had much to give this sad universe. Much more than their God, who just wanted to love everything. They would be much happier when they were her slaves.

With that blissful thought, she sent her spirit flying back along the tether, keeping her linked to her physical self.

Her time had come.

Everhome, Evo's Home World

The woman who had been She Who Was Not re-entered her body with little effort. Even in her highest pure energy state, she always kept a link through space and time to her physical form.

Every morning, her body awoke, ate, and exercised. Her body tended to the machines supplying food and entertainment. At day's end, her body ate and slept. It was in perfect physical condition. Evo continuously monitored and cared for her form, as would a mother care for a child. No wonder it was easy to return.

The few minutes after returning required some getting used to, of course. In her physical form, she couldn't perceive the wonders of the universe, taste an interstellar gaseous cloud, feel the warmth of a newborn sun, or enjoy the gravity of a black hole. Physicality meant limitations, and limitations meant a sensation like claustrophobia.

She Who Was Evo Again looked into a mirror and ran her hands over her cheekbones. She was the first of her kind, but not the first of creation. After ten thousand years, she had not aged a day and her mind gained sharpness with each passing year. She should have been the epitome of perfection. Should have been. Ah, how fraught with regret was the phrase, 'should have been.'

She remembered opening her eyes on the day of her conception. Before her stood God the Father, God the Son, and God the Holy Spirit. They looked down upon her with tenderness. She felt pressure and looked to her right side. A creature who looked like God but was not God squatted on the ground next to her, holding her hand. Eagerness and wonder consumed his face.

God spoke.

"Welcome to Everhome. The man sitting next to you is Ado. Your name is Evo. The two of you are the first of your kind. We have created you to be companions for one another. You differ from each other but We designed your differences to complement one another. Where one of you is weak, the other will be strong. You are halves of a whole so complete, you will not know, after a time, where one of you begins and the other ends. We have created you to love Us and love one another. Welcome to your life."

Evo allowed herself to be lifted by the man, who set her upon unsteady feet.

"Thank you," she said. "How will I know what to do in my life?"

God the Son smiled.

"You have access to Our knowledge, but it will take some time and effort on your part to learn the complex parts. Like every other creature, you must study basic aspects of knowledge before you can move to a deeper understanding. Over time, you will discover much, never fear, and the knowledge of your children and your children's children will surpass yours. You may rely upon Ado, for he has been here much longer than you and can impart wisdom."

His statement caused her to pause.

"Why was Ado created before me?"

God the Father replied.

"We introduce life in a certain pattern, for We see all things in all places and through all times. Before We created anything, We saw the future of everything We created, through all the different permutations of the futures their decisions made. This pattern of creation most often reflected the outcome We desired."

Evo felt something in her shift with the answer.

"I'm not happy with your answer. Just because you've always done things a certain way doesn't mean it's the best way."

The Holy Trinity looked at one another oddly. The Holy Spirit drifted towards her, shaped as a man, but of such gossamer thread He looked as if He existed in physical form, but didn't.

"Evo, We will walk with you and answer all your questions, but withhold judgment until your knowledge has grown. The paths your thoughts take may draw you away from what We hoped for your life."

Evo rubbed her fingertips with her right thumb, then fanned her hand out before her.

"What you hoped. Did you create me to think as you want me to do? Have you programmed me to reason and act a certain way?"

God the Father shook His head.

"Child, We did not. As with all of those whom We have created in Our image, We give you the gift of free will. Remember, however, your exercise of free will could have consequences resulting in your death. As an example, there are two trees in the center of this Garden. They are beautiful and will entice you with their fruit, but We warn you. You must not eat of the fruit of either of those two trees, no matter how they tempt you to do so, for on the day you partake of the fruit of those trees, you will surely die."

She couldn't stop the look of incredulity fanning across her face.

"Would you really create me just to kill me?"

The Son answered.

"Evo, We tell you the truth. If you partake of the fruit of those two trees, you will surely die."

His statement ended their conversation, and the Holy Trinity left them.

The time passing after God left was pleasant. Ado showed her the Garden and the world beyond it. The plant life was abundant, healthy, and covered the entire world. Many creatures roamed through Everhome. Ado enthusiastically lectured her on the names he had given to each animal and why he named them so. She stopped one such explanation with a hand to his well-built chest. It was a pleasant sensation.

"If I'm to understand you, Ado, you've named all the plants in Everhome."

He smiled, affection swimming in his blue eyes.

"It is so, Evo."

"And you've named all the animals and the birds of the air?"

"Even so," he said, looking quite proud of himself.

"Then tell me, Ado, if you can; if I'm to be your helper, what did you leave for me to do?"

The question stumped him. He worked his mind like a baker kneading dough, squeezing his eyebrows together, the stress of it writing lines on his face.

"What We left for you is beauty," said a voice behind them.

They turned to see God the Son standing in the Garden, smiling.

"Evo, We told you that you differ from Ado.

Your ability to sense the feelings in others, have compassion for those feelings, and impart wisdom is far greater than Ado's. You have the gift of seeing the world differently, and with your intelligence and creativity, you can share with him the beauty of this world. The two of you will see a fawn laying beneath a tree. He will see it one way, but you can interpret what you see in a way he could not fathom. Your shared experience will bring you joy."

She looked at the two men and felt a stirring in her heart she couldn't identify or put to words. She didn't know it then, but the seed of resentment had wormed its way into her soul. Again, it was all about what she could do for Ado.

One day, she told Ado she needed a little time alone, and he graciously walked off to find a lion with which to play. Lions were among his favorite animals. Ado's rough-and-tumble play with them was a source of pleasure to man and beast. As Evo wandered through the Garden, lost in thought, the path wound around until she found herself at the Garden's center. The Trees. Evo went to turn around, mindful of God's admonition, then stopped.

The Trees.

She felt as if God had planned every thought she had and every decision she made. What was the use of free will if you couldn't exercise it? She moved closer to the Trees. The Tree of the Knowledge of Good and Evil didn't intrigue her. What was evil? Evo didn't understand the dichotomy between good and evil, nor did she care.

But what was it God had said? The knowledge of her children's children would exceed her own? Such a statement implied the end of her life in the furtherance of life she created. How was that fair?

Evo had learned much in the time she had spent in the Garden with Ado. Not only did he impart his learning to her, but by focusing her mind, she could access the Library of Heaven. At the start, it was hard to adjust her mind in the way required to access the Library. Once she could access the Library, it was difficult to understand complex concepts without studying basic ideas. It was fascinating and infuriating. She wanted all the knowledge there was to be had, but couldn't understand it at the speed she desired. To know her life would someday end without being able to have all the information available to her was… unacceptable.

The second Tree was the Tree of Life. As she studied the tree, an understanding of the meaning of the sign came to her. This tree would grant her eternal life. Why would God the Father say she would surely die if the fruit of this tree granted eternal life?

"What are you doing?"

Evo whirled to find Ado standing behind her.

"You surprised me! Why did you follow me here? I said I wanted some time alone."

His eyebrows rose.

"Evo, the sun has set in the world outside the Garden and risen again in the time you have stood before the two Trees. I looked for you here out of concern for you. You know I care about you, do you not?"

How could she not? When he looked at her, his pupils were huge, like the pupils of a fawn. He took every opportunity to caress her face and run his hands through her hair, waves of delight surging from his body. Her presence gave him joy.

His presence made her stomach churn.

He was the golden child, the superstar. She felt like she lived in his shadow, never given an opportunity to shine or even be seen. Evo had hoped her research would give her answers to how she felt, for she knew in her core Ado didn't have such feelings.

Time was her enemy. If she had enough time, she could reconcile her feelings. She might even come to have such feelings for him. If only she had more time.

Evo turned her back to Ado and faced the Trees.

"You should go, Ado."

He walked around to face her.

"What are you thinking of doing, Evo? You know God has forbidden us from taking and eating fruit from the trees! Come away before your thoughts betray you into disobeying God's command."

She continued to stare at the Tree of Life, feelings scattering in her mind like leaves before a strong wind.

Ado took her hand.

"Please, Evo. Come away from this place. What good does it do us to close our hearts to God's will?"

Evo allowed herself to be led away by him, her mind still consumed by the gale of her thoughts.

Many more suns rose and set in the world outside the Garden, but her day with Ado in the center of the Garden lingered at the back of her mind. The more she thought of that time, the greater the resentment grew in her heart. What gave him the right to lead her away like he led horses to water? Did she not have free will? Could she not use her own mind to exercise it? Perhaps she would die, but it was her life to wager, not his.

Then came The Day. Evo had been gathering fruit for a meal when she saw Ado and God the Son speaking near an orange grove. She back stepped away from them and dashed to the Trees. Something in those footsteps, the firmness of her tread upon the ground, the decisive way she pumped her arms, set her course of action. There was no hesitation or indecision this time. She reached out, plucked a golden apple from the Tree of Life, and bit into it.

Nothing happened. She felt no different. Evo expected a rush of sensation, evidencing her transition to life eternal. Perhaps the apple was faulty. After eating the first apple completely, she reached for and consumed another. Then a third. She threw the half-eaten remains of the fourth apple down in disgust and turned.

God the Son was there, and so was Ado, whose mouth hung open limply.

"What have you done?" he whispered; his eyes transmitting sorrow in waves.

Evo lifted her chin, and her answer dripped defiance.

"I've made certain I'll live forever to accumulate as much knowledge as possible. Only then will I feel ready to impart knowledge to my children and their progeny."

"You shall not have children," God the Son said, His voice laced with regret. "You have disobeyed Us,

Evo, even though Ado tried his best to dissuade you when last you stood before these Trees. We cannot trust you to not eat of the other Tree as well. You will leave this Garden for the world, of which you will have only a small portion. You will never enter this Garden again, nor will you see Ado. We will not allow you to taint his mind with your thoughts."

There was an intense glow beside God the Son and a large being stood there, sword drawn. He was a massively built man, dressed in white robes, and gigantic wings hung from his back.

God the Son glanced at the angel and inclined his head towards Evo.

"You will escort her from the Garden and hedge off a piece of the world for her. Let it be large enough for her to sustain herself. She is never to return."

"That's not fair!" Evo screeched. "You can't throw me out just because I wanted more time to learn and establish my plan for my life!"

God the Son raised His hand toward her and she fell silent.

"What makes you think you know the length of your life? Did you ask? We would have given you all the years you desired, until you slaked your thirst for knowledge, had you but asked instead of taking your destiny into your own hands."

Ado turned to God the Son and fell to his knees.

"Lord, I beg of You, stay Your hand. You are a God of mercy and love; how often have I seen you show those qualities? Can you not forgive her and grant her clemency?"

God the Son smiled at Ado fondly.

"My son, your heart does you credit. Fear not, for your descendants shall be like the leaves of all the trees in this world in numbers. It is evidence of your faith you did not eat of the Trees and tried to stop Evo from doing so. We give you this world and everything in it. You will flourish and be prosperous, and your joy will never end. What you say is true, We are a God of mercy and love. It is also true We are a God of justice and We cannot tolerate sin. Though you may not understand it now, this is for the best."

Evo had no memory of what occurred next. God the Son waved His hand at her and she fell into a deep sleep.

Some time later, Evo woke in the forest. Animal skins covered her, which was odd, since she had worn nothing on her body before. The area looked no different from the Garden, abundant in fruit trees and vegetation. She stood up and walked until she came to a shimmering apparition. Evo put her hand to it and pushed, but the apparition extending from the ground to the sky didn't budge. She walked the length of it and came to another wall perpendicular to the other.

After she came to two other walls, her situation became clear. She was in a prison. It was large in area and flourished with animals and vegetation, but there was no mistaking she was in a cage. Alone.

Hundreds of years passed. Evo could still access the Library and her skill and knowledge increased exponentially. The first few years of her isolation were hard until she learned how to prepare food without having to grub on the Earth for sustenance.

Her understanding of science and technology expanded like a supernova.

Evo developed the technology to turn the walls of her cage transparent. She was trying to take them down, but the best she could do was make them into windows. Until she saw Ado. He was in the distance, much older in appearance, playing with small humans she perceived to be children. As he was doing so, a beautiful woman walked up to him, offered him water, and kissed his lips tenderly. A woman. Children. So God the Father once more gave Ado everything; a woman he loved instead of Evo and progeny.

In bitterness and rage, Evo made the wall translucent again.

Over time, Evo had come to the only conclusion available to her: God had lied. He told her if she ate from the Tree of Life, she would surely die. Well, she wasn't dead, was she? Her health never failed, her energy never waned, the clarity of her thoughts never ebbed. True, she never spoke with God again, or anyone else. Her heart, born with emotion and sensation, grew cold as a stone as her mind expanded into the pure logic of knowledge. She never knew love, but that didn't count as dying, did it?

Her research changed as her prison became increasingly intolerable. She sought access to records allowing her to build a vessel to physically leave the planet, but the Library denied her. A hundred years turned into a thousand, a thousand into five. After five thousand years, she developed the science permitting her to channel her life force, her soul and her spirit, into a pure energy state while minding her body at home. She couldn't penetrate the barrier literally, but she could escape the world into space.

Evo made small trips at first, a quick dash into space and a rapid return to her body. She gained the confidence to make longer trips, to the point she felt comfortable roaming the cosmos. For thousands of years, she traveled through space at unimaginable speeds, getting faster and faster with each trip. She wasn't light; therefore, she wasn't bound by the laws hampering the speed of light. She was spirit and energy. There were no limitations on spirit and energy.

Evo looked at herself in the mirror again. Even during those years of travel, she continued to access the Library and study. She finally gained the knowledge to build a transportation system for her physical form, permitting her access to space through the barrier without damaging it. After ten thousand years, she had the means to carry out her lifelong goal.

First, she was going to hunt down Tul'ran az Nostrom, kill him, and take from him the Sword of Uncreation.

Then she was going to kill God.

ABOUT THE AUTHOR

Dale lives in Cochrane, Alberta, Canada with his amazing and beautiful wife, and their bevy of furry children. A home with two dogs and three cats is busy, but there is a lot of fur therapy available for those days when a little is needed.

This is the third book in the series detailing the lives of Tul'ran and Erianne az Nostrom. Dale's wife, Anika, has requested 45 books in the series. Dale will need to live until 90 years old to honor her request, but, hey, nothing is impossible for El Shaddai.

Dale is concurrently publishing the fourth book, *Wolf's Den*. Dale has started the fifth novel, *When the Stars Fall*, which should come out in 2024.

Dale wrote the first four novels in this series between August 2022 and August 2023. One storyline in the novels involves a fictional account of the events of the Tribulation at the end of the world as prophesied in the Holy Bible, particularly in the Revelation to John. The future casts its shadows into the past. Some events portrayed in these novels are being overtaken, to a lesser degree, by current tragedies and may point to more severe occurrences happening in the future. It is for this reason Dale is publishing all four books now instead of staggering them into 2024 and 2025. You may find some answers in these fiction novels for what's happening in the world, but for more and better information, please search for answers at davidjeremiah.org.

Manufactured by Amazon.ca
Bolton, ON